DICKENS and MESMERISM

The Hidden Springs of Fiction

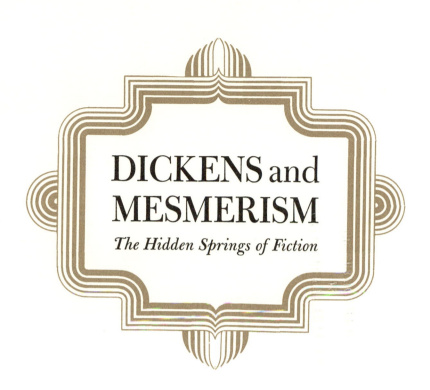

DICKENS and MESMERISM

The Hidden Springs of Fiction

Fred Kaplan

PRINCETON UNIVERSITY PRESS

Copyright © 1975 by Princeton University Press

ALL RIGHTS RESERVED

*Library of Congress Cataloging in Publication Data will
be found on the last printed page of this book
Publication of this book has been aided by a grant from*

THE ANDREW W. MELLON FOUNDATION

This book has been composed in Linotype Baskerville

Printed in the United States of America

by Princeton University Press

Princeton, New Jersey

To Gloria,
Ben, Noah, &
Julia

ACKNOWLEDGMENTS

I am particularly indebted to the resources and assistance of the Henry W. and Albert A. Berg Collection of the New York Public Library, Astor, Lenox and Tilden Foundations, and its curator, Lola Szladits, and to The Wellcome Institute for the History of Medicine and its former and present Librarians, Eric Gaskell and Eric J. Freeman. The Pierpont Morgan Library, through the offices of Herbert Cahoon, and The Huntington Library, through the offices of Jean Preston, were kind enough to sanction quotation and summary from unpublished letters by John Elliotson and Chauncy Hare Townshend. The Wellcome Institute, by courtesy of the Wellcome Trustees, permitted quotation and summary from its Elliotson letters, and generously provided many entertaining and illuminating illustrations. The Editors and Trustees of the Pilgrim edition of *The Letters of Charles Dickens*, to whom Mr. Christopher Dickens has turned over the common-law copyright for Dickens' unpublished letters, have permitted the use of summaries and very short quotations. The Berg Collection and The Pierpont Morgan Library were most kind in making accessible to me unpublished letters by Dickens and for granting their permission for my use of these letters within the restrictions imposed by the heirs to the common-law copyright. Mr. John S. Mayfield, Curator of Manuscripts and Rare Books at Syracuse University Library, generously permitted me to quote extensively from Monkton Milnes' unpublished poem "Mesmerism in London." Part of Chapter 1, substantially revised, is reprinted from *Journal of the History of Ideas*, Vol. xxxv, No. 4 (1974), pp. 691-702, with the permission of the *Journal of the History of Ideas*, Inc.

ACKNOWLEDGMENTS

Through the skillful resources of Mrs. Mimi Penchansky, of the Paul Klapper Library of Queens College, the City University of New York, many far-flung libraries provided books and periodicals. My own personal appearances and letters provided assistance from the libraries of Columbia University, the New York Academy of Medicine, the New York Public Library, the Richard Gimbel Dickens Collection of the Beinecke Library of Yale University, the British Museum, the Victoria and Albert Museum, the Bowdoin College library, and the typing service of the Office of Graduate Studies, Queens College, particularly its able director, Mrs. Florence Waldhetter. A superb English typist, Mrs. Patricia Nossek, deserves my appreciation both for her competence and her reasonable rates. Of the individuals who responded to my inquiries and gave assistance in one form or another, those who deserve special acknowledgment are Vineta Colby, Christopher C. Dickens, Morris Dickstein, Leslie Epstein, Martin A. Fido, K. J. Fielding, Norman Fruman, Dolores Greenberg, Mark Greenberg, Robert Greenberg, Dora Greenspan, Madeline House, Gloria Kaplan, David Kleinbard, Michael Kowal, Hedy Kraus, John S. Mayfield, Jonathan Miller, Carol Molesworth, Charles Molesworth, A. N. L. Munby, John Podeschi, F. N. L. Poynter, Edwin Seaver, Charles H. Shattuck, Harry Stone, Graham Storey, H. P. Sucksmith, Michael Timko, Kathleen Tillotson, Alan Trachtenberg, Harley Williams, Carl R. Woodring, and Marjorie G. Wynne. R. Miriam Brokaw, Associate Director and Editor of Princeton University Press, gave this book much of her personal attention and shared with me the year-long adventure of publication through the approval of my academic peers.

FRED KAPLAN
1975
Great Neck, New York

viii

ABBREVIATIONS

These abbreviations are of the most obvious kind, for the purpose of facilitating reading through an exposition as free as possible from eye-impeding long parentheses or frequent footnote numbers. The historical and biographical material with which the first four chapters are largely concerned demands extensive footnoting. The references in the remaining five chapters are mostly of a different kind, preponderantly references to passages within Dickens' fiction. Because each of these chapters in a sense deals not with one or two novels but with the Dickens opus as a whole, the citations come thick and fast. To facilitate matters I have presented these references by abbreviated book title in parentheses after the quotation. I myself have used *The Oxford Illustrated Dickens*, except in the four cases in which superior editions are available: *Oliver Twist* and *The Mystery of Edwin Drood* in *The Clarendon Dickens* (1966, 1972), *David Copperfield* in the Riverside Edition (Boston, 1958), and *Hard Times* in the Norton Critical Edition (N.Y., 1966). I have referred to quotations from the novels by section and/or chapter, not by page number (except in the case of *Pictures from Italy*), since readers are certain to draw upon disparate editions. Following the list of abbreviations of Dickens' novels there appears a list of books and manuscript sources referred to by short title in the footnotes.

SB	*Sketches by Boz*
PP	*The Posthumous Papers of The Pickwick Club*
OT	*Oliver Twist*
NN	*Nicholas Nickleby*

OCS	*Old Curiosity Shop*
BR	*Barnaby Rudge*
MC	*Martin Chuzzlewit*
CC	*Christmas Carol*
TC	*The Chimes*
HM	*Haunted Man*
BL	*Battle of Life*
PFI	*Pictures from Italy*
AN	*American Notes*
DS	*Dombey and Son*
DC	*David Copperfield*
BH	*Bleak House*
HT	*Hard Times*
LD	*Little Dorrit*
TTC	*Tale of Two Cities*
GE	*Great Expectations*
OMF	*Our Mutual Friend*
ED	*The Mystery of Edwin Drood*

Berg MS — Letters in the Henry W. and Albert A. Berg Collection of the New York Public Library

Braid — James Braid, *Neurypnology or, The Rationale of Nervous Sleep, Considered in Relation to Animal Magnetism* (London, 1843)

Clarke — James Fernandez Clarke, *Autobiographical Recollections of the Medical Profession* (London, 1874)

Dexter — *Mr. and Mrs. Charles Dickens. His Letters to Her*, ed. Walter Dexter (London, 1935)

Dupotet — Baron Dupotet de Sennevoy, *An Introduction to the Study of Animal Magnetism* (London, 1838)

Huntington MS — Letters in The Huntington Library, San Marino, California

Johnson   Edgar Johnson, *Charles Dickens, His Tragedy and Triumph* (N.Y., 1952)

Life   John Forster, *The Life of Charles Dickens* (London, 1872-1874), ed. J. W. T. Ley (London, 1928)

Morgan MS   Letters in The Pierpont Morgan Library, New York

Nonesuch   *The Nonesuch Edition of the Letters of Charles Dickens,* ed. Walter Dexter (London, 1938), 3 vols.

Pilgrim   *The Pilgrim Edition of the Letters of Charles Dickens,* ed. Madeline House and Graham Storey (Oxford, 1965, 1970), Vols. 1 and 2

Townshend   Chauncy Hare Townshend, *Facts in Mesmerism* (London, 1840)

Toynbee   *The Diaries of William Charles Macready,* ed. William Toynbee (London, 1912), 2 vols.

Wellcome MS   Letters or prints in The Wellcome Institute for the History of Medicine, London

TABLE OF CONTENTS

LIST OF ILLUSTRATIONS

following page 142

John Elliotson.

Hospitals and Medical Schools of London, 1836-1837.

Mesmerism, woodcut, c. 1840.

Mesmeric Session, woodcut, c. 1840.

Frederick Manning, The Murderer.

Maria Manning, The Murderess.

Valentine Greatrakes, Curing . . . by the stroke of his hand only.

Opposite top: Le Mesmerisme Confondu, 1790.

Animal Magnetism, The Operator Putting His Patient into a Crisis.

Opposite bottom: Magnetic Dispensary, 1790, etching by Barlow.

Opposite top: Robert Macaire magnétiseur, H. Daumier.

Opposite bottom: Le Magnétisme, L. Boilly, 1826.

Establishing the Electro-Biological Circuit Between Mesmerist and Subject.

Making the Magnetic Pass, D. Younger, 1887.

The Reverse or Upward Pass, D. Younger, 1887.

The Cataleptic State, D. Younger, 1887.

DICKENS and
MESMERISM
The Hidden Springs of Fiction

"The Mesmeric Mania"

⟦ 1 ⟧

At least as early as January of 1838 Charles Dickens was
persuaded to attend a demonstration of the "mighty curative powers of animal magnetism" or mesmerism given by
John Elliotson, the outspoken senior physician and Professor of the Principles and Practice of Medicine at the University of London.[1] The invitation did not come in a vacuum. Undoubtedly Dickens, in his role of artistic London
gentleman in a vivacious circle of successful men like William Macready, William Harrison Ainsworth, and George
Cruikshank and up-and-coming stars like John Forster,
Daniel Maclise, Robert Browning, Edward Bulwer, and
Richard Monckton Milnes, had his fingers to the pulse of
all the fashionable obsessions of the last years of that decade.
London had been his family, school, and home for almost
ten years of adult consciousness—his familiarity with its
physical and intellectual byways was an essential element in
his first employment, his work in the House, his journalistic
training, and his cosmopolitan *Sketches by Boz.* Certainly
Dickens had seen even before 1838 such advertisements as

[1] The specific date, January 14, 1838, is established from the clinical
notes in "Case Book, No. 17," University College Hospital, referred to
in T. R. E., "John Elliotson, M.D. Camb., F.R.S." *University College
Hospital Magazine*, Vol. I, No. 1, July 1911, 272-284.

"Treatment of Acute and Chronic Diseases by Animal Magnetism at No. 20 Wigmore Street, Cavendish Square. Experimental Seances, for the treatment of Chronic and Nervous Affections, are conducted by Baron Dupotet De Sennevoy, every day (Sundays excepted) from half-past One to Three o'clock. Entree, 2s.6d."[2] He had written in 1835 a vignette for *Sketches by Boz* that jokingly referred to "magnetism." He had had numerous opportunities much before 1838 to pay his entrance, and the unavailability of evidence to document such experiences at that time may be more a comment on Dickens' finances, employment exigencies, and historical accident than on his intellectual curiosity.

For when Dickens' impressive Gad's Hill library was auctioned after his death in 1870, the extent of his reading experiences, though undervalued ever since, should have become clear, particularly his special interest in mesmerism and what shrewd booksellers today call "the occult." At least fourteen volumes on these subjects were evicted from Gad's Hill under the impetus of the auctioneer's hammer, two of them, Samuel Hibbert-Ware's *Sketches of the Philosophy of Apparitions* (1824), and R. Dale Owen's *Footfalls on the Boundary of Another World* (1860), extensively annotated by their owner.[3] Prominent on the list are two of John

---

[2] This advertisement appears as an unnumbered page in Dupotet.

[3] See *Catalogues of the Libraries of Charles Dickens and W. M. Thackeray, Etc.*, ed. J. H. Stonehouse (London, 1935). Among the other volumes were such classics on mesmerism as Baron Von Reichenbach's *Researches on Magnetism and on Certain Allied Subjects* (1846), such mesmeric-occult landmarks as Joseph Ennemoser's *History of Magic* (1854), Jung-Stilling's *Theory of Pneumatology* (1834), Count de Gabalis' *A Diverting History of the Rosicrucian Doctrine of Spirits* (1714), Augustin Calmet's *A Phantom World* (1850), John Abercrombie's *Inquiries Concerning the Intellectual Powers* (1840), Catherine Crowe's *Night Side of Nature* (1848), Henry Bell's *Selections of the Most Remarkable Phenomena of Nature* (1827), and even *The Principles of Nature, her Divine Revelations and a Voice to Mankind* by the "Poughkeepsie Seer" A. J. Davis, inscribed to "Charles Dickens, Esq., with the Author's respects. . . ."

Elliotson's most influential books on mesmerism, his text-book *Human Physiology* (1840) and *On Numerous Cases of Surgical Operations Without Pain in the Mesmeric State* (1843), the latter with a hand-inscribed dedication "To Charles Dickens, from his sincere friend, John Elliotson."

What the auctioneer sold in 1870 were in many instances books purchased or received in Dickens' middle and late years. Except for those volumes definitely thumbed and annotated, there is rarely evidence that Dickens read any specific volume, regardless of when it first came into his possession. But Dickens was a much more perceptive reader of a wider variety of books than he has been given credit for, particularly if we grant that he read even a small portion of those he owned on travel, economics, social sciences, and Italian literature. Certainly between 1834 and 1845 Dickens read a rather large number of books and articles on mesmerism, among them Elliotson's two books, *Human Physiology* and *Numerous Cases*, probably the Baron Dupotet de Sennevoy's *An Introduction to the Study of Animal Magnetism* (1838), and definitely his friend Chauncy Hare Townshend's *Facts in Mesmerism* (1840). He was in close contact from its inception with the Victorian "mesmeric mania"[4] that dominated the headlines of the public consciousness for over twenty years.

[2]

Victorian historians of mesmerism conveniently fall into three categories: those who defended the phenomenon on spiritual and metaphysical grounds, those who defended it as scientism, and all those who opposed it, whatever their reasons (and they varied widely), though indeed the most common attacks were naturally the reverse positions of its supporters. Its historians were always partisans. Many de-

---

[4] This phrase is taken from *The Mesmeric Mania of 1851, with a physiological explanation of the Phenomena produced*. A Lecture by John Hughes Bennett, M.D., F.R.S.E., Edinburgh, 1851.

manded, many pleaded for, dispassionate inquiry, an open mind on an open subject. But neither the early Victorian conception of historiography nor the passionate partisanship of the experts would permit it. All those who grappled with the subject had much to gain and much to lose, since fundamental values and principles were at stake. A-priori assumptions of mechanism or spiritualism seemed to determine not only the procedures but the logic of innumerable attempts to prove "Mesmerism True—Mesmerism False."[5] The disputants almost always manifest a sense of nervous defensiveness or argumentative excess, as if they are aware that their claims to objectivity suit neither the stage of development of historiography nor their own intense emotional commitments. Consequently most histories of mesmerism in the first half of the nineteenth century are small sections, often only a chapter or two, of works that either attempt to defend and explain or confound and explain. In many ways the Victorians loved a controversy and a scandal more than they loved fact, despite the frequent claim that we "want . . . nothing but Facts" (*HT*, 1).

The facts of mesmerism and the origin of self-conscious concern about it are not hard to come by. The controversy was and still is in the attempt to explain through comprehensive theory the cause and the behavior of the phenomena. It is on this point that the Victorians fought bitterly, even to the inevitable internecine war between believers. But they did not dispute Mesmer's claim that he had been the first to draw to mesmerism elaborate and self-conscious attention and to give it a name.

In 1779, having settled in Paris after fleeing the hostile atmosphere of Vienna, Franz Anton Mesmer published "Sur La Découverte Du Magnétisme Animal."[6] In the balanced phrases of a still classical French he found his language; in the ferment of pre-revolutionary Paris he found a temporary

---

[5] John Forbes, *Mesmerism True—Mesmerism False, A Critical Examination of the Facts* (London, 1845).

[6] Franz Anton Mesmer, *Mémoire Sur La Découverte Du Magnétisme Animal* (Geneva, Paris, 1779); translated by V. R. Meyers with an introduction by Gilbert Frankau (London, 1948).

home and a permanent audience.[7] For Mesmer's doctrine caught the historical currents of both intellect and emotion as they moved forward, often in conflict, from the rationality and the sentimentality of the eighteenth century. It offered science and progress, almost instant solutions to ancient problems. Disease, corruption, discord, war could be cured and eliminated. But like other utopian visions of the period, mesmerism appealed to the heart as well as to the head. And consequently it had not only a strand of scientific but also an elaborate weave of Romantic and revolutionary utopianism that contained threads from western society's inheritance of religion and magic. Like many eclectic movements, mesmerism could appeal to an astoundingly diverse population. Not only did its therapeutic aspect cut across ideologies but its multi-layered psychological and ideological complexities could be embraced selectively. One could pick and choose what one wanted and needed.

Mesmer's claims, concisely stated in his twenty-seven propositions, insofar as they became part of the Victorian controversy can be reduced to two basic principles: (1) Mechanical laws, working in an alternate ebb and flow, control "a mutual influence between the Heavenly bodies, the Earth, and Animate Bodies which exist as a universally distributed and continuous fluid . . . of an incomparably rarified nature." (2) Since all "the properties of matter and the organic body depend upon this operation" whose influence or force may be communicated to animate and inanimate bodies, it is possible to create a new theory about the nature of influence and power relationships between people and between people and the objects in their environment. If that theory is true and put into practice, "the art of healing will thus reach its final stage of perfection." Because Mesmer believed that magnets were particularly good conductors of this force or influence, and to distinguish it from mineral magnetism, he named the phenomenon Animal Magnetism.[8]

[7] See Robert Darnton, *Mesmerism and the End of the Enlightenment in France* (Cambridge, Mass., 1968; New York, 1970).

[8] Mesmer, *Mémoire*, pp. 54-55.

7

His followers were to invest the phenomenon with the name of its discoverer, an unwise nomenclature; and the Victorians were to use interchangeably Mesmer's term and the abstract noun formed from the Viennese doctor's name.

Mesmer did indeed conceptualize this force in the language and the concepts of his eighteenth-century medical training. Though his instinct for gain was well developed, there is ample evidence to suggest that he was no charlatan; that his training, perception, and temperament had led him to the exploration of what he and others considered a legitimate scientific tool with overwhelming therapeutic possibilities.[9] But in the late eighteenth and early nineteenth centuries specific practical results could not exist without the attempt to explain the force behind the power. The scientific and the metaphysical mind had not been separated. No cure could exist without an explanation of why the cure worked; without an explanation the cure could not be tolerated. And, of course, the frequent coexistence in the same mind of both mechanistic and transcendental assumptions often assured that a pragmatic and demonstrable phenomenon would be at least partially explained in metaphysical terms.

Regardless of metaphysics, however, mesmerism particularly fascinated an age almost obsessed by the possibility of curing all illnesses and that suffered various epidemics of its own, particularly plagues of the nervous system and the psyche.[10] The Victorians not only consulted doctors but be-

[9] For modern accounts of Mesmer and his movement, see J. Milne Bramwell, *Hypnotism, Its History, Practice, and Theory* (London, 1903), R. Tischner, *Franz Anton Mesmer* (Munich, 1928), Stephan Zweig, *Mental Healers* (London, 1934), Margaret L. Goldsmith, *Franz Anton Mesmer: The History of an Idea* (London, 1934), F. Schurer-Waldheim, *Anton Mesmer* (Vienna, 1938), Bernard Wolfe and Raymond Rosenthal, *Hypnotism Comes of Age. Its Progress from Mesmer to Psychoanalysis* (New York, 1948), B. Milt, *Franz Anton Mesmer und seiner Beziehungen zur Schweiz* (Zurich, 1953), Frank Podmore, *From Mesmer to Christian Science* (New York, 1909; 1963), and D. M. Walmsley, *Anton Mesmer* (London, 1967).

[10] Harriet Martineau, *Harriet Martineau's Autobiography*, ed. Marie Weston Chapman (London, 1878), and John Stuart Mill, *Autobiography*

gan to believe in them. At the same time, they were intensely aware of their limitations, especially in dealing with certain forms of human abnormal behavior, an awareness that so increased among the medical profession itself that, interestingly, almost all the major mesmeric theorists and innovators in England in the first half of the nineteenth century were medical practitioners. Perhaps Mesmer himself sensed or anticipated the coming psychological crisis of western man, the illness of the nerves and the nervous system that was to become the characteristic disease of a society attempting to grapple with the problems of personal and public identity that the new age forced on many of Victoria's subjects. Perhaps he did not. But he believed that he had discovered a power that could cure a wide range of diseases that had seemed previously an inevitable part of man's burden, and that he could exert this power for progress across a wide range of human activities—personal relationships, individual health, economics, government, and national well-being. Most importantly, Mesmer and his followers were possessed by the energy, certitude, and ambition that often accompany a new vision of ultimate reality. They believed that they had discovered not simply *a* truth or *a* useful method but that they had discovered *the* fundamental and irreducible truth that underlay all surface truths and methods. They had a clue to ultimate reality, to the power behind *all* things. Their metaphysical and religious vision convinced them that in the long run their doctrine would be recognized and accepted, and for almost seventy-five years the mesmeric movement in England and on the continent was inspired with an energy born of optimism and a blindness born of higher vision.

Mesmerism came to England on the winds of the revolution, tainted with its European and particularly its French

---

(London, 1873), are classic representatives of this Victorian experience. But the pages of *The Lancet* and *The Zoist*, particularly the latter, are filled with similar cases, though those which came to the attention of the medical profession usually involved severe physiological symptoms.

origin, often resented by a proud and suspicious island nation as a dubious foreign import. The scientific community, with which Mesmer himself had been in communication, rejected it almost out of hand, as much out of indifference and general lethargy as out of disapproval and politics. Englishmen studied with Mesmer, and especially with his disciples, Bergasse, Deslon, Puységur, Deleuze, and the Abbé Faria, who advanced Mesmer's major theories and procedures with minor modifications to suit their needs.[11] At the turn of the century a number of disciples, both French and English, attempting to make their fortunes and spread the doctrine, established mesmeric salons in Hammersmith and Bristol. Rumor advertised that fortunes up to five thousand pounds were easily made.[12] But the attitude of the establishment, when it took notice, was condemnatory,[13] and one of the first English pamphlets on the subject, John Pearson's *A Plain and Rational Account of the Nature and Effects of Animal Magnetism* (1790), strikes the characteristic satiric note:

"If the minister fears opposition in some favorite motion from a turbulent orator, he may by the eloquence of his fingers, consign the troublesome member to sleep; or if the gentleman be already upon his legs, thundering out invec-

[11] See Charles Deslon, *Observations* (Paris, 1781), Nicolas Bergasse, *Observations de M. Bergasse sur un écrit du Docteur Mesmer* (London, 1785), Marquis de Puységur, *Mémoires pour servir à l'histoire du magnétisme animal* (Paris, 1784) and *Rapport des cures opérées à Bayonne par le magnétisme animal* (Bayonne, 1784), Joseph Deleuze, *Histoire Critique du magnétisme animal* (Paris, 1813) and Abbé Faria, *De la Cause du Sommeil lucide* (Paris, 1819).

[12] See Podmore, pp. 122-124, and George Winter, *History of Animal Magnetism* (Bristol, 1801), pp. 318-320. For the earliest work in English by a direct disciple, see Monsieur le Docteur Bell, *The General and Practical Principles of Animal Electricity and Magnetism, & c.* (London, 1792).

[13] Hannah More wrote to Horace Walpole (September 1788): "I give you leave to be as severe as you please on the demoniacal mummery which has been acting in this country. . . . Mesmer has got a hundred thousand pounds by animal magnetism in Paris. Mainduc is getting as much in London" (*Memoires of the Life and Correspondence of Mrs. Hannah More*, ed. William Roberts, London, 1834, II, 120).

tives against mal-administration, he may find this Demos-
thenes other employment, by throwing him into a Crisis.
You may say that this power may prove a dangerous engine
in the hands of a corrupt administration; but remember,
Sir, the Patriots may avail themselves of the same weapon,
so that on a day of public business, St. Stephen's would ex-
hibit a motley scene of members sound asleep, or rolling in
convulsions. This would form a new era in the history of
ministerial influence. . . ."[14]

The mesmeric movement in England from 1800 to 1837
was a pale and scattered shadow of continental activities.
The movement had no public presence of any consequence
in England for almost forty years. There were no active
mesmeric salons, retreats, societies, professional medical
controversies, publications of pamphlets, articles, and books,
and no heightened public consciousness of the phenomenon
of the kind that in France and Germany made the subject
one of sensationalized discussion. Much that was French
was anathema to Englishmen during these years, the result
of centuries of antagonism and rivalry brought to a climax
by the Napoleonic Wars. Though ideas did move westward
across the channel even during the war years, intellectual
currents from France were resisted by the English community with even more hostile and condescending tenacity
than those from anyplace else, except perhaps America,
where lectures on mesmerism had become commonplace oc-
currences during the 1820's.[15] Characteristically, when a
small circle of London enthusiasts, mostly wealthy Jewish
merchants, supported the private publication of a translation in 1822 of M. Loewe's *A Treatise on the Phenomena
of Animal Magnetism*, it was to Germany and a German

14 John Pearson, *A Plain and Rational Account of the Nature and
Effects of Animal Magnetism* in a series of Letters with Notes and an
Appendix by the Editor (London, 1790), p. 32.
15 See Joseph Du Commun, *Three Lectures on Animal Magnetism*,
as Delivered in New York, at the Hall of Science, on the 26th of July,
2nd and 9th of August by Dr. Joseph Du Commun, 2d Teacher of
French at the U.S. Military Academy, West Point (New York, 1829).

11

author that they had turned, not to France or a French mesmerist. And Shelley's familiarity with animal magnetism in a poem of the same year as the English translation of Loewe's book is the product of his European rather than his English experiences, though the reversal of the normal genders of the subject-operator relationship in "The Magnetic Lady to her Patient" is more expressive of the poet than the movement:

> Sleep, sleep on! forget thy pain;
> My hand is on thy brow,
> My spirit on thy brain;
> My pity on thy heart, poor friend;
> And from my fingers flow
> The powers of life, and like a sign,
> Seal thee from thine hour of woe;
> And brood on thee, but may not blend
> With thine.[16]

Despite the comparative failure of De Mainaduc, George Winter, and other disciples of Mesmer in starting an influential movement in England at the beginning of the century, mesmerism was one of a number of new scientific-metaphysical systems that did begin to find English proponents by the 1820's, men who had read closely the occult and scientific literature of the Christian tradition. For magic and science, the transcendental and the mechanistic, often produced equally imaginative explorations of phenomena, creating a literature during the eighteenth and the first half of the nineteenth century that made natural companions on Dickens' library shelf of books as seemingly diverse as the Count de Gabalis' *A Diverting History of the Rosicrucian Doctrine of Spirits: Sylphs, Salamanders, Gnomes, and Daemons* (1714), John Abercrombie's *Inquiries Concerning the Intellectual Powers and the Investigation of Truth* (1840), and John Elliotson's *Human Physi-*

---

16 *The Complete Poetic Works of Percy Bysshe Shelley*, ed. Thomas Hutchinson (London, 1960), p. 667.

12

ology (1835-1840).[17] Indeed, until at least the 1860's these were hardly strange bedfellows, variations on a widespread concern with the relationship between mind and matter, explorations of what H. G. Bell and so many others called *Selections of the Most Remarkable Phenomena of Nature* (1827).[18]

Though mesmeric activity in England did not become formidable until the end of the third decade of the century, early in the 1820's phrenology, whose fortunes were soon to be closely allied with those of mesmerism, came to England as part of the larger interest in the relationship between mind and matter. Dickens' friend, John Elliotson, the Englishman most responsible for the "mesmeric mania" in England, founded and became the first president of the London Phrenological Society in 1824.[19] When he began publishing *The Zoist* in 1843, he gave it the subtitle *A Journal of Cerebral Physiology and Mesmerism, and Their Application to Human Welfare*. In March 1825 "the justly-celebrated Dr. Spurzheim . . . commenced a course of eighteen lectures on the Science of Phrenology . . . at the Crown and Anchor Tavern, Strand," where the London Phrenological Society met every Saturday evening with Dr. Elliotson in the chair at eight.[20] When Dickens in 1835 wanted his newspaper audience to laugh with him, he utilized a shared language on connected topics:

"Some phrenologists affirm, that the agitation of a man's brain by different passions, produces corresponding developments in the form of his skull. Do not let us be understood as pushing our theory to the full length of asserting, that any alteration in a man's disposition would produce a visible effect on the feature of his knocker. Our position

[17] See *Catalogue of the Libraries of Charles Dickens and W. M. Thackeray*, ed. J. H. Stonehouse (London, 1935).

[18] Also in Dickens' Gad's Hill Library.

[19] The only work of any usefulness on Elliotson's life appears in John Hargreaves Harley Williams, *Doctors Differ* (London, 1946), pp. 13-80.

[20] *The Lancet* (March 19, 1825), 349.

13

merely is, that in such a case, the *magnetism* which must exist between a man and his knocker, would induce the man to remove, and seek some knocker more congenial to his altered feelings" (*SB*, "Our Parish," vii).

Phrenology and animal magnetism went hand in hand after 1838. Indeed, the strength of the phrenological movement was sharply divided in the early 1840's when Elliotson and others insisted, despite the convictions of many scientists who had accepted phrenology but not mesmerism, that the phrenological societies affirm an unalterable link between the two. The new compound science was to be called Phreno-magnetism or Phrenomesmerism. Elliotson claimed that a patient in mesmeric trance would evidence knowledge and/or behavior directly corresponding to the phrenological stimulation applied by the mesmeric operator to the specific area of the cranium that phrenology had identified with a certain human quality or trait of personality.[21] When the Phrenological Association met at the end of July in 1842, "Mr. Donovan rose, and expressed his sincere gratification at seeing the association in a state of bankruptcy, inasmuch as such a position would prevent a repetition of the disgraceful proceedings of this session, when mesmerism and materialism were so mischievously mixed up with phrenology, in obedience to the purposes of the party who had so unfortunately obtained a preponderating influence in the association." A debate ensued in which "Mr. James Simpson entered into a narrative of mesmeric operations which he had witnessed that morning at Dr. Elliotson's house." Mr. Donovan maintained "then, as he had at first, that the Phrenological Association did not afford a fit theatre for such discussions."[22]

Elliotson himself first became directly aware of the mesmeric claims and possibilities in 1829, when one of Mesmer's disciples, Richard Chenevix, demonstrated the potential

21 See *The Zoist*, I, 2 (July 1843), 134-142.
22 *The Lancet* (June 25, 1842), 459-460; (July 2, 1842), 486.

medical use of the phenomenon at St. Thomas's hospital and published a series of articles on the subject in the *London Medical and Physiological Journal* to which Elliotson added a brief "memoranda" (October, 1829).[23] The medical profession immediately denounced Chenevix's claims and rejected his plea for dispassionate inquiry, attacking with what was to become its characteristic satiric animosity the movement's accounts of its origin and history.[24] Elliotson reserved judgment, impressed by the results of Chenevix's experiments but busy with the exigencies of his own extraordinarily full professional career as lecturer, phrenologist, physician at St. Thomas's, private practitioner, and author of medical textbooks.

Building a formidable reputation, Elliotson was not to return to his interest in mesmerism until 1837. As Professor of the Principles and Practice of Medicine at the University of London, popular teacher, recognized authority on diagnosis and drugs, widely published in textbooks and medical journals, he gave the Baron Dupotet de Sennevoy the same opportunities at the newly formed University Hospital that he had given Chenevix at St. Thomas's. In the summer of 1837 Elliotson began to experiment with mesmerism on ward patients; this culminated in public exhibitions held in May and June of 1838 in the theater of the hospital, attended by innumerable notables from the London medical, scientific, and literary worlds, including Dickens. The notorious O'key sisters and others provided sensationalized demonstrations of Elliotson's commitment to exploring the power of animal magnetism. The controversy involved public scandal, allegations of sexual impropriety, bitter warfare within the faculty of the University and its board of trustees, the condemnation of mesmerism as quackery, and finally the pressures that motivated Elliotson to resign his

---

[23] Elliotson describes his contact with Chenevix in his *Human Physiology*, 5th edition (London, 1835-1840), pp. 680-681.

[24] *The Lancet* (June 13, 1829), 341-344.

professorship and leave forever the world of academic medicine for the public espousal of the "mighty curative powers" of animal magnetism.[25]

In 1843 *The Zoist* became the official voice of the movement in England. But beginning in 1836 a torrent of pamphlets and books on the subject, many written in English, some translated from French and particularly German, appeared in England and were widely read and reviewed. The most significant of these books in characterizing the movement and capturing the texture of the mesmeric mania are Jung-Stilling's *Theory of Pneumatology* (1834), James Campbell Colquhoun's *Isis Revelata* (1836), Dupotet's *An Introduction to the Study of Animal Magnetism* (1838), Elliotson's *Human Physiology* (1835-1840), Chauncy Hare Townshend's *Facts in Mesmerism* (1840), James Braid's *Neurypnology* (1843), Harriet Martineau's *Letters on Mesmerism* (1845), and James Esdaile's *Mesmerism in India* (1847).

Published in London in 1834, Jung-Stilling's *Theory of Pneumatology* made its way to many shelves, including Dickens', because it seemed an authoritative refutation of the materialistic philosophies that were threatening Christian belief in the supernatural world. "In Reply to the Question, What Ought To Be Believed Concerning Presentiments, Visions, and Apparitions According to Nature, Reason, and Scripture," the late Professor of the University of Heidelberg and Marburg claimed that "the whole creation consist solely of essential realized ideas of the Deity" or "original existences" and that "spirits, angels, and men" are some of the various and infinite classes of these original existences.[26] Though the assumptions are Platonic and Christian, the enemy is materialism and science, both the philosophies and the professions that throw doubt on the credibility of transcendental views of reality.

[25] The events of 1837-1838 at University College Hospital are recounted in *The Lancet* for those years, in Dupotet's book, in Clarke, and in scattered sources.
[26] Jung-Stilling, p. 370.

Long dead before the Victorians began their matter-and-mind, body-and-soul debates, Jung-Stilling appeared in England at the crucial beginning of the battles, emphasizing the independence and permanence of the soul in an imaginative manner. He represented the attempt to absorb the new science into Christian eschatology. Devoting only a short section to the mesmeric claims, he vouched for their actuality, asserting that "light, electric, magnetic, galvanic matter, and other, appear to be all one and the same body. . . . This light or ether, is the element which connects soul and body, and the spiritual and material world together."[27] In the battle against anti-Christian materialism and against Christian naturalists, magnetism was a potent weapon that "undeniably proves that we have an inward man, a soul, which is constituted of the divine spark, the immortal spirit, possessing reason and will, and of a luminous body, which is inseparable from it."[28] As if providing a rationale for a sophisticated ghost story, Jung-Stilling imagined that animal magnetism could enable an individual "in the present life" to "detach his soul" from his body, obliterating the restrictions of time and space, and make contact with "the world of spirits." The ghost story, then, for Jung-Stilling, was not only metaphor but context, an attempt to weave together the new science and the old religion on the assumptions that were always implicit in Christian supernaturalism. The anti-materialistic and anti-mechanistic emphasis of Carlyle, Bulwer, Dickens, Tennyson, Browning, et al., embraced the excitement of this societal ghost story, though perhaps of this distinguished group only Carlyle did not believe in either magnetism or spirits. But Jung-Stilling's English publisher and translator were right when they posited an audience for theories about both.

It was an audience that read with sanguine and scandalized avidity John C. Colquhoun's *Isis Revelata, An Inquiry Into The Origin, Progress, and Present State of Animal*

[27] *Ibid.*, p. 372. [28] *Ibid.*

Magnetism (1836). Colquhoun had the distinction of being denounced by both Christian eschatologists of the
school of Jung-Stilling and scientific materialists such as
Elliotson, Braid, and Esdaile. Both schools objected to his
amiable eclecticism; each found in him little or nothing
of its own preoccupations. Colquhoun was a gentleman
amateur who initiated a widely imitated type of book on
mesmerism whose main purpose was to touch all bases—
historical and phenomenological—in an attempt to demonstrate that the phenomenon was real and worth investigat-
ing. The formula, copied with variations by Henry Hall
Sherwood, William Lang, John Forbes, William Newnham,
Spencer Hall, Thomas South, George Barth, and Thomas
Capern, among others,[29] produced a leisurely account of the
origin of the movement, a theory of the nature of the force,
discussion of the relationship between magic and animal
magnetism, a review of the great literature that contained
statements relevant to mesmerism, a description of the relationship between subject and operator, a catalogue of the
various mesmeric phenomena, including trance and previ-
sion, and frequent long accounts of cases, either read about
or observed by the author, in support of his conclusions. If
Colquhoun's book has any special significance of its own,
other than that it was widely read and became the model
for similar works, it is in the emphasis that it placed on
the importance of the will in mesmeric relationships and
in including in toto the report of the French Academy's
commission on mesmerism of 1828. Englishmen who had
accepted the damning report of the first commission of 1784

[29] See Henry Hall Sherwood, *The Motive Power of Organic Life*
(London, 1841), William Lang, *Mesmerism: Its History* (London,
1843), John Forbes, *Illustrations of Modern Mesmerism* (London,
1845), William Newnham, *Human Magnetism; its claim to dispassionate inquiry* (London, 1845), Spencer T. Hall, *Mesmeric Experiences* (London, 1845), Thomas South, *Early Magnetism* (London,
1846), George Barth, *The Mesmerist's Manual* (London, 1851), and
Thomas Capern, *The Mighty Curative Powers of Mesmerism* (London,
1851).

were disconcerted to learn that the new commission had strongly ameliorated the earlier condemnation.

Though Colquhoun proclaimed many of the same eschatological assumptions that characterize the Christian transcendentalists who accepted mesmerism as another proof of the reality of the invisible and the existence of the soul, it is in his references to the importance of the will in mesmerism that he helps create a major Victorian tradition. Many Victorian mesmerists, including Elliotson, continued to believe in the existence of an external invisible fluid or pervasive magnetic force suffusing the universe. But as early as Colquhoun it began to be claimed that the magnetic force was also an internal power, existing within the human body and transmitted from mesmeric operator to subject by the force of will. Magnetism was like human energy, invisible except in its results, and within and under the control of gifted individuals. "The will is the grand agent in the production of magnetic phenomena."[30]

Dupotet's *An Introduction to the Study of Animal Magnetism* (1838) emphasizes that "it is not to be forgotten that great mental energy, sustained concentration of the will, is necessary to control its influence."[31] Dickens' good friend Chauncy Hare Townshend, in *Facts in Mesmerism* (1840), remarks that "Even the swimmer, who learns at length to surmount the boisterous surf, or to stem the adverse stream, will revel in the consciousness of awakened power. How much more must the mental enthusiast riot in the display of energies so long concealed, so wondrously developed."[32] A characteristic Victorian triad—energy, will, and power—emerges from the discussion, and is relentlessly accompanied in the larger context by problems of morality. It becomes widely recognized that these three concerns are potentially both destructive and constructive. In the very first year of "the mesmeric mania" in England, when Elliotson and Dupotet were under attack for their experiments at Univer-

[30] Newnham, p. 377.   [31] Dupotet, p. 341.
[32] Townshend, p. 36.

sity College Hospital, Dupotet tried to make clear the fundamental moral and benevolent essence of the new force:

"And if anyone should ask what is the moral tendency of the doctrine of animal magnetism, I should answer, that it obviously tends to establish the spiritual ascendency of man over . . . material conditions . . . and affords a precursory evidence of a future state of being, which belief in itself cannot fail to suggest those principles of self-government and moral conduct which alone can promote the real welfare and happiness of society."[33]

Great forces, great energies, had been released; and now, assured of their moral constructiveness, the Victorians desired to use this infusion of energy and this new power for the good of individuals and society.

Among the different paths to progress within mesmerism the most controversial was that of the scientist. In addition to being damned by the transcendentalists for their particular species of foul materialism, the mesmeric scientists, mostly physicians, were equally condemned by their scientific peers for departing from the normal rules of evidence and verifiability. Colquhoun, who was accused by Elliotson of "nonsense, credulity, and coarseness," and Dupotet and Townshend were amateur anti-materialists, neither theologians nor scientists.[34] Trained in nothing in particular, their imaginations had become inflamed with the possibilities of a new idea, and each played a significant role in popularizing it. But without the concern and commitment of John Elliotson it is doubtful that their movement would have received in England the serious attention given it by the educated and the public as a whole. Elliotson's reputation as scientist was solidly secure by 1837; mesmerism, however, was deeply suspect. While Dupotet maintained that it had become accepted as a legitimate medical tool on the

[33] Dupotet, p. 341.
[34] John C. Colquhoun, *Hints on Animal Magnetism* (Edinburgh, 1838), p. 86, and Elliotson, *Human Physiology*, pp. 689, 692-693.

continent, he expected "to encounter the same obstacles, the same prejudices, even the same personal hostility which I had to contend against twenty years ago in Paris."[35] He was absolutely correct, though Elliotson, whose reputation was so high, bore the brunt of the criticism; in the end his career was laid low, and from 1840 to his death in 1868 his medical contemporaries hardly missed an occasion to denounce him. But Elliotson, followed by James Esdaile and James Braid, represents the serious scientific approach to the phenomena: the attempt to categorize its various manifestations, to apply scientific standards of evidence and verifiability, to incorporate the results into larger diagnostic and prognostic theories (particularly in respect to diseases of the nervous system), to use the new force as a curative agent in the treatment of illnesses (which resulted in the foundation of the London Mesmeric Infirmary in 1849), and to present to the medical world the claims of mesmerism as an effective anaesthesia in surgical operations.

Elliotson's textbook *Human Physiology* (1835-1840), which went through more than five editions in a short period, had started as far back as 1815 as a translation of the esteemed German physician J. F. Blumenbach's *Institutiones Physiologicae*. (Dickens refers to the "Blumenbach theory" about the swinish qualities of the "descendents of Adam" in *Martin Chuzzlewit*.) Blumenbach's work had in later editions been reduced to footnotes, and, finally, Elliotson in 1835 produced a full medical textbook. Like many such Victorian endeavors, though scientific by the standards of the period, it was an encyclopedia of human teleology, ontology, and physiology, all medical knowledge and history against the larger humanistic background. Between 1835 and the completion of the fifth edition of 1840 Elliotson added to his explanation and defense of phrenology and to his rather brief material on mesmerism a long assertive chapter on the truth of mesmerism and its utility in medical science, particularly in the treatment of nervous

[35] Dupotet, p. 2.

disorders like epilepsy. The argument was supported with examples from Dupotet's and his own clinical and public experiments. Whereas in earlier editions Elliotson had admitted being impressed with the minimal mesmeric claims, in the fifth edition he presented an account of his own involvement with mesmerism between 1827 and 1838 and an assertion of his new commitment to the larger claims of the movement in regard to the nature of mesmeric force, the best means of conducting and communicating it, and its role in the treatment of illness. Widely read by the serious public, the book had substantial impact in medical circles particularly. A generation of medical students could not avoid giving consideration to the subject. Few of Elliotson's professional peers could escape the pressure to have some opinion on it.

The official organs of the profession reacted with abrupt and definitive hostility, declaring that Elliotson's acceptance of mesmerism was an astounding aberration in the scientific discipline and procedures of a doctor previously notable for his scrupulosity. While there seemed some substance worth investigation in the phenomena of sleep-waking and mesmeric trance, scientists as materialistic and positivistic as Elliotson saw nothing but deception in many of the major mesmeric performances, such as those by the "primadonna of the magnetic stage." They saw utter absurdity in the claim of clairvoyance.

While the mesmeric anti-materialists spared Elliotson the condemnation that would naturally result from the confrontation of opposing doctrines (they could ill afford to defame a general supporter of such prominence), Elliotson's scientific materialism seemed much too worldly and Church of England for many of the mystic temperaments that had made mesmerism their enthusiasm. In criticizing Colquhoun's "inordinate love of the marvellous, whether true or false, instead of knowledge and judgment," Elliotson dramatized the division:

"Materialism is as great a horror to him [Colquhoun] as

phrenology; and he fancies that mesmerism proves the existence of soul independent of body, and is doing wonders
by weaning people 'from the deadly errors of materialism
and infidelity.' . . . He is thus ignorant that materialists
may not only believe in God, but in the divine authority of
Scripture, and more honour Scripture by looking implicitly
in full faith to it alone, as God's authority, for their belief
in a future state, than those who endeavor to make its decla-
rations more probable by fancying a soul immortal in its
own nature and independent of matter, when the Scripture
tells us we shall rise as matter,—with bodies, and go to
heaven with bodies, where Christ, God himself, sits bodily,
—as matter, flesh, blood, and bones, in the word of the
Church of England."[36]

Elliotson's scientific materialism simply refused to admit
of the existence of soul independent of body, a position that
the Jung-Stilling camp abhorred. But mesmerism could be
the soul for many different bodies or the body for many
different depictions of the soul. Like the good doctor he
was, Elliotson preferred to remain with the facts of the body
without rejecting the Christian tradition that the Victorians
generally accepted as the larger context of reality.

The work of James Esdaile in India, which Elliotson
published in *The Zoist* and then as a separate pamphlet
under the title *Mesmerism in India*, exemplifies one of the
approaches for which the scientific materialists had great
hopes. Elliotson himself had published in 1843 *Numerous
Cases of surgical operations without pain in the mesmeric
state with remarks upon the opposition of many members
of the Royal medical and chirurgical society and others to
the reception of the inestimable blessings of mesmerism.*
Both physicians were astounded and horrified that the medical profession, particularly surgeons, among them Elliotson's former colleagues and bitter opponents at University
College Hospital, refused to make use of mesmeric trance as
an anaesthetic in surgical operations. Both books consist of

[36] Elliotson, *Human Physiology*, p. 691.

case after case in which Elliotson and Esdaile claim that surgical operations had been performed without pain under the
influence of mesmerism. The doctors were accused of fraud,
and of having themselves been its victims. But it was not
opposition but progress that had the strongest role in dis-
couraging if not eliminating the possible anaesthetic uses of
mesmerism. Despite Elliotson's and Esdaile's claim that mesmerism was less disruptive to the physical system than chlo-
roform, the introduction of ether in 1847 made the obstacles
too great to overcome: even in Victorian medicine and philosophy an instant and consistent physical agent was to be
preferred to a time-consuming and inconsistent psychological one. The enemies of Elliotson and mesmerism gloated
euphorically "that one of the limbs of mesmerism was cut
away by ether." Richard Liston, Elliotson's former colleague,
proclaimed: "Rejoice! mesmerism, and its professors, have
met with a heavy blow and great discouragement. An American dentist has used ether (inhalation of it) to destroy sensation in his operations, and the plan has succeeded in the
hands of Warren, Hayward, and others in Boston. Yesterday,
I amputated a thigh . . . without the patient being aware of
what I was doing, so far as regards pain. . . . Rejoice!"[37]

One final twist in the scientific approach to the mesmeric
phenomenon was to suggest new directions for its utilization
at a time when its defeat as a potential scientific-medical
tool was becoming clearly apparent, despite the continuance
of the public mania throughout the 1840's and 1850's. When
James Braid in 1843 published his *Neurypnology or, The
Rationale of Nervous Sleep, Considered in Relation with
Animal Magnetism* he initiated a series of essays and books
that eventually brought him to conclude in public that the
mesmeric fluid did not exist. It was not an external force.
There was no separate power or entity that had a physiological existence, visible or invisible. He claimed that the
phenomena produced by mesmerism or animal magnetism

[37] *The Zoist*, Vol. VI, No. XXII (July 1848), 210-211.

24

were the result of strong suggestibility between the mesmeric operator and the subject.

What the movement from Mesmer to Elliotson had vigorously denied, despite the differences of assumption and method from group to group within the movement, was now being presented as true, though the terminology had been altered. Critics of mesmerism for seventy years had declared that the phenomenon was not real in the material sense, that there did not exist some invisible but identifiable force outside of man but simply a mental or imaginative force not independent of the ordinary workings of the mind. Mesmerism was like poetry, an example of the inventive powers of the human imagination. All of the performances of subjects under the influence of mesmerism were the result of powerful imaginations working in congruence, not of an all-pervasive fluid or force that had a separate and permanent existence of its own. Braid, rejecting the language of metaphor for that of a newly developing science, invented the word "hypnosis" to describe what the mesmeric operator did to his subject. He insisted that "the manifestations were entirely attributable to the mechanical pressure operating on an excited state of the nervous system," that suggestion was the key process, and that "hypnosis" could play an important medical role as a curative agent.[38]

The details of the conflicting claims were eagerly followed by a public avid for explanation and education. But despite the attraction of the intricacies of position within the mesmeric movement, the press at large was naturally more interested in the titillation of sexual scandal, sensationalized accounts of various well-known personalities, and the claims of astounding, almost miraculous, cures. The avalanche of claims, discussions, and accusations throughout the 1840's and 1850's created a public consciousness about the phenomenon that made the terminology and assumptions of mesmerism part of the air the early Victorians breathed.

[38] Braid, p. 99.

Dickens' own involvement with mesmerism and his friendships with Elliotson and Townshend simply epitomize the widespread interest that claimed the attention not only of the medical profession and the general public but also that of serious poets, novelists, critics, painters, the upper middle class, and the aristocracy. Among the literary famous, Coleridge, Wordsworth, Browning, Tennyson, Arnold, Clough, Collins, Thackeray, Trollope, and both Carlyles became interested to varying degrees, in the case of Tennyson to the extent of practicing mesmerism himself. Mesmeric salons proliferated; select demonstrations became a parlor game for the fascinated elite. Monckton Milnes wrote "Mesmerism in London" (1840). Mary Russell Mitford wrote to Elizabeth Barrett that "certainly what is wanted of mesmerism is, not the wild notions of girls of nineteen, but the power to alleviate disease and perform operations without pain." Elizabeth asserted that, "for my own part, I have long been a believer, *in spite of papa*." Harriet Martineau intensified the public scandal by publishing in *The Athenaeum* and then in her pamphlet *Letters on Mesmerism* (1845) all the details, rehashed again in the *Autobiography*, of her miraculous cure by mesmerism and her firm belief in its "mighty curative powers."[39]

⟦ 3 ⟧

Some time at least as early as January 1838, Dickens, not quite twenty-six, having finished *Pickwick Papers*, in the process of writing *Oliver Twist* and about to write four more novels in the next five years, became fascinated by

[39] See Monckton Milnes, "Mesmerism in London," unpublished ms., Syracuse University Library; *The Life of Mary Russell Mitford*, ed. A. G. K. L'Estrange (N.Y., 1870), p. 273; *Letters of Mrs. Browning*, ed. F. Kenyon (London, 1897), p. 197; and *Harriet Martineau's Autobiography*, ed. Marie Weston Chapman (London, 1878), I, 437-521. A brief general account of the fascination of some distinguished Victorians with the mesmeric phenomenon appears in Arno L. Bader, "Those Mesmeric Victorians," *Colophon* (Vol. II, N.S., No. 3, 1936), 335-353.

Elliotson's experiments.[40] The novelist and his frequent companion, George Cruikshank, who had done the illustrations for *Sketches by Boz*, visited the wards of North London Hospital or, as it was becoming commonly called, University College Hospital, on January 14, 1838. From 48 Doughty Street, just north of Gray's Inn, where Dickens had moved in March of the preceding year, it was a comparatively short carriage ride to Gower Street, where the new hospital had been constructed and opened for patients on Nov. 1, 1834.[41]

William Wood, Elliotson's assistant, was the primary operator in the wards on that day. Hannah Hunter, "a delicate-looking little girl" who "was admitted on January 1, 1838," was one of the half dozen or so patients being treated by "mesmeric operations." Having suffered for many years from "disorders of the nervous system . . . pains in the left ear," and attacks of asthma, she had become about six months before "subject to fits of convulsions, rigidity, with insensibility . . . and . . . has now complete paralysis of the lower extremities. . . . She has never menstruated." Though "genuine mesmeric sleep" was not induced in Hannah until January 20th, as with the other patients who had been daily

[40] Though specific indebtedness is always acknowledged in a footnote, there is a general indebtedness for biographical information and ambiance that transcends citable instances to John Forster's *Charles Dickens* (London, 1872) and Edgar Johnson's *Charles Dickens: His Tragedy and His Triumph* (N.Y., 1952). However, Forster seems to have censored from his account almost all his knowledge of Dickens' involvement with mesmerism. Johnson's account is helpful but incomplete and diffuse. He indicates that "Dickens met Dr. John Elliotson and first became interested in mesmerism . . . around this time"—which seems to be the summer and fall of 1838 (p. 221). The date is at least six months earlier.

[41] Many of my facts concerning the hospital, the medical school, and some of the detailed accounts of Elliotson's professional career and activities, especially in regard to the mesmeric controversy, come from the pages of *The Lancet*, which published weekly beginning in 1823 and is still in existence. Wherever it has seemed reasonable to do so, I have given the specific reference from *The Lancet*. In certain cases, in order not to overburden reader, printer, and text, I have simply indicated the sources of my account with a general reference.

undergoing mesmeric therapy the basic procedure was rather simple, though there were many imaginative variations in the case of Hannah and others: William Wood's hands were extended towards her head while Miss Hunter sat in a chair facing him. After a minute and a half "she became insensible." With other patients on that day Wood and Elliotson used other procedures also, more likely than not the common practice of moving the hands or "making passes" in a steady, rhythmic pattern of the operator's choice, to be varied on the basis of effect from subject to subject. On February 6 in Hannah Hunter "sleep was induced by Mr. Wood merely fixing his attention on her for the space of four minutes, without the hand being even extended." The most common method of awakening the subject from the mesmeric sleep was moving the two thumbs or any two corresponding fingers in transverse movements across the subject's eyebrows. On February 8 "Dr. Elliotson . . . proposed to ascertain how many of the transverse movements were required to awake her." Two movements failed. "In another minute a third movement was made, and she instantly awoke."[42]

Dickens' reactions to these first experiments are unrecorded, but he must indeed have been fascinated, for his friendship with Elliotson dates from about this time. He returned again and again to witness experiments and demonstrations. He studied mesmerism closely and learned from Wood and Elliotson how to function as an operator and induce mesmeric sleep. Watching Hannah Wood early in January he probably felt the same sense of awesome mystery, of hidden natural powers in the process of demonstration and revelation, and the same thrill of dangerous exploration and potential scandal that a large number of his contemporaries were beginning to feel as Elliotson brought the new science more and more to the attention of the public through his demonstrations. At the end of April, Dickens' friend, the actor William Macready, whose family doctor Elliotson had

[42] *The Lancet* (May 26, 1838), 314-315.

become in 1836, went "to the North London Hospital, where we saw Dr. Elliotson's exhibition of his epileptic patients under a course of animal magnetism. It is very extraordinary, and I cannot help thinking that they are partly under a morbid influence and partly lend themselves to a delusion."[43] Dickens had initial doubts. In the same month, in what was probably a pattern of constant visits, he went with William Harrison Ainsworth, who wrote to his cousin: "Are you at all interested in the subject of animal magnetism? The other day I accompanied my friend Dickens to see some girls magnetized by Dr. Elliotson, and a more curious exhibition I never beheld. Unless there was some collusion, which I can scarcely imagine, the effects of the magnetizer were truly surprising—almost magical. . . ."[44]

There was no reason to doubt Elliotson's honesty. His career before 1837 was a record of extraordinarily solid and adventuresome professional accomplishments.[45] The short, lithe, dark-eyed, dark-haired Londoner, born in 1791, had risen in the corrupt, nepotic world of London academic medicine through his talents, his courage, and his passion for reform. He was assisted by *The Lancet*, an influential medical journal founded in 1823 by Thomas Wakley for the purpose of exposing the abuses of corrupt and contented

[43] *Macready's Reminiscences and Selections From His Diaries and Letters*, ed. Sir Frederick Pollock (N.Y. 1875), p. 429.

[44] Stewart Marsh Ellis, *William Harrison Ainsworth and His Friends* (London, 1911), I, 335.

[45] The facts of Elliotson's life are increasingly difficult to ascertain. There is no standard biography. Though Mr. Williams' essay in *Doctors Differ* does not cite sources, he has informed me that to the best of his memory he has relied almost exclusively on *The Lancet*. My sources are mainly the pages of *The Lancet, The Zoist*, a journal founded and edited by Elliotson which published from 1843 to 1856, unpublished letters at The Pierpont Morgan Library, The Huntington Library, and The Wellcome Institute for the History of Medicine, surviving portraits and other visual representations, and the many scattered references that appear throughout Victorian autobiographies, lives, and letters, and in modern editions of the letters of those contemporaries who thought Elliotson interesting and/or important enough to mention.

29

professionalism.[46] When *The Lancet* began publishing Elliotson's clinical lectures in 1828, he advanced in a short
time from a relatively unknown junior physician at St.
Thomas's Hospital to a nationally known exponent of the
experimental use of new drugs and a widely popular teacher
who was the first physician in a London medical school to
base his lectures on actual ward cases. He transformed his
thrice weekly ward-rounds into teaching experiences. Within
a short time after the beginning of the publication of his
clinical lectures, Elliotson's reputation was such that *The
Lancet*, rather proud of its role in the transformation, reported that his income from his private practice had risen
from £500 to £5,000 per annum.[47]

In July of 1837 Elliotson was introduced to the "Baron"
Dupotet de Sennevoy, a rather "plain, intelligent, unassum-
ing-looking" Frenchman, "a small, spare man, with a pale,
intellectual face" who "did not speak English."[48] The mysterious "Baron" had played a role in French mesmeric-med-
ical circles since the early 1820's, associated both with private salons and with the wards of the Hôtel-Dieu in Paris.
His activities had figured prominently in the report on mesmerism made by a select committee appointed by the French
Academy in 1828.[49] Dupotet did his best to convince the
committee, with partial success, and early in 1837 he had
come to England to teach, practice, and spread the doctrine.
Elliotson "had long been of opinion that if medicine were to
be improved in its practical value it must be by therapeutics." He "immediately entered heart and soul into the
subject" and "placed at the disposal of Dupotet several cases
of epileptic girls then under his care. . . ."[50]

[46] See Samuel Squire Sprigge, *The Life and Times of Thomas Wakley*
(London, 1912) and *The Lancet: A Brief Historical Account of The
Lancet* (N.Y., 1921).
[47] *The Lancet* (Sept. 2, 1837), 836.　　　[48] Clarke, p. 161.
[49] The "Report on the Magnetic Experiments made by a Committee
of the Royal Academy of Medicine at Paris" is reprinted in its entirety
as "Appendix No. 1" in J. C. Colquhoun, *Isis Revelata, An Inquiry Into
The Origin, Progress, and Present State of Animal Magnetism* (London,
1836), II, 193-293.
[50] Clarke, pp. 160-161.

Dupotet wrote at the beginning of September 1837 that he had been "introduced nearly two months since to the University College Hospital by Dr. Elliotson, to demonstrate the existence of magnetism. . . . I at first made some essays before that distinguished physician, which did not present very great results, but we soon after began to arrive at the object of my researches."[51] Naturally the experiments attracted attention and controversy. Both Dupotet and Elliotson agreed that they were to be open to gentlemen of culture, the better to insure by the light of public scrutiny their objectivity. Publicity brought what both experimenters considered premature conclusions, based on ancient prejudices rather than on demonstrable facts. *The Lancet* reserved judgment and assigned its sub-editor, Mr. George Mills, to follow the experiments closely. He was responsible for most of *The Lancet* accounts of the mesmeric activities of the next year.[52] He watched Dupotet carry on almost daily experiments during the months of July and August. At the end of August Elliotson no longer had any doubts and, before departing on his annual holiday trip to the continent, delivered a clinical lecture in which he affirmed his commitment to the value of pursuing such experiments. *The Lancet* published the lecture in full on September 9th, and while Elliotson was away it was read by the magazine's large medical audience. The popular journals carried the subject to the general public.

The lecture was a sober account of various ward cases in which standard procedures had failed to produce therapeutic results, particularly in cases of epilepsy, followed by a discussion of somnambulistic activities manifested by a female epileptic patient, a phenomenon Elliotson called "sleep-waking." Elliotson then made a crucial leap, pointing out the resemblance between naturally produced somnam-

51 *The Lancet* (Sept. 16, 1837), 905.

52 Clarke, pp. 159-160, identifies himself as the reporter of Elliotson's clinical lecture on mesmerism. "G. M.," the author of *The Lancet* accounts of Elliotson's public demonstrations and ward experiments, is obviously George Mills, the sub-editor of the journal who was present at the August experiments at Wakley's home.

bulism and artificially produced mesmeric sleep-waking or trance. This perception was of major importance to Elliotson and to the history of magic and medicine. Two worlds that rational science had desperately tried to keep apart were suddenly brought together. "Now the question arose, whether these states" and the unusual powers and activities inherent within them "could be produced by means of art. . . . Whether to believe these things or not, he (Dr. E.) did not know, but he was determined to see for himself. . . . There was no collusion, he felt convinced, in this case." Supernatural explanations were not to Elliotson's training or taste. Since the phenomena were scientific, "there could be no disgrace in taking the trouble to inquire into the effect of mesmerism; not, of course, going to anything supernatural, but only as to its production of such effects as we observed in other cases, such as sleep, coma, sleep-waking, loss of power and sensation in the limbs, etc. So, also, we had seen persons who appeared to be asleep, but who were sensible to external objects; and, again, we saw some faculties possessing extraordinary sensibility, while others were more obtuse than natural. This was the extent to which the inquiry would be carried."[53]

Elliotson continued the practice he had introduced in the early 1820's of keeping detailed case-book records of his patients' entire hospital regimen. He left for the continent in full confidence that Dupotet would continue to amass relevant data from his ongoing experiments in the wards— and returned at the beginning of October to discover that in his absence the medical committee had closed the hospital to Dupotet. Dupotet had been informed "that the experiments should be discontinued."[54] On Elliotson's authority Dupotet continued through much of the next year to attend the ward experiments and the theater demonstrations. But Elliotson, assisted by Wood, now became the main operator. The Doc-

[53] *The Lancet* published this clinical lecture in full on Sept. 9, 1837, 866-873.
[54] *The Lancet* (Oct. 14, 1837), 99.

tor maintained that he did not believe "a ten-thousandth part of what had been asserted respecting mesmerism . . . but . . . his conclusions were, that certain circumstances which were observed to take place in health and disease, such as sleep, and somnambulism, might be produced by mesmerism." Those who believed that during the past summer he had committed himself to the most extravagant curative and diagnostic claims for this phenomenon were purveyors of scandal, as well as remiss in scientific objectivity since they themselves had not witnessed the experiments.

Despite opposition, the experiments continued. Elliotson, Dupotet, and Wood trained clinical clerks to perform mesmeric therapy in the wards under Elliotson's authority. From July 1837 to Dickens' first visit in January 1838 the experiments had been conducted regularly, with particular emphasis on first exhausting standard medical remedies, concentrating on cases of epilepsy and other disorders of the nervous system (among them hysterical paralysis), and collecting a body of data that might establish the facts about what effects mesmerism actually produced. Could these effects be repeated on a statistically regular basis in order to provide data for credible generalizations about the actuality of these phenomena? Elliotson believed that only frequent experiments could provide the answer; he continued to conduct them, under public scrutiny, though he was much criticized by his colleagues. Not only did Dickens attend, but, as word spread about these activities, a large cross-section of London academic, medical, aristocratic, and literary life began so to crowd the wards with visits by "gentlemen of education" that Elliotson decided to hold certain demonstrations in more commodious surroundings.[55]

[55] See the general accounts of mesmeric activities in *The Lancet* (Sept. 1837 to March 1838).

CHAPTER

II

Dickens Discovers Mesmerism

⟦ 1 ⟧

On the 4th of April 1837 "a girl sixteen years of age, a house-maid" named Elizabeth O'key, who had been subject for the twelve previous months to attacks of epilepsy, had been admitted to University College Hospital under the care of Elliotson.[1] Her sister Jane followed, also epileptic, but lacking the abilities that were soon to motivate hostile critics to call Elizabeth "the prima donna of the magnetic stage." She was unusually small and physically undeveloped.[2] On the back of her right hand, "she had several inflamed spots . . . sites of large warts . . . which she frequently picked, and prevented from healing."[3] She "was of a stunted and spare stature, her countenance being of a chlorotic sickliness, looking pale and melancholy . . . there was no evidence of her having made any approach towards puberty."[4]

For Elliotson, the physical deficiencies of such patients were functions of their diseases; for many hostile observers, the O'keys lent themselves to mesmeric activities not because of their diseases but as an extreme manifestation of certain psycho-sexual peculiarities. In the public mind, potential sexual power and exploitation were implicit in the

[1] *The Lancet* (Sept. 9, 1837), 866.   [2] *Ibid.* (June 23, 1838), 457.
[3] *Ibid.* (July 21, 1838), 587.   [4] *Ibid.* (Aug. 18, 1838), 727.

relationship between the operator and his subject, between the strong-willed Victorian male and the potentially hysterical female. "An Eye-Witness" pointed out that "several male epileptics have . . . been experimented on, and in no one instance has any sensible effect been produced." Not only were operators always male but subjects were hardly likely to be affected unless they were female. The same observer claimed that since "Dr. Elliotson has been away," for his September vacation of 1837, "the scenes exhibited have been most absurd; in fact, they have bordered on the disgusting."[5] Even an anonymous correspondent, who "entirely" gave "up the idea of collusion on the part of the patient," produced as evidence for the authenticity of the O'keys the theory that "one of the first symptoms by which cerebral affections in general demonstrate themselves and particularly in women . . . is a diminution of the ordinary restraint on language. . . . Everybody knows that when ladies faint, there is a hustling of gentlemen; which is not so much on account of the necessity of cutting laces, as for fear of what might be said by the patient during the temporary suspension of restraint. The purest-minded woman upon earth, might talk of her innocent preferences, her state of health, or many other subjects on which witnesses would not be desirable."[6] *The Lancet* was later to retail scandalous antimesmeric stories of rape, debauchery, and orgies, and Elliotson was to be the victim of an anonymous pamphlet called *Eyewitness, A Full Discovery of the Strange Practices of Dr. E. on the Bodies of his Female Patients! At his house . . . with all the secret experiments he makes upon them. . . . The whole as seen by an eye-witness, and now fully divulged!*[7]

The O'keys were experienced in a specialized form of public performance. Both girls had taken part in the rituals of the controversial evangelical preacher Edward Irving, Carlyle's good friend, who found religious and spiritual sig-

---

[5] *Ibid.* (Oct. 14, 1837), 100.   [6] *Ibid.* (Sept. 2, 1837), 839.
[7] *Eyewitness*, London, 1842, British Museum, 6495bb.3.(40).

nificance in the phenomenon of babbling or talking in tongues, a variant of the Methodist emphasis on enthusiasm and public conversion. At Islington Green, where Irving preached, Elizabeth O'key "first developed her powers as an enunciator of the 'unknown tongues.' "[8] When Elliotson came to give the first public demonstration of the forces of animal magnetism with Elizabeth O'key as the star and her sister in a supportive role, both O'keys had had considerable experience in performances, and both had already exhibited talents of a special sort, engaging in a kind of mental-spiritual concentration and role-playing, sincere or not, before large public meetings conducted by Irving.

Elizabeth had already been mesmerized at least one hundred times in the little over a year in which she had been a patient in the Hospital under Elliotson's care. This "patient par excellence, the prima donna of the 'magnetic' stage," was accused of having come to the hospital with a predisposition to cooperate, "having seen accounts of M. Dupotet's experiments in the papers; she was, therefore, not entirely ignorant of what was to be done, nor of the effects that were to be expected." Wood responded that though "she had applied to the hospital in consequence of having heard that M. Dupotet had the power of curing epilepsy, and for this purpose she was anxious to submit to his experiments . . . I should say she was totally ignorant of what was to be done," a claim that some were to believe and many to deny.

Dickens attended either the first demonstration on Thursday, May 10, 1838, or the second on Saturday, June 2nd, perhaps even both. "Amongst other distinguished persons" was "Charles Dickens, then just becoming famous as the author of the 'Pickwick Papers,' " attending with his friend George Cruikshank. "I well remember him, with his smooth reflecting face, his long black hair, his fine expressive eyes, and his noble forehead," a Dickens much like the one of Maclise's "Nickleby Portrait" of the next year.[9] In that novel

8 Clarke, pp. 162-164.
9 *Ibid.*, pp. 155-156.

Dickens describes Nicholas as having "as much thought or consciousness of what he was doing as if he had been in a magnetic slumber" (*NN*, VII). But the audience of over two hundred on May 10 were alert, buzzing with anticipation and excitement. "The company, so many of them as could find sitting-room," were "seated in the area of the theatre." Undoubtedly the crowded room was warm as Dickens jostled shoulders with the distinguished guests, among them several Members of Parliament, various members of the nobility, distinguished scientists, physicians, and surgeons from the hospital staff, members of the London University Board of Trustees, and literary and artistic gentlemen of the town. Certainly Sir William Molesworth was present, the editor of Hobbes, who had recently donated thirty guineas to University College Hospital in appreciation for the "pleasure and instruction which he obtained in witnessing the experiments of Dr. Elliotson in Mesmerism" and as affirmation of his belief "that the researches now being made . . . will add considerably to our knowledge of the phenomena of Nature, extend the bounds of science, and afford explanations of numerous facts previously inexplicable."[10]

The audience immediately focused on the three figures who occupied the center stage, the well-known doctor, his familiar assistant, and "a girl named O'key." Elliotson prefaced the demonstration with a crucial speech that was to become the prototype of his constant public repetition of his aims, methods, and principles:

"He was," he said, "fully aware that in prosecuting his

[10] Though specific quotations are usually cited, as in this case, *The Lancet* (May 26, 1838), 320, these accounts of the large public demonstrations of May 10 and June 2 and the following accounts of the ward experiments of these and the following months are taken from the seven special reports on Elliotson's activities that appeared in *The Lancet* (May 1838 to Aug. 1838). The account of the experiments conducted at Wakley's home on four occasions in the month of August were published in full, and later republished, in *The Lancet* (Sept. 1, 1838). In all instances in which I give a running historical account without frequent footnotes, the account has been reconstructed from *The Lancet* of these months.

inquiries into the subject, he exposed his character to risk, many persons believing that magnetism was a mere deception, or an absurdity. . . . He was firmly convinced of the reality of the facts which he had seen, and having since himself verified them, he considered it to be his duty to show them to the students, to the medical profession at large, and to any men of education who might take an interest in the matter. . . . Yet he had been asked to take the patients on whom the experiments were tried, away from the hospital, on these occasions, to a private lodging, or an hotel in the neighborhood. But he knew very well that if he had prosecuted his inquiries with closed doors, suspicion would have arisen that he was afraid of publicity, and of the testing of his assertions. . . . The institution, however, under whose roof they were now assembled, was established for the promulgation of truth, and the promotion of education founded on facts, and if the views which he taught were correct, then it was the duty of the other professors also to adopt them, whether the 'institution' was supposed to suffer or not from so doing. For the hospital was not founded in order to fill the pockets of the professors, but to throw light on truth and nature, and to expose fallacies. The question, then, to be decided was this, 'Is animal magnetism based on facts or fallacies?' "[11]

[2]

What the audience viewed on May 10th, to be repeated with variations on Saturday, June 2, before an even larger audience, were a series of experiments performed mainly between Elliotson and the O'keys to demonstrate Elliotson's growing belief that not only were the mesmeric phenomena real but that he had detected certain laws that governed their manifestations. While Elliotson spoke his introductory remarks on May 10, Elizabeth O'key sat impassively, as if unaware of the scrutiny of "spectacles, eyeglasses, and opera-glasses." Gradually the girl seemed to pass into the stage "of inoffen-

[11] *The Lancet* (May 26, 1838), 283.

sive delirium or sleep-waking." She was attracted by "a worn oak chair in the middle of the area." "The question of deception was at once met by a conviction, derived from appearances, that the most accomplished actor that ever trod the stage could not have presented the change with a truer show of reality." After exclaiming, "what a dirty-white chair," she turned to the Marquis of Anglesea and greeted him familiarly as "white trowsers." She then turned to Sir Charles Paget, asked "Why do you wear your hat?" and was proceeding to take his hand when "Dr. Elliotson approached her, and, unseen by the girl, waved his hand from the head downwards, behind her, without touching her. She instantly closed her eyes, tottered for a moment on her heels and fell backwards, in dead sleep. She was caught before reaching the ground." Awakening after half a minute, she was put to sleep again with a pass of the hand and then awakened by Elliotson's blowing twice in her face. She continued her expressions of pleasure with all bright things which she referred to as "such a white thing"—an ivory opera-glass, a breastpin from the handkerchief of a gentleman, a polished chair.

Her activities were constantly punctuated with familiar expressions, oblivious of polite class distinctions, usually accompanied by the expression, "How do ye?" After Elliotson had demonstrated what he called a state of catalepsy by showing that the blindfolded girl would move her fingers and limbs in response to movements of his own hands, the girl declared: "Don't be silly . . . you silly man. Oh, but you're a fool, Dr. Ellisson. Ha! Ha! How do ye? Mine won't go like yours. They ain't so silly. Oh, Dr. Ellisson, leave off, it's no use." Finally "they began to open and shut like the Doctor's, upon which her eyes closed, her head fell back, and she went fast asleep, from which state she was awoke by blowing in the face, instantly saying, as she did almost invariably, on every recovery from stupidity of sleep, 'Oh! How do ye?' "

Elliotson then attempted to demonstrate the first of the

laws that he believed he had discovered: that mass or surface has a directly increasing intensity in communicating the mesmeric fluid. For he had concluded in agreement with Mesmer and his main disciples that the mesmeric manifestations were due to a natural phenomenon like electricity that took the form of a pervasive magnetic field or fluid, almost like air, that could be brought under control and that could act on individuals with a power in direct proportion to the mass or surface through which the fluid was acting. Whereas one finger produced sleep-waking of a short duration, only seconds in fact, the more fingers or surface and mass that were brought to bear, the greater the length and intensity of the sleep-waking produced.

Experiments were tried on Elizabeth O'key involving the immovability of muscles and the lifting of unusually heavy weights. Within certain limitations, they seemed successful. After variations of the previous experiments, another "patient was now introduced, about two hours having elapsed from the commencement of the exhibition." This was Jane O'key. "The crowd was so dense in the area of the theatre, that . . . we could not note, with the same undeviating precision, the few experiments that were next performed." These were generally successful. But both Elliotson and Wood had the greatest difficulty in awakening her from "somnambulistic sleep." Wood decided to test "the alleged phenomena of clairvoyance" that "Dr. Elliotson afterwards remarked, had never before been tried upon her." Wood asked her when she would awake. After a few repetitions of the question, she answered in five minutes. Wood asked whether she would awake herself, and since the answer was no, requested instructions. The barely audible reply was that "You must awake me . . . By rubbing my neck." "The prophecy was tested by a watch, and just before the expiration of the time involved, Dr. Elliotson began to pass his thumbs transversely on the neck, continuing the process, but in vain, for half a minute, when Mr. Wood took it up, and in a few seconds the girl awoke to her natural state."

40

She complained that she had a headache. The crowd parted to let her pass out. As she walked through the audience, "many gentlemen, won by her apparent amiability, shook hands with her."

Elliotson had concluded "that respecting the influence of 'mass,' 'surface,' and 'numbers,' in magnetism, he recognized the existence of a law which permitted him to believe that this 'science' would, at some future day, be reducible to certain fixed principles. . . ." At the public demonstration on June 2 he wanted to demonstrate that his hypothesis was correct and to speculate further in such a way as to bring other aspects of the phenomenon under the rule of scientific law. The doctor knew of many cases in which "although no sensible effect was produced, yet the disease was disappearing." The O'keys were brought onto the stage.

First, some of the experiments of May 10th were repeated to provide the audience with illustrations of the four distinct states of mind and body produced by the mesmeric sleep-waking phenomenon: (1) The natural state of quiet rational reserve. (2) A state of harmless but vocal delirium produced by mesmeric passes. (3) A state of fixed paralysis produced by a further pass or so. (4) Either recovery within a minute or two or, if further passes were made, profound sleep from which the subject might be aroused by rubbing the eyebrows or blowing into the eyes, which usually resulted in a return to the second stage. But Elizabeth and Jane were most often during experiments semi-permanent inhabitants of the second stage, so that "to the spectator" it appeared to be their "natural condition." The results of the experiments were similar to those of May 10th. During one of Jane's voluble narrations "she was repeatedly pinched by visitors, without evincing the least sensation." After repeatedly failing to lift a weight over fifty pounds in her normal state, on the advice of her "negro . . . a spirit which she says constantly attends her, and whom she consults on various occasions," she lifted a weight of seventy pounds some three or four inches from the ground "as all eyes but her own

41

were fixed on the weights." Elizabeth, in her natural state, disapproving of Jane's volubility, was caught around the waist by her sister, whose eyes suddenly lighted on the crowd in the upper rows and exclaimed: " 'Only look! What a lot of heads! And faces of all sizes! Oh, there!' pointing to some- [one] who was gazing very curiously at her, 'Look at the fool.' " The audience laughed.

In the next few months Elliotson tried to prove that "mucous surfaces are much more sensible to the magnetic influence than cutaneous," that the insensibility produced during sleep-waking had anaesthetic potential, that magne- tism could be effected between an operator and his subject by indirect means, from a distance and through the use of magnetized objects, and that certain subjects while mag- netized had special powers of prediction that might have im- portant diagnostic uses. These experiments produced vol- uble opposition from the already hostile and expressions of incredibility from those who claimed to have open minds. Much of the hospital and university staff expressed fears for the reputation of the institution as a serious and respectable center of science. But Elliotson maintained the logic of his initial commitment: if the phenomenon was real, then there followed the necessity of testing the extent and in- tensity of its manifestations. If it were true that the pressure of her hands against those of another person would send Elizabeth to sleep, then it was only reasonable to test and demonstrate this. If his theory that the effective intensity of mesmeric phenomena was increased by mass or surface was accurate, then it followed that it made scientific sense to experiment with chains of linked human hands. And if it were true that certain substances could contain and trans- mit the mesmeric fluid, then it seemed perfectly reasonable to conduct experiments in which the intensity of such trans- missions could be measured.

But the most controversial of all the experiments was an extension of the assumption that if the power underlying the phenomenon was mental and invisible, then it seemed reasonable to determine if the sisters could "see," that is know and recount some event or fact occurring while blindfolded. The sisters had begun, in May 1838, to act out dramatically the manifestations of special visions in which they claimed the power of clairvoyance. Through mesmeric trance they could know accurately specific events that had not yet occurred, even those concerning life and death. This was naturally a matter of concern in a hospital. Could the girls be better diagnosticians than the doctors?

Early in May the O'keys had begun claiming contact with special guides who provided them with a power of predictive accuracy. After being ill on the 14th of May, Jane "inquired of her negro," whom she quite confidently revealed had told her "that the attack in her side was a swelling, in consequence of two ribs being strained in lifting heavy weights some days before." Towards the weary end of the three-hour public demonstration in the theatre on June 2, while the rain "was rattling in torrents on the skylight," she answered that her "negro" had told her that lifting eighty pounds would hurt her ribs. At 3 p.m. on Friday, June 1, Wood transcribed and put into a sealed envelope a statement made by Elizabeth while in a state of mesmeric somnambulism in which she predicted that she would be drowsy for the next forty-eight hours, after which she would fall into a twenty-four hour sleep from which she would be awakened into delirium by Wood's pressing his thumbs on the palms of her hands. In this state of delirium not only would she not know anyone but she would be "very ill tempered, cross, spiteful and mischievous . . . would say very bad things" and "if she got hold of knives she will cut anybody." In the ward at 4:30 on the afternoon of June 3 Elizabeth proceeded to perform in the manner predicted in the sealed letter "in the care of the matron of the hospital, with a direction on the outside 'that it might not be opened before Dr. Elliotson applied for it.' "

While it was noted that the predictions almost never involved information known beforehand to the audiences for these prophecies, Elliotson and Wood were becoming increasingly hopeful about the possibility of sensitive subjects through some special sensing apparatus being able to detect conditions affected by the magnetic fluid that could not be detected by those not under mesmeric trance. If the earlier demonstrations had actually proved the existence of special mesmeric powers and if any of the theories concerning their origin were correct—particularly the theory of a pervasive invisible fluid much like electricity—then it made good scientific sense for the doctor fearlessly to explore all possibilities of pre-vision. For if this pre-vision could be demonstrated to be an accurate predictive power, the consequences for the broadening of diagnostic capabilities would be immense.

[3]

Meanwhile the Hospital Committee, already having castigated Elliotson at a meeting early in June, had passed a resolution requesting that the doctor "refrain from further 'public exhibitions' of mesmerism." His written response requested that the committee agree to determine from lists Elliotson would submit "the names of such gentlemen as might in future apply for permission to witness the experiments." The committee responded that it refused to "sanction any exhibition."[12] The last large public demonstration was on June 2. But "numerous small parties" continued to be "entertained in corners of the wards . . . and the clinical clerks were employed . . . in manipulations upon epileptic and other patients." Throughout June, July, and August *The Lancet* reporter continued his weekly accounts, in which he constantly affirmed that if the O'keys are "impostors, there has never been forgetfulness of the part to be acted, even for a moment, on any occasion," and that all witnesses of the events, "however doubtful of other phenomena . . . say that at least the sleep is real." Elliotson con-

12 The various communications between the Hospital Committee, the College Council, and Elliotson appear in *The Lancet* (Jan. 5, 1839), and in Clarke, p. 177.

tinued to invite appropriate visitors who were still in town during the hot summer season.[13] *The Lancet* reporter continued to report to the medical world, the popular journals to the general public.

But Mill's employer, the influential Thomas Wakley, who had been a schoolfellow of Elliotson's, had grown increasingly suspicious. Probably prompted by the prestigious forces opposing Elliotson's experiments at the hospital, he decided that he wanted to see for himself. Wakley was a major power in the London medical world. As a pugnacious, caustic, and crusading medical journalist, himself a doctor, he had founded *The Lancet* in order to reform a complacent and self-serving profession. His strident reporting and editorials were widely read, the fear of the old guard and the hope of young idealists to whom he had endeared himself by cracking the profitable monopoly of the old medical schools, publishing verbatim accounts of lectures. His publication of Elliotson's clinical lectures was instrumental in establishing Elliotson's reputation, and he had joined with Elliotson and others in the foundation and support of London University Hospital. Such was Elliotson's confidence and Wakley's power that, after an initial postponement, a private demonstration was held on August 2nd at Wakley's home in Bedford Square.[14]

On "an early day in the month of August" Elliotson, accompanied by William Wood, demonstrated the full range of mesmeric phenomena "not as tests of the reality of the phenomena displayed, but as demonstrations of the supposed discoveries and the real opinions of the Doctor." Wakley was unconvinced. "The experiments were again commenced . . . and a second time rejected by Mr. Wakley." At the third demonstration Elliotson explained that the first tests would demonstrate that of the two identical pieces of

[13] Toynbee, I, 469.
[14] The fullest account of the four sessions appeared in *The Lancet* (Sept. 1, 1838), 805-811, and is supplemented by Clarke's account, pp. 183-192.

45

metal he had brought with him, one of lead, the other of nickel, the effects of the nickel would prove "quite astounding." He claimed that "lead might always be applied with impunity, as no magnetic effect ever resulted from the application of that metal to the skin." Elizabeth O'key was brought into the room. Wakley sat in a chair directly in front of her and certainly no more than three feet distant. "A piece of thick pasteboard was placed in front of her face, and held in the situation by two of the spectators . . . so that it was impossible that she could see what was passing either below or in front of her."

First Wakley rubbed the lead alternately against Elizabeth's hands in a way that raised the possibility that both metals were being used. This produced no effect. Then Elliotson held the nickel in his hand to charge it with magnetic influence; Wakley held the lead in his for an equal length of time, to keep the temperatures of the metals equal. Wakley touched O'key's palm with the lead. Nothing happened. He then touched it with the nickel. Again nothing happened. The lead was then used twice more, with the same results. The nickel was used again, and this time mesmeric trance immediately ensued. Wakley incredulously wanted to know how the experiments could possibly be of any value if there were no certainty at all in the results and "if the effects were to be attributed to one metal so long after another had been employed."

After some tense conversation it was agreed to try again, using only the magnetized nickel. But Wakley secretly arranged a control over the experiment. He substituted for the magnetized nickel a piece of lead and a farthing, slipping into an observer's hand the magnetized nickel he had received from Elliotson. The observer, "unseen by any person, placed it in [his] waistcoat pocket, and walked to the window, a distance of at least eighteen feet."[15] Wakley leaned forward. Another observer said, "with much sincerity of feeling, in a whisper, but loud enough to be heard at a

15 Clarke, p. 186.

short distance, 'Take care; don't apply the nickel too strongly.' " Elizabeth immediately fell into trance with even a
more striking distortion of the body than had occurred in
her previous paroxysm. She remained that way for a half
hour, Elliotson remarking that the effects were "extraordinary" and that "they presented a beautiful series of phenomena." With self-confident solemnity Wakley presented
Elliotson with the facts. Elliotson frankly admitted that he
could not explain the results but maintained that "he had
not the slightest doubt that the whole would yet admit of
a satisfactory explanation." Wakley stated that as far as
he was concerned the results were perfectly conclusive.

Nevertheless, on Elliotson's "earnest request," they agreed
to meet at the same place at 9 a.m. the next day to try what
effects nickel would produce. Elliotson had concluded that
the experiments had failed because the lead had been
touched to a spot where the nickel had previously been
applied. No one was convinced, and Wakley replied that "he
believed that O'key could herself give a better explanation
of the supposed phenomena than any other person." He re-
luctantly consented to play his former role again, but used
the lead instead of the nickel. Mesmeric trance resulted.
Elliotson slowly said that "he must admit that he had been
deceived in supposing that lead could not convey the magnetic influence." Wakley replied peremptorily that, on the
contrary, for experimental purposes it would be fully justi-
fied to use the lead only and the nickel not at all, since if
the effects of the nickel lingered, as Elliotson had claimed,
then any metal used afterwards would produce the results
of the nickel. The tensions of this confrontation were suddenly relieved by an interruption. Wakley had to leave to
see a person on business, "and before he could return Dr.
Elliotson, who was pressed for time, left with Mr. Wood."
A half hour later, when Wakley returned, he suggested that
for the purpose of presenting a report to the medical world
all the experiments be repeated. Wakley and his associates
remained with the O'keys, performing twenty-nine experi-

ments with magnetized water and coins. The results were consistently contradictory and unpredictable. By 10 p.m. "there did not exist amongst the spectators two opinions as to the character and the causes of the symptoms." The experiments ceased and in the hot night the girls were sent back to the hospital.

They were not to remain in their foster home much longer. The climate of opinion in the hospital was turning against Elliotson, due, among other causes, to the venomously anti-mesmeric editorials in *The Lancet* with the publication of a full account of the experiments in August. The London sensation had become a London scandal. What had been a subject of professional interest and experiment had now become the cause of extreme partisan contentiousness. *The Lancet* announced to all its correspondents that "we cannot undertake to give publicity to any communications on Animal Magnetism." The innuendos of sexual impropriety became explicit accusations. When Elliotson returned in October from his holiday he discovered that not only had he already been "exposed" but that the denunciations were becoming ad hominem: "Is it true that any physicians or surgeons of any one of the London Hospitals are insulting public decency, and abusing the confidence reposed in them by parents and guardians, by still practising animal magnetism on the sick and deluded patients . . . ? After the exposure . . . accomplished to the satisfaction of every sane spectator, at a private residence in London—we had thought that the humbug would no longer be tolerated." Ironically, Wakley's attacks were partially defenses of the new medical school and hospital that he and Elliotson had been both so instrumental in founding: "If there be such a hospital . . . the medical school with which it is connected must be speedily and irreparably ruined, unless the immoral quackery be at once put down . . . in which the heinous enormity against common sense and female delicacy is perpetrated."

The sexual slander soon became more explicit. Mesmerism was a seducer's art by which the nervous systems of "young and artless females" are excited "by a series of manipulations which not only injure the body but lead to a loss of virtue." Young, wealthy Russian rakes had come to England to learn the art in order to seduce "unsuspecting females who might fall within their power." The guests at such exhibitions "in the private wards of one of our public hospitals" were "wealthy and, perhaps, libidinous men." The daughter of a banker, placed under the care of a Polish quack, a follower of Mesmer, "was thrown into a profound sleep, and the quack stole her honour." Macready noted in his diary when he received an invitation on November 23, 1838, to attend "an exhibition of phenomena in animal magnetism on Sunday next" that his physician was certainly "infatuated with the subject."[16] But certainly he had no moral criticism of his friend. And Dickens, neither wealthy nor libidinous, on November 24th wrote to Cruikshank that "Elliotson has written to me to go and see some experiments on O'key at his house at 3 o'clock tomorrow afternoon. He begs me to invite you. Will you come?"[17]

Undoubtedly Dickens and Cruikshank went to this exhibition at 37 Conduit Street, Elliotson's residence and office from the early 1830's until shortly before his death in 1868. "An elegant mansion" with "a splendid suite of rooms," the house was later the scene of thrice-weekly mesmeric exhibitions and of frequent dinner and music parties, many of which Dickens attended.[18] As Elliotson wrote to a correspondent in December, 1838, "I rarely return from my round till seven, and consequently can never dine out except at very late hours and then in my own immediate neighborhood. Invitation after invitation is thus declined and my friends are all so good as to see this necessity and come and visit me without expecting me to go out. . . . I shall not hesitate to invite you to my next good music party."[19] But many of the invitations were for mesmeric exhibitions. The O'keys

16 Toynbee, I, 478.
17 *Pilgrim*, I, 461, to George Cruikshank, 11/24/38.
18 See *Chambers' Edinburgh Journal* (Sat., Oct. 26, 1839), 337-338.
19 Wellcome MS, Elliotson to unknown correspondent, 12/17/38.

were still Elliotson's patients at the hospital; they were shuttled between the wards and his home for treatment and exhibition. What Dickens saw on November 28th most likely was an intimate demonstration of the standard mesmeric experiments with trance, water, metals, and perhaps clairvoyance that he had seen before and that had been reported on in full in the press.

Suddenly a new element of controversy arose, an extension of the previous summer's experiments with clairvoyance as a tool of medical diagnosis. Elizabeth O'key occasionally offered rather crude but definitive opinions on the future health of her fellow patients; one of Elliotson's clinical clerks, all of whom had been trained to perform mesmeric manipulations for therapeutic purposes, had noticed that on some occasions, "when passing the bedsides of persons dangerously ill, she shuddered." Elliotson decided to experiment with the possibility that the O'keys could through their mesmeric sensitivity accurately diagnose the future course of an illness.

First he consulted with the nurse in charge to determine whether or not in her opinion there would be any impropriety in bringing O'key into the men's ward. The visit was scheduled. "One night late, the lights being all but extinguished, O'key was led into Ward 1, occupied by men." The beds of the patients were arranged around the sides of the oblong room. "O'key was led carefully and slowly around the room." Nothing happened. When she came opposite the bed of a man expected to die imminently, suddenly she began to shiver violently, and, being asked why, exclaimed emotionally that "Great Jacky"—the "angel of death"—"is on the bed!" She moved to the bedside, before leaving the ward, of another gravely ill patient and shuddered slightly. "What's the matter, O'key?" "Little Jacky is on the bed." The first man "died before the morning, the second escaped scarcely with his life." *The Lancet* reported, without mentioning the fates of the patients, that Elliotson accepted these prophecies "as correct indications of the fate of the

50

patients." There is no direct evidence to prove that Elliotson actually did, however, and within the next few years, growing gradually more incredulous about clairvoyance, he was led finally to express serious skepticism about the phenomenon.

But strong doubts about mesmerism's being practiced in the hospital exploded into turbulent opposition on the morning after. Many were outraged by what they considered such impropriety and the probability of the incident's being used to support further rumors about sexual indiscretions. The patients were alarmed as wild rumors swept the hospital. The issue was one of life and death. Who would O'key prophesy about next? The students were "in a state of wild excitement," some of them eagerly waiting to see the " 'inspired girl.' " Arriving earlier than usual that day, Elliotson immediately went to the theatre, followed by a large crowd. He seemed oppressed "but not daunted," demonstrating the usual courage of his convictions despite criticism. He explained that there was a physiological explanation for the events: that a person near death exuded a "peculiar effluvia" that could not be detected except with an unusually strong sense of smell and that the O'keys, through their preternaturally acute senses, could detect the "effluvium even at some distance from the dying person."[20]

Throughout December the furor continued. Hospital politics, in which Elliotson had taken an important part, intensified, one faction headed by Elliotson, the other by Liston. The two men disliked one another intensely. The scenes in the medical committee room had often been turbulent, the two doctors frequently making offensive remarks to one another, so much so that on one occasion Liston said that he was so furious "that he would never enter the hospital again."[21] But Liston's party, which had been in the minority, suddenly found itself the beneficiary of the general

[20] *The Lancet* account appears in the issue for Jan. 5, 1839, 561-562. Clarke's account appears on pp. 173-177.

[21] Clarke, p. 176.

hostility amongst the staff and of the pressures of public scandal created by Elliotson's experiments.

In October the hospital house-committee had met to consider whether or not Elizabeth O'key should be discharged. She had remained beyond the prescribed time limit. Elliotson argued that Elizabeth had been readmitted for a new illness and consequently was within the rules: it was his professional opinion that "it was still necessary to retain O'key in the hospital." The hospital committee complained to the college council, which, after discussion, resolved "That the House-Committee do forthwith discharge O'key." The house-committee sent a letter to Elliotson "respectfully requesting him to discharge" her. He took no action. Finally, on December 27th, 1838, the council of University College met and resolved formally "That the Hospital-Committee take such steps as they shall deem most advisable to prevent the practice of mesmerism or animal magnetism in future within the hospital." On the next day, in the morning, Elliotson submitted his resignation, and in the evening, at 6:30 p.m., he and Dickens dined together.[22]

[4]

Eight days after this dinner party, the University College council accepted Elliotson's resignation, despite the spirited efforts by his friends and his large contingent of student supporters to influence a majority to decline it. To that same dinner party in Conduit Street came a group of Elliotson's student supporters, invited by the doctor. "He addressed them very energetically on the step he had taken." With the assistance of the other guests, they formulated a strategy of student meetings and protests. Dickens was probably incapable of resisting making some contribution to the plans. The strategy focused on a mass student meeting and the passage of a sweeping resolution of support that would compel the council to refuse Elliotson's resignation in the best interests of the hospital.

22 *Pilgrim*, I, 480, to George Cruikshank, 12/28/38 and I, 637, Diary entry for Friday, Dec. 28, 1838. "Dr. Elliotson—Dinner—½ past 6."

In his letter of resignation Elliotson had stated that he had resigned because of undue interference of the house-committee and the council with a patient under his care. He had added that he would never again enter either the hospital or the college. He was threatened now with being taken at his word. It was announced that Dr. Copland was to finish the course of lectures and that Dr. Carswell had been appointed physician at the hospital. On Friday, January 4, nearly 300 people, mostly students, met in the Anatomical Theatre at 1 p.m. Three resolutions were submitted to the floor, two extreme, the third comparatively neutral. After a good deal of sharp debate, in which William Wood again and again stood to defend the doctor, and much parliamentary manipulation, those in favor of a vitiated version of the resolution supporting Elliotson seemed to be equal in number to those against it. The chairman moved "that the question be put to the ballot, between the hours of 1 and 3 o'clock, in the beadle's room, on the next day, Saturday," and that all enrolled students should be permitted to vote. The council was scheduled to meet at 4 p.m. on that Saturday to decide on the resignation.

At 1 p.m. a large number of students gathered in the beadle's room. An argument between the two factions ensued on the propriety of the place of voting and on who had the right to vote. Wood's urgent request that the place of balloting "be removed to the theatre" was accepted. Great efforts seem to have been made to round up voters, particularly, *The Lancet* claimed, by Elliotson's supporters, who canvassed "every avenue leading to the Theatre," as "at the old elections." As it came close to 3 o'clock the tensions increased. The time for closing the voting was extended to 3:30 p.m., though there is no indication of who instigated the delay. The voting closed amidst bitter words between both factions.

The tally resulted in the passage of the moderate, neutral resolution: "That the students of University College, duly appreciating the high professional acquirements of Dr. Elliotson, and the inestimable value of his services here, do most sincerely regret the circumstances which necessarily led to his resignation as Professor of the Principles and Practice of Medicine in the College, and as Physician to the Hospital." The vote was so close, 124 to 113, that both factions considered it a victory. Debate immediately ensued about whether or not to forward to the council not only the resolution but the tally also. "Much cheering attended the observations of either party . . . amidst which a friend of Dr. Elliotson kept calling out, 'It's just four o'clock, we shall be too late.' " The resolution to forward the tally was quickly defeated "and the resolution . . . was conveyed to the council. But that body had just disposed of the resignation of Dr. Elliotson, by accepting it."[23]

Now, no longer having the facilities of hospital and college available to him, at the age of almost fifty, Elliotson began to make himself constantly available to the cause he believed in and to the needs of his large private practice. Without the demanding requirement of daily lectures and rounds, his always busy social life expanded excitingly. Among his patients and friends were to be some of the most prestigious Englishmen of the day, particularly writers such as Dickens and Thackeray; and his friendship with Dickens was to last until his death, two years before Dickens' own. Dickens, and certainly others, were stirred by the sincerity, almost the nobility, of Elliotson's high principles, and by his persuasiveness. Dickens wrote in 1842 "that I have closely watched Dr. Elliotson's experiments from the first—that I have the utmost reliance in his honour, character and ability, and would trust my life in his hands at any time—and that after what I have seen with my own eyes, and observed with my own senses, I should be untrue to myself if I shrunk for a moment from saying that I am a believer, and that I became so against all my preconceived opinions and impressions."[24]

[23] The account of these meetings is from *The Lancet* (Jan. 12, 1839), 590-597.
[24] *Nonesuch*, I, 376, to Dr. R. H. Collyer, 1/27/42.

CHAPTER

III

"A Believer"

⟦ 1 ⟧

Between January 1839 and June 1844, when Dickens departed with his entire family for a year's stay in Italy, where he was to have his most significant mesmeric experiences, he and Elliotson saw one another frequently. Dickens began to talk about and practice mesmerism with an enthusiasm that found its way into the letters and memoirs of these years. Though he was feverishly busy with the writing of *Nicholas Nickleby, The Old Curiosity Shop, Barnaby Rudge,* and *Martin Chuzzlewit,* the occasions on which he refused dinner invitations "to keep on" at his writing were balanced by those on which he could not refuse recreation and excitement.[1] The first few months of 1839 were intensely busy ones for both the doctor and the writer. Dickens had on hand the obligation to complete *Nicholas Nickleby,* his anxieties with the publisher Richard Bentley concerning his editorial duties and the promised manuscript of *Barnaby Rudge,* and the urge for a new form of publication that resulted in *Master Humphrey's Clock.* But at least it was one of the periods during these four and a half years in which he was not to be writing two novels simultaneously. Elliotson was involved in the painful termination of his hospital affairs

---

[1] *Pilgrim,* I, 508, to John Forster, 2/14/39.

and in the search for new patterns of discipline and productivity in a life that had unexpectedly become his own to arrange.

The first two months of the year were marked for Elliotson by the refusal of one of his former students to read at a mass meeting a farewell letter of some thirty-six pages that the doctor had written. On January 14 one of Elliotson's replacements, making his first appearance as a lecturer, had been greeted by a well-organized claque of Elliotson supporters who attempted to prevent the replacement from being heard, "stamping upon the floor . . . from the upper benches" every time he attempted to speak. "Every now and then a cry was raised, but feebly responded to, of 'Dr. Elliotson,' which was met by a general clapping of hands . . . and cries of 'No Elliotson; no humbug; no magnetism.' "[2] Elliotson was not to address any large group of medical professionals again, outside mesmeric circles, until 1846. Then he took the occasion of his being invited, over much opposition, to deliver the Harveian Lecture to the Royal Society to compare himself implicitly to John Harvey and to defend mesmerism against the scientific philistines.[3]

The friendship between Dickens and Elliotson intensified during 1839. Despite their being intensely preoccupied with their own work, they reciprocated invitations and met at the parties of society's and art's elite. Dickens declined dinner invitations, in order to "get on" with *Nicholas Nickleby*, from "Talfourd, Milnes, Elliotson. . . ."[4] Late in March, Macready entertained Elliotson at a dinner attended by Darwin, Carlyle, and Harriet Martineau. Whenever these dinners materialized, mesmerism was a topic of conversation, for as early as 1839 Richard Monckton Milnes, among others, had become an intense enthusiast. So too had

[2] From *The Lancet* (March 9, 1839), 388.
[3] Published as *The Harveian Oration*, delivered before the Royal College of Physicians, London, June 27, 1846. With an English version and notes. London, 1846.
[4] *Pilgrim*, I, 508, to John Forster, 2/14/39.

Bulwer-Lytton.[5] The next year Milnes wrote a comic poem, "Mesmerism in London," whose main character was the protégé of a man whom Dickens met through Elliotson in 1840 and who was to become a life-long friend. The poem circulated in manuscript, a conversation piece at least at Milnes' famous breakfast parties.[6] Dickens attended mesmeric demonstrations at 37 Conduit Street. As he wrote to so many, Elliotson wrote to a correspondent: "If ever you are at liberty at twelve o'clock (except on Tuesday or Friday) or on Sunday at three, and can drop in, I will show you another beautiful case . . . a youth who never saw a person mesmerized. If you come on Sunday we will try you. I heard a second time from Mr. Dickens: and Mr. and Mrs. Dickens were well then, though she had been indisposed."[7] At about this time Elliotson seems to have become the Dickens' family doctor. In the autumn of 1839, having finished *Nickleby*, Dickens sent Elliotson an inscribed copy with a note requesting him "to accept" it "as a very feeble mark of my lasting esteem and admiration."[8]

Struggling with his vexation over his unwise commitment to deliver a manuscript to Bentley and mistakenly enthusiastic about the potential success of a new journal, Dickens embraced a whirl of work, social activities, and family engagements as 1840 began. By April he had begun his own contribution to the new magazine. It was to be transformed under pressure into *The Old Curiosity Shop*.[9] When the hectic spring turned summer, Dickens took short vacation trips. Returning from Devonshire, he found on his desk "two kind notes" from Mr. Chauncy Hare Townshend

[5] Toynbee, I, 504; II, 20, 33. See C. Nelson Stewart, *Bulwer Lytton As Occultist* (London, 1927) and Robert Lee Wolff, *Strange Stories, Explorations In Victorian Fiction—The Occult and The Neurotic* (Boston, 1971).

[6] See James Pope-Hennessy, *Monckton Milnes, The Years of Promise, 1809-1851*, Vol. I (N.Y., 1955).

[7] Morgan MS., Elliotson to unknown correspondent, 5/4/39 (?).

[8] *Pilgrim*, I, 593, to John Elliotson, 10/23/39.

[9] *Pilgrim*, II, 60, to Daniel Maclise, 4/18/40.

and a note from Elliotson asking him to dinner to meet Townshend. Their major subject of discussion was mesmerism, for Townshend had six months earlier published *Facts in Mesmerism*, dedicated "To John Elliotson, M.D. Cantab. F.R.S.," whom he had "never had the pleasure of seeing . . . till within the last two months . . . but the greater part of the London, I may say of the English, world have derived their ideas of mesmerism from *your* experiments, which so many have personally witnessed."[10]

Townshend was fourteen years older than Dickens and three years younger than Elliotson. The Doctor and the Reverend had missed one another at Cambridge, Elliotson passing quickly into professional activities, Townshend staying at Trinity as a scholar, gentleman, and poet. Renowned for his "beauty of countenance," delicacy, and sensibility, Townshend became a friend of Hartley Coleridge, cultivated the friendship of Southey, and then later the Wordsworths. He published poetry and criticism without the inevitable success that his mannerisms implied. Sometime in the 1830's, though he was to make frequent return visits, he left England for residence on the continent, establishing himself finally in a lovely villa, Mon Lorici, in Lausanne, which Dickens visited many times, particularly during his Switzerland holidays in the late 1840's and 1850's. While on the continent, Townshend became fascinated with mesmerism and began the experiments that led to his extremely popular account of its powers. He searched for receptive subjects to use in public and private demonstrations. He obviously had such a keen eye for prospective sensitives that when their friendship had intensified he cajoled Dickens to "give me a mesmeric trial." He was impatient with those engagements which kept him "from mesmerizing you—which I am sure I could do, and which I long to do."[11]

Townshend was aggressive in his courting of Dickens. Though their mutual passion was mesmerism, their friend-

10 Townshend, IV:VI.
11 Huntington MS., Townshend to Dickens, 6/7/41.

ship began with Townshend's presenting to Dickens a sonnet addressed to "Man of the genial mind!" Dickens probably was flattered, for he was thanked for his "high services
. . . in the name of human kind."[12] Townshend may have
read the sonnet across the dinner table to Dickens and Elliotson on August 8. Though it was their first meeting,
Townshend came well prepared with admiration, enthusiasm, and knowledge of Dickens' attendance at mesmeric
demonstrations. Though it was near the end of his short stay
in England, Townshend urged an invitation for August
10th, which Dickens felt he could not refuse, partially due to
the power of the sonnet: "I owe a visit to a gentleman who
leaves England tomorrow for a long time; and as the said
gentleman addressed a sonnet to me, have been obliged to
engage myself."[13] Townshend returned to the continent
soon after, not to be in England again until the spring of
the next year, when his demonstrations were to become the
talk of the town. Both Dickens and Elliotson left London
in September, Elliotson for his annual visit to the continent,
Dickens for Broadstairs, his favorite resort. Autumn found
Dickens intensely involved in *The Old Curiosity Shop*,
Elliotson in his mesmeric and phrenological activities. Elliotson frequently sent Dickens urgent notes: "I am anxious
that you should see human nature in a new state, and if you
can come to my house tomorrow at four precisely I will
show a very curious and perfectly genuine case of mesmerism." And probably Dickens had on more than one occasion
to decide that "At the last minute—I had not the resolution
to breathe it to myself before—I am obliged to decide *not
to go* tonight. You know how hard this is upon me as we
[Macready] were to have gone together—and I have a high
regard for Elliotson. . . ."[14]

[12] Chauncy Hare Townshend, "To the Author of Oliver Twist, Nicholas Nickleby, & c.," *Sermons in Sonnets and Other Poems* (London,
1851). See *Pilgrim*, II, 112.
[13] *Pilgrim*, II, 112, footnote.
[14] *Ibid*., 148, to W. C. Macready, 11/4/1840.

One of Elliotson's saddest duties during the late fall and winter was to attend daily the slow death of Macready's favorite daughter and the almost fatal illness of his son. On November 26th, "Elliotson called to see Henry—my blessed, withering, wasting babe. . . . Received a dear and most affectionate note from Dickens, which comforted me as much as I can be comforted. But I have lost my child." Elliotson during this difficult winter became, as he was to remain, a close friend of the actor; it was a kind of total friendship in which there was no distinction made between professional concern and attendance on the one hand and emotional compassion and commitment on the other.[15] The doctor could be relied on for medicine with compassion and competence; and though Macready would have none of it except as entertainment, Dickens also shared a commitment to a strange and marvellous phenomenon that promised to reveal secrets of the most mysterious sort about life and people. The visits to 37 Conduit Street continued, and even Macready went. Dickens wrote to him on January 6th, though he was in the process of "murdering that poor child [Little Nell]": "Are you going to Elliotson's on Friday? If so, I'll take you there, and call for you."[16]

[2]

Two particular affairs brought Elliotson, Townshend, and Dickens together in 1842: Dickens' fascination with Townshend's demonstrations and his implication of Elliotson in his attempt to assist the impoverished carpenter-poet, John Overs. Elliotson's role as a private practitioner and as the leading public voice of mesmerism had begun to impose a new pattern on his daily activities. Though his home had become the recognized center for demonstrations of a subject that continually attracted widespread curiosity, he also carried on a medical practice in which mesmerism was only one therapeutic tool. But he began to use it frequently, keeping

[15] Toynbee, I, 98-113; II, 448.
[16] *Pilgrim*, II, 180, to W. C. Macready, 1/6/41.

a careful record of all the facts of the cases with which he dealt. This later formed the basis of detailed reports on the role of mesmerism in medical practice that he was to publish beginning in 1843 in *The Zoist*, whose origin and continuance for thirteen years was to be mainly the product of Elliotson's efforts.[17]

Dickens' admiration for the doctor increased, and in February 1841 he invited him to be godfather with Walter Savage Landor to his second son. Elliotson replied that "I shall be delighted to become father in God to your little bo peep." Elliotson's sense of humor was aroused, and he insisted that Dickens should still retain the title "of his father in the flesh, with all the rights, privileges, perquisites & duties thereto annexed, from the moment you determined to construct him to the end of life." Dickens' non-purposefulness in these matters of child creating was soon to become painfully clear, the subject of his own awkward private jokes. The joke was one that the liberated bachelor-doctor and the novelist could share, as they could share Elliotson's humor about other Victorian sacred things: "I should, however, have been compelled to forego this delight had you not absolved me from religious duties & every thing vulgar—For nothing could I consent to teach him in the vulgar tongue— nor would I have spoiled him for arithmetic by teaching him that three are one & one is three, or defaced his views on the majesty of God by assuring him that the maker of the Universe once came down & got a little jewess in the family way." Though Elliotson did not write sonnets, his appreciation of Dickens' genius was often fulsomely expressed: "Oh, how as a human being I thank you for your delightful Clock. I look forward to every Friday night with impatience; for after dinner one of us reads the new number aloud. But last Friday week we were beaten to the earth—Symes,[18] who

---

[17] *The Zoist* was published by Balliere in London from 1843 to 1856, with Elliotson as the first among equals on the editorial staff.

[18] Edmond Sheppard Symes, a student of Elliotson's at University College, supported his former professor both in his devotion to mesmerism

reads most beautifully, at last threw down the book & sobbed, & Wood & myself cried a deluge: & we all agreed that you must be a good man to be able to write thus—Not that I ever heard your goodness doubted."[19] Dickens was to write strongly of his affection on many occasions.[20]

One such occasion was a planned visit to the Westminster Bridewell, Tothill Fields, a prison whose enlightened administration by Augustus Frederick Tracey had prompted Dickens to awaken Elliotson's "utmost interest . . . by a very imperfect description of . . . humane and wise governance."[21] For Elliotson, like Dickens, had a lifelong interest in the improvement of the institutions that dealt with criminals and the insane, intensified in the doctor by insights into these problems derived from his professional exploration of mesmerism and phrenology.[22] Both visited asylums and attended public executions, and in 1849 they witnessed the execution of the Mannings, which, though it was the occasion for Dickens' most publicized comments on the evils of capital punishment, was one among many occasions for Elliotson to denounce such spectacles. He claimed that they were based on mistaken assumptions about the nature of the human mind.[23] This additional common concern brought

---

and in his enduring personal loyalty. Symes and Elliotson were the closest of friends and when, sometime in the 1860's, Elliotson could no longer look after himself, he became a permanent guest in Symes' home, where he died in 1868.

[19] Huntington MS., Elliotson to Dickens, 2/11/41. See *Pilgrim*, II, 210, footnote.

[20] *Ibid.*, p. 281, to Augustus Tracey, 5/11/41.

[21] *Ibid.*

[22] See Philip Collins, *Dickens and Crime* (London, 1962), pp. 53-93.

[23] See Collins, pp. 235-255. Elliotson wrote at great length on the evils of capital punishment. As a phrenologist, interested in cerebral psychology and physiology, he believed that criminal tendencies could be physiologically located in the brain and nervous system and scientifically analyzed. Criminal tendencies were thus inherited, not learned, and the criminal was to be dealt with as were the insane—with treatment for the disease rather than with punishment for acts for which he was not responsible in the normal sense. The implications for free

the two men together a number of times and increased Dickens' respect for Elliotson's insight and integrity. The psychology of the criminal mind was a topic of mutual fascination, and undoubtedly each learned from the other.

The visit to Tothill Fields took place, and Townshend, who had recently returned to London for his annual spring visit, joined the party. As soon as he had become set in his chambers, Townshend urged Dickens to "come and see me tomorrow . . . anytime between 12 & 3." In addition to a music party at which "two young protégés" of his were to play on the flute & piano, one of his "young friends is the celebrated clairvoyant somnambulist, mentioned in my book. Perhaps we may have some mesmerizing."[24] Dickens seems to have taken seriously Townshend's reminder to him of his "*pledge* to cultivate my *friendship*. I only lack *opportunity* to do the same by one who had lightened many a weary hour of my life, and whom I *love* in his works." Townshend was "vexed" to have been out when both Dickens and his wife paid a call, complaining that he was being "literally torn to pieces" by tedious obligations, so much so that he had not even had time "to read Humphrey's Clock." He expected in a short while to go to the country and to "sit out of door, and read my dear book—as it *ought* to be read." True to the Romantic anti-urbanism of his youth, Townshend complained of "heartless London—where idle business chokes

---

will and determinism involved Elliotson in frequent and lengthy controversies. Elliotson's statements on capital punishment and his analysis of specific cases, like the Mannings, appear in *The Zoist* during the 1840's. It is likely that Dickens, who was quite interested in and familiar with the Mannings, read Elliotson's long article "On the Brains of Manning and his Wife, the Bermondsey murderers" (*The Zoist*, Vol. IX, No. XXXVI, Jan. 1852, 335-356). See illustration section. At the end of the article, Elliotson corroborates Dickens' account of the crowd: "The conduct of the crowds who went to witness the execution was, as usual, disgusting, and was described by Mr. Dickens in *The Times* of Nov. 14 of that year [1849]. . . . I hope that, while the punishment of death disgraces our statutes, executions will be perfectly public."

[24] Huntington MS., Townshend to Dickens, 5/11/41.

the affections" and keeps friends apart. "But the chief purpose of this note is to ask you, at what hour we are to go to the prison tomorrow, & whether I shall come to your house?"[25] Soon after Dickens showed Elliotson and Townshend the enlightened administration of the prison, the latter began to show Dickens the miracles of Alexis.

The young flutist, who had studied the instrument professionally, had first come under Townshend's influence in 1837 in Antwerp. Fifteen years of age in 1839, Alexis, according to his father, had for many years been a natural sleepwalker, with a tendency to clairvoyance, capable of performing while seemingly asleep the most beautiful improvisations on the flute. Alexis' powers were such that "on one occasion, while his father was watching him . . . the only light in the apartment, a lamp, went suddenly out; but the sleepwalker continued to play as before, and was heard to turn over the leaves of his music until he had come to the end of the piece, which, moreover, he could not execute without book."[26]

When Alexis entered Francis Kemble's drawing room, two days after Dickens' party's visit to the prison, Fanny came to the conclusion that Alexis was "one of the first of the long train of mesmerists, magnetizers, spiritualists, charlatans, cheats, and humbugs who subsequently appealed to the notice and practiced on the credulity of London society."[27] Alexis' performance on that occasion "consisted principally in reading passages from books presented to him while under the influence of mesmeric sleep, into which he had been thrown by Mr. Townshend, and with which he was previously unacquainted," his eyes of course tightly bandaged, a variant of Alexis' standard clairvoyant performance that Dickens marvelled at. "Have you seen the magnetic boy?" he wrote to Lady Blessington. "You heard of him no doubt from Count D'Orsay. If you get him to

25 *Ibid.*, 5/18/41.   26 Townshend, p. 236.
27 Francis Ann Kemble, *Records of Later Life* (N.Y., 1882), pp. 228-230.

Gore House, don't, I entreat you, have more than eight people—four is a better number—to see him. He fails in a crowd, and is marvellous before a few."[28] Early in May Dickens had called on Macready and lauded the "wonders of this boy, under the effect of magnetism, producing such wonderful effects."[29] Dickens' enthusiasm intensified his relationship with Townshend; and before he left to visit Scotland, and Townshend to visit relatives in the country towards the end of June, Townshend urged Dickens "to give me a mesmeric trial." They continued to correspond, but did not see one another again until the end of July. Dickens accepted Townshend's invitation to dine, though "he dare not be mesmerized, lest it should damage me at all. Even a day's headache would be a serious thing just now.—But a time will come. . . ."[30]

The time never did come, for Dickens always found reasons to avoid putting himself in the power of an operator's manipulations, born as he was to be an operator rather than a subject. When Kate "has a girl stopping here, for whom I have conceived a horrible aversion, and whom I *must* fly," Dickens felt that "she is the Ancient Mariner of young ladies. She 'holds me with her glittering eye,' and I cannot turn away. The basilisk is now in the dining room and I am in the study, but I *feel* her through the wall."[31] But Townshend promised "to keep my hands off you, however much they may be itching to perform mesmeric evolutions about your head—& I will try to get up a case for you to *see*. It would be a shame there should be 2 operators present (for Elliotson makes one of my party) and no stigmatising, as a little boy of one of my friends calls it."[32] A poor substitute for Dickens was brought in, a Miss Critchly whom Elliotson used for some experiments he performed in August. Townshend, however, continued to demonstrate mostly

[28] *Pilgrim*, II, 291, to The Countess of Blessington, 6/2/41.
[29] Toynbee, II, 135-136.
[30] *Pilgrim*, II, 342, to Chauncy Hare Townshend, 7/23/41.
[31] *Ibid.*, pp. 103-104, to Daniel Maclise, 7/22/40.
[32] Huntington MS., Townshend to Dickens, 7/24/41.

with Alexis, who became an English and then European celebrity.[33] Monckton Milnes caught the flavor of Dickens' and his contemporaries' fascination with the boy's powers:

Alexis & his Mesmerism
Have thrown fair ladies into fits
And made a formidable schism
Among Philosophers and Wits:
Many, to no conclusion come,
Some few in perfect credence revel,
The most cry out "it's all a bum(?)"
And Ashley murmurs "it's the Devil!"

No wonder that the [people?] feel
Some tremor at this power displayed,
This reading letters with one's heel,
This ogling with one's shoulder blade:
On secrecy however set
You reckon now without your host,—
No place is safe—not Cabinet
Nor Boudoir—no—not even the Post![34]

Dickens also took to verse and attacked Sir Robert Peel and the Tories with a similar comic enthusiasm in a political squib that appeared in *The Examiner*:

He's a magnetic doctor, and knows how to keep
The whole of a government snoring asleep. . . .

. . . .

33 As emphasized by Jeanne Carol Owen in her dissertation *Dickens and Mesmerism: With Special Reference to the Comic and Horrific in the Novels* (Queensland, Australia, 1970), Alexis is not to be confused with the Alexis whose feats *The Zoist* detailed in 1844-1845. Ms. Owen's dissertation, which I discovered toward the end of my project, covers a small portion of this biographical ground, though without the resource of the most important manuscript materials. Ms. Owen's dissertation is mainly devoted to identifying mesmeric allusions in Dickens' novels. Like any writer who discovers that another author has written on what a title may suggest is the same subject, I was both sorry and delighted that "seems" was not "is."
34 MS., "Mesmerism in London," Syracuse University Library.

He's a *clairvoyant* subject, and readily reads
His countrymen's wishes, conditions, and needs. . . .[35]

Before going to Broadstairs Dickens had ordered from his wineseller two dozen bottles of his "Illustrious Punch" to which present Elliotson had responded that Dickens seemed resolved to "punch out all my wits—*Two dozen* punches! I had made up my mind to half a dozen: But two dozen who shall stand! I would send you two dozen Judies in return— but what would Mrs. Dickens say!" Never for a moment forgetful of Dickens' fascination with mesmerism, he concluded with a description of his success with a woman suffering from epilepsy whom Dupotet had tried to cure some "three years before. . . . In *one* minute at the utmost, she was senseless & rigid, & so remained."[36]

Dickens' high opinion of Elliotson increased substantially as the result of their involvement with John Overs—"a poor cabinet maker, who in the intervals of his work has taught himself to think and feel like a man, and has written some pretty ballads and good little prose sketches."[37] Overs' case involved not mesmerism but money and medical assistance. Having contracted what was diagnosed as a chronic "affection of the pleura," Overs was informed by his doctors that he could no longer endure the long hours on foot and the physical labor as "foreman to a manufacturer of medicine chests."[38] Dickens sent him to Elliotson, exclaiming the wonders of a man from the working class who not only had literary aspirations but "really writes."[39] Dickens had told Overs that "I never knew him [Elliotson] to fail in any case where cure was possible, or care, humanity, and strong interest in his patients coupled . . . with greater skill than any other man possesses, could be of any avail." Elliotson examined Overs for a full hour "and had gone into his case

[35] *Miscellaneous Papers, Plays and Poems*, ed. Andrew Lang, Vol. II (London, N.D.), 467-470.
[36] Huntington MS., Elliotson to Dickens, 8/4/41.
[37] *Pilgrim*, II, 363, to W. C. Macready, 8/21/41.
[38] *Ibid.*, to W. C. Macready, 8/21/41.
[39] *Ibid.*, p. 362, to John Overs, 8/20/41.

as if he were Prince Albert."[40] As he wrote of Elliotson's exertions, Dickens' anger at his friend's ill-treatment by *The Lancet* for the mesmeric beliefs that he himself shared rose to a dramatic pitch: "When I think that . . . every rotten-hearted pander who has been beaten, kicked, and rolled in the kennel, yet struts it in the Editorial We once a week—every vagabond that an honest man's gorge must rise at—every live emetic in that nauseous drug-shop, the Press—can have his fling at such men and call them knaves and fools and thieves, I grow so vicious that with bearing hard upon my pen, I break the nib down, and with keeping my teeth set, make my jaws ache."[41]

Elliotson informed Overs and Dickens that the case was curable with treatment and rest. Dickens lauded Elliotson; if Overs knew "of his skill, patience, and humanity," as Dickens did, "you would love and honor him as much as I do. If my own life, or my wife's, or that of either of my children were in peril tomorrow, I would trust it to him implicitly."[42]

Despite Dickens' efforts to help, including arranging light employment with Macready at the theatre, the Overs affair ended in querulous misunderstandings, Overs believing he had been insulted by Macready and the employment arranged for him. Dickens and Elliotson patiently attempted to act constructively, explaining that they had "no desire or intention to speak harshly on this point."[43] Overs, having expected that Dickens and his friends would do more, blamed them for doing less; and the gift horses having been looked in the mouth, they soon went about their own business. But the affair served to strengthen the bond between Dickens and Elliotson. Throughout the rest of 1841 they saw one another frequently.[44]

40 *Ibid.*, p. 368, to W. C. Macready, 8/24/41.
41 *Ibid.*
42 *Ibid.*, p. 369, to John Overs, 8/24/41.
43 *Ibid.*, pp. 427-428, 434-435, to John Overs, 11/23/41, 11/30/41.
44 *Ibid.*, p. 426, footnote; Toynbee, II, 148. As with their lasting interest in mesmerism, Dickens, Elliotson, and Townshend were to be

[3]

When the novelist and his wife left for America in January 1842, Dickens had already learned from Elliotson and Townshend how to perform as mesmeric operator. Soon after he arrived in Boston, an invitation came from an American mesmerist to observe his cases. Dickens responded that he would be very "much interested" in doing so.[45] How did Dr.

---

linked together for the rest of their active lives, Dickens surviving both friends by only two years. The dinners, the visits, and the travels together, the controversies and the mesmeric exhibitions, the attendance of Townshend as one of the three witnesses to Katey Dickens' marriage to the brother of Wilkie Collins, even the concern in the 1860's for Elliotson's failing health and fortune and the editing of "Townshend's Hiccoughs" after his death in 1868, were an important part of Dickens' life. He admired Elliotson's convictions, particularly on mesmerism and phrenology, which he shared ("I hold phrenology, within certain limits to be true . . ."), and his loyalty both as friend and doctor. Elliotson remained faithful to mesmerism and his professional commitments. In the 1850's he wrote to T. A. Shaw in Paris: "If you can purchase for me an engraving of Mesmer, an undoubted likeness, I shall be greatly obliged. I should indeed like a profile and a full face. I shall be happy to give you autographs of Townshend, Sandby, Miss Martineau and any others I may have." His interest and his sense of the enemy never flagged: "Any mesmerism and other news will always be most acceptable to me. The new *Zoist* of today is capital full of important facts. Mesmerism has made astounding progress here in the last six months, and is the general talk, and universally admitted, except, of course, among the doctors who are as intolerant and blindly selfish as any roman catholic priest" (Wellcome MS., Elliotson to T. A. Shaw, 1/2/51). Dickens' faith in his friends and in their discovery remained as staunch: "I have asked Elliotson and Townshend (an accomplished man, who has written better of mesmerism than any one else), to dine here next day. I have a strong belief that if you try that remedy under good superintendence on Henry, it will do him an amount of good that nothing else will, humanly speaking." But Macready was probably just as much the doubter in 1854 as he had been earlier. And certainly Townshend's admiring worship of Dickens increased as the years went by, for "he radiates the force of his mind into the saddest and most difficult circumstances. If ever I am out of humour with human nature (and I have had some sad experiences) there are two persons on whom I think. One of them is Mr. Dickens" (Morgan MS., Townshend to Angela Burdett Coutts, 11/10/55).

[45] *Nonesuch*, I, 376, to Dr. R. H. Collyer, 1/27/42; for a brief account, mainly of Dickens' phrenological experiences in America, see Noel C. Peyrouton, "Boz and the American Phreno-Mesmerists," *Dickens Studies*, III (1967), 38-50.

Collyer know of Dickens' interest in mesmerism? Perhaps it was simply well known; perhaps the communication had come through Elliotson, whom Dickens took the opportunity to praise lavishly in a firm statement of his beliefs on the subject. He had no hesitation in standing with the believers. At the end of March, in Pittsburgh, for the first time Dickens tried his powers as magnetizer. Naturally he began with a subject strongly under his powers already, his wife Catherine.

In a burst of letter writing he wrote to Macready, gravely concerned by the news that the actor's health was becoming increasingly precarious: "But if Elliotson be the man I take him to be (and if he be not, the whole human race wears masks and dominoes), he will already have administered the necessary restoratives."[46] To learn of his "extraordinary success in magnetizing Kate," which Dickens hoped he "will be a witness of many, many, many, happy times," Macready should consult Forster, to whom Dickens had written the details. Before leaving Pittsburgh by steamboat for Cincinnati, Dickens, in the presence of two temporary acquaintances, had decided to try to magnetize Kate, after "holding forth upon the subject rather luminously, and asserting that I thought I could exercise the influence. . . ." Within six minutes of passes about her head with his hands, Catherine became hysterical. Then two minutes later she fell asleep. Dickens found that he could awaken her quite easily, imitating what Elliotson and Townshend had demonstrated to him: transverse movements of his thumbs across her eyebrows, and blowing softly on her face.

Astounded by the rapidity of his success, Dickens was "rather alarmed" on "the first occasion." Despite his prefatory boasting, he had not been prepared for such sudden results. Indeed, the sense of power and mystery must have given him pause for a moment. But he implied that on the occasions that followed, his sense of certainty increased, his

46 Toynbee, II, 169-170.

"alarm" replaced by confidence and fascination.[47] Soon after his return to England, he demonstrated his powers, and began to mesmerize members of his family and friends, both in circumstances of social levity and in serious instances of illness. Macready, always the skeptic on the subject, found Landor, Maclise, and Forster visiting Dickens, who "had been mesmerizing his wife and Miss Hogarth, who had been in violent hysterics. He proposed to make a trial on me; I did not quite like it, but assented; was very nervous, and found the fixedness of the position—eyes, limbs, and entire frame—very unpleasant, and the nervousness at first painful. Reasoned myself out of it, and then felt it could not effect me."[48]

Despite Macready's escape, Dickens was to mesmerize men successfully. His good friend, the artist John Leech, hurt himself severely in a fall at Bonchurch in September 1848. Leech recovered, seemingly with Dickens' assistance.[49] The novelist had already long before realized the great powers he possessed, and had quite seriously played the role of physician. Fortunately he could also see himself in comic terms that helped relieve the serious forces beneath. He wrote to Forster, after his success with Leech, "What do you think of my setting up in the magnetic line with a large brass plate? 'Terms, twenty-five quineas per nap.' "[50] But as was frequently the case with Dickens, the comic request described an established fact. He already had.

⟦ 4 ⟧

Dickens' major experience as mesmerist, which was strongly to influence his life and his fiction, took place in Italy, on the long year's sabbatical from the exhaustion of having completed not only *American Notes* and *Martin Chuzzlewit* but more major novels than any English novelist had ever writ-

[47] *Nonesuch*, I, 426, to John Forster, 4/1/42.
[48] Toynbee, II, 179-180.
[49] *Nonesuch*, II, 174-177, to John Forster, etc., 9/23/49-9/27/49.
[50] *Ibid.*, p. 175, to John Forster, 9/26/45.

ten in a comparable period of time. After the return from America and a large welcome-home banquet, Dickens embraced a hectic routine of social rounds, family responsibilities, and creative work, not only novels and *American Notes* but the Christmas stories that were to become a regular part of his annual productivity, and another fling at journalism. Dickens the mesmeric operator was also Dickens the manipulator and manager of men, Dickens the administrator, Dickens the social critic and reformer, Dickens the actor, and certainly Dickens the editor. He was a man who loved activity, and activity's usual concomitant, power. He was used to getting his way, dominating through his talent and his will. He absolutely refused to be second in anything or to give in to anyone on the occasions on which he felt he was right. Like most self-assured men, he rarely ever thought that he was wrong. He was used to controlling and manipulating people just as he was used to creating and manipulating characters in fiction.

Dickens had begun to exert his own mesmeric powers for what he thought were good and therapeutic ends. He had learned from Elliotson and Townshend, and from his reading, something about these forces and their possibilities that suited the kind of man he had already become through birth and environment. At a crucial early moment in his career he had been opened up to new experiences and theories about personality, will, dominance, and control, the relationship between the conscious and the unconscious, reality and dreams, the visible and the invisible, mechanistic science and transcendant forces. Exhausted with work and the financial and psychological problems of his growing family, perhaps encouraged by his American experience, he suddenly had an idea that would open him to further new experiences. On November 1, 1843, he revealed his plan to Forster. "I shall take all the family, and two servants—three at most—to some place which I know beforehand to be CHEAP and in a delightful climate, in Normandy or Brittany. . . . During that time, I shall walk through Switzerland, cross the Alps, travel through France and Italy; take Kate perhaps to Rome and Venice; and in short see everything that is to be seen."[51] He would produce a book of travel sketches based on his letters to Forster, as he had done during his trip in America. He was already taking Italian lessons.

While finishing *Martin Chuzzlewit*, he wrote to his friend Felton of his secret plans, which hardly anyone yet knew about, and of "strange thoughts of Italy and France, and maybe Germany."[52] Preparations began in the late winter and early spring of 1844. Elliotson undoubtedly learned of the plans when he visited the house to look after "his patient."[53] The rest of his circle was informed. By March the extensive travel fantasy had been reduced to sharper focus, Italy the country to be spotlighted, and then, after some alternatives were considered, Genoa the city. "For on the first of July, please God, I turn my face towards Italy. . . . Dick turns his head towards the orange groves."[54] Almost like a magnetic force, Italy attracted him as he turned his face towards its power. He was not to be disappointed.

[51] *Ibid.*, I, 544-545, to John Forster, 11/1/43.
[52] *Ibid.*, p. 554, to C. C. Felton, 1/1/44.
[53] *Ibid.*, p. 556, to T. J. Serle, 1/2/44.
[54] *Ibid.*, p. 584-585, to T. J. Thompson, 3/24/44.

CHAPTER

IV

Dickens and the de la Rues

[1]

Even before the Dickens entourage arrived in Italy, the de la
Rues were part of their fate. Dickens' bumbling well-inten-
tioned friend, the Scots sculptor Angus Fletcher, who had
been residing in Genoa, knew Emile de la Rue well enough
to consult him about renting a palazzo for the visiting English celebrity. The Swiss banker, who had made Genoa his
permanent home, was a man of acute practicality. He re-
sided with his English-born wife, her mother, and later their
children, with frequent visits from one of Madame de la
Rue's brothers, in a top-floor apartment in the Palazzo or
Brignole Rosso, "an ascent a trifle shorter than" the "ascent
of Mont Blanc," with an extensive view of, among other
things, the famous Palazzo Peschiere and its grounds.[1] His
knowledge of all things Italian, including its politics and
real estate, was extensive. He had contacts among the au-
thorities at Turin; he knew the country and the language as
if it were his own; he had the authority and reputation of a
prominent banking firm of which he was the chief representative in Italy, with headquarters in a quiet but expanding commercial seaport. De la Rue urged Fletcher to take
the "old palazzo of the Doria . . . one of the strangest old

[1] Berg MS., Dickens to Emile de la Rue, 8/19/57.

palaces in Italy . . . surrounded by beautiful woods of great trees," maintained at the expense of the owner, "a wonderful house" for the Dickens family. In a poem of 1887, "Genoa and the Mediterranean," Thomas Hardy praised the consoling peacefulness of "Palazzo Doria's orange bowers." The palazzo was on the sea, six miles from the center of Genoa.[2]

But the impractical, lovably stubborn Fletcher, whom Dickens had later to restrain himself from damning for his foolishness, had set his mind on the Villa Di Bagnerello in the inconveniently located suburb of Albaro, "the queerest . . . place that ever was anywhere."[3] By October, Dickens had gotten out of a bad arrangement (not only were they living in the "pink elephant"—but Fletcher with them in some distant wing) and become the close neighbor of the de la Rues. They had rented the "Palazzo Peschiere, in Genoa; which is surrounded by a delicious garden, and is a most charming habitation in all respects."[4] If de la Rue's original advice had prevailed, they would have been distant neighbors and perhaps less close friends.

More likely than not their formal acquaintance began, through Fletcher, early in Dickens' Genoese sabbatical. Visits between the two families became common as soon as they were close neighbors. Dickens apologized to Madame because he was "obliged to deny" himself "the pleasure of coming to you this morning. . . . Kate and Georgy will leave here at a quarter before 2 and will come straight to you."[5] On November 5, 1844, the day before he was to leave for a month-long trip through Italy and to England for the reading of *The Chimes*, Dickens gave a dinner-party for fourteen, and the de la Rues were naturally included.[6] By the end of December, Dickens entreated Emile de la Rue to "eschew" formality in their relationship. He was to come

[2] *Nonesuch*, I, 679-680, to John Forster, 6/2/45.
[3] Berg MS., Dickens to Frederick Dickens, 7/22/44.
[4] *Nonesuch*, I, 614-615, to Rev. Edward Tagart, 8/9/44.
[5] *Ibid.*, p. 630, to Madame de la Rue, "Wednesday Morning (1844)."
[6] *Ibid.*, p. 640, to John Forster, 11/17/44.

and go in the Dickens household and Dickens in theirs without formal notice.[7] Dickens seemed pleased to have found this unexpected opportunity for friendship and sought to surround it with the protection of total family involvement. He was delighted to have people outside his family with whom to involve himself.

Madame de la Rue attracted Dickens' interest immediately. This "excellent little woman," small, dark, with long hair, had frequently suffered from a nervous tic, a "sad invalid" whose alternations between nervous headaches and painful indispositions on the one hand and voluble sociability and cheerful good humor on the other must have reminded Dickens of many of Elliotson's patients. He had seen similar cases at the exhibitions at London University Hospital and at 37 Conduit Street. His experience with mesmeric theory and therapeutics and his wide reading in its literature made it easy for him to identify the psychosomatic nature of Madame de la Rue's condition and to wonder whether or not his own mesmeric powers might not be sufficient to the task. He sensed the possibility that she might be ready for a new doctor and a new medicine. In addition, he found that he had time and energy on his hands. He had written *The Chimes* in October but was to write nothing other than correspondence during the rest of the stay in Italy. Though he released some of his energy with long walks with Emile and by constantly smoking cigarettes, "good large ones, made of pretty strong tobacco," he missed London streets and stimulations; he could not settle down to a writing routine; he had a pain in his side and dreamed of his dead sister-in-law Mary; he felt restless with unexorcized energy.[8]

Soon after his return from England at the beginning of December Dickens began to mesmerize Madame de la Rue, with the consent and cooperation of Emile. By the end of the month Dickens' easy, informal companionship with the

7 Berg MS., Dickens to Emile de la Rue, 12/26/44.

8 *Nonesuch*, I, 813, to John Forster, "(November 1846)"; *Nonesuch*, I, 795, to John Forster, 10/3/46.

husband had expanded into a new relationship with the wife. She had become his patient; he her "humble servant and physician."[9]

Madame de la Rue's "severe" attacks "of her sad disorder" produced convulsions, distortions of the limbs, aching headaches, insomnia, and a plague of neurasthenic symptoms, including catalepsy, that Dickens knew Elliotson, Dupotet, and Townshend had treated successfully. Cure was possible, alleviation certain. Dickens cautioned the de la Rues that initial treatment might intensify disorder: this would be a good sign. It was his hope that mesmerism would increase it temporarily, evidence of the applicability of its power to this patient. It would imply the probability of alleviation in the future, after longer treatment. Dickens was eager to continue the next morning at eleven, ready and happy to come to her not only then but at any other time or season when he could entertain the smallest expectation of rendering her the slightest service. He volunteered to Emile an assertion of his selfless sincerity, which he and the de la Rues certainly believed in. There was to be nothing self-serving in his commitment, for he had the truest interest in her and her suffering and boasted that if he could lessen them in any degree, he would "derive great happiness from being the fortunate instrument of her relief."[10]

Dickens placed reliance on standard mesmeric techniques: sleep-waking (mesmeric sleep) and mesmeric trance, within which the patient, stimulated by the doctor, explored fears, fantasies, and dreams through verbalized free association. The first was to alleviate pain and exhaustion; the second, to discover and come to terms with the underlying causes of the disorder and illness. Madame de la Rue must have seemed to Dickens every bit as good a subject as the O'keys had seemed to Elliotson. The technical procedures were a success from the very beginning. Dickens had no trouble

---

[9] Berg MS., Dickens to Emile de la Rue, 12/26/44; *Nonesuch*, I, 745, to Madame de la Rue, 4/17/46.
[10] Berg MS., Dickens to Emile de la Rue, 12/26/44.

inducing mesmeric sleep through his usual procedure of quiet, steady, rhythmic passes over the head and face of the patient with constant verbal emphasis on concentration and calmness. He solicited her "gentle trust . . . in my power to help her" and insisted ultimately on "her subservience to me."[11] She would have to give herself to the domination of his will and efforts with the same commitment with which he devoted himself to her cure.

By the beginning of January Dickens and Madame de la Rue were deeply involved in a relationship of intensive mutual need that had suddenly broken the boundaries of normal rules of proportion. Emile de la Rue and Catherine Dickens watched from the sidelines, the former nervous and hopeful, the latter nervous and threatened. By the middle of January Dickens was being summoned, and eagerly hastening, at all hours of the day and night to Madame de la Rue's bedroom, where a psychodrama of the most stimulating kind frequently occurred.[12]

Having put her into mesmeric sleep for some twenty minutes on the night of Wednesday, January 15, Dickens, with great difficulty and through repeating the identical question three or four times, finally drew Madame de la Rue into conversation. Dickens asked her where she was today, perhaps as usual on the hillside, to which she answered yes. Was she quite alone? No. Were many people there? Many indeed. Male or female? Both. Dickens inquired about their dress and activity. Madame could not see. But then there was so much to look at. The people were walking about and talking. To whom? Not to me, she answered. To one another. Dickens wanted to know what they were saying, but Madame claimed that she didn't know. She had so much to do. But they were a large crowd? Yes. Madame suddenly cried out, terribly agitated, "Here's my brother!" She repeated her exclamation, breathing quickly, becoming stiff. Dickens wanted to know where he was. Was he part of the

---

[11] *Ibid.*, 1/25/45; 2/4/45; 1/27/45.
[12] *Ibid.*, 1/15/45; *Nonesuch*, III, 752, to J. S. Le Fanu, 11/24/69.

crowd? No, he was in a room. Was anyone with him? No. Did she know what he was doing? Yes. He leaned against a window. He looked through it. She repeated twice that he looked so sad. Madame began to cry, overwhelmed with sympathy for his sadness. Dickens wanted to know which brother this was. Was it the one he knew? No. Not him at all. Was it a different brother? His name? Charles. He was so sad. But why was he sad, Dickens asked? Madame said that she did not know, but that she would try to find out. Dickens urged her to watch the door. Someone might come in. Yes, yes, she said, she would, she was busy looking, she was attempting to see. Dickens' persistent questioning elicited from Madame de la Rue, who envisioned her brother "Charles" standing against a window with the sea visible through it, that the poor fellow was so sad because he was thinking of her and thought himself completely forgotten.

Dickens' account of this mesmeric session is in a letter to Emile, who was probably out of town briefly on business. Regardless of his whereabouts, Emile gained all his knowledge of the sessions between his favorite patient and physician from the physician, since he did not appear at the sessions himself, perhaps out of a sense of tact or warned by Dickens of possible interference with the process. His wife, like most mesmeric subjects, could remember little or nothing once awakened. But Dickens, acting on the novelist's as well as the physician's impulse, like Elliotson, who kept careful case records of treatment in the hospital wards, wrote down in long letters almost verbatim accounts of some of the sessions. He reported to Emile that Madame de la Rue spoke earnestly, as if the scene had been actually visible to her, in the special tone of voice naturally used by someone who is concentrating intensely on something that she can see and fears to miss any sight of. She wiped away the tears a number of times, as if to see her brother "Charles" more clearly. But this mysterious brother "Charles" was not the only male who inhabited this trance landscape in which the pathetic figure of Madame de la Rue shed tears, standing on a hillside in the pleasant breeze under a blue sky. Despite its pastoral atmosphere, the landscape was threatening, with indifferent or hostile crowds, a lost brother who was like another self, "unseen people" who were rolling "stones down this hill, which she is much distressed in her endeavors to avoid, and which occasionally strike her," and another man who was "haunting this place." She saw him mostly, but sometimes she could only hear him talking. She feared him and dared not look at him. Dickens connected this figure with the man Madame de la Rue called her "bad spirit." She begged Dickens to say nothing about him. On Dickens' request, since the spirit had been talking of him, she attempted to hear what he was saying. But she could not understand his words and suddenly warned Dickens not to leave her on a Monday. "It's not he who says that. *I* say it." She then complained that she was tired and begged Dickens to awaken her from mesmeric trance.[13]

The next day Dickens followed the same line of questioning, and in a series of daily mesmeric sessions pursued the significance of the estranged brother and the dark stranger. Perhaps he had in mind the relationship between the O'key sisters, the frequency with which family members, particularly siblings, appeared as doubles in mesmeric literature and in the trance responses of Elliotson's patients, and the controversial role Elizabeth O'key's "Great Jacky" had played in the clairvoyant predictions of the fates of patients in the hospital wards. This "bad spirit," like Elizabeth's, could be summoned instantaneously in mesmeric trance and did not hesitate to make predictions not only about the patient but about the fate of the doctor and others.[14] Dickens considered the possibility that Madame de la Rue was clairvoyant.[15] He had been warned by her not to go away on a Monday. The Dickens and the de la Rue household knew that the novelist had planned to leave on Sunday, January 19th, for an extended trip through Italy. But by this time Dickens and Madame de la Rue had entered into

[13] *Ibid.* [14] *Ibid.* [15] *Ibid.*, 1/27/45.

a relationship of such mutual dependency that the doctor could not give up the patient any more than the patient could give up the doctor. Dickens wrote to Emile that the length of his stay in Naples would be determined completely by what he heard from the de la Rues. It was his intention to return to Rome within ten days or two weeks, certainly before Holy Week began. But his plans were flexible and he intended to be "guided solely by your letters."[16]

To further communication and to keep him in as close touch with his patient as possible, Dickens and Emile decided that the latter would keep a daily journal, forwarding the relevant pages to each one of the towns on Dickens' schedule in time to arrive there when he did. In that way Dickens would have a reasonably up-to-date casebook. He could occupy himself with the problems of his patient, exert influence through letters, and be notified immediately in case of emergency. Much of Dickens' mental energy went into the planning of the fullest benefits of mesmerization for Madame de la Rue. Even their separation was to be therapeutically beneficial, for Dickens speculated that the distance between them would increase Madame de la Rue's receptiveness to his power and its permanent influence. He wanted her to adjust to the necessity of relying on "her anxious physician." She would then be "more prepared" to "confide in, and to yield to, the reality, when it is at hand."[17] From various cities in the last weeks of January, 1845, Dickens responded to de la Rue's journal—letters supplemented by letters from Madame herself, the gloss and the text. He urged on de la Rue that it was essential that the Phantom should not for an instant regain its power. For Dickens could not help noticing how remarkably obsessed Madame was with the Phantom, and how deep into her consciousness and trust his influence and effect on it had penetrated.[18]

For Dickens, Madame de la Rue was a weak innocent, the

[16] *Ibid.*, 1/15/45.   [17] *Ibid.*, 1/25/45.   [18] *Ibid.*

victim of merciless forces, "so needing to be helped and tenderly and carefully directed." If for any reason the de la Rues could not meet Dickens in Rome together, he urged that Emile consider the quickest, most expeditious method of persuading her to come without him.[19] So confident was Dickens of his power to control this vital fluid, this life force, and to use it for beneficial ends, and so oblivious was he, in his sincerity and enthusiasm, of the world's sense of proprieties, that he proclaimed to Emile: "we have every reason for Hope, Courage, Confidence, Resolution, and Perseverance."[20] Dickens seems to have had no hesitation in taking under his protection the complexities of this "little" woman and her problems, much as he was attracted to and attracted the dependencies of a series of "little" women in his life and fiction, including his two sisters-in-law, his wife, his daughters, and Ellen Ternan. The depth of his involvement was not a cause of hesitation to him, so invincible was his own sense of integrity and self-worth. When taxed later with even the implication of amorous let alone sexual motives, not to speak of impropriety, he reacted with outraged imperviousness.[21]

By the end of January Catherine had begun to make her disapproval known. Perhaps she was only jealous of her husband's time. Perhaps she already sensed the potential sexual basis of the power relationship between a male operator and a female subject in Victorian mesmerism. The closeness of the relationship had begun to verge on the uncanny, the telepathetic. From Siena, Dickens, who had begun to answer Emile's journal "day by day," wrote that he had "a strange and uncommon anxiety upon me all day." He was deeply distressed, fearing that Madame de la Rue was ill. The de la Rues' silence made him feel in his "apprehension" that they were twice as far away from him as they in fact were.[22]

19 *Ibid.*   20 *Ibid.*
21 Dexter, pp. 227-229, 12/5/53.
22 Berg MS., Dickens to Emile de la Rue, 1/26/45.

Reading de la Rue's "Diary" "for the hundredth time" the next night in his lodgings in La Scala, Dickens had an astounding story for de la Rue's consideration, which was to be told to Madame only to the extent that her husband thought wise. What had happened "was really quite a fearful thing, and the strangest instance of the strange mysteries that are hidden within this power, that I have ever seen or heard of." Aware of how difficult of belief the occurrence was, Dickens wrote to de la Rue that if he read it in print it would seem unbelievable. He and Madame had agreed that at eleven o'clock each morning Dickens would concentrate for one hour on his patient. On the road to La Scala, Dickens sat within the carriage, not on top, as was his usual custom. Instead, Mrs. Dickens had "been hoisted up" for the fresh air. Dickens paid no attention to her, remaining absolutely still and concentrating his entire being with absolute and unwavering intensity on mesmerizing "our patient." No one could possibly know what he was doing, particularly Catherine. Would anyone believe that after about five or ten minutes he was startled to hear Catherine's muff fall and that when he looked up at her he found her "in the mesmeric trance, with her eyelids quivering in a convulsive manner peculiar to some people in that state"? Her extremities were cold, all her senses numbed. He was able to awaken her only with considerable effort and, in response to his question, she said that "she had been magnetized." Until the magnetic effect wore off, she trembled badly.[23]

Dickens' astonishment was at the demonstration of his own powers more than at the existence of the powers themselves and their modes of transference. He was at pains to assert that he had not fictionalized or dramatized the event: "For it is Truth itself. I have purposely stated it in the plainest manner, and have not presented it to you in anything like the remarkable aspect in which it actually occurred."[24] The readers of the mesmeric literature of the

[23] Ibid., 1/27/45.　　　　　[24] Ibid.

previous ten years, particularly of the Elliotson-Dupotet-Townshend experiments, many of which Dickens witnessed, would have found nothing extraordinary in the episode. Elliotson had conducted many "successful" experiments with mesmerizing at a distance, through walls and buildings, sometimes across miles. In the pages of *The Zoist* he was to recount instances of patients being mesmerized without any awareness that the process was occurring. Occasionally observers, in some special proximity to the operator, would become mesmerized themselves. Sometimes totally ignorant that such a process was being attempted upon someone else, a chance passer-by—a servant, for example, coming through the room—would suddenly fall into mesmeric trance. Often the Elliotson accounts involve some object that assists in the communication of the mesmeric fluid, such as a mirror or a metallic substance. Interestingly, Dickens wrote to de la Rue that he had been teaching Catherine some Italian vocabulary in their travelling carriage just prior to his attempt to mesmerize Madame de la Rue. He assumed that Catherine was still repeating the words when he was startled by the fall of her muff.[25] Perhaps the object of transference of power in this case was language. The rocking carriage, the repetition of the foreign words, the quiet but suggestive presence of a man who had already mesmerized her many times—the results were unexpected because unsought, but certainly quite explainable, especially to Dickens, who had at hand a relevant series of experiences and references.

And what about Madame de la Rue? Did she benefit from this mesmerizing at a distance? The implication seems to be that she did, though Dickens found it quite natural that the longer they stayed apart, the weaker his influence grew. Elliotson had explained to doubters that mesmerized metals gradually lost their potency. The effect had to be renewed. Dickens agonized over the possibility that "prolonged separation" would decrease his influence over her.[26] He urged the necessity of Madame's coming to meet him in Rome. He

25 *Ibid.*
26 Morgan MS., Dickens to Emile de la Rue, 1/31/45.

speculated that as the time for the journey came closer, she might protest and find reasons not to go. But the greater her disinclination to come, the more formidable the danger and the more evident the absolute necessity for her to be "brought" by force if necessary. Dickens underlined the word "brought" for Emile's consideration. He believed that Emile was in sympathy with him.[27]

For Madame de la Rue's suffering had increased; she was engaged in a titanic battle between Manichaean forces represented on one side by the dark Phantom, on the other by Dickens and the force of his approach, the power of magnetism. Dickens placed all trust in her gentle confidence in his power to assist her. Emile, who had had to play a secondary role in these dramatics, was assured that she had not told him of the extent of her terrible mental suffering and her horrible nightly trials because of her unwillingness to have him suffer sympathetically more than absolutely necessary. But it was the dark Phantom who was the key to her illness; it was he who bound her "to the disease and the disease to her." But, Dickens assured Emile, through Madame's full revelation to her physician of all her former secrets about that dark Phantom, "the chain is utterly broken." His power was gone. Dickens speculated on the origins of the Phantom:

"I cannot yet quite make up my mind, whether the Phantom originates in shattered nerves and a system broken by pain; or whether it is the representative of some great nerve or set of nerves on which her disease has preyed—and begins to loose its hold now, because the disease of those nerves is itself attacked by the inexplicable agony of the magnetism. I think upon the whole I incline to the last opinion; but I would not make up my mind without more observation of, and more conversation with, herself."

As an afterthought, he added that he should like to discuss it at full length with Emile.[28]

Though Dickens' speculations are consistent with many of

27 *Ibid.*, 2/10/45.
28 Berg MS., Dickens to Emile de la Rue, 1/27/45.

Elliotson's pronouncements on the relationship between magnetism as a cure and the diseases it alleviates, the main thrust of the diagnosis is original and demonstrates the psychological perceptiveness of Dickens the novelist, who frequently used some symbolic projection of the inner life and the imagination to represent a central illness of the spirit. The effect of the disease on some great central nerve had been to set loose this Phantom who lived within. The magnetism would free the central nerve from its pain, and imprison or destroy the evil force. Madame de la Rue was doing battle with herself; the Phantom who lived with such fictional vividness was like "the dread companion of the Haunted man . . . an awful likeness of himself" (1847).[29] It was this Phantom whom Dickens feared, for that figure was so intimately connected with the hidden pains and anxieties of her being and its effect so inseparable from her belief in Dickens' benevolence and power and in her general knowledge of the force of magnetism *"that it must not make head again."*[30] He imagined relapse and madness if that power should reassert itself.

Madame de la Rue seems to have become a battleground on which two potent figures fought: Dickens and the Phantom. For, in characteristic manner, Dickens had made someone else's battle his own. But in doing so in this case he had made such a total commitment in such a delicate situation that undoubtedly he had become not only Madame de la Rue's physician but her psychotherapist, and in the many transferences that obviously occurred he himself became a surrogate for the patient, internalized her struggles, and took the Phantom as his personal enemy. At the same time, however, his level of awareness was sufficient enough, and the language and tools of mesmerism adequately distancing, so that at some times and at some level of consciousness he seemed to have known precisely what he was doing.

The challenge of the experience, the conflict of wills, the

29 *HM*, I.
30 Berg MS., Dickens to Emile de la Rue, 1/27/45.

extension and growth of the powers of the self, the thrill of the danger, the excitement of a total passion and a total commitment, despite the obstacles of time, place, and situation, demanded Dickens' involvement. He could not resist; he had no desire to resist. Letter after letter in the last days of January and all through February flew from his pen in response to Emile's journal. When it came, he answered immediately; when it did not come, he worried incessantly about the possible negative significance of no news. The Dickens family arrived in Rome on the night of the next to the last day of January. Letters from both Emile and Madame de la Rue awaited them, Emile inquiring about some books, probably on mesmerism, Madame indicating that the beneficial effects of the mesmerism were wearing off and imploring Dickens not to visit the St. Trinita di Monto. She had a "fevered dream" set in the church, filled with sights and sounds so dreadful that she could not yet bring herself to tell him the details. Though she could not explain to herself why, she dreaded his going there without her.[31] In a sense, of course, Dickens could go no place in those days without Madame de la Rue's being with him. He extracted from her letter this warning and included it in his response to Emile, who learned about his wife's dream from Dickens. It was presented as evidence of the need for Emile to hasten the news from his head office in Geneva and his partner in Turin that would clarify the date of the de la Rues' arrival in Rome. The power of the Phantom might reassert itself, Dickens feared, and the longer they were apart the less effective the force of magnetism would be day by day. Dickens was horror-struck, remembering that one night Madame de la Rue had proposed to stop the mesmeric treatments without explanation, though she had only recently begun to feel the relief and advantages of the sessions. A horrible thought struck him. What if it were the case that this Phantom who pursued her every night threatened that he would take some horrible revenge not only upon herself but

[31] Morgan MS., Dickens to Emile de la Rue, 1/31/45.

on him also unless she gave up the mesmeric treatments? And what if that idea became fixed in her mind? He believed that her nature was so unselfish and self-sacrificing that she would in such a circumstance suffer miserably without any explanation rather than permit him to be endangered.[32] At this point Dickens needed his patient and mesmerism as much as his patient needed him.

A few days later he found support for his anxiety about the ascendant power of the Phantom in the news from de la Rue that Madame had not fulfilled her promise to Dickens that she had laid great stress on in her last letter. They had agreed that she would make herself receptive at precisely one o'clock each morning to Dickens' long-distance mesmerizing. She wrote that she would leave the casino precisely at that time on a particular night. But, despite her promise, her fear of the Phantom was so great that she disregarded her pledge to Dickens and stayed out far into the morning to avoid their mesmeric session. Though Dickens admitted that this was a trivial incident, he found it significant nevertheless, a sign of the increasing power of the evil figure. Dickens cautioned de la Rue not to believe his wife's assertions that she no longer needed mesmeric treatment, pointing out her inconsistencies, which he suggested were a natural part of her unnatural state. But the Phantom must be beaten down. Everything depended on this. And it could not be done at a distance. Dickens was confident that if he could exercise his magnetic power "near her and with her," he could shatter the dark figure "like glass."[33]

But other complications had to be attended to. De la Rue worried that Dickens did not appreciate the full extent of his own devotion to his wife. Dickens wrote from Naples to assure him that he had no cause to think that he had "the faintest doubt of the truth, intensity, and earnestness of your devotion . . . or of the affectionate and zealous watch you have kept over her in all her sufferings." He felt ad-

[32] *Ibid.*   [33] *Ibid.*, 2/4/45.

miration for de la Rue's constancy and patience. He pleaded that his words and his actions not be misunderstood. Catherine's growing dissatisfaction with her husband's commitment to Madame de la Rue hovered over his request for Emile's understanding. At great length he reviewed for Emile the threat of the Phantom, the inconsistencies of purpose and mind that naturally resulted from the disease, the danger that the Phantom might use his possible power over Dickens as blackmail against Madame. But the magnetism from a distance had been working, though direct renewal must not be delayed much longer. De la Rue confirmed that on the past Sunday, when Dickens had been concentrating for one hour on magnetizing Madame, she had indeed been magnetized. For Dickens it was all "part of such a strange and mysterious whole," an explanation of cosmic energy and order.[34]

A remarkable incident had occurred on the previous Monday and Tuesday, the last day of carnival in Rome, which correlated with de la Rue's comment that Madame had been particularly restless that Tuesday in Genoa. Dickens, somewhat moody, though not depressed, had been wandering through the streets all afternoon. At about one or two o'clock at night he awakened suddenly, feeling an inexplicable anxiety, a state of "horror and emotion." He was quite sure that it had not been caused by a dream. It even seemed as if the feeling had come over him after he had awakened, rather than that he had been awakened by the feeling caused by some experience while asleep. The anxiety was so severe that he lighted candles and walked about his room, thinking constantly about Madame de la Rue. He thought about her "while awake and asleep" for the next three nights. What struck him as extraordinary was that he had a constant anxiety about her without dreaming of her in the common way, "a sense of her being somehow a part of me, as I have when I am awake."[35] Perhaps Dickens was close to the truth when

34 *Ibid.*, 2/10/45.   35 *Ibid.*

he implied that Madame de la Rue and her Phantom were extensions of him, "part of me," the result partially of Madame's creations and of his own suggestions. Dickens was treading on the threshold of a new response to the objection that critics of mesmerism had been raising for seventy years: that there did not exist some mysterious force outside of man but simply a mental or imaginative force not independent of the activities of the human mind; that mesmerism was like poetry, an example of the inventive powers of the imagination. Though Dickens, like Elliotson, believed throughout his life in the existence of an independent fluid, he came close at times to implying the same doctrine that James Braid enunciated in *Neurypnology or, The Rationale of Nervous Sleep, Considered in Relation with Animal Magnetism* (1843): that suggestion was the key process and that mesmeric "manifestations were entirely attributable to the mechanical pressure on an excited state of the nervous system."[36]

Undoubtedly, both operator and subject in this case were people with sensitive and excitable nervous systems. As the days of separation extended throughout the rest of February 1845, Dickens (who joked through his pain that "I have the perfect conviction that I could magnetize a Frying-Pan")[37] and Madame de la Rue lived in a state of frenzied anticipation of their reunion. "Good God," Dickens wrote, "how glad I am, you made your arrangements in good time . . . I was desperately mindful of my Patient yesterday and the day before. Intensely so, last night. I half expect some reason for it in your next journal."[38] As an experiment, Dickens gave up keeping his morning hour, without telling Madame about the change. He lived in the hope that they would start for Rome on the third of March. He feared that she had had "a bad attack." He made arrangements with Emile to ride out on horseback to surprise Madame as they approached

36 Braid, p. 99.
37 Morgan MS., Dickens to Emile de la Rue, 2/10/45.
38 Berg MS., Dickens to Emile de la Rue, 2/14/45.

the city and alerted them to "watch out for a gallant figure, apparently possessing an angelic nature. All others are counterfeit."[39] In this Manichaean battle with dark forces, Dickens had no doubt what side he was on. And he had no doubt that he could overcome this evil creature, for it was a creation of the imagination, of the sick mind; it was a self-delusion, not a reality: "it is in its nature a false thing—an unreal creation; a lie of her eyes and ears." He was certain that if he "could call it up, when she and I were together, and could represent it as letting fall the Blade of a Guillotine upon my head, I would do so, and would have her look on immoveable: triumphant in the conviction that it was a powerless shadow." With the confidence of Sydney Carton on the guillotine platform, Dickens asserted the supremacy of a reality principle over an illusion.[40]

They were finally reunited in Rome. Madame de la Rue, who had begun to sleep calmly at night, had become a "sad invalid" again.[41] She was ill through a good part of the month, pursued "by myriads of bloody phantoms of the most frightful aspect" who "after becoming paler . . . all veiled their faces."[42] Dickens applied himself energetically to his task, and the entire Dickens family had to adjust its schedule to the needs of the physician and his patient. As on many other nights, the corridors of Meloni's hotel at which both families were lodged were busy with hastening footsteps until four in the morning on March 19th.[43] Sightseeing was curtailed. Dickens did no writing, other than occasional entries in his own diary and his correspondence. "One night . . . she was rolled into an apparently impossible ball, by tic in the brain, and I only knew where her head was by following her long hair to its source. Such a fit had always held her before at least 30 hours, and it was so alarming to see that had hardly any belief in myself with reference to it.

---

[39] *Ibid.*, 2/25/45.
[40] Morgan MS., Dickens to Emile de la Rue, 2/10/45.
[41] *Nonesuch*, I, 667, to Charles Bodenham, 3/24/45.
[42] *Ibid.*, III, 752, to J. S. Le Fanu, 11/24/69.
[43] *Ibid.*, I, 745, to Madame de la Rue, 4/17/46.

91

But in half an hour she was peacefully and naturally asleep, and next morning was quite well."[44]

Dickens' confidence and energy seemed inexhaustible, Madame de la Rue's needs insatiable. So inseparable were the two that both families travelled together back to Genoa at the beginning of April, much to Catherine's discomfort. "From that time, wheresoever I travelled in Italy, she and her husband travelled with me, and every day I magnetized her; sometimes under olive trees, sometimes in vineyards, sometimes in the travelling carriage, sometimes at wayside taverns during the midday halt."[45] Catherine became increasingly jealous and visibly hostile to both her husband and to the de la Rues.[46] She certainly imagined that she had lost her husband's love and affection. Quite possibly, she imagined a sexual affair between him and Madame, perhaps conducted with the tacit approval of Emile. Years later, at another moment of crisis in the Dickens marriage, he was to write, significantly to Emile de la Rue, in his best serious-joking strain: "She has been excruciatingly jealous of, and has obtained positive proof of my being on the most confidential terms with, at least fifteen thousand women of various conditions in life, every condition in life, since we left Genoa. Please to respect me for this vast experience."[47] Undoubtedly in Catherine's mind the first such infidelity had been with Madame de la Rue. Miserable, threatened, hysterical, Catherine forced her husband "to make that painful declaration of your [Catherine's] state of mind to the de la Rue's." Emile seemed to understand, with sophistication and sympathy. Dickens continued mesmerizing Madame throughout April and May. When the turmoil of their preparations for departure from Italy scheduled for June became too much for Dickens, he settled himself in the Palazzo Rosso and watched the hectic activities at the Peschiere from

[44] *Ibid.*, III, 752, to J. S. Le Fanu, 11/24/69.
[45] *Ibid.*
[46] Dexter, pp. 227-229, 12/5/53.
[47] Berg MS., Dickens to Emile de la Rue, 10/23/57.

the de la Rues' window.[48] His temper with Catherine was short; he blamed her for misunderstandings and inconveniences.[49] He attempted to teach de la Rue how to mesmerize his wife and later consoled him through the mail, sympathizing with his failure: "I feel how natural it is, that you should be grieved at not being able to exert the influence. But it dwells with this person and it does not dwell with that person, unaccountably. . . ."[50]

If this were science then, it was personal science, a special talent of the elect; and the chosen physician was about to leave. Immediately before their departure, while in mesmeric trance, Madame suddenly called out to Dickens that he must remember to mesmerize her when he would be in England on December 23rd, at exactly eleven o'clock in the morning for fifteen minutes. He should do it without fail.[51] Dickens wrote the statement in a short note to Emile de la Rue so that it would not be possible for Madame to overhear. The methodical Emile, whose annotations of date, place, and situation appear on almost every Dickens letter to him that has survived, wrote at the bottom of the sheet of paper over six months later that "on the 23X the affect took place upon her from 11 to ½ past." He wondered whether Dickens in London had mesmerized her that day.[52]

⟦ 2 ⟧

How often Dickens concentrated on this long-distance mesmerizing in the weeks and months and years after his

---

[48] *Nonesuch*, I, 681-682, to John Forster, 6/7/45.

[49] *Ibid.*, p. 680, to T. Yeats Brown, 6/3/45.

[50] Morgan MS., Dickens to Emile de la Rue, 6/29/45.

[51] *Ibid.*, 6/8/45.

[52] A check of various allusions and habits of writing ("X" for December, for example) in the instances in Dickens' letters in which he paraphrased or quoted Emile de la Rue with those of the annotations on each letter makes it certain that the handwriting on the letters other than Dickens' is Emile's. He seems to have saved and filed each letter he received from Dickens, with identifying file annotations. This is one of the few cases in which the annotation is of any substantive significance. None of Emile's or Madame's letters to Dickens seems to have survived.

departure from Genoa, "dear old Genoa" which he could never forget, "where . . . the best part of me is . . . shaking hands with you."[53] "I have only the dregs here," he lamented, like Byron bewailing the lost "flowers and fruits" of life. In the initial year of separation he wrote frequently, both to Emile and to Madame de la Rue. The first letters were in transit, from Zurich and Brussels, to those "friends of mine in a red palace," and then from Devonshire Terrace.[54] Dickens was pleased with the results of his sessions with Madame and fully expected to continue his treatment in the future. He felt that he had good reason to believe that he would find his power "greatly increased and intensified" whenever he had the opportunity to continue the treatment that had done her so much good already. He had absolutely no doubt of that.[55] He marvelled over the change in her "*moral* influence" over the shadow, so striking in comparison to the shadow's influence over her when he first went to Rome. The shadow, though not finally defeated, had been temporarily discomfited. Madame de la Rue had seen the shadow momentarily, but it seemed only "the shadow of the Bad shadow," passing quickly, unwilling to be seen, ashamed, exhausted.

Dickens felt this an even more favorable sign than if she had not seen it at all. It seemed prescient to him of an eventual final cure. If the disease should return, he assured de la Rue, though the earth be large, he would journey to wherever might be necessary. He would think ill of Emile, and believe that Emile thought such of him, if there should be any hesitation in putting Dickens to the test or any suggestion that they did not trust one another fully. "Ours is not a common knowledge of each other." To keep the image of the knowledge bright, he planned to have a watercolor done of "the Inimitable B" at work in his study at Devon-

[53] Berg MS., Dickens to Emile de la Rue, 6/15/45.
[54] Morgan MS., Dickens to Emile de la Rue, 6/29/45.
[55] *Ibid.*

shire Terrace for his friends. But "you must come to England. That's clear. And I must come back to Genoa too."[56]

Finally settled again in London, Dickens reported to Emile that there was nothing new, but by mid-summer he was hectically immersed in varied social, literary, and theatrical activities. His letters to the de la Rues were less frequent, his apologies charming. His left ear had been burning considerably since last Monday, when he failed to write to Emile, and "as I sit with the right side of my face towards Genoa, I am inclined to think you must have been anathematizing me . . . for not keeping my promise." Dickens hoped and trusted that the positive effects of the mesmerism would last and sustain Madame's morale, at least until his next visit, which he expected to be no later than one year after he had departed unhappily from his friends. He would receive any account of his distant friends with "new and higher interest than ever."[57]

Madame de la Rue wrote frequently during the summer and fall of 1845. Emile requested that Dickens send him books difficult to get in Italy, among them "Brewster and the *Philosophy of Apparitions*," obviously pursuing an interest in the occult and the mesmeric that Dickens had awakened. The novelist sent a large box of his own books as a present to Madame, but when he attempted to add a few volumes for Emile the binder remonstrated that the box was a present to a lady that had been devoted entirely to Dickens' works. The binder considered the box a completed entity. He would include in the box anything that he was ordered to place there. But if he were forced to include any book that was not written by Dickens, "the completeness of that 'ere box is gone, and I don't care no more for it myself than if it was a Tea Kettle." So affected was Dickens by this logic that he had the lid nailed on instantly, without including the books for Emile.[58]

[56] *Ibid.*   [57] Berg MS., Dickens to Emile de la Rue, 7/28/45.
[58] *Ibid.*, 7/29/45.

95

By October happy Genoa days seemed long ago and far away. They exchanged presents and gossip. Dickens generously offered the hospitality of the de la Rues, "who would die to serve me," to friends bound for Italy. He constantly alluded to his imminent coming, sometimes in comic and extravagant terms, as if he himself were indirectly accepting the implausibility of a foreseeable reunion. Not only would Catherine object and create obstacles but his duties with the *Daily News* and the first stirrings of *Dombey* demanded his attention. Still, he daydreamed about that year of happiness and glory, as he was to do increasingly as the years went by. He wondered how all his old walks were and whether or not the old idle man with the broom still loitered on the palace steps. Was he himself ever "an idle man in a plaid coat" sunbathing each day high in the box of his travelling carriage with his happy friends? Perhaps it was all a dream. Did he "never magnetize a little somebody, with all my heart in her recovery and happiness?"[59] But the real question of moment was whether he would see them again soon. It was one thing to correspond, to employ Emile as a kind of executive courier for the *Daily News*,[60] to exchange gossip, to implore the de la Rues to visit London, quite another actually to arrange a visit.

The opportunity came in August of 1846. Dickens was staying with his family at Rosemont near Lausanne, near Townshend's villa, restless and unhappy with his progress on *Dombey*, though he put a brave face on it to Emile and claimed that "my troubles are not greater, thank God, than they usually are, when I am plunging neck and heels into a new book. It is always an anxious and worrying time."[61] But he would certainly find time to see his friends. He found time to see Townshend and Elliotson and to have "great success again in magnetism."[62]

But Catherine's antagonism to the de la Rues and Dick-

59 *Ibid.*, 10/28/45.
61 *Ibid.*, 8/20/46.
60 *Ibid.*, 1/28/46, 2/16/46.
62 *Nonesuch*, I, 804, to Douglas Jerrold, 10/24/46.

ens' fear of domestic discord made secret, elaborate plans necessary. He cautioned de la Rue that neither he nor Madame should say anything about their meeting in letters to mutual friends. "It seems a course that will suit anything and save a whole world of chances." He arranged to meet the de la Rues at Vevey the last Wednesday in October, indicating that he must return home "that night," explaining that it was important "with a view to my next day's work." Perhaps it was also important to call as little attention as possible within his household to the trip. He assured de la Rue that if he did not understand the alternatives they should take if some circumstance changed, "*She* will."[63]

He went alone and met them on Wednesday morning between nine and ten for breakfast. It was a brief meeting, and by the middle of the next month he was settled in Paris for an extended stay. He confided to Forster that "I was in that state in Switzerland when my spirits sunk so, I felt myself in serious danger."[64] Perhaps the brief meeting with the de la Rues was therapy for the physician. He continued to correspond with them. From Paris he reported to the de la Rues on his attendance at a play "called Irene ou le magnétisme . . . I was quite fascinated by it, and delighted Scribe [the playwright] by bringing it over to Elliotson."[65] He wrote to confirm Emile's question about a recent instance of telepathic mesmeric sympathy between them: "it is unquestionably true that at the time . . . I *was* thinking more than usual about you. . . ."[66] In March ot 1847 he sent them all the available numbers of *Dombey* and boasted that "I magnetized a man at Lausanne among unbelievers, and stretched him on the dining-room floor."[67]

As the months went by, his less frequent letters were filled with apologies, gossip, and nostalgia for the Genoa days. He

---

[63] Berg MSS., Dickens to Emile de la Rue, 8/17/46, 8/20/46.
[64] *Nonesuch*, I, 813, to John Forster, "(November 1846)."
[65] Berg MS., Dickens to Emile de la Rue, 3/24/47.
[66] *Ibid.*
[67] Morgan MS., Dickens to Emile de la Rue, 3/25/47.

referred to the power of his eyes and his magnetism as his "visual ray," to de la Rue's eyes as his "optic ray" or nerve. He wondered about Madame. "Does she ever think of her old doctor, and do you think of his visual ray—and stands Genoa where it did in those exciting times?"[68] He kept the possibility of reunion in the near future alive, mentioning that he and Maclise had been talking about going to Italy together on the first of May. He assured de la Rue that if it were only he, "I should say I was pretty certain to come." But Maclise was indecisive and the plan might not mature, though, regardless, "I have strong hopes of seeing you in Genoa before the autumn."[69] The hopes did not materialize, and Dickens amused himself with many things in addition to hard work, among them his performance as the doctor in one of his favorite farces, Mrs. Inchbald's "Animal Magnetism," which he had read as a boy.[70] But Madame de la Rue's "case" and its implications for the relationship between mind and body had become for the adult Dickens a central and constant example of mysterious psychological forces. He even published his own analysis of this special disease. "It has happened to ourselves to be closely acquainted with a case, in which the patient was afflicted with a violent and acute disorder of the nerves, and was, besides, continually troubled with horrible spectral illusions. . . . The patient, a lady, perfectly acquainted with the nature and origin of the phantoms by which she was haunted, was sometimes threatened and beaten by them; and the beating, which was generally upon the arm, left an actual soreness and local affection there. But, experience had taught her, that the approaching real effect suggested the imaginary cause. . . ."[71]

The Great Exhibition of 1851 brought innumerable vis-

[68] Berg MS., Dickens to Emile de la Rue, 2/29/48.
[69] Ibid.
[70] Nonesuch, II, 87, to John Leach, 5/7/48.
[71] Philip Collins, "Dickens on Ghosts: An Uncollected Article, with Introduction and Notes" (from Examiner, Feb. 26, 1848), The Dickensian, LIX (1963), 11.

itors to London, among them the de la Rues. Emile's banking concerns made it possible for them to combine business
with pleasure. In April Dickens sent his "love to my dear old
patient" and insisted that if it were not for theatrical activity on behalf of the Guild of Literature and Art he would
have seen them both that "Spring; for I had made up my
mind to run over to Genoa and Venice."[72] The transporta-
tion time between London and Genoa had been reduced to
twenty-four hours.[73] But it was the de la Rues who took advantage of the new schedule. At the end of June, Emile was
in London and dined with Dickens at Richmond. Perhaps
Madame de la Rue made the trip also. At the beginning of
October they were both in town for the Exhibition. But
Dickens' need for the de la Rues and his sense of urgency
about seeing them had decreased considerably. He was busy
with varied obligations and feared that he might not be able
to get to town to visit them at Jermyn Street, where they
were staying. "But, as it is quite clear to me that you will be
perpetually and constantly coming backwards and forwards
in future, I shall hope, on the occasion of our next visit, to
welcome you to my own home, and install you in my own
Den." He seems to have assumed that Catherine would not
object.[74]

Whether or not she would have, that visit did not take
place. But Dickens himself finally got his chance to go to
Italy again. Early in 1853 he decided that he was going "to
desert his family and run about Italy" for two months in
the fall "until Christmas" with Wilkie Collins and Augustus
Egg. He offered to "execute any little commission" for various friends.[75] The de la Rues were delighted and wrote as
if he were going to stay in Genoa "at least a month."[76] On
the twenty-eighth of October he finally saw them and his

[72] Berg MS., Dickens to Emile de la Rue, 4/25/51.
[73] Ibid., 10/8/51.
[74] Ibid.
[75] Nonesuch, II, 483, 486-487, to Mrs. Richard Watson, 8/27/53; to
W. S. Lander, 9/7/53; to John T. Delano, 9/12/53.
[76] Nonesuch, II, 493, to John Forster, "(September 1853)."

other Genoese friends again in their own city. In his long letters to Catherine he hardly mentioned the de la Rues, though he wrote detailed descriptions of their other friends and of his visit in a hard rain to the Peschiere, which had been turned into a school, the gardens neglected, the fireplaces closed up, the rooms "full of boarding school beds." He had only two days or so to spend in Genoa, which had changed to his amazement into an expanding commercial city filled with bustling activity. He let Catherine know that de la Rue was acting as his business and travel agent.[77] When he left Genoa he wrote detailed letters to Emile, with elaborate directions for the transference of money and the arrangement of couriers, travel accommodations, and the forwarding of mail. From Rome he sent gossip, particularly an account of his stay at the same hotel they had all stayed in eight years before.[78] He was deeply conscious of the changes in both places and people. From the window he looked down on the "Piazza del Popolo. The electric telegraph shoots through the Coliseum like a sunbeam—in at one ruined arch, and out at another. It looks otherwise as it grandly looked when your visual ray last beamed upon it."[79]

But he had spent a considerable portion of his stay in Genoa with the de la Rues. Madame was still suffering from her old illness. The effect of Dickens' mesmeric treatment years before had been temporary. Without hesitation, he offered to begin the treatment again. But this time Madame de la Rue declined. "She replied that she *felt* the relief would be immediate; but that the agony of leaving it off so soon, would be so great, that she would rather suffer on."[80] If she had not declined, would Dickens have stayed only two days in Genoa? Possibly the surge of commitment and enthusiasm from the past, the excitement and the challenge,

[77] Dexter, pp. 194-201, 10/28/53, 10/29/53.
[78] Berg MSS., Dickens to Emile de la Rue, 11/14/53, 11/25/53, 12/4/53.
[79] Berg MS., Dickens to Emile de la Rue, 11/14/53.
[80] *Nonesuch*, III, to J. S. Le Fanu, 11/24/69.

might have returned. Dickens' life might have taken a sharp turning five years before his break with Catherine. But conditions had changed, and so had his relationship with the de la Rues. From Rome Dickens' note of farewell seems to reflect the changes. "Give my love to Madame de la Rue," he wrote, "and tell her that it was a great happiness to me to see her again even for so short a time, and to see her looking so well and to find her in her old brave spirits." He sent a present to Madame, wrote from Venice and Turin, but seemed reconciled to the tentativeness of "perhaps we may meet in England before long."[81]

From Turin Dickens sent Catherine a devastating letter, filled with bitter truths both expressed and unexpressed, bristling with the implacable will and determination of an aggressive man asserting his moral rights. He had never forgotten the embarrassments that Catherine's jealousy had created over eight years before, both the private anguish and hostility between them and the public pain of his having to explain to the de la Rues. The visit to Genoa and the marital events of the intervening years intensified the pain. Perhaps the rejection inherent in Madame de la Rue's refusal to enter into a mesmeric relationship with him again emphasized the penalties he had to pay for Catherine's limitations. He had become painfully aware of the things that he had missed in life. But, whatever his failings, they were the other side of the coin of his strengths, and he wanted Catherine to know that his commitment to mesmerism, to exploring the nature of power, to asserting himself, his will, and his personality, to testing deeply the possibilities of all kinds of human relationships—all these things were inseparable from his art and his life. For "the intense pursuit of any idea that takes complete possession of me, is one of the qualities that makes me different—sometimes for good; sometimes I dare say for evil—from other men." He was now possessed with the notion that Catherine must apologize to

Madame de la Rue for her actions of almost nine years before, just as five years later he was to be unalterably possessed
with the conviction that they must separate:

"Whatever made you unhappy in the Genoa time had no
other root, beginning, middle, or end, than whatever has
made you proud and honored in your married life, and
given you station better than rank, and surrounded you with
many enviable things. This is the plain truth, and here I
leave it.

"But since the time when you constrained me to make
that painful declaration of your state of mind to the de la
Rues, I have been, in all the correspondence I have ever
had with him, deeply impressed by the delicacy and gratitude which has invariably restrained him from the least
allusion to it, and has always led him to references to you
and the children which none but a generous and affectionate
man could possibly have been so natural and so instinctively
manly in. I come back to Genoa after that long time, and
find her, with all the change upon her of those many years
of suffering—and all the weariness of attendance, night and
day, upon her foolish sick mother who wears out everybody
near her body and soul—alluding in the same manner to
you—easily, gratefully, and full of interest—from the first
moment of my setting eyes upon her. When sending some
brooches Egg and Collins had commissioned her to buy, yesterday, and begging to be recalled to Mamie's and Katey's
remembrance, and to send her love to you and Georgina.
Now I am perfectly clear that your position beside these
people is not a good one, is not an amiable one, a generous
one—is not worthy of you at all. And I see that you have it
in your power to set it right at once by writing her a note to
say that you have heard from me, with interest, of her sufferings and her cheerfulness—that you couldn't receive her
messages of remembrance without a desire to respond to
them—and that if you should ever be thrown together again
by any circumstances, you hope it will be for a friendly association without any sort of shadow upon it. Understand

above all things, that I do not ask you to do this, or want you to do this. I shall never ask whether you have done it or not, and shall never approach the subject from this hour. My part in it was settled when we were in Switzerland, and there an end. But I am confident that if you could do this without any secret reservation in your own mind, you would do an unquestionably upright thing, and would place yourself on a far better station in your own eyes, at one time or other. And I am absolutely confident that they both deserve it, and would both be very sensitive to it. But I most earnestly repeat, for all that, that it would be utterly valueless and contemptible if it were done through a grain of any other influence than that of your own heart, reflecting on what I have written here."[82]

Catherine, it seems, did send the letter of apology, sometime at the end of February, though she did her best to disguise it in a letter requesting the recipes for certain "Italian dishes."[83] Dickens had concocted his own recipe for Madame de la Rue's continuing illness: that she come to London for treatment by Elliotson.[84]

Dickens was to see Emile at least three times more, Madame probably only twice. As the years went by, he had more to say to the husband and less to the wife, though whenever he wrote he apologized for his unreliability as a correspondent and affirmed the constancy of his affections. If only Emile knew how reliable a correspondent Dickens was in spirit, how frequently he thought of Emile and Madame de la Rue, how steadfast he was in his heart and memory to his beloved friends, he would never be angry with him for his failure to write regularly.[85] When de la Rue and his wife were in Paris in 1855, Dickens, who was living there at the time, though temporarily on a trip to London, wrote indignantly that "how you ever can have been so near London

[82] Dexter, 225-229, 12/5/53.
[83] *Nonesuch*, ii, 545, to Emile de la Rue, 3/9/54.
[84] *Ibid.*, p. 544, to Emile de la Rue, 3/9/54.
[85] Berg MS., Dickens to Emile de la Rue, 8/19/57.

and never told me, is one of those marvels, far beyond the
wildest mesmerism, which I can by no means comprehend."[86] He sent gossip and travelling friends to visit the
de la Rues. They exchanged news, political and otherwise,
of London and Italy. He confided to Emile in 1857 his diffi-
culties with Catherine, his "skeleton . . . in the cupboard,"
with whom "I don't get on better in these later times . . .
than I did in the earlier Peschiere days. Much worse! Much
worse!" She got on with no one, he claimed, neither with
the children nor with herself, and she had "positive proof
of my being on the most confidential terms with, at least
fifteen thousand women of various conditions in life . . .
since we left Genoa."[87] Undoubtedly Dickens meant de la
Rue to understand (and certainly he did) that Catherine accused Madame de la Rue as the first and perhaps even the
cause of the subsequent "fifteen thousand" intimacies.

In late 1858 both de la Rues were in town and Dickens
invited Elliotson, whom he had told about his success in
mesmerizing Madame, to dinner with them at his home.[88]
The de la Rues stayed into December and Dickens and
Emile had opportunity for friendship and conversation. In
the 1860's a trip to Genoa began to become one of the favorite daydreams of an overworked man. He wrote to his sister
Letitia from Paris that "It is likely enough that I may go on
from here to see some friends in Genoa."[89] But he did not.
In August 1863 the de la Rues visited Gad's Hill for three
days.[90] Throughout September and October, with Catherine
no longer an impediment, they saw one another frequently,
and Dickens took advantage of Emile's influence with the
headmaster of Tunbridge Wells School to have his youngest
son, who had been unhappy at Wimbledon School, placed
there.[91] When Dickens, on the morning of Friday, June 29,

[86] *Ibid.*, 12/1/55.   [87] *Ibid.*, 10/23/57.
[88] *Nonesuch*, III, 75, to John Elliotson, 11/25/58.
[89] Morgan MS., Dickens to Letitia Austin, 12/20/62.
[90] *Nonesuch*, III, 359, to Wilkie Collins, 8/9/63.
[91] Berg MSS., Dickens to Emile de la Rue, 9/13/63, 9/22/63, 9/24/63,
10/28/63; *Nonesuch*, III, 370-371, to Rev. W. C. Sawyer, 11/6/63.

1866, found the card of "the Secret Visual Ray whom I love" awaiting him at the office of his journal, *All The Year Round,* he invited him to Gad's Hill and implored him not to "spirit" himself "away mysteriously."[92]

That seems to have been the last meeting, though the letters continued, always with nostalgic plaints by Dickens for his "beloved Genoa . . . It would gladden my heart indeed to look down upon its bay once again from the high hills."[93] At the end of 1869 Madame wrote to Dickens, remarking how convincing and true to her own experiences she had found a story by J. S. Le Fanu, "Green Tea," that Dickens had published in *All The Year Round* in 1859 and that centered around the powers of mesmerism. He wrote to the author a very brief account of his experiences with Madame de la Rue, when he had magnetized her "every day" and urged Le Fanu to respond through him to her queries in a brief note. She still experienced the old illness; it had never left her completely; "her sufferings are unspeakable."[94] So too were Dickens', though of a different kind. His old energy and willful enthusiasm, depleted by time and change, and the exhaustion of his magnetizing readings, in which he did en masse what he had done before only to individuals like Madame de la Rue, were almost gone. But his favorite daydream, expressed in a letter to T. A. Trollope, who lived in Italy, remained: "Walk across the Alps? Lord bless you, I am 'going' to take up my alpenstock and cross all the Passes, and I am 'going' to Italy; I am also 'going' up the Nile to the Second Cataract, and I am 'going' to Jerusalem, and to India, and likewise to Australia. My only dimness of perception in this wise is that I don't know when. If I did but know when, I should be so wonderfully clear about it all. . . . But whenever (if ever) I change 'going' into 'coming,' I shall come to see you."[95]

[92] Berg MS., Dickens to Emile de la Rue, 6/29/66.
[93] *Nonesuch*, III, 489, to Mrs. Cowden Clarke, 11/3/66.
[94] *Ibid.*, pp. 752-753, to J. S. Le Fanu, 11/24/69.
[95] Berg MS., Dickens to T. A. Trollope, 11/4/69.

105

The Discovery of Self

[1]

Catherine's fear that her husband was indeed having an affair with Madame de la Rue may have been unfounded in fact. She had, however, not only personal grounds for her suspicions but wide support from the sensational literature of the period that insisted on associating mesmerism with sex. For Dickens the intensity of his experience with Madame de la Rue was a crucial step in the process of self-discovery. More so than any great writer in our literature, he conducted his education in public, publishing serial fictions whose life and vivid substance were the results of dramatizing his deepest concerns. Mesmerism was not a stale science or a metaphysical-spiritual parlor game. It was more than a theory by which to explain strange extrasensory phenomena or a clever functional stratagem for mystification in sophisticated ghost stories. Dickens' fascination with Elliotson's and Townshend's experiments, his wide reading in the subject, his own practice of mesmerism, seem natural for a man who from his earliest adulthood was predisposed by talent, situation, and personality to surmise that there existed special clues to his and his contemporaries' behavior.

There were questions that Dickens had to ask himself, central to his self-understanding and to the fiction he was writing: what is the nature and the power of self and of mind? what is the relationship between childhood and the life-energy potential of the adult? what is the source of energy within human beings? what are the origins and nature of evil and mental disease? how and why are certain individuals able to influence, even to dominate, others for good and often for evil? and what role does willpower play in human affairs?[1] These questions were not asked with the

[1] Elliotson took the occasion in July 1849 (*The Zoist*, Vol. VII, No. XXVI, 117-121), in a phrenological article on "The Head of Rush the Murderer," to give his own answer to one of these central questions of Victorian religious and philosophical conflict. His eloquent phrasing of the questions and the starkness of his answers, though they are not necessarily Dickens', deserve extensive quotation:

"Why was such a monster, such a monstrous organization, made? But why is the whole world a scene of suffering and wickedness? Why are innocent babies tortured with endless varieties of disease? Why are they agonized with the natural process of obtaining their teeth? Why do epidemic poisons devastate nations, the good and the bad equally? Why do agonizing and fatal hereditary diseases attack the virtuous? Why do countless causes of misery assail the just and the unjust? There is little happiness which is not produced with the unhappiness of others, toiling and anxious. . . . As to the miseries occasioned by ourselves, why are we not so made as to wish and be able to act better? Why have we not more intellect and more virtuous brains? Why is mankind so organized and situated that ignorance, superstition, vice, and suffering, are the prevalent lot of humanity. . . . Not only while beholding the glitter and happy excitement of our parks and streets have we merely to turn our heads and see the famishing and diseased beggar, or visit the hospitals or the dirty alleys and back streets and behold want and agonizing and wasting disease: but, while we are enjoying the most glorious landscapes, the dwellings of the destitute and almost houseless are at hand, some victim of disease is never far off, and some suffering birds, fish, beast or insects. . . .

"For the innocent brutes suffer too. Look at the miseries of the toiling horse—that docile and affectionate animal—cruelly forced to excess labour for our advantage. . . . Truly, 'the whole creation travaileth and groaneth.' The insensible department of nature is no less exposed to injury and destruction. . . . In the vegetable and inanimate department there is no suffering, and all appears a magnificent circulation of changes: but the *same general laws* which disturb them reign throughout. . . . Good comes out of evil every moment. But the question presents itself, Why the evil at all? And next comes the greater question, Why is anything at all? For what end this strange and suffering spectacle of nature?

"The head of Rush is no greater mystery than the rest of sentient

objective purposefulness of the philosopher or the scientist but as the developing artist asks them, intuitively, in terms of personal experience; and they were asked within artistic forms, in dramatized situations within a fictional world in which the nuances of style often convey meanings truer to human experience than the doctor's casebook or the logician's syllogism.

Dickens' daughter Mamie vividly recalled that her father "was always . . . much interested in mesmerism, and the curious influence exerted by one personality over another. One illustration I remember his using was, that meeting someone in the busy London streets, he was on the point of turning back to accost the supposed friend, when finding out his mistake in time he walked on again until he actually met the real friend, whose shadow, as it were, but a moment ago had come across his path."[2] Dickens was constantly searching for that "shadow" both in his life and art. Like Coleridge, Dickens often gazed "with unclosed lids . . . to watch that fluttering stranger"

> For still I hoped to see the *stranger's* face,
> Townsman, or aunt, or sister more beloved . . .

---

nature. To give a shadow of a reason is impossible. The purpose of all this is past finding out. We must be content with beholding and submitting in silence, conscious of our own littleness and inability; and not foolishly and presumptuously attempting an explanation. We must be satisfied that it could not be otherwise than it is, and this is my own sole consolation. But while we thus encourage a humble spirit, let us do all the good in our power.

"From Rush's head we must learn charity. Let every man remember that, if he had such a charge of cunning, acquisitiveness, &c., &c., as Rush was burthened with in the possession of such massive organs, and a corresponding deficient charge of higher feeling and intellectual power, he would be a Rush. Let us detest such organizations as we detest the organizations called wolf, tiger, rattlesnake, scorpion, or vermin; and let us defend ourselves and others from them by all means which are absolutely necessary and as little cruel as possible. But let us pity the individual, for he did not make himself,—no, not a hair of his head."

2 Mamie Dickens, *My Father as I Recall Him* (N.Y., n.d.), pp. 20-21.

108

Using Dickens' words in "Travelling Abroad," Forster emphasizes the identity of that stranger. Riding in a coach between Gravesend and Rochester, Dickens "noticed by the wayside a very queer small boy." After discovering that he went to school at Chatham, Dickens took the boy up and they drove into sight of Gad's Hill. " 'You admire that house?' said I. 'Bless you, sir . . . ever since I can recollect, my father, seeing me so fond of it, has often said to me, "If you were to be very persevering and were to work hard, you might some day come to live in it." Though that's impossible. . . .' I was rather amazed to be told this by the very queer small boy; for that house happens to be *my* house, and I have reason to believe that what he said was true." Forster concludes that "The queer small boy was indeed himself." Of course, "on the coincidences, resemblances, and surprises of life, Dickens liked especially to dwell. . . . The world, he would say, was so much smaller than we thought it; we were all so connected by fate without knowing it; people supposed to be far apart were so constantly elbowing each other; and tomorrow bore so close a resemblance to nothing half so much as to yesterday."[3]

From Dickens' earliest maturity, mesmerism was a vehicle of self-discovery as well as a tool to explore the nature of the self as a concept and as an active force in determining personality and human relationships. He believed, despite the comic facetiousness of his earliest reference to mesmerism, that there is a "magnetism which must exist between a man and his knocker" (*SB*, "Our Parish," VII). One can in moments of insight discover one's self; there is such a self to be discovered by "a magnetic and instinctive consciousness" (*MC*, VIII). Like Scrooge, who "sat down upon a form, and wept to see his poor forgotten self as he used to be," the self has a past and a future as well as a present. And to understand the complexities of the present self, its

---

[3] The incident appears in *The Uncommercial Traveller and Reprinted Pieces* (London, 1958), "Travelling Abroad," pp. 61-62. Forster's account and the following quotation appear in *Life*, I, 5.

actualities in the past must be explored; to guide the relationship of the self to the self in the present, glimpses of the possible alternate states of the self in the future may be invaluable. Caleb Plummer in *The Cricket on the Hearth*, Dickens' only sustained achievement while restlessly searching for unexplored facets of himself in his year in Italy, "had a wandering and thoughtful eye which seemed to be always projecting itself into some other time and place, no matter what he said. . . . ."

The strain is not only toward self-definition but often toward simple affirmation of the existence of a self. The urge toward self-discovery sometimes comes out of some moment in the still center, an ineffable second of quiet revelation that is mainly the promise of redefinition rather than its actuality. Esther Summerson "had stopped at the garden-gate to look up at the sky, and when we went upon our way, I had for a moment an undefinable impression of myself as being something different from what I then was" (*BH*, xxxi). For Esther there seems to have been some former but forgotten self, some other whom she once was, whose existence is brought to her consciousness by a special collocation of time and place, a moment filled with suggestions from a consciousness so distant that it now seems mostly subconscious.

But some individuals can articulate the tensions between present reality and the lost selves of the past. Miss Pross responds to Mr. Lorry in *A Tale of Two Cities* that Dr. Manette's mindless vacuity in the present is the result of his fear of keeping alive in his mind the dreadful experiences of his former self. " 'Not knowing how he lost himself, or how he recovered himself, he may never feel certain of not losing himself again' " (II: vi). For self-discovery is often threatening, particularly to the equilibrium of the self in the present. Some of Dickens' characters have the courage to face this pain, others do not. Some seek self-discovery, some have it thrust upon them. Dr. Manette's friends have no wish to cause him pain; they prefer the vacuity of the

110

present to the potential suffering and madness of the future. Mr. Jasper has no such concern for Edwin Drood. But it is Jasper the mesmerizer who is sometimes so directly in touch with the complexities of his self that he can use them as a manipulative weapon in his control of Edwin, who is convinced that his uncle has revealed himself to him: " 'I hope I have something impressible within me, which feels—deeply feels—the disinterestedness of your painfully laying your inner self bare, as a warning to me' " (II). Self-discovery can be salvation and harmony; it can also be damnation and disintegration. "As the gloom and shadow thickened behind him, in that place where it had been gathering so darkly, it took, by slow degree—or out of it there came, by some unreal, unsubstantial process—not to be traced by any human sense,—an awful likeness of himself" (*HM*, I).

Dickens was sometimes face to face with that "awful likeness of himself," though he was more likely to evade the confrontation in his life than in his fiction, as he seems to have done when presented by Madame de la Rue with the "Charles" of her mesmeric trances. The Dickens whom other people saw, whether in their waking moments or in their "magnetic slumber (s)" (*NN*, VII), had less reality to Dickens than the self of his own projections. Certainly he would never accept, hardly even admit, a vision of himself that was not consistent with his own. His sense of his own self was so strong, so filled with possibilities of realization, that attempts to impose definition on it from outside the self often produced outrage and hostility. Dickens could be stubborn, assertive, "imperious in the sense that his life was conducted on the *sic volo sic jubeo* [so I want, so I command] principle, and that everything gave way before him. The society in which he mixed, the hours which he kept, the opinions which he held, his likes and dislikes, his ideas of what should or should not be, were all settled by himself, not merely for himself, but for all those brought into connection with him, and it was never imagined they could be called in question. Yet he was never regarded as a tyrant: he had immense power of will, absolute mesmeric force, as he proved beneficially more than once."[4] Catherine hardly had a chance against such force of will, regardless of the degree of marital pressure she might have been capable of exerting. "Charles" saw what he wanted to see and often he did not want to see "Charles."

[2]

But the complications and the tensions of these problems that were often evaded in Dickens' life were rarely evaded in his fiction. There the opportunities for the fullest dramatization of self-definition could be given the objectivity of character, plot, imagery, and tone, the resources of art added to those of psychology. Dickens' education in public was self-analysis through art, drawing upon the experiences he had had with Elliotson, with Townshend, with Madame de la Rue, with his wide reading in mesmeric literature. Dickens' fiction is a process of self-discovery parallel to and drawing upon the processes of mesmerism: the recall of the past, the free flow of feelings, the interaction between the conscious and the unconscious mind, the modes of dialect, conversation, wit, honesty within deception and deception within honesty, and illuminations of perception that the mesmeric trance produces. Mesmerism provided Dickens not only with a rationale for the working of personality and mind, for the relationship between "a man and his knocker" and

4 Edmund Yates, *Recollections and Experiences* (London, 1884), II, 94. Dickens' beneficent but domineering role-playing as doctor, whether medical or mesmeric, is recorded in an anecdote by Mrs. E. M. Ward in *A Supplement to Charles Dickens: By Pen And Pencil*, ed. F. G. Kitton (London, 1889-1890), p. 12: "On one occasion my husband met with an accident to his hand, which necessitated the attendance of Dr. Elliotson. Before the arrival of the medical man Dickens took charge of the patient himself, doing everything that was necessary,—bathing the injured part with vinegar, binding it up, and performing to perfection the combined functions of surgeon and nurse. He even appeared on the scene at midnight, provided with medicines and liniments ordered by the doctor to be administered at that hour, and, feeling perhaps that no one else could be trusted, thus ventured to continue his kind attention to the grateful invalid."

a man and the cosmos, but with a language and an imagery that could be dramatically utilized in fictional creations. It is a language of self-discovery.

It is, among other things, a look in the mirror, a tool that Elliotson and other mesmeric operators experimented with, fascinated by the possibilities of what one could see, particularly under special conditions of vision and reflection. Elliotson concluded that mirrors could focus and intensify the mesmeric force. The audiences in the wards and in the drawing room at 37 Conduit Street frequently watched with excitement as Elliotson demonstrated the power of the mesmeric fluid as it was transmitted and intensified through a reflecting surface.[5] The mirror itself could be used not only to heighten reality but to reveal the actual. One could see in the mirror a reality that was not accessible in the illusions of unreflecting surfaces. For Dickens, art is such a mirror on which the real can be condensed and intensified; the artist is like the mesmeric operator, staring into the mirror, seeing within it heightened truths and powers, and transmitting them to the subjects, his audience.

Sometimes it is a revelation of self, as controlled and momentary as a gesture of defiance, depicted by the narrator from the outside so that we have two selves, the real self and the public self. Arthur Clennam is shown a portrait of the Meagles' twins, one long dead, the other the spoiled "Pet." That lost double or second self has left a void in the family that the adopted servant Tattycoram would fill, if the family and her own sense of inferiority would permit. But she is bitter with hostility and frustration because forces within her will not let her create this new identity. "The picture happened to be near a looking-glass. As Arthur looked at it again, he saw, by the reflection of the mirror, Tattycoram stop in passing outside the door, listen to what was going on, and pass away with an angry and contemptuous frown upon her face that changed its beauty into ugli-

[5] For the use of mirrors and other reflective surfaces in mesmeric experiments, see *The Lancet* (June 23, 1838), 454-455.

113

ness" (*LD*, I:xvi). Quilp plays his schizophrenic games with his mother-in-law, using the mirror as a tool of control, to affirm for himself and for her his mastery: "Mr. Quilp now walked up to the front of a looking-glass, and was standing there, when Mrs. Jiniwin, happening to be behind him, could not resist the inclination she felt to shake her fist at her tyrant son-in-law. It was the gesture of an instant, but as she did so . . . she met his eye in the glass. . . . The same glance at the mirror conveyed to her the reflection of a horribly grotesque and distorted face with the tongue lolling out: and the next instant the dwarf, turning about, with a perfectly bland and placid look, inquired in a tone of great affection, 'How are you now, my dear old darling?' " (*OCS*, v). Charles Darnay confronts himself with a civilized version of Quilp's posturing: "When he was left alone, this strange being took up a candle, went to a glass that hung against the wall, and surveyed himself minutely in it. 'Do you particularly like the man?' he muttered at his own image; 'why should you particularly like a man who resembles you?' " (*TTC*, II:iv). Darnay is alienated from himself, intent upon remaining calm with this distant double. But he is not a man who completely avoids self-creation in the mirror, ultimately creating a new self through a gesture of unification.

Sometimes the "broad bend-sinister of light" (*BH*, xii) strikes a mirror that affirms the separateness of identities that should be one. When the unhappily married Lammles stood before "a mirror on the wall before them . . . her eyes just caught him smirking in it. She gave the reflected image a look of the deepest disdain, and the image received it in the glass. Next moment they quietly eyed each other, as if they, the principals, had had no part in that expressive transaction" (*OMF*, II:iv). The entire communication occurs through the intermediary of the mirror, which creates its own reality, a momentary pause in the mask of falsity, a revelation of true feeling. Not only do they see themselves in the mirror; they see themselves in each other. In this marriage of identical falsities, the two penniless, unscrupulous fortune hunters have deceived one another into believing that the other has what each does not. But they have equal possessions; they are both possessionless. One is the alter ego, the double of the other. Their images of "disdain" are "looks" of fear and self-hate. Neither likes what is seen in the mirror. Neither has the power to change what the mirror reveals. Some force outside themselves works through the intermediary; when they look at one another directly, without the mirror's intervention, it is as if they "had had no part in that expressive transaction." It is as if the selves that had been momentarily revealed through the mirror had been obliterated from consciousness the way a mesmeric subject loses knowledge of his visions when he awakens from trance.

Esther Summerson in *Bleak House* particularly knows the power of mirrors. She has good reason to approach them with fear. In the mirror of her natural features there may be some clue to her origin and in the mirror of her distorted, pockmarked face after her illness there is the threat of a new untried self. " 'I miss some familiar object. Ah, I know what it is, Charley! It's the looking glass.' " Tottering unsteadily into the next room, she notices that " 'The mirror was gone from its usual place in that room too; but what I had to bear, was none the harder to bear for that' " (xxxv). As a little girl she had " 'stood on tiptoe to dress myself at my little glass, after dressing my doll.' " She remembers this at the moment when with an unexplained surge of excitement she responds to the first meeting of her eyes with Lady Dedlock's. " 'There was something quickened within me, associated with the lonely days at my godmother's. . . .' " For Lady Dedlock intensifies Esther's sense of the fragile indefiniteness of her present self and the threat of the future. " 'I was rendered motionless . . . by a something in her face . . . the fascination that overpowered me' " (xxxvi).

The mirror can be used to destroy another self, to split a hoped-for single identity into two separate selves. One exists in the world of looking into the mirror; the other exists in the mirror world itself. The potential single self of matrimonial unity splits in the Dombey marriage. Edith demands that her husband accept their separateness. The stranger who might have been one's found self is now the permanently estranged other. " 'Nothing can make us stranger to each other than we are henceforth.' " Dombey speaks coldly. "She turned her back upon him, and . . . sat down before her glass." He speaks again. In her mirror world she reduces him to non-existence. "She answered not one word. He saw no more expression of any heed of him, in the mirror, than if he had been an unseen spider on the wall, or beetle on the floor, or rather, than if he had been the one or other, seen and crushed when she last turned from him, and forgotten among the ignominious and dead vermin of the ground" (*DS*, XL). Edith's form now exists only "as the glass presented it to him." But when the self is strong, such as with the Reverend Septimus Crisparkle, "the looking-glass presented . . . a fresh and healthy portrait" (*ED*, VI); when the lost or dull self has the assistance of a person beneficent enough to help in the search for self-discovery, the discovery may come as a step in a process of growth and maturity: "It was new and strange to him to have himself presented to himself so clearly, in a glass of her holding up" (*ED*, XIII). But when the substance of the self is weak and permanently corrupted, the image created in the mirror is "dusty," unclear, sometimes horrible, fragmented and death-like.

The larger mirrors are in the hands of an artistically quite purposeful Dickens, making dramatic use of his own resources of experience and self. The hand mirror or the bedroom glass shows the individual; the famous "great looking-glass above the sideboard" in *Our Mutual Friend* "reflects the table and the company," the society as a whole, a conglomeration of individual selves and those things with which this collectivity without community has surrounded

itself. Under this panoramic mirror that "reflects" fragments, the story of "that popular character whom the novelists and versifiers call Another" is told. He has no name.
He is the anonymous but well-known stranger. His is the
collective epithet for all those "queer small boy" (s), and
that awaited completion of our partial selves that never
comes, the "one friend and companion I have never made."[6]
The man from "Nowhere" is discussed, equally anonymous
as "the man from Somewhere." Under the great mirror, abstract stories with dehumanized personifications of selflessness are appropriate. The mirror cannot gather up and focus
the energy of individuals or of the group. It cannot intensify
vacuity. But it can "reflect" the devitalized reality of those
who do not look in the mirror. For the mirror almost seems
to look at them, as if it were Dickens' eyes, eyes affected by
the scene they receive on their retinas. The characters round
the table under the great mirror have minimal self-consciousness; they do not look at their reflections. Consequently the mirror can do nothing for them; it cannot be
a tool or instrument of revelation; it cannot be an active
agent in a process of self-awareness; it cannot intensify and
transmit mesmeric powers; it cannot even depict an active
and changing process of disintegration or self-hate. The
mirror in the constant present tense "reflects" ten times in
a single paragraph this static world of frozen selves separate
from one another, a shiny surface world of superficial people
and things in which self and essence are never discovered
because never sought. The mirror seeks nothing. It helps no
one to discover because no one searches.

This image is totally inappropriate for Dickens. Like
Little Dorrit, Our Mutual Friend is about the possibility of
discovering the self, of finding satisfactory completion,
through trial and pain; and many of the moments of revelation in these searches are like hard looks into the mirror of
self and society. Ultimately the mirror of society does noth-

[6] *Nonesuch*, ii, 620-621, to John Forster, 1/55.

ing but "reflect"; the mirror of self creates a new reality. The mesmeric mirror promised focus, concentration, intensity, the power and dominance of the will; the mirror of society produced dispersion of energy, clouding of focus, surface reality. As Dickens' career progressed, his concentration on socially directed liberal commitments decreased. His involvement with the exploration of the problem of the self within himself and others remained at its constant high intensity. Reaching out to large audiences, through his readings, he was not, like the Veneering's mirror, a reflector, but like a mass mesmerizer, exploring and expanding himself through imposing himself and his vision on others. He wrote less but he found another complementary way to continue to create and define himself. Behind the public readings were the public mesmeric demonstrations of 1837 and 1838, the crowded theaters at University Hospital in which Elliotson demonstrated the existence of this magnetic force to large audiences of the most disparate kind. Dickens did to his audiences what a mesmeric operator did to his subjects.

[3]

In mesmeric trance the subject was often like an actor, playing a number of roles, the single conscious personality split into multiple, seemingly disharmonious parts. In instances in which the subject in trance in Elliotson's experiments did not disintegrate into fragments, the self that emerged was often radically different from the conscious self, as if inhibitions and repressions had been lifted. Reflective white surfaces, especially mirrors, caught Elizabeth O'key's attention. She saw unusual things in them. Both sisters became extremely voluble, even garrulous, in trance, sometimes ill-tempered, vindictive, hostile; other times affectionate, vulgar, playful. Like great actresses, these "prima donna" (s) of the magnetic stage played many moods and roles. They created second selves, projections like Elizabeth's diagnostic "negro," who had special insight into the mortality of other

human beings.[7] The two sisters themselves were an inseparable entity in a special sympathetic relationship in which
they could communicate without the normal stratagems of
gesture and language. They insisted on staying together;
both managed simultaneously to have the appropriate diseases that would permit their being admitted to and remaining in University Hospital. Both were small, with
nervous tics, not quite mature, not completely childish,
hovering on the border of sexuality though not sexually
developed into womanhood, partaking of both roles. Sometimes they would become completely childish, unself-con-
scious, other times womanly and aggressive. The doctors of
the period made much of the claim that they had never
menstruated, child-women indeed.[8]

Madame de la Rue and most mesmeric patients experi-
encing this Victorian version of psychotherapy were often
schizophrenic, divided in their behavioristic patterns. Dickens observed the disparity between Madame's trance personality and her condition when awake, her characteristics
when in frenetic convulsions and when seemingly normal.
In her mesmeric trances there was the second Madame de
la Rue, available for analysis of the kind that Dickens
poured out in his letters to Emile. And in her trances there
was also that "Another," that "man from Someplace," that
dark shadow who pursued and threatened her, and of course
her brother "Charles," who was or was not there, sometimes indistinctly, about whose purposes and motives she
was not sure.

For Dickens, beginning with *Oliver Twist* but becoming
intense after 1845, the image of the double, of the second
self or the lost or the found other, became central to his fiction. Often the individual in the mirror's focus or under
mesmeric observation becomes split into two parts, two separate characters in the plot, two parts of a single larger

[7] See *The Lancet* (June 9, 1838), 382; (June 16, 1838), 401; (July 21,
1838), 590; (Dec. 28, 1838), 561-562; (Jan. 12, 1839), 593-594.
[8] See *The Lancet* (June 23, 1838), 457; (Aug. 18, 1838), 727.

metaphor. Of course, the theme of the double pervades nineteenth-century literature and the nineteenth-century imagination in all its forms of expression. But it is nowhere more expressive of the subject-operator relationship in the search for the discovery of self than it is in Dickens.

The epitome of doubleness is to have another existent self precisely like oneself. It may be disturbing to look in a mirror and see another version of oneself, a part necessary for the completion of the whole. It is quite another thing to see someone else absolutely indistinguishable in physical appearance from oneself. At least four sets of identical twins appear in Dickens' fiction. To be such a twin is to be part of a larger metaphor of doubleness, but an exemplary part, unavoidable and dramatic. The least dramatic of these twins are the bland Cheeryble brothers, who are like an identical blob of protoplasm, split into indistinguishable extensions of the same principles of benevolence. They are not complementary oppositions. There are no parts to the Cheeryble twins' unity, no depths of opposing and complementary forces that need for the fulfillment of each the unity of both into a balanced whole. Dickens has created a single individual, with an equal distribution of all his characteristics throughout the whole, and divided the whole into two. So the Cheeryble twins seem manufactured and unreal, psychological nonentities. Rather than expressive of the division of the self into two, dramatizing conflicts of self, soul, and society, they represent the simple increase, the doubling of what was already completely there in one. It is the difference between doubling and doubles. They have lost nothing; they will gain nothing. They are statically and undividedly one.

The Flintwinch twins also exist mainly to function as a cog in the plot. But the plot of *Little Dorrit* is more complex and threatening than the plot of *Nicholas Nickleby*. One Cheeryble brother would have sufficed; two identical Flintwinches are necessary. They are simultaneously the product of a trance vision of Affery Flintwinch, under the mesmeric power of her manipulative husband, and of the dramatizing of the splitting apart of all the natural unities of human relationships until the one central unity of Little Dorrit and Arthur Clennam is achieved. Affery Flintwinch, half-asleep, observes a scene that fills her with wonder. She is unaware of the existence of her husband's twin. Again, a mirror image is used to help heighten the focus on split selves, and the problem of distinguishing between illusion and reality, between false selves and real ones:

"Mr. Flintwinch awake, was watching Mr. Flintwinch asleep. He sat on one side of a small table, looking keenly at himself on the other side with his chin sunk on his chest, snoring. The waking Flintwinch had his full front face presented to his wife; the sleeping Flintwinch was in profile. The waking Flintwinch was the old original; the sleeping Flintwinch was the double. Just as she might have distinguished between a tangible object and its reflection in a glass, Affery made out this difference with her head going round and round" (*LD*, I:iv).

Like the Cheeryble brothers, these twins are alike, scoundrels both, but true doubles in that they fit together; they complement one another in their fulfillment of their functions in the plot. Each brother does what the other cannot do, in the furtherance of a single scheme. But together they are one personality. Jeremiah Flintwinch is sober, industrious, scheming, prudent, brutal, immoral, a permanent resident of England and an embodiment of the spirit of the Clennam household; his brother Ephraim is intemperate, alcoholic, dissolute, unstable, brutal, immoral, a wanderer whose habitat is the dissolute waterfronts of continental ports like Antwerp. For a short time Ephraim had been a "lunatic keeper (I wish he had had himself to keep in a strait-waistcoat)," until he lost the job through "over-roasting a patient to bring him to reason." His jobs had been legion since. Jeremiah has had only one job, also a kind of lunatic keeper, the resident guardian and provocateur of Mrs. Clennam's madness. Both make their living from other

121

people's loss of self. When Jeremiah turns valuable papers over to his brother for temporary safe-keeping, he is fulfilling through the vehicle of the plot the appropriate function of a double—to accomplish himself through his other self.

The twins most dedicated to the fulfillment of one another are Helena and Neville Landless in *Edwin Drood*. They are the single psychological self divided, each incomplete alone, two parts of a metaphor of wholeness. They have special means of sympathetic communication, a kind of mesmeric telepathy or clairvoyance. Their communications are carried on special waves of fluidic sympathy. Mr. Crisparkle remarks that Neville has spoken not only for himself but for his sister also, though he has "had no opportunity of communicating" with her. " 'You don't know, sir, yet, what a complete understanding can exist between my sister and me, though no spoken word—perhaps hardly as much as a look—may have passed between us. She not only feels as I have described, but she very well knows that I am taking this opportunity of speaking to you, both for her and for myself.' " The mesmeric theory that Dickens believes in insists that the waves of mesmeric power across the fluid that pervades the cosmos make possible such communication between two sympathetic individuals. It is a form of talking to oneself, to that part of you which is alive in the other. Neville proudly announces that "we are twin children" *(ED,* vii).

But there are differences between them. They are not a simple replication of the original bit of protoplasm. They are different and complementary. They must be joined together to make one, but that joined one is different from each separate one. Helena is courageous, bold, unsubduable, best in conditions of adversity, a person of immense will power. Neville concedes that "nothing in our misery ever subdued her, though it often cowed me." He is vacillating, hot-tempered, without mastery of his own will and imagination. Together weakness and strength may be comple-

mentary; she may give him strength, he may give her gentle-
ness. He is the possibility of Helena's weakness; she is the
possibility of his strength. The realization of both can come
through the metaphor of their twinness. By containing both
it may turn into advantage what was disadvantage in personalities that contained only one of the extremes. In the
mechanism of the plot it is Helena who is called upon to
help her brother. Crisparkle reminds Helena that " 'you
came into this world with the same dispositions, and you
passed your younger days together surrounded in the same
adverse circumstances. What you have overcome in yourself, can you not overcome in him? . . . You have the wisdom of Love . . . and it was the highest wisdom ever known
upon this earth . . .' " (*ED*, x).

Is it, then, self-love that the Minor Canon recommends?
Are not these twins inseparable aspects of a single self?
In Dickens' late fiction, to love another is to have power over
that other and to give that other power over you. It is to
enter into a special kind of subject-operator relationship.
" 'The true lover' " must be represented " 'as having no
existence separable from that of the beloved object of his
affections, and as living at once a double life and a halved
life' " (*ED*, xi). To love is to search for one's double. It is
an inward journey as well as an outward one. It is an extension of self-love. Dickens seems to accept this, in fact
ultimately to insist upon it. It is not sexual, certainly not
masturbatory. So many of the successful loves are sexless in
Dickens' fiction, so many of the unsuccessful ones filled with
sex and the rhetoric of domination, exploitation, and sadism. The successful loves are the merging of two separated
parts of the same self into a created whole, a new and better
self. The separated parts of the single self need not be lovers
in the physical sense.

The implications of Dickens' concern are even more
pronounced in the case of the Meagles twins, Pet (Minnie)
and Lillie in *Little Dorrit*. For " 'Pet had a twin sister who
died when we could just see her eyes—exactly like Pet's—

above the table, as she stood on tiptoe holding by it.' " These twins were identical. When Clennam observes Tattycoram's distorted face in the looking-glass in the Meagles' parlor he has just admitted the impossibility of telling the sisters apart, in the portrait done seventeen years before "of two pretty little girls with their arms entwined" (*LD*, I:xvi). The similarity between the two has not created the traditional crisis of identity in Pet because Lillie has died at an early age. But the crisis has been transferred to the foundling, Tattycoram, whom the Meagles have taken into their household in the indeterminate position of half maid, half adopted child. She was to be a maid to Pet, but also to take the place of her lost sister.

For the Meagles, however, this sister has not been lost. She has been given psychological and imaginative life, a permanent place in the family: " 'Pet and her baby sister were so exactly alike, and so completely one, that in our thoughts we have never been able to separate them since. It would be of no use to tell us that our dead child was a mere infant. We have changed that child according to the changes in the child spared to us, and always with us. As Pet has grown, that child has grown; as Pet has become more sensible and womanly, her sister has become more sensible and womanly, by just the same degrees. It would be as hard to convince me that if I was to pass into the other world to-morrow, I should not, through the mercy of God, be received there by a daughter, just like Pet, as to persuade me that Pet herself is not a reality at my side' " (*LD*, I:ii). Tattycoram has not been allowed to take her place. So deep is the need of the Meagles for this lost child that they continue to create her in the present with the involuntary assistance of the surviving twin. Without her, they are not their complete selves; their own identities are diminished.

So they seem compelled to this act of surrogate creation, despite the adverse effect it has on Tattycoram and their relationship with her. They cannot understand her sense of loss and diminishment. And when Pet herself marries foolishly and unhappily, the Meagles do not realize that through keeping alive the dead sister they have permanently harmed both Pet and Tattycoram. Tattycoram should have been given the opportunity to fill the role of the lost sister, as she herself desires; Pet should have been given the opportunity to have had a lost sister. The sense of loss would have created the need for search, and Pet would have created a personality and a meaning for herself in the pains and the pleasures of the search. But because the Meagles insist on keeping the dead Lillie alive in a self-indulgent fantasy, both living girls are less than what they might have become.

Non-biologically related look-a-likes are rare in Dickens' fiction. Even in the Victorian novel of artifice such coincidence was beyond the possibility of credibility except in the rarest cases. Plots of connection and coincidence like Dickens' can snap under the weight of the patently absurd. So outside of the world of the dreams, trances, and fantasies of Dickens' characters, where doubles abound, there appears only one set of identical doubles who do not come from the same womb, Sydney Carton and Charles Darnay in *A Tale of Two Cities*. The artifice of their being literal twins would have strained credulity less. But they are as psychologically opposite as most of Dickens' doubles, each part of what should be a unified self. Dr. Manette recognizes his daughter as "my other and far dearer self." But Charles Darnay is thrown into confusion by his discovery that he has another self, a double. Sydney Carton does not complement him; he does not seem to be a desired completion. On the contrary, he seems to Charles to be like a "Double of coarse deportment, to be like a dream" (*TTC*, II:IV). Carton is drifting, unloved and unloving; Darnay has work, love, purpose, future. But Carton initially makes the mistake of imagining that Charles Darnay and he are look-a-likes in every way. He looks into the mirror of self and imagines that any man who looks so like him must be like him in essence, an essence that he himself is unhappy with.

" 'Do you particularly like the man?' he muttered, at his own image; 'why should you particularly like a man who resembles you? There is nothing in you to like; you know that.' " He concludes as he gazes into the mirror that he hates Charles Darnay. Obviously, he also hates himself.

But he is eventually awakened to the possibility of good within himself. This special kind of self-love may become self-respect. Through his involvement with his double, his own dormant impulses to love self and others are brought to life. That part of him which his double represents has indeed been a part of him always, but suppressed and lost. Conditions aid in his self-discovery. When Sydney Carton ascends the steps to the guillotine, the two aspects of self have been united. They are both to live on in Charles Darnay, whose continued existence ensures the continued existence of a unified Sydney Carton. The actualities of the physical grave become less real than the needs of the life of the emotions.

Beyond the artifice of biological twins or look-a-likes are the created doubles or second selves, like Mrs. Gamp's Mrs. Harris and the chemist Mr. Redlaw's "awful likeness of himself," created in a world of "powerful, and apparently, mesmeric influence" (*HM*, ii). Both Redlaw and Mrs. Gamp teeter on the brink of instability, paralytic schizophrenia. They are divided into two, Redlaw tormented by the happiness he has lost, Mrs. Gamp maintaining through her fiction the balance between her loneliness on the one hand and her need for companionship on the other. The long days and nights of solitude and menial treatment are made bearable by gin and the company of the talkative imagined Mrs. Harris. When Betsey Prig attempts to destroy Mrs. Gamp's fragile balance between her two selves by denying the existence of Mrs. Harris, Mrs. Gamp's sense of self is deeply disturbed, for "the shock of this blow was so violent and sudden, that Mrs. Gamp sat staring at nothing with uplifted eyes, and her mouth open as if she were gasping for breath" (*MC*, xlix). Her speech quickly returns. " 'Well you mayn't believe there's no sech a creetur, for she wouldn't demean herself to look at you.' . . . Mrs. Gamp was heard to murmur 'Mrs. Harris' in her sleep" that night, so much a part of both her waking and her dream world is this creation. But her waking and her dream worlds are the same. She cannot split them apart, except at a penalty so severe that one doubts that she would survive. She has divided herself into two in order to be one and to deprive her of that other is to deprive her of herself.

In addition to twins, look-a-likes, and created second selves, there are the innumerable partial doubles of Dickens' fiction: the siblings, the friends, the lovers, so many of whom Dickens creates in relationships in which one represents an opposite or a similar aspect of the other. They are all part of Dickens' exploration of the possibilities of self and self-discovery. Some are partial doubles, related biologically, each pair in some way important to the novel in which they appear. Some are lovers who must fulfill a similar drive towards wholeness through the discovery of self in another, the way all "true lovers" live "at once a doubled life and a halved life." False lovers are halved; instead of discovering the self through another, they have lost themselves, unlike Arthur Clennam and Little Dorrit, Eugene Wrayburn and Lizzie Hexam, who find completion in one another.

The search for the self begins in childhood; that "stranger" of Coleridge's vision, like Dickens', is needed from the earliest age of consciousness of incompletion. For some the need remains until old age and death. Children like David Copperfield and Em'ly Peggotty, Bitzer and Cissy Jupe begin it; it is carried into maturity by David and Steerforth and Eugene Wrayburn and Mortimer Lightwood; Mortimer "is but the double of the friend on whom he has founded himself" (*OMF*, II:xvi); and in old age Scrooge looks back towards Jacob Marley and implores his spirit to unite with him again, so that his fragmented self can be whole once more. These are all types of the "Charles" who is in search of "Charles," but who sees the problem and possible solutions more clearly in his fiction than in Madame de la Rue's mesmeric trances or in his own life. Like Tennyson's (who discovered that he also had the mesmeric power), like Wordsworth's, who insisted that "We Poets in our youth begin in gladness; But thereof come in the end despondency and madness," Dickens' search for self was not always successful: the self discovered was not always a happy one.

[4]

But there is a discoverer making this discovery of self in Dickens' fiction, a creator of mirrors, a center of consciousness with the attributes of human or extra-human physiognomy and psychic powers. He is the operator, the mesmerizer, the physician, the man possessed of special powers of the eye. He often relies upon images derived from mesmeric experience. The eye is the key organ of transmission, that "special visual ray" which Dickens seriously joked about with Emile de la Rue. In Dickens' case, his own eyes were physically weak. But they had special mesmeric force: "those wonderful eyes that saw as much and so keenly, were appreciably, though to a very slight degree, near-sighted. Very few persons, even among those who knew him well, were aware of this, for Dickens never used a glass. But he continually exercised his vision by looking at distant objects, and making them out as well as he could. . . . It was an instance of that force of will in him, which compelled a naturally somewhat delicate frame to comport itself like that of an athlete."[9] The mesmerizer keeps his "visual ray" steady, the

[9] T. Adolphus Trollope, "Recollections of Mr. T. Adolphus Trollope," *A Supplement to Charles Dickens: By Pen and Pencil*, ed. F. G. Kitton (London, 1889-1890), p. 14. Ernst Robert Curtius, *Balzac* (Bern, 1951), calls attention briefly to Balzac's commitment to mesmeric theory and imagery, particularly the "magnetic stare" (pp. 55-58). The many parallels between Balzac and Dickens (who makes no reference to Balzac in his available letters, etc., but whose library did contain a copy of Balzac's *Contes drolatiques*) are illuminating and deserve a focused study beyond the kind of linkage of their names in studies such as Donald Fanger's *Dostoevsky and Romantic Realism: A Study of Dos-*

way the eyes in the Portrait on the wall "seem fixed" upon Oliver (*OT*, xii), the way John Willet "gradually concentrated the whole power of his eyes into one focus" (*BR*, i). The image may be comic, as "the power" of Simon Tappertit's "eye. Indeed he had been known to go so far as to boast that he could utterly quell and subdue the haughtiest beauty by a simple process, which he termed 'eyeing her over'; but it must be added, that neither of this faculty nor of the power he claimed to have, through the same gift, of vanquishing and heaving down dumb animals, even in a rabid state, had he ever furnished evidence which could be deemed quite satisfactory and conclusive" (*BR*, iv). But Dickens himself gave full credence to the experiments that reported the mesmerization of animals, like Harriet Martineau's infamous cow.[10] The fault is not in the force but in Tappertit himself: " 'He's got his eyes on me . . . I feel 'em though I can't see 'em. Take 'em off, noble captain . . . they pierce like gimlets . . . a kind of ocular screw.' " Bumble, like Simon Tappertit, believes that he has such power; in fact he has only an institution and its authority behind him. It is a societal rather than a mesmeric force, a group authoritarianism rather than a cosmic power working through a favored individual that permits him to cow others, though he confuses them. " 'Have the goodness to look

toevsky in Relation to Balzac, Dickens, and Gogol (Cambridge, Mass., 1965). The only other major nineteenth-century novelists who made direct use of mesmerism in their fictions are Edgar Allan Poe in a number of stories (see Sidney E. Lind, "Poe and Mesmerism," *PMLA*, LXII [1947], 1077-1094 and Doris V. Falk, "Poe and the Power of Animal Magnetism," *PMLA*, 84 [1969], 536-545), and Nathaniel Hawthorne in *The Blithedale Romance* and *The House of the Seven Gables*.

10 Accounts of Harriet Martineau's intense involvement with mesmerism appear in her *Autobiography*, her *Letters on Mesmerism* (London, 1845), originally published in the *Athenaeum* (November-December 1844), and in Robert K. Webb, *Harriet Martineau, A Radical Victorian* (N.Y., 1960), which refers to the incident of the cow (p. 251). Elliotson authored an article, incorporating a letter from Miss Martineau, on "Mesmeric Cure of a Cow, by Miss Harriet Martineau," *The Zoist*, Vol. VIII, No. XXXI (Oct. 1850), 300-303.

at me,' said Mr. Bumble, fixing his eyes upon her. 'If she stands such a eye as that,' said Mr. Bumble to himself, 'she can stand anything. It is a eye I never knew to fail with paupers; and if it fails with her, my power is gone' " (*OT*, xxxvii). What never existed fails with the shrewish Mrs. Corney. But Hugh indeed does have "an evil eye"; Lord George Gordon's "very bright large eye" was "striking to observe"; and the evil mesmerizer of *Barnaby Rudge*, Mr. Gashford, has "a pair of eyes that seemed to have made an unnatural retreat into his head, and to have dug themselves a cave to hide in." Monks has a "fierce gaze" which can work its will on others; he is to be taken seriously. Oliver believes that his sight of Monks and Fagin may have been a trance. He explains: "We had our eyes fixed full upon each other."

When Dickens presents the feigned domination of old Martin Chuzzlewit by Mr. Pecksniff he does so in the imagery of ocular control, the steady stare of the mesmeric sleep-waker who is under the power of an unscrupulous operator: " 'You hear what has been said,' replied the old man, without averting his eyes from the face of Mr. Pecksniff: who nodded encouragingly. 'I have not heard your voice. I have not heard your spirit,' returned Martin. 'Tell him again,' said the old man, still gazing up in Mr. Pecksniff's face . . . an exclusive and engrossing object of contemplation" (*MC*, xliii). That Chuzzlewit is feigning does not alter the impact; Dickens has an imagery to draw upon, a framework in which to place the relationship of domination and control, of operator and subject. A man's eyes are "the windows of his soul" (*BH*, xxv); through them is an entranceway to his deepest recesses. And through the eyes of an operator the resources of willpower can be brought to a focus of concentration and communication.

When Mr. Tulkinghorn meets Lady Dedlock, just prior to his mesmerizing her, he has felt "a rather increased sense of power upon him." Their confrontation comes through their eyes: "He is suddenly stopped in passing the window by two eyes that meet his own . . . looking in through the glass from the corridor outside" (*BH*, XLI). The transparent glass becomes an agent of focus and intensity. In the battle between two aggressive women, all the force of each is brought to bear upon the other through the eyes: Miss Pross and Madame Defarge stare intently: "Neither of them for a single moment released the other's eyes" (*TTC*, III: XIV). But neither can completely control the other through mesmeric power.

The man whose "optic vision" is extraordinary is John Jasper. He has been given a full armament of mesmeric weapons: the power of his music, eyes, hands, touch, voice, presence. This is complicated by his addiction to opium and his schizophrenic habitation of both an ordinary world and one of dream-waking. His eyes clearly are the passageways to his soul. Under the influence of opium, "a strange film comes over [his] eyes," like the old opium dealer who stares with a "strange blind stare . . . an unwinking, blind sort of steadfastness" (*ED*, XIV).

But the mesmeric stare is different. It is not blind and opaque. So powerful are Rosa Dartle's eyes that innocent David Copperfield must evade their mesmerizing force: " 'So surely as I looked towards her, did I see that eager visage, with its gaunt black eyes and searching brow, intent on mine; or passing suddenly from mine to Steerforth's; or comprehending both of us at once. In this lynx-like scrutiny she was so far from faltering when she saw I observed it, that at such a time she only fixed her piercing look upon me with a more intent expression still. Blameless as I was, and knew that I was . . . I shrunk before her strange eyes, quite unable to endure their hungry lustre' " (*DC*, XXIX). There are eyes that are closed in upon themselves, which see nothing, and stare with a blindness to self and others that is the result of loss of power to communicate. And there are eyes that reach outward toward others to establish a subject-operator relationship, intent upon the transmission of mesmeric influence.

Dickens knew the difference between the two; he had seen

and experienced both. He had taken opium and administered it; he had seen friends and relations under its influence: "Two of our women were taken in a queer way last week, but I drove them both raving mad immediately, with opium and ether—and with the greatest success."[11] His pleasure in the experiment was an expression of his profound amazement at the complexities of human beings: "The perverseness of that clan and their unholy joy in eating and drinking what is bad for them, are wonderful phenomena."[12] Dickens never confused the two. But he gave Jasper both. "Fixed as [is] the look" Edwin meets, "there is yet in it some strange power of suddenly including the sketch" of Rosa Bud, who is the prime subject of Jasper's mesmeric operations (*ED*, ii); Jasper's look "is always concentrated"; in his mesmeric intensity of communication all the power of his body is focused in his eyes: the "steadiness of face and figure becomes so marvellous that his breathing seems to have stopped"; when he plays accompaniment to Rosa's singing, "he followed her lips most attentively, with his eyes as well as his hands," producing a strange music of subliminal sounds that becomes unbearable to the girl, for as Jasper stared he "ever and again hinted the one note, as though it were a low whisper from himself. . . ." So powerful is this transmission of influence through the eyes that "all at once the singer broke into a burst of tears, and shrieked out, with her hands over her eyes: 'I can't bear this! I am frightened! Take me away!' " (*ED*, vii). She must "Beware! Beware! His flashing eyes. . . ."

Except when he is under the influence of opium, nothing blocks Jasper's view. Rosa laments that " 'he has made a slave of me with his looks. He has forced me to understand him, without his saying a word; and he has forced me to keep silence, without his uttering a threat. When I play, he never moves his eyes from my hands. When I sing, he never moves his eyes from my lips.' " There is no escape from this

11 Morgan MS., Dickens to Henry Austin, 8/20/54.
12 *Ibid.*

mesmeric power: " 'he himself is in the sounds . . . I avoid his eyes, but he forces me to see them without looking at them' " (*ED*, VII). Then no wonder Jasper despises Deputy or "Winks," the boy employed by Durdles, and fears that he will shed his blood. Deputy pursues him with the threat, " 'I'll blind yer, s'elp me! I'll stone your eyes out, s'elp me! If I don't have yer eyesight, bellows me!' " (*ED*, XII). Jasper would lose the key image, focus, and vehicle of his power if Deputy's metaphor of invective would become a literal reality. Rosa would be freed from his influence. The seeing mesmeric eye would become the blind opium eye.

But the eye does not operate alone. The "visual ray" must be supplemented by other organs of focus and transmission of this power. Dickens gave the running heading "such eyes and such hands" to the key chapter in *Great Expectations* in which Pip realizes that Jaggers' servant, the "wild beast" he has "tamed" through the force of his will, is Estella's mother. The eye and the hand are linked. Their powers are joined. Jaggers dominates others not through physical strength alone but through the strength of his knowledge and his personality. He has a steady vision. But his hands are the conductors of his power; they are his own obsessive concern. He constantly washes them. Aware of their strength, "suddenly, he clapped his large hand on the housekeeper's, like a trap, as she stretched it across the table. So suddenly and smartly did he do this, that we all stopped in our foolish contention" (*GE*, XXVI).

The imposition of his own power on Molly is the imposition of his hand on hers: " 'I'll show you a wrist. . . . Molly, let them see your wrist. . . . There's power here.' " His own is a symbol of his power. When Pip is strolling into Cheapside, "a large hand was laid upon my shoulder. . . . It was Mr. Jaggers's hand, and he passed it through my arm" (*GE*, XLVIII). All his powers are in that hand, which seems almost to have autonomous life. But his eyes function as similar instruments. He draws all other eyes to him. He forces their concentration and their submission: " 'Master,'

Molly says, in a low voice, with her eyes attentively and entreatingly fixed upon him. . . . The moment he ceased, she looked at him again. 'That'll do, Molly,' said Mr. Jaggers, giving her a slight nod; 'you have been admired, and can go.' She withdrew her hands. . . ." (*GE*, xxvi). She had been held by his hands, as if in a mesmeric chain, with the power passing from his hands to hers; she had been held by his eyes, as if the mesmeric force of his will had captured hers.

A man of some will and principle, Gabriel Varden, is able to exert power over Barnaby through a combination of the eye and hand: "the locksmith held up his finger, and fixing his eye sternly upon him caused him to desist" (*BR*, iii). Bella Wilfer hardly knows the source of the power that Dickens jokes with when he has her point "a rallying finger at" her father's "face" and pronounce that " 'I have got you in my power' " (*OMF*, II:viii). In *Hard Times*, Mr. Gradgrind's "square finger, moving here and there," which "lighted suddenly on Bitzer," is not a random image but the product of Dickens' experience with the use of hands in mesmeric experiments. Like Dickens attempting to relieve the tic-like convulsions of Madame de la Rue curled up into a ball so that one could not tell where her head was,[13] so too another doctor, Allan Woodcourt, "knows that by touching her [the injured nameless woman from St. Albans] with his skilful and accustomed hands, he can soothe her yet more readily" (*BH*, xlvi).

Another man intensely conscious of the mesmeric power of his hands is Mr. Bucket. His "fat forefinger" and he are "much in consultation together." It is a finger almost with life of its own. It is a finger that thinks. In his confrontation with Sir Leicester, "Mr. Bucket feels his way with his forefinger," as if it were a force of intellection and intuitive responsiveness. "He puts it to his ears, and it whispers information; he puts it to his lips, and it enjoins him to secrecy; he rubs it over his nose, and it sharpens his scent;

[13] *Nonesuch*, iii, 752, to J. S. Le Fanu, 11/24/69.

he shakes it before a guilty man, and it charms him to de-struction" (*BH*, LIII). It mesmerizes Sir Leicester, who "sits like a statue, gazing at the cruel finger that is probing the life-blood of his heart" (*BH*, LIV). Even Mr. Smallweed quails before "the dread power of the man," as Bucket assails him, "instantaneously altering his manner . . . and communicating an extraordinary fascination to the fore-finger" (*BH*, LIV). So quick are his flashes of intuitive un-derstanding (as he reads Mrs. Rouncewell's mind) that he seems to less gifted men to be almost clairvoyant. The power of his mind and the power of his forefinger are inseparable. They transfix, fascinate, pierce. No one can oppose them successfully.

Hands may not only touch but talk. They may create a language of their own, so potentially powerful are they as vehicles of communication. Jasper himself is a musician, whose organ is his art, his special language. In this sense he is a charismatic figure who can through touch and sight and song attempt bold works. He is a Prospero figure, but a tainted, fallen Prospero whose moral capabilities and con-trols are not strong enough to channel his desires construc-tively. He uses his art in an attempt to dominate Rosa Bud, for he "ever and ever again hinted the one note." When Rosa hysterically collapses in the midst of a recital, "Jas-per's hands had, in the same instant, lifted themselves from the keys, and were now poised above them, as though he waited to resume." His art is inseparable from his desire to control. Edwin half-seriously jokes that " 'Jack, you are such a conscientious master, and require so much, that I believe you make her afraid of you' " (*ED*, VII). His art like his hands is a language of mesmeric communication.

This language is often the language of control without touch, though the language of the laying on of hands is common in mesmeric literature and in Dickens' fiction. But the power need not be communicated through the direct application of physical contact. The vibrations and force of the fluid can leap across space, for space is not empty. It

135

is not only a conductor but is itself always suffused with the mesmeric fluid, like an ether surrounding all things. It is an hospitable environment, simultaneously a conductor and a reinforcer. There may be "delicate fingers that are formed for sensitiveness and sympathy of touch" (*DS*, XLVIII). But there are other organs or vehicles that do not need the reinforcement of actual contact.

In a fictional world in which characters are "detained . . . by some magnetic attraction" and enter into unions as if "by magnetic agreement" (*DS*, VIII and XXXVI), James Carker has been given powers that do not depend on the touch of hands. When Florence learns that there is still no news of Walter's ship, Carker "said this with his widest smile. . . . Meeting his eyes, [she] saw, rather than heard him. . . ." It is not his eyes or his touch that are the vehicles of communication, but his smile. Florence feels "confused, frightened, shrinking from him, and not even sure that he had said those words, for he seemed to have shown them to her in some extraordinary manner through his smile, instead of uttering them" (*DS*, XXIV). White, gleaming, reflective, like glittering surfaces, almost mirrors themselves, Carker's teeth are his dominant feature. Hardly a description of Carker omits reference to them; hardly a scene or action occurs involving Carker in which his smile and his teeth are not prominent.

Like Jasper, though without his complexities, his drive is towards dominance. He controls through terror and fear, no one more successfully than Rob the Grinder, the fallen son of the Toodles. The power flows through his smile and his teeth. He turns Rob into a slave: "Inmate of Mr. Carker's house, and serving about his person, Rob kept his round eyes on the white teeth with fear and trembling, and felt that he had need to open them wider than ever. He could not have quaked more, through his whole being, before the teeth, though he had come into the service of some powerful enchanter, and they had been his strongest spell. The boy had a sense of power and authority in this patron of his that engrossed his whole attention and exacted his most implicit submission and obedience. . . ." (*DS*, XLII). Rob believes that Carker can "read his secret thoughts." He hardly dares to think. He empties his mind of everything but the need to be submissive. Dickens and his readers knew that Carker's power was mesmeric.

⟦ 5 ⟧

This image of the operator and his necessary counterpart, the subject, is frequent in Dickens' fiction. The operator may be successful or unsuccessful in his attempt to control others, depending on the extent of his powers and whether they are used in Dickens' judgment for good or for evil ends, and depending on the strength of the forces that oppose them. But they are all active figures, dominant and aggressive personalities, who have, like Dickens, made one of the great discoveries of the nineteenth century: the primacy of energy and will.

It is essentially a discovery of the self, of the definition, exploration, and assertion of the self.[14] But it does not rely on the self alone. It turns outward as well as inward, toward other men and their powers, and especially toward the universe at large, toward some scientific or spiritual explanation of the existence of the will and of individual energy. The answer is not only in ourselves but in our stars. Certain men are graced with special powers; often they are artists; but they are always physicians of sorts, some of whom drastically misuse their power. Dickens drew frequently upon this metaphor not only in his fiction but in his life. He saw himself as a doctor to other people's needs. He was Madame de la Rue's "physician"; she was his "patient." But this extraordinary power suffuses the universe. It exists within us and without us, within our bodies and psyches, and also in the atmosphere, like electricity or ether.

[14] Lionel Trilling in *Sincerity and Authenticity* (Cambridge, Mass., 1972) emphasizes the identification of man's concern with authenticity and the authentic private self with modernism.

Mesmerism offered Dickens the terminology and the imagery to discover and explain himself and others in terms that promised universal applicability and perhaps even physical verifiability. The phenomenon was real. The Victorians observed innumerable examples of its existence. Dickens was absolutely convinced, though indeed there were many doubters. But by and large there was a wide acceptance of the existence of the phenomenon, though great differences from individual to individual, from camp to camp, in the explanation of its nature, origin, and possibilities. Dickens seems to have accepted Elliotson's and Townshend's approach. It seemed right. But more than anything else it seemed apposite and useful, not only true to his experience but true to his imagination.

It was a source of imagery for the depiction of character and the dramatization of the relationships between people. It was a theory and a rationale that suited Dickens' personal needs. His involvement with mesmerism was concomitant with his discovery of the great resources of energy and will within himself. He felt not only graced with the healing powers of a doctor in touch with the deepest forces of the universe, but like some great magician who specialized in the magic of psychic insight and manipulation; he felt himself as artist to be a kind of Prospero, who had discovered his "charms . . . Spirits to enforce, art to enchant." This discovery energized him while drawing out from within him the resources of energy that the demands of his art and life had sent him in search of.

CHAPTER

VI

The Past Illumined

[1]

The search for self demands an exploration of one's past. But how is one to get at it? Through what techniques is the elusive past accessible? Dickens assumes that one's distant past is central to one's sense of oneself and one's powers in the adult present and future. The years of infancy and childhood are formative; the mature present cannot be understood without coming to terms with the inheritance that genetics and environment have forced upon the child, who in Dickens' world comes not "trailing clouds of glory . . . from God who is [his] home," but shorn, often like the Blakean lamb, the inheritor of a "prison-house" of limitations. There are mysteries bequeathed from the past, anxieties like dark phantoms that haunt one with prohibitions, warnings, diminishments of one's sense of security in the present. To create a viable present life the past must be explored as the key to our psychic frustrations and imbalances now, so the world of Dickens' fiction assumes. And that past can be made accessible through the use of techniques that heighten consciousness, such as mesmeric trance, putting us in touch with hidden springs of the self that are inaccessible to us in our waking states. In mesmeric crisis the constraints that the self has imposed upon the self may be thrown off; the mind may be put in touch with aspects of the mind that are otherwise hidden; we may be given mesmeric sight; we may be given the language with which to express ourselves to those who have the skill to understand us.

Not every character in Dickens' fiction has a past, though indeed most do. When "Pickwick burst like another sun from his slumbers, threw open his chamber window, and looked out upon the world beneath" (*PP,* ii), he has no psychic inheritance to weigh down his sense of himself in the present and the future. He floats like a bubble of inconsequentiality across the landscape of a present that mocks him gently, then harshly. His only past is that of vague historical abstraction, the man of impractical reason from an eighteenth-century ethos who believes in the dominance of order, "domestic economy," and truth. He has dismissed relativism within himself and others. He has no autobiography—no mother, father, family, story of origins, childhood impressions, defeats, triumphs, frustrations, anxieties, self-doubts—and the past that he creates for himself in the present of the novel is one from which he learns almost nothing. On retirement from the woes of this world he employs "his leisure hours in arranging the memoranda which he afterwards presented to the secretary of the once famous club" (*PP,* lvii). The memoranda epitomize his elimination of meaningful pastness from the past by transforming human experience into "Transactions of the Pickwick Club" and "Theories of Tittlebats." If the past exists, it does so as dry arrangement of abstractions. Consequently Pickwick has no tools for discovering and exploring it. He does not need them. At the beginning of Dickens' involvement with mesmerism, Pickwick refuses to make the beginning he does not need, and Dickens, who desperately needs it, leaves him behind.[1]

[1] For relevant discussions of *Pickwick Papers,* see J. Hillis Miller, *Charles Dickens, The World of His Novels* (Cambridge, Mass., 1958), pp. 1-35, and Steven Marcus, *Dickens from Pickwick to Dombey* (N.Y., 1965), pp. 13-53.

First there is the general past, available through memory and evocation. It is the past of the days of our fathers, particularly significant because it is the time when we were children, impressionable and vulnerable. But there is also the past that skips the generation of our fathers, finding some special identification in the search for self in the milieu of our grandfathers, as in *Barnaby Rudge* and *A Tale of Two Cities*, Dickens' only attempts to write something that his Victorian contemporaries would clearly recognize and label as "historical."[2] From Scott on, and among Dickens' contemporaries and friends like Ainsworth and Thackeray, the historical novel was widely popular. Dickens himself was only sufficiently attracted twice to venture into a period evocation reverberating with the specificity of historical events so important that their influence could easily be detected in the society of his readers.

For in both Dickens' historical novels, the emphasis is on continuity, not only on the events of the past and the conditions of the present but on the absolute continuity of the human personality. There is hardly a character in Dickens' two historical novels whose central passions and means of expressing them are not perfectly suitable for transference into any other Dickens novel, with the exception of *Pickwick Papers*. All it would take would be a different suit of clothes. *Barnaby Rudge* and *A Tale of Two Cities* exist as historical novels with much less immediacy and power than they do as Dickens novels, expressive of the themes with which Dickens cannot avoid dealing. They are movements into a past into which Dickens twice chose to go back a little further than he normally did. His time-machine usually insisted on back-pedaling only a single generation.

Usually our own pasts can best be illumined through a return to those crucial moments of childhood and early

[2] Discussions of historical fiction and of historicity in fiction have been minimal. The seminal work is George Lukas, *The Historical Novel* (1937; London, 1962). For a recent general account, see Avrom Fleishman, *The English Historical Novel, Walter Scott to Virginia Woolf* (Baltimore, 1971).

adulthood when our sense of ourselves in all its varied forms was being shaped. That past for Dickens is about "thirty years ago" when "Marseilles lay burning in the sun, one day" (*LD*, I, 1), though within any Dickens novel time may pass so quickly (or so slowly) that an infant like the newly-born David Copperfield or Pip or Nicholas Nickleby may provide us within his chronicle with an advancement from those "thirty years ago" to the present of Dickens' actual writing of the work. There are exceptions, of course. In such a huge opus there must be an exception to everything.[3] But even in *Our Mutual Friend* and *Bleak House,* novels of "these times of ours," the same themes are approached in other ways.

There is the past of one's immediate youth, the birth and childhood of consciousness and self-identity, as if by focusing on the sensibilities of developing children Dickens could get closer to the formative mysteries that are hidden from the adult during his normal functioning. Adult consciousness interferes with confronting unevasively crucial incidents from the past and dealing with complex problems in the present. The "queer little boy" whom Forster claims was Dickens himself is the prototype of a vast gallery of boys (and occasionally girls) in Dickens' fiction whose anxieties are so effectively depicted that for many readers they are the most memorable characters he creates. The mere mention of Oliver in the workhouse, Smike at Squeers' school, Paul and Florence Dombey in the darkness of the older Dombey's shadow, David dominated by a new father in his dead father's home, Pip alone on the threatening moors, often invokes in readers the feelings of anxiety that these characters feel as vulnerable children in hostile environments. Dickens seems at his best when he can make

[3] This "huge opus" has been the catalyst for a large and growing body of critical commentary, some of it notable. But Dickens scholarship has suffered an insufficiency of historical and contextual studies, particularly those that would place Dickens' assumptions and themes in the larger cultural and intellectual perspective.

John Elliotson. From *The Lancet*, 1831.

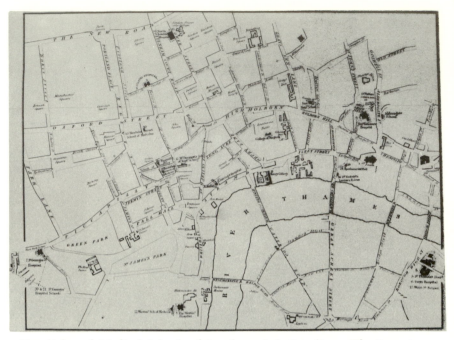

Hospitals and Medical Schools of London, 1836-1837. From *The Lancet*, 1836.

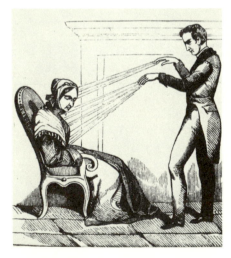

Mesmerism, woodcut, c. 1840.

Mesmeric Session, woodcut, c. 1840.

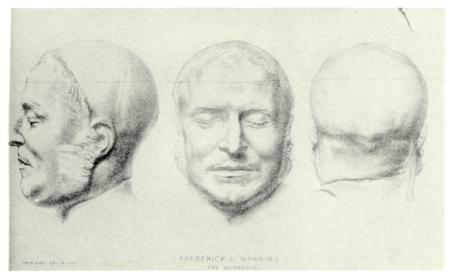

Frederick Manning, The Murderer. From *The Zoist*, 1849.

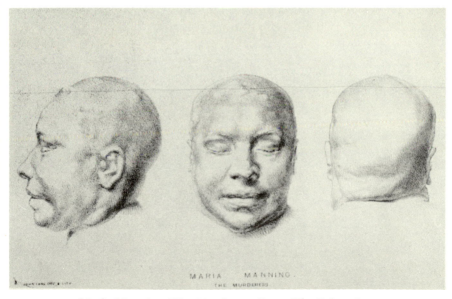

Maria Manning, The Murderess. From *The Zoist*, 1849.

The true and lively Pourtraicture of Valentine Greatrakes Esq of Affane in ý County of Waterford in ý Kingdome of Ireland famous for curing several Defeases and diftempers by the ftroak of his Hand only.

Pub.d March 20th 1794 by W. Richardson Caftle St Leicester Square

Valentine Greatrakes, Curing . . . by the stroke of his hand only.
From *The Zoist*, 1845.

Opposite top: Le Mesmerisme Confondu, 1790. From E. Hollander, *Die Karikatur und Satire in der Medizin*, Stuttgart, 1921.
THE WELLCOME INSTITUTE.

Opposite bottom: Magnetic Dispensary, 1790, etching by Barlow. From a drawing by Collings, Bentley, London, 1790. THE WELLCOME INSTITUTE.

LE MESMERISME CONFONDU.

MESMER.

Drawn by Collings.   Published as the Act directs by Bentley & Co Jan. 1.st 1790.   Etch.d by Barlow.

MAGNETIC DISPENSARY.

Animal Magnetism, The Operator Putting His Patient into a Crisis. From E. Sibly, *Key to Physic*, London, 1810. THE WELLCOME INSTITUTE.

Opposite top: Robert Macaire magnétiseur, H. Daumier. From H. Mondon, *Les Gens medecine dans l'oeuvre de Daumier*, Paris, 1960. THE WELLCOME INSTITUTE.

Opposite bottom: Le Magnétisme, L. Boilly, 1826. From E. Hollander, *Die Karikatur und Satire in der Medizin*, Stuttgart, 1921. THE WELLCOME INSTITUTE.

Robert Macaire magnétiseur.

Imp Mourlot Frères

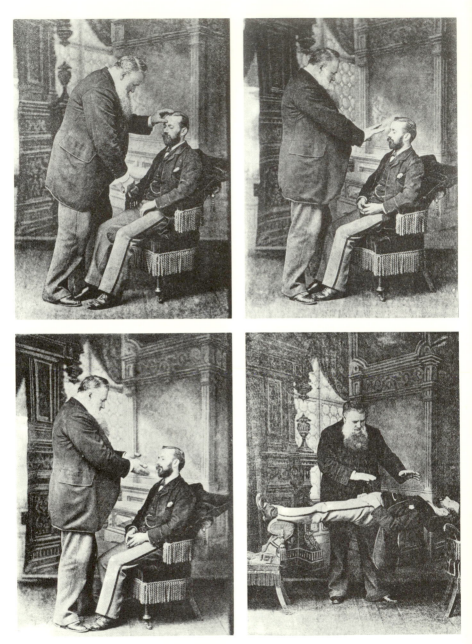

Top left: Establishing the Electro-Biological Circuit Between Mesmerist and Subject.
Top right: Making the Magnetic Pass.
Bottom left: The Reverse or Upward Pass.
Bottom right: The Cataleptic State.
From D. Younger, *The Magnetic and Botanic Family Physician*, 1887.

adult consciousness and its problems understandable as a product of the past.

It is not simply a matter of those notorious blacking bottles in the warehouse, Dickens' account of his desolation when sent out as a child by his impoverished parents to work as a factory menial in Warren's Blacking House.[4] It is also Dickens' consciousness of the possibilities of the experience, not all of which he saw by any means as negative. Nicholas remarks to Tim Linkinwater, " 'There is a double-wallflower at No. 6, in the court, is there?' 'Yes, is there!' replied Tim, 'and planted in a cracked jug, without a spout. There were hyacinths there, this last spring, blossoming in—but you'll laugh at that.' 'At what?' 'At their blossoming in old blacking-bottles,' said Tim. 'Not I, indeed,' returned Nicholas. Tim looked wistfully at him, for a moment, as if he were encouraged by the tone of this reply to be more communicative on the subject . . ." (*NN*, XL). Out of the blacking-bottles grew flowers, a potential that Dickens fully appreciated. Out of the pains of the past come good things. But they can arrive only if the anxieties of the past are explored and confronted. And the question is how.

[[2]]

Dickens' awareness of the problem may not have originated with his contacts with mesmerism in the early 1830's. Indeed, such awareness and its results would have occurred even if Dickens had never come into contact with Elliotson, Townshend, and Madame de la Rue, and had never developed an interest in the literature and practice of mesmerism. Certainly he would have found some other framework within which he would have been offered useful tools to explore questions ineradicably a part of his being from childhood on. The novel itself is such a tool, even without the particular theories of consciousness, force, influence, and origins that Dickens came to believe in. The novel in the

---

[4] See *Life*, I, 19-33, and Johnson, I, 31-46.

hands of such a genius is a vehicle of self-discovery. But the vehicle itself needs subsidiary vehicles to create networks of significance and comprehension for the movement of the main traffic. Mesmerism was such a tool for Dickens, an intellectual movement whose currents were not only readily available to him but whose primary concern was to establish the validity and importance of the very kinds of assumptions that Dickens was making about human beings and their relationships.

For the mesmerists promised that the mind had special powers which, if properly stimulated, could put the individual in touch with his past, his present, and his future. The phrenologists of the period, some of whom also were mesmerists, claimed that through a close analysis—mainly observation and touch of the anatomical features of the cranium—the basic character and consequently the future behavior of human beings could be determined.[5] Dickens had no argument with them, often remarking on the "phrenological attributes" of his characters (*BH*, xxi). The narrator of *Martin Chuzzlewit* jokes about "the development of an entirely new organ, unknown to phrenologists, on the back" of Mr. Pecksniff's head (ii). David Copperfield refers to a pie crust as "a disappointing head, phrenologically speaking: full of lumps and bumps, with nothing particular underneath" (*DC*, xxviii). Dr. Chillip has observed the "strong phrenological development of the organ of firmness, in Mr. Murdstone and his sister" (*DC*, lix) with as

---

[5] The pages of *The Lancet* and *The Zoist* contain articles and letters on phrenology and accounts of the meetings of the London Phrenological Society of which Elliotson was a founding member and president for many years. Elliotson's belief in a connection between cranial anatomical features and moral and intellectual qualities was shared by Dickens (see "Boz and the American Phreno-Mesmerists," by Noel C. Peyrouton, *Dickens Studies*, iii [1967], 38-50, for an instance in which Dickens became the subject of a phrenological analysis), and undoubtedly Dickens and Elliotson shared an interest in the cranial attributes of the criminal and murderer (see the illustrations). See David A. De Guistino, *Phrenology in Britain, 1815-1855: A Study of George Combe and His Circle* (Dissertation Abstracts 30: 5375A).

much wryness as Mr. Crisparkle observes that " 'as to the phrenological formation of the backs of their heads . . . the Professing Philanthropists were uncommonly like Pugilists' " (*ED*, XVII). Even Mr. Smallweed's "phrenological attributes" are "unimpaired" (*BH*, XXI). Through phrenology the criminal type could be identified, and Dickens avidly read accounts by Elliotson and others in *The Zoist* of the cranial attributes of great criminals like Courvoisier, whose execution they attended together in 1840. But mesmerism promised more, an actual transference of consciousness from the limited world of physical reality into a state of existence in which all the normal boundaries to both mental and spiritual experience were lifted. Jung-Stilling's claim that mesmerism could provide the vehicle to free one from one's body and put one in touch with the transcendent world of spiritual and supernatural phenomena was to be taken seriously.[6]

Through mesmerism the mind indeed could know its own powers, and Dickens believed them to be great. For mind is not the sum of its physical-chemical parts but a potentially immense force. These special powers, however, are too often hidden and undeveloped. Mesmerism provided a technique, mesmeric trance or sleep-waking, through which human beings could discover themselves and their mental powers.

In the summer of 1837, whether or not he had attended any mesmeric sessions yet, Dickens had already taken the subject into his creative consciousness. Pickwick has only one mental fix, static, contained, rational. For Oliver there are vaster possibilities. He "had roused himself from sleep, he was not thoroughly awake. There is a drowsy state, between sleeping and waking, when you dream more in five minutes with your eyes half open, and yourself half conscious of everything that is passing around you, than you would in five nights with your eyes fast closed, and your

---

[6] See Jung-Stilling, *Theory of Pneumatology* (London, 1834), pp. 370-372.

sense wrapt in perfect consciousness. At such times, a mortal knows just enough of what his mind is doing, to form some glimmering conception of its mighty powers, its bounding from earth and spurning time and space, when freed from the restraint of its corporeal associate" (*OT*, IX). In mesmeric trance special knowledge or power comes. One's ordinary mental state is changed radically and a new reality appears. Nicholas figuratively mesmerizes himself through reading a tutorial responsum with questions and statistics "with as much thought or consciousness of what he was doing as if he had been in a magnetic slumber" (*NN*, VII). In such a state, the normal mind is obliterated temporarily, as if "he might have been in a trance, or under the influence of opium" (*NN*, L) or "like men in a dream or trance" (*NN*, LIV).

Often, of course, Dickens uses this imagery metaphorically. In moments of great tension about the self and others, Dickens' characters, like Pip stunned by the thought of what Magwitch may reveal to him, often are "in a sort of dream or sleep-walking" (*GE*, XL). Such states are not induced by some special effort by an operator to create mesmeric trance in a subject but mainly by the press of circumstances. They are not mesmeric in the literal sense. Dickens draws upon the imagery of mesmerism to dramatize the relation of the self to the self and the world under conditions of particular stress. When the mob invades and destroys John Willet's tavern he is not actually in a state of mesmeric trance but he acts as if he were. He "stared round at the mass of faces . . . and while he was, as he thought, in the very act of doing so, found himself, without any consciousness of having moved, in the bar; sitting down in an arm-chair, and watching the destruction of his property, as if it were some queer play or entertainment, of an astonishing and stupefying nature, but having no reference to himself" (*BR*, LIV). This is not the search for self but the temporary loss of self for self-protection.

But it is *as if* he were in a trance. This kind of experience produces the trauma that results in conditioned mesmeric behavior in situations that threaten to revive the pains of the past. Doctor Manette is Dickens' best example of the power of the past to produce trance in the present to avoid reliving pain. To discuss his past with Mr. Lorry, Manette and Mr. Lorry enter into the protective pretense that they are talking about someone else. Manette creates another self, and makes him a fictive stranger. Otherwise he could not talk about himself. " 'I believe,' returned Doctor Manette, 'that there had been a strong and extraordinary revival of the train of thought and remembrance that was the first cause of the malady. Some intense associations of a most distressing nature were vividly recalled, I think. It is probable that there had long been a dread lurking in his mind, that those associations would be recalled—say, under certain circumstances—say, on a particular occasion' " (*TTC*, I:xix). The behavior is mesmeric, just as "if I hide my watch when I am drunk, I must be drunk again before I can remember where" (*ED*, iii).[7] Here it is the metaphor that counts, just as in the case of Eugene Wrayburn, so exhausted with his night's work that he "had become a mere somnambulist" (*OMF*, I:xiv) or Stephen Blackpool, who observes the suicidal movements of his wife "as if a spell were on him . . . motionless and powerless, except to watch her" (*HT*, I, 13).

But in other instances it is not the metaphor but the actuality, the formal mesmeric experience itself that is crucial for the metaphors it produces and the assumptions it communicates. David Copperfield approaches the actuality, though in a disguised form. The vehicle is Rosa Dartle's music. David's mind is brought to the threshold of a new reality, an insight into special ways in which people reveal

[7] *Edwin Drood* is the only Dickens novel in which the role of mesmerism has been widely discussed, mainly as an attempt to complete and solve the unfinished mystery. See Arthur J. Cox, "If I hide my watch—," *Dickens Studies*, iii (1967), 22-37, and Aubrey Boyd, "A New Angle on the Drood Mystery," *Washington University Studies* (1921), pp. 35-85.

themselves and control others: "I don't know what it was, in her touch or voice, that made that song the most unearthly I have ever heard in my life, or can imagine. There was something fearful in the reality of it. It was as if it had never been written, or set to music, but sprung out of the passion within her; which found imperfect utterance in the low sounds of her voice, and crouched again when all was still. I was dumb when she leaned beside the harp again, playing it, but not sounding it, with her right hand. A minute more, and this had roused me from my trance" (*DC*, XXIX). David comes within the circumference of Rosa's mesmeric emanations and, unlike Steerforth, is vulnerable, to his credit. For Steerforth's imperviousness is a sign of the callous, cruel self that he and his mother have created for him. Rosa's powers are less than those of Jasper but also those on whom she would exert them have more strength to resist. Steerforth's playful, ironic response, " 'Come, Rosa, for the future we will love each other very much,' " produces an explosion that is not simply the passion of rejected love. It is the anguish of someone who has used her maximum force of will (so strong that David, not its object, has been affected), and found her subject impervious. Such a fundamental rejection suggests Steerforth's rejection of belief in vital power in the universe at large and makes it possible for him to maintain a cold cruelty on the surface level of ego and charm alone.

The mesmerists were surprised to discover that in many instances an individual who was not the subject of the mesmerist's exertions but who happened to be present in the same room was thrown into mesmeric trance, so great was the power, so specially susceptible certain chosen people.[8] But not everyone has the special capabilities to transfer and receive this force. Steerforth is impervious, David susceptible, just as Dickens himself felt his own susceptibility as

[8] Dickens' account of his inadvertent mesmerization of Catherine on their trip to Rome is a dramatic example of the forces involved. See Berg MS., Dickens to Emile de la Rue, 1/27/45.

subject and refused to permit Townshend "to give" him "a mesmeric trial. . . . I dare not be mesmerized."[9] For the powers of mesmerism are the powers of irresistible attraction, the trance a moment that often reveals some hidden aspect of the self that one may prefer to keep controlled and disguised, in the interests of self and society.

Bradley Headstone is also under the control of a mesmeric power that is not purposely directed towards him. Lizzie Hexam is in touch with the hidden forces of life. She gazes, like Paul Dombey, into the fire, and sees "wise fancies" (*OMF*, II:ii). She is gifted with special insight, an unselfconscious embodiment of "vital force." With no conscious notion that she has done anything to attract Bradley, she is at a loss to understand the implications of the language he uses to describe his passion for her: " 'You know what I am going to say. I love you. What other men may mean when they use that expression, I cannot tell; what *I* mean is, that I am under the influence of some tremendous attraction which I have resisted in vain, and which overmasters me. You could draw me to fire, you could draw me to water, you could draw me to the gallows, you could draw me to any death, you could draw me to anything I have most avoided, you could draw me to any exposure and disgrace' " (*OMF*, II:xv).

This is the language of mesmeric attraction. Lizzie is to Bradley like "the Loadstone Rock" to Charles Darnay. It "was drawing him, and he must sail on, until he struck. . . . The unseen force was drawing him fast to itself, now" (*TTC*, II:xxiv). She is to Bradley like the "Mace and Seal" to the litigants in the Chancery Court. " 'There's a cruel attraction in the place,' " Miss Flite says, " 'You *can't* leave it. . . . It's the Mace and Seal upon the table.' What could they do, did she think? I mildly asked her. 'Draw. . . . Draw people on, my dear. Draw peace out of them. Sense out of them. Good looks out of them. Good qualities out of them.

---

[9] *Pilgrim*, II, 342, to Chauncy Hare Townshend, 7/23/41, and footnote.

I have felt them even drawing my rest away in the night. . . . First, our father was drawn . . . then our brother was drawn . . . and I was drawn to stay there. . . . I have seen many new faces come, unsuspicious, within the influence of the Mace and Seal, in these many years' " (*BH*, xxv). People may possess this pulling force. But the process of attraction and the special trance that results usually reveal certain previously hidden possibilities of the self that unbalance and destroy, turning one potential for obsession into a cancer that grows and becomes the whole. Many of Dickens' characters are exemplifications of the tyranny of some special need over all else.

An important variant of trance in Dickens' fiction is achieved through the self mesmerizing force of language, the powers of rhetoric to create a second self who becomes the self that one cannot live without. Of course this is a metaphoric use of the term "mesmerism." But in many Dickens characters the overwhelming need to discover a self who provides a reality that fulfills the needs of the ego is satisfied through a purposeful use of language to create this other being and to keep him viable. Some attempt to keep themselves and others in a constant state of suspension of disbelief in the self. They are usually verbal prestidigitators, magicians of rhetoric, like the novelist himself, who can use language to create the illusion of the existence of a number of levels of reality or can give substance and perhaps credibility to what turns out to be purely a fantasy. Some of Elliotson's subjects, particularly the O'keys, had this great rhetorical facility under mesmeric influence. In sleep-waking the mesmeric subject loses most verbal inhibitions, producing a flow of language that in effect seems to create a new personality for the speaker, quite different from his waking personality. Characters like Mrs. Gamp, Mr. Micawber, Mr. Pecksniff, and Flora Finching seem to have the volubility of permanent sleep-waking. But the restraints are not so loosened (under Dickens' control) that they commit any of the verbal-sexual improprieties that an anonymous observer feared, in a letter to *The Lancet,* inevitably would occur when females were under the influence of mesmerism or some other liberating excitement such as a fainting spell or general hysteria.[10]

Mrs. Gamp has created not only Mrs. Harris but a special self for herself, both pure creations of language. But her efforts at persuasion are directed mostly at herself. She does not particularly need position in the world. She has no need to use her rhetoric to manipulate others. She must minister to her own unhappiness. By constantly addressing herself, she emphasizes that she has a self, even if only a created one. By creating Mrs. Harris, she amplifies herself. Through language she gives texture and context to a self that would otherwise have minimal presence. Through her language she not only helps others to believe in her existence but mainly persuades herself that she exists. It is a form of self-hypnosis, with special privileges. Like Elliotson's babbling patients, she gains license to express herself. Her constant drunkenness acts in consonance with her verbal flow. Poor as her being is, through language she at least has a being, a past and a present, like Micawber, Pecksniff and Flora Finching.[11]

Many of Elliotson's mesmeric patients awed his audiences with their epileptic convulsions. But actual mesmeric trance is unmistakable. It is not simply a matter of being "drawn" irresistibly towards some person or thing or having "desperate fits" like Monks. In mesmeric trance the order of human experience is distinctly different from that of ordinary consciousness. But there are varied possibilities of reaction; and Elliotson was acutely aware of the general unpredictability of the responsum from instance to instance, from subject to subject, though indeed he hoped to discover certain stable patterns that would permit verifiable generali-

[10] See *The Lancet* (Sept. 2, 1837), 839.
[11] For a comparison of Flora and Molly, see Fred Kaplan, "Dickens' Flora Finching and Joyce's Molly Bloom," *Nineteenth-Century Fiction,* 23 (Dec. 1968), 343-346.

zations. Dickens was aware of this, and it suited his needs as novelist perfectly. The possibilities were protean. He need not feel his credibility questionable if he changed the details from instance to instance as the particular fictional situation demanded. For example, at some times "there is a kind of sleep that steals upon us . . . which, while it holds the body prisoner, does not free the mind from a sense of things about it, and enable it to ramble at its pleasure" (*OT*, xxxiv). This mesmeric consciousness is different from that in which you "form some glimmering conception" of the mind's "mighty powers: its bounding from earth" (*OT*, ix). This is heavier, more earth-bound and threatening. "So far as an overpowering heaviness, a prostration of strength, and an utter inability to control our thoughts or power of motion, can be called sleep, this is it." But now also, as when Oliver had been earlier in mesmeric sleep-waking, there is a special consciousness: "And yet we have a consciousness of all that is going on about us; and if we dream at such a time, words which are really spoken, or sounds which really exist at the moment, accommodate themselves with surprising readiness to our visions, until reality and imagination become so strangely blended that it is afterwards almost a matter of impossibility to separate the two."

Dickens at the very time of writing these words had been a frequent observer of Elliotson's patients, and was rich with things to say on the matter. For "nor is this, the most striking phenomenon incidental to such a state. It is an undoubted fact, that although our senses of touch and sight be for the time dead, yet our sleeping thoughts, and the visionary scenes that pass before us, will be influenced, and materially influenced, by the *mere silent presence* of some external object: which may not have been near us when we closed our eyes: and of whose vicinity we have had no waking consciousness" (*OT*, xxxiv). As in Elliotson's experiments, here too Dickens affirms that the mesmerized subject can see with his eyes closed. He is in a special state of receptive consciousness in which communication can be effected through means other than through physical organs. In this case, it is an instance of double consciousness. "Oliver knew, perfectly well, that he was in his own little room; that his books were lying on the table before him; that the sweet air was stirring among the creeping plants outside. And yet he was asleep. Suddenly, the scene changed; the air became close and confined; and he thought, with a glow of terror, that he was in the Jew's house again." Fagin sits in his usual place and whispers to Monks, whose face, like that of Madame de la Rue's dark shadow, is "averted . . . 'Hush, my dear!' he thought he heard the Jew say; 'it is he, sure enough, come away.'" The man with "averted face" speaks with "dreadful hate." He would know Oliver under any circumstances, even "if you buried him fifty feet deep," so strong is this magnetic attraction between these two brothers, split aspects of a single self. "As, in some cases of drunkenness, and in others of animal magnetism, there are two states of consciousness which never clash, but each of which pursues its separate course as though it were continuous instead of broken . . ." (*ED*, III). In mesmeric trance Oliver confronts the inheritance of Monks and Fagin, of the fallen and corrupted world, and of his sweet dead mother and her pain, the possibility that she still may bequeath him redemption through those who loved her (or damnation through those who hated her).

States of mesmeric trance are frequent in *Edwin Drood*, in which the plot mechanism itself seems to depend on the creation of sleep-waking in a number of characters. Jasper is often in "a delirious state between sleeping and waking" (*ED*, X) and "subject to a kind of paroxysm, or fit" (*ED*, XIII). He attempts to mesmerize Rosa Bud, who constantly feels the threat of his domination. He attempts to mesmerize Edwin, with what success only the unwritten portion of the novel could reveal. Helena Landless, who also seems to have mesmeric power, perhaps would have attempted herself to use it, perhaps even to mesmerize Jasper. But through some mechanism that was to have been explained in the final sections of the book, undoubtedly Jasper was to have been revealed as self-mesmerized, through some vehicle, perhaps music or opium. Jasper could have conditioned himself to go into mesmeric trance while under the influence of opium; the mesmeric tool might have been the drug itself. But whatever the agent, Jasper lives in double consciousness, with two separate states of being: his everyday mind and his mesmeric state, in which he performs actions that his normal consciousness may be unaware of, may indeed purposely suppress because of the immoral and unsocial needs that are being gratified. He has kept them separate even from himself, though occasionally words and actions from his trance consciousness surface and appear in normal states. Indeed, sometimes the mesmerized subject does not know that he is acting in the present under the power of suggestions previously implanted. Mr. Crisparkle, for example, "walked to Cloisterham Weir. He often did so, and consequently there was nothing remarkable in his footsteps tending that way. But the preoccupation of his mind so hindered him from planning any walk, or taking heed of the objects he passed, that his first consciousness of being near the Weir was derived from the sound of the falling water close at hand. 'How did I come here!' was his first thought, as he stopped. 'Why did I come here!' was his second" (*ED*, xvi). Though the method and time of the placement of the suggestion in his mind are unclear, undoubtedly Jasper has put it there for his own ends.

Cloisterham is a city of origins and ends. *Edwin Drood* trys to make some sense of the relationship between them. It is a dark, autumnal novel, which takes its tone from the mystery of double consciousness that reverberates with the mystery of death and perhaps no consciousness at all. It is a city in which no children play. On Christmas Eve, which should anticipate the reconciliation of the old self and the new, the past and the present, there are a "few strange faces in the streets; a few other faces, half strange and half familiar, once the faces of Cloisterham children, now the

faces of men and women who come back from the outer
world at long intervals to find the city wonderfully shrunken
in size. . . . To these, the striking of the Cathedral clock,
and the cawing of the rooks from the Cathedral tower, are
like voices of their nursery time. To such as these, it has happened in their dying hours afar off, that they have imagined
their chamber-floor to be strewn with the autumnal leaves
fallen from the elm-trees in the Close: so have the rustling
sounds and fresh scents of their earliest impressions revived
when the circle of their lives was very nearly traced, and the
beginning and the end were drawing close together" (ED,
xiv). These "half strange and half familiar faces" are one
indication of the schizophrenia of Cloisterham and of its
foremost magician.

But the city itself is a city of the past, of endings and
murder and death. The four young people who come there
are victims of the past. Edwin and Rosa Bud have been imprisoned by the wishes of their parents for a marriage that
neither of them desires. Neville and Helena are exiled
orphans in a foreign land, children of youthful adversity.
Jasper has been entrusted with the care and guardianship
of the former, Crisparkle with that of the twins. Undoubtedly Dickens intended to work out the fates of both pairs
as moral indicators of these two different men entrusted
with a similar responsibility. But Jasper himself is a man
with a hidden past. What Jasper's double consciousness
makes indubitable is that—like Oliver Twist, David Copperfield, Estella Magwitch, Esther Summerson, and John
Rokesmith—he possesses a past with which he must come
to terms in order to create a viable and constructive present
for himself. His violence, jealousy, bitterness, addiction, all
have a history. His double states of consciousness are states
of refuge as well as states of disguise for aggressiveness. They
must come from somewhere. And it is just this history that
is suppressed. The combination of opium and mesmerism
potently affects a John Jasper without a psychic past, without remorse, without a rationale. His own mesmeric trances

as well as his use of mesmerism on others are not instruments of self-discovery but murderous weapons to destroy himself. Undoubtedly the novel would have ended with death and the loss of consciousness. For the most mysterious state of consciousness and potential of mind is no consciousness at all.

[3]

The powers of the mind are often revealed not only in direct mesmeric trance but in unusual states of consciousness brought on by natural stimulants. One of these is fear. The inebriated Orlick plans to murder Pip, who is imprisoned in the old sluice-house and aware that every drop in Orlick's bottle is a drop of his life. "I knew that when I was changed into a part of the vapour that had crept towards me but a little while before, like my own warning ghost, he would do as he had done in my sister's case." Suddenly Pip's mind accelerates: "it was not only that I could have summed up years and years and years while he said a dozen words, but that what he did say presented pictures to me, and not mere words." His mind becomes extraordinarily imagistic: "In the excited and exalted state of my brain, I could not think of a place without seeing it, or of persons without seeing them. It is impossible to over-state the vividness of these images, and yet I was so intent, all the time, upon him himself . . . that I knew of the slightest action of his fingers" (*GE*, LIII).

This special state of mind is a form of double consciousness. Activated by the adrenalin of fear, Pip does two things simultaneously: he concentrates fully on the details of his present situation while, with the imagination of a novelist, he actually sees in his mind's eye his past experiences as if they were being perceived by his physical senses. Pip's mind then is capable of at least two levels of activity at the same time: one the normal functioning in regard to every day needs, the other some special functioning in which the past becomes a living part of the present. Pip experiences on this second level of consciousness not thoughts but images, visually perceived experiences: "wonderful the force of the pictures that rushed by me instead of thoughts" (*GE*, LIII), suggesting mesmeric trance-talkers like the O'keys, who in their states of double consciousness told with vivid clarity the things that they were seeing actually as if they were seeing them with their open eyes. Pip's comment echoes a thought of Esther Summerson's: "I had never known before how short life really was, and into how small a space the mind could put it" (*BH*, xxxv).

Another vehicle to reveal the powers of mind in Dickens' fiction is illness, the traditional Romantic sickness-unto-death. At some moment of crisis of self-identity, often after a great exertion of the will on behalf of someone whose needs one has responded to in a process of self-definition, the mind and body lose their normal balance. Some great symbolic illness threatens to defeat life. When Oliver is rescued by Mr. Brownlow, he sinks into a fever that brings him close to death. Little Nell cannot recover from her final illness. Dick Swiveller at a moment of crisis is "seized with an alarming illness . . . always shadowy and dim, but recognisable for the same phantom in every shape it took" (*OCS*, LXIV). In such states, special phantoms like Madame de la Rue's dark shadow challenge one's continued existence. The illness is an attack of the self upon the self, and the continued existence of the individual is open to question. Louisa Gradgrind falls insensibly ill in a special form of crucifixion, like Lawrence's "the man who died" (*HT*, III:I). Pip becomes sick "with a heavy head and aching limbs, and no purpose, and no power" (*GE*, LVII). Such illnesses represent a concentration of all the psychic diseases of the individual's life. In his illness Pip "confounded impossible existences with my own identity," searching for some other better self acceptable to his new moral sense. In his attempt to obliterate his former detested self he imagines that he is an insensible, inanimate object, first "a brick in the house wall," then a "steel beam of a vast engine." He entreated "to be released from the giddy place where the builders had set me . . . and . . . implored in my own person to have the engine stopped, and my part in it hammered off" (*GE*, LVII). In this heightened state of consciousness many Dickens characters can confront the often contradictory drive of the psyche both toward self-annihilation and toward life. For Pip, the past and the present can be brought into a new balance through a heightened awareness of what he has done wrong and what he can do right.

Kate Nickleby remarks to the unhappy Madame Mantalini that "bodily illness is much easier to bear than mental" (*NN*, XXI). Dickens believed that mental power could be brought to bear on bodily illness. That was an essential element of mesmerism and crossed all lines of theory within the movement. For those who believed, as did Dickens, that there existed an invisible fluid whose powers could be transmitted for therapeutic ends, indeed the role of mind and will in the process was central. The mesmerist had special powers that enabled him to control the beneficial effects of this force. Dickens believed that he was doing this in his mesmeric communications. Those mesmerists who began to emphasize that the mesmeric effect, particularly trance or sleep-waking, was produced through suggestion from the mesmerist acting on the sensitive nervous system of the subject, of course believed that the mind played the central role in the process. Dickens obviously realized that in his attempts to ministrate to Madame de la Rue he was dealing with an illness whose manifestations were physical but whose cause was mental.[12] The mind has extraordinary powers. It is the mind that must be ministered to. It is in the mind that the crucial battles must be fought.

But the risk is great. One's life itself is in jeopardy. The vision is gained only at risk to survival, for the forces are threatening, except perhaps to the mesmerist, who has an explanation of, and believes he has the power to control,

[12] Berg MS., Dickens to Emile de la Rue, 1/27/45.

these strange experiences. Esther thinks that "it may be that if we knew more of such strange afflictions, we might be the better able to alleviate their intensity" (*BH*, xxxv). Dickens believed that he did, for those forces at work in mental illness are the same forces the mesmerists believed that they could control. Dickens, attempting "to alleviate" the "intensity" of Madame de la Rue's "strange afflictions," perhaps recognized that the "afflictions" were in other forms his own as well.

[4]

So important is the inheritance from the past that it not only deeply disturbs the psychic life of many Dickens characters, but involves them in an actual search for the formative people and events of their hidden lives. From *Oliver Twist* on, almost every Dickens novel depends for some level of its impact on the discovery of lost or hidden parentage. Children have been born to parents who cannot sustain them. From their earliest moments of consciousness they are aware of the paucity of their environment and the constant threat to even minimal security. They mature into childhood and beyond, suffering the direct consequences of their deprivations, constantly aware of something crucial that has been lost. It is not that it has never been there. Such bleak necessitarian pessimism rarely dominates the Dickens world. It was indeed there once, surviving in some dim remembrance from earliest infancy. Sometimes the promise is vaguely intuited in the noble looks of faces in portraits, the whisper of a resemblance between the ugly duckling and some lovely more fortunate swan. It is glimpsed in the actual charity and love of strangers who sometimes become foster parents. But that which has been lost must be searched for and revealed. It is the only way in which we may know ourselves. The plots of lost parentage are in the service of an exploration of the theme that the new personality must be forged out of a confrontation with the conditions that have created the frustrations and anxieties of the old.

There is the constant sense of expectation in Dickens' novels that the discovery will come, sooner or later. The vital link between past and present will be revealed. These moments of revelation are often special moments of heightened consciousness. But they are prepared for by the slow accumulation of impressions and intuitions, by some special emphasis within the sensibility of the hero on the possible happiness that will come from something that is about to be learned. This knowledge will produce a more harmonious future. Significantly, then, the past and its connection with the present are all aspects of the future. The expectations of the oppressed consciousness in the present are focused on some new qualitative life that will be the achievement of one's deepest hopes and dreams. " 'Wouldn't you like to be a book-writer?' " Mr. Brownlow asks Oliver, a question that David Copperfield and Charles Dickens answer in the affirmative. But the question is rich with resonances, for it is a question whose emphasis on futurity provides insight into the question that Dickens asks repeatedly: given where we have come from, what indeed can we be? Oliver's expectations for the future have been suppressed by the heavy mulch of his past. But, of course, flowers may grow in the empty blacking pots, though he can for the moment only answer that it would be a much better thing to be a bookseller (*OT*, xiv), a good but painful joke for the author and reader.

Exploring the past is an attempt to foresee and create the future. Dickens had a strongly developed sense of prescience, a predilection for premonition that bordered on a commitment to clairvoyance, if only as a metaphor for the powers of the mind. One of the special powers in mesmeric trance was clairvoyance. Elliotson experimented with its efficacy as a diagnostic tool. When the O'key sisters created anxiety and scandal at University Hospital by predicting the fates of fellow patients, Elliotson theorized that each disease gives off a special identifiable effluence from the body that the mesmerized subject in a state of heightened sensitivity can detect.[13] Townshend experimented with the possibility that the subject in mesmeric trance could see with eyes closed, with no physical possibility of the normal organ of sight being used. This special vision, this "visual ray," could even see what had not yet occurred. Clairvoyance, many believed, was a fact. But many did not, including Elliotson, who gradually became convinced that the phenomenon did not exist. Elliotson and his circle, however, continued to believe that under certain conditions special sensitivities permitted the mesmerized subject to become aware of actualities so quickly that it seemed as if he could see into the future.[14] In fact, they had simply shortened the gap between actuality and perception.

But, for the novelist particularly, to narrow this gap is to discover a mechanism that gives one the opportunity to create the future, to use special states of consciousness to discover what the mind wants the future to be. One need not believe literally in clairvoyance; one can utilize the assumptions that help to create metaphors that are true to the psyche's sense of the connectedness between past, present, and future. The mind, knowing the past, aware of the present, seeks a future that is not simply the passage of time from the present to some new present but is indeed the created moments that are the result of all that we have done and thought previously. The search for a past is the search for a future, but a future that must be created from the past as an act of self-discovery and self-definition.

In moments of special consciousness both past and future may be revealed. Such moments occur in dreams, such as the ones "no less prophetic and equally promising" that "haunt-

[13] *The Lancet* (Jan. 5, 1839), 561-562. Clarke, pp. 173-177.
[14] The assumptions of clairvoyance are set out in an account "collected by Dr. Elliotson" of "Reports of various trials of clairvoyance of Alexis Didier, last summer, in London," *The Zoist*, Vol. II, No. VIII (Jan. 1845), 477-537. Elliotson's sober doubts about clairvoyance are expressed in *The Zoist*, Vol. IX, No. XXXV (Oct. 1851), 234 *passim*.

ed" Mrs. Nickleby's sleep (*NN*, xxvii). They occur in mesmeric trance, when prophetic powers sometimes become so strong that the future is revealed. Clairvoyance is the process of seeing more clearly what one has done and is doing. For what one can see of the future has often already been determined by the past. Lady Dedlock's "eyes are on the fire. In search of what? Of any hand that is no more, of any hand that never was, of any touch that might have magically changed her life? Or does she listen to the Ghost's Walk, and think what step does it most resemble? A man's? A woman's? The pattering of a little child's feet, ever coming on—on—on?" (*BH*, xxviii.) The interrogative mood is the future-seeking mood. Dickens uses it often. What was seen? What was thought? Did she know? Did he remember? From novel to novel, above and beyond the mere rhetorical exercise of interrogating neat solutions to obvious plot problems or affirming some sentimentality, Dickens uses it as a connection between past and future. Lady Dedlock is constantly on the edge of futurity. She frequently anticipates the next sequence of events. As her predicament worsens, her nervous anticipations are dramatized by her unanswered questions. We know what she knows and just a little more: that the "touch that might have magically changed her life" will never come unless it comes to transform her into no life at all. She has no future because she cannot reconcile her past and her present. The past must destroy her because of her knowledge that her present self is at war with the past on which it must be based. She sees in the fire what once was and what can never be.

When Dickens told the story of "meeting someone in the busy London streets" whom he assumed to be a friend and "walked on again until he actually met the real friend, whose shadow, as it were, but a moment ago had come across his path," he was affirming his commitment to the metaphors of double consciousness and clairvoyance. The mind knows certain things before it has a right to know them. Physical laws are the lesser laws, partial restrictions on certain of our faculties, not to be taken as total reality. But what would Dickens have answered to the question, was it clairvoyance or was it creation? Had the mind anticipated what was necessarily to come, or had the needs of the mind created the future that it naturally knew of at the moment of creation and inevitably found confirmation for in the reality?

The question is, of course, unanswerable in any formal sense. But novels do not exist on that level of reality. They have a created reality as their very essence. They are attempts not to answer such a question but to dramatize the centricity of the powers and the needs of the mind in terms of the human experience in which the past and future are central to what we are and what we can become. The defeated Mr. Bounderby "stood before the fire; projecting himself after his old explosive manner into his portrait— and into futurity." But Mr. Bounderby's egomania and insensitivity are indomitable. Nothing can defeat them except death. His sense of self may be assailed but it will never be defeated or even altered by human conflicts. He can stare intently into the fire. But what can he see? "Into how much of futurity?" Dickens asks, as the first of a series of such questions in the concluding paragraphs of *Hard Times* (III:ix). "Did he catch any glimpse of himself making a show of Bitzer to strangers. . . . Did he see any faint reflection of his own image making a vainglorious will. . . . Had he any prescience of the day, five years to come, when Josiah Bounderby of Coketown was to die of a fit in the Coketown street . . . ? Probably not." Since Bounderby will not look at his past, he cannot see the future, which means, in effect, that he cannot create a worthwhile future for himself. He cannot be transformed into a better self.

The series of questions is taken up again. "How much of futurity did [Mr. Gradgrind] see? Did he see himself . . . making his facts and figures subservient to Faith, Hope and Charity. . . ?" And then for a third time, "How much of the future might arise before [Louisa's] vision?" Clairvoyant power increases from Mr. Bounderby, who has none; to Mr. Gradgrind, who has renounced his former mechanism but has but small "foreknowledge"; to Louisa, who can see certain future things "plainly"; to Cissy Jupe, who has a sure knowledge that "these things were to be." The concluding emphasis is unmistakable. "Dear reader! It rests with you and me, whether, in our two fields of action, similar things shall be or not" (III:ix). The future is to be created, not discovered. Made, not received. Foreknowledge is simply an extension of the power of the mind in the present to extend itself confidently into the future because it knows that the future is its creation. Dickens, of course, had great faith in such powers, in his own and in the possibility of ours. Mesmerism helped him "to form some glimmering conception of [the mind's] mighty powers, its bounding from earth and spurning time and space" (*OT*, ix).

CHAPTER

VII

The Sources of Evil

The mesmeric force that pervades the universe is volatile
and seemingly inexplicable. How is it to be brought under
control? And will it be used for ends positive or negative in
respect to Dickens' conception of human welfare and the
Victorians' sense of consonance with universal harmony?
Dickens' vision demanded that he explore both the faculty
that permits the operator to harness this energy and the
quality of his use of it. A wide range of human personalities
and relationships could be the substance of this exploration,
for every conceivable facet of human activity lent itself to
description and analysis in the language that Dickens had
learned from his mesmeric experience. To the mesmerists,
the faculty that controls this universal fluid is "will" or
"will power." Human beings are the fortunate and graced
possessors of "will": great expectations for the individual
and society are plausible in direct ratio to the resources of
"will" available to both.

The earliest English mesmerists, like Chenevix and Elliotson, initially maintained that the mesmeric fluid could
be tapped and communicated with the operator acting only
as a mediator, creating the contact but hardly controlling it.
Mesmerists with scientific backgrounds found the theory

suitable, amenable to their standards of objectivity. It would not do to put excessive power into the hands of the operator. Rumor suggested that mesmerism could be used for self-serving ends. The power the mesmerist could exert over his subjects through the exercise of his will could lead to results that might be destructive both to subject and operator and to the general safety of society. One of the earliest of the opponents of mesmerism in England feared that it would be used for political advantage as a tool of mass persuasion.[1]

Elliotson felt such objections sharply. He assured a concerned friend of Dickens' that "It is not necessary to will— I have seen the effects produced when the operator knew not his object was not aware of what he was doing—still this will is thought by many to increase the effect decidedly; and that this will is influential is proved by the undoubted fact of the effect being produced on a distant, absent person." Elliotson could not deny the centricity of the controlling mechanism: "The will, I presume, works upon the brain—though, possibly on other parts of the nervous system directly." So potent is the force that "the blind person may be mesmerized, I often do it with the eyes of the person shut. I have frequently done it behind the patient's back, with or without his knowledge." And the mesmeric force is not structurally complex or difficult to focus: "The power is apparently elementary: for it may be communicated through the means of inanimate objects, applied to the patients when the operator is not aware of it. . . . Many phenomena are sympathetic. The patient will taste, smell, and feel when and as the operator is . . . affected."[2] And also, as many feared, do precisely what the operator requests. Such a request would indeed be a command.

By the mid-1840's most of the professionals and all of the amateurs of mesmerism had vaguely grasped what Dickens

[1] See John Pearson, *A Plain and Rational Account of the Nature and Effect of Animal Magnetism* (London, 1790), pp. 30-32.
[2] See Morgan MS., Elliotson to unknown correspondent, 5/4/39 (?).

had seen with clear and almost instantaneous intuition, the novelist leaping ahead of the intellectual movement from which he had learned: "will power" was the agent that harnessed this force of universal energy. He felt himself a gifted individual, possessing the ability to focus and transmit such power. His own will was indisputable, verging on the tenacity of a stubbornness so extreme as to be an act of constant self-definition. In his life he constantly expanded his capacity for energy and control. In his fiction the emphasis on energy and will began to become paramount as early as when the oppressed Oliver summoned up the potential resources of force within himself and "defied" Noah Claypole "with an energy he had never known before" (*OT*, VI). For the quality and achievement of a man are inseparable from the degree of force of will within him, his capacity to rouse himself into dominating action.

The amount of the mesmeric fluid in the cosmos, however, is given, neither to be increased nor decreased by human effort or manipulation. It is the raw potential for human doing, ultimately measurable, if only adequate tools are available. Perhaps some individuals have this potential within them more than do others. It was also possible that the potential was equally distributed. The Victorians disagreed on this point. The mechanism of control, the will power, however, differed from person to person. It was the only agent through which the force could be seen in operation at all. Without will, then, the mesmeric fluid was not only non-quantifiable; it was not observable ever. Only in the context of human actions could one observe and describe the force. By its effects, it could be known—no other way. So here, then, was the challenge to the novelist as well as to the scientist, to Dickens as well as to Elliotson. Casebooks were necessary. A record of the various manifestations of the force within human behavior has to be established in order to be able to make generalizations and come to conclusions. But for the novelist there was a creation, not a record, a novel, not a casebook, to be composed. By its effects it can be known is the novelist's maxim. Not that Dickens ever created fiction to demonstrate a theory, but his fiction was inevitably based upon his assumptions about the nature of human beings and the powers available to them.

[2]

Energy seems to sparkle on the pages of Dickens' fiction, under the control of a purposeful will and in the interest of the exertion of power for some vision of how things might be as well as how things are. The act of creation demands the fullest use of this vital force, inseparable from "the triumphs of . . . art" upon which David Copperfield bestowed ". . . every energy of [his] soul" (*DC*, LXI), "a patient and continuous energy . . . which I know to be the source of my success" (*DC*, XLII). But the force can be destructive as well as creative. When men have repressed it, often for self-serving ends, and when the restraints are loosened in circumstances of crisis, the result may be disastrous: "the wild energy of the man, now quite let loose, was absolutely terrible" (*OMF*, II:xv). Bradley Headstone has suppressed his natural energy, like Jeremiah Flintwinch, whose "natural acerbity and energy, always contending with a second nature of habitual repression, gave his features a swollen and suffused look" (*LD*, I:III). Not given its head, the force literally takes Flintwinch's head, distorting it into a twisted manifestation of self-destructiveness. But "less" than "ordinary natures may lie by for years, ready on the touch of an instant to burst into flame" (*OMF*, II:XI), so ultimately irrepressible is the "motive power" of all things.[3]

When the energy level of an individual is low or nonexistent, it is because he is cut off from this basic power. Energylessness in the Dickens canon is even worse than "misdirected energy," with which the self-indulgent Harold Skimpole charges Jo the Crossing Sweep: "At our young friend's natural dinner hour" he "says . . . 'I am hungry;

[3] Henry Hall Sherwood, *The Motive Power of Organic Life* (London 1841).

will you have the goodness to produce your spoon, and feed me?' Society . . . does *not* produce that spoon; and our young friend, therefore, says, 'You really must excuse me if I seize it.' Now, this appears to me a case of misdirected energy'' (*BH*, xxxi). But Skimpole has no energy at all and resents the waste of resources by Jarndyce on someone who has the ability to look after himself. Without energy, however, his self is diminished, fallen, corrupt. To serve his needs, he would dehumanize others, particularly competitors for society's spoon, preferring to view Jo as an abstract illustration of a principle rather than as a person. His reproach, disguised as compliment and self-deprecation, is that " 'You are ready at all times to go anywhere, and do anything.' " But doing, Skimpole recognizes, is directly related to the desire to control and communicate such force, for " 'Such is Will!' " But " 'I have no Will at all—and no Won't— simply Can't.' "

The simple matter of the rejection of "doing" is a rejection of mesmeric fluid, the force suffusing all things, even oneself; consequently it is a denial of oneself and others. It is the Dickens version of Coleridge's "death-in-life." The absence of energy indicates enervation and purposelessness. Sometimes it is the self-indulgence of irresponsible pseudo-artistic gratification, as in the case of Skimpole. At other times, such absolute staticism is the result of some great shock to the psyche, so severe that a kind of psychological paralysis results, as with Miss Havisham, perpetually isolated in her wheelchair at Satis House, rejecting all but the most minimal confrontation with the world of the present. Sometimes, even in such withdrawal, a dialectic between paralysis and energy continues, such as the occasional spurts of frenetic plotting of Mrs. Clennam, seemingly immovable in the house of her hidden crimes. Or sometimes a complacent psyche finds the most unshakeable satisfaction in its position in society. Consequently lassitude and indifference to the problems of others become a suitable projection of self-image, as in the case of Sir Leicester Dedlock, whose marmoreal solidity is immovable; as in the instance of Sir John Chester, who finds raw energy, like Barnaby's, vulgar, and whose favorite retreat is the quietude of his comfortable bed.

But this is energylessness by choice. Many characters in Dickens' fiction are not blessed with such alternatives. Their fate is more pathetic. Some circumstance beyond individual control has reduced them to inactivity. Wemmick's "Aged P" is made almost inoperable as a human being by senility. "Mr. F's Aunt" is reduced to irrational but bitterly aggressive comments on those who represent to her some insult to her condition. Mr. Wickfield's alcoholism has made him the energyless slave of Uriah Heep, scarcely more capable of exertion for himself than Dr. Manette, imprisoned in the Bastille and driven mad by his isolation. For there are states of consciousness like senility, insanity, alcoholism, opium trance, and eventually death, in which energy is completely denied and the human being reduced to much less than human stature.

Purposeful denials of energy, however, are more to be feared and eventually more destructive and damning. They are a perversion of natural forces self-consciously undermined as an act of irresponsible self-destruction by those who may have the power to recreate themselves as superior human beings. To deny energy is to deny the value of work, and to throw doubt on the significance of human achievements in a wide variety of fields. It is, of course, to discredit art and the artist through the implication that art is no more worth doing than anything else; it is the ultimate nihilism, an attack on the very basis of the artist's life, the one activity that for Dickens remains unchallengeable.

The energyless often deny the existence of projects worth exerting one's energy for. Dickens will not permit such nihilism without exposure: " 'Then idiots talk,' said Eugene, 'of Energy. If there is a word in the dictionary under any letter from A to Z that I abominate, it is energy. It is such a conventional superstition, such parrot gabble!' 'Precisely my view of the case, Eugene. But show me a good opportunity, show me something really worth being energetic about, and *I'll* show you energy.' 'And so will I,' said Eugene" (*OMF*, I:III). But Eugene is to discover, through a catastrophic experience, that the energy that he has suppressed must find expression. He learns that his mysterious energy is inseparable from sympathetic identification with others. It connects all things and all people, and consequently is particularly consonant with relationships of love. This energy may direct one outwards toward others.

But to do this one must first establish an active identity through the exertion of energy under the control of will. Without such self-identity one is at the mercy of external forces that may diminish one even more. Georgiana Podsnap "has no strength of will or character to help herself, and she is on the brink of being sold into wretchedness for life" (*OMF*, II:xvi). The corrupt strong prey on the innocent weak. Affery Flintwinch has no "Will or way of her own," and "her personality was swallowed up," her self-identity lost (*LD*, I, v). She finds herself again through an act of the will: " 'No, I won't, Jeremiah—no, I won't—no, I won't! I won't go! I'll stay here. I'll hear all I don't know, and say all I know. I will, at last, if I die for it. I will, I will, I will, I will' " (*LD*, II:xxx). Arthur Clennam has been cut off from internal and external sources of energy. He is "liable to be drifted where any current may set." When Mr. Meagles urges him to go directly to London "with a will," he responds that " 'I have no will. That is to say . . . none that I can put in action now. . . . Will, purpose, hope? All those lights were extinguished before I could sound the words' " (*LD*, I:II). Dickens began by suggesting that " 'where there's a will, there's a way' " (*NN*, xxii). But Smike's grave is not a monument to success. Some insurmountable circumstance may ensure that an individual's willpower will not be strong enough for the task.

There are people whose power of will is indomitable, who have a superabundance of that force. They are Dickens' heroes and his villains, in contact with the vital force of the universe and with the potential to use it for either good or evil. They are characterized by the manifestations of their great energy under the control of their desires, strong magnets in a gravitational field weaker than their magnetism. They are forces to reckon with, strong in their sense of purpose, like George Rouncewell, " 'as self-willed and as determined a man, in the wrong way, as ever put a human creature under Heaven, out of patience! You could as soon take up and shoulder an eight-and-forty pounder by your own strength, as turn that man. . . .' " (*BH*, LII). So strong can this power of will be that it can almost literally raise the dead. When Mr. Inspector in *Our Mutual Friend* applies his will to the removal from the river of a snagged corpse he directly addresses the hidden prize: " 'I mean to have it. Come!' he added, at once persuasively and with authority to the hidden object in the water, as he played the line again; 'it's no good this sort of game, you know. You *must* come up. I mean to have you.' " And he does. "There was so much virtue in this distinctly and decidedly meaning to have it, that it yielded a little, even while the line was played. 'I told you so,' quoth Mr. Inspector, pulling off his outer coat, and leaning well over the stern with a will, 'Come!' " (*OMF*, I:XIV).

Dickens' heroes succeed when they discover their will to be energetic and use that energy for beneficial purposes. However, in the Dickens world, energy, will, and power are perplexingly distributed, not according to the dictates of some morally purposeful distributor but in a pattern that threatens to persuade us that guided benevolence in the universe is minimal. George Rouncewell may be stubborn, "self-willed . . . in the wrong way." His blunt self-affirmation, though, is in the service of a constructive moral vision. But the forceful energy level and will power of many of the most fascinating and vivid Dickens characters are in the service of total self-interest. The Victorian codes of convention may demand the defeat of evil. Dickens himself may need to demonstrate the superiority of moral force over immoral energy. But the defeat can never be reassuring when the villains as a total impression manifest more energy and will than the heroes and heroines. Certainly this is a perplexing and complicated moral world.

For Dickens is deeply concerned with the nature of evil, the problems of dramatizing the complex reality of human motivations. The minor villain of hypocritical self-definition may boast of his machismo in terms of his will, like Walter Bray, who claims " 'that there was a time, when I carried every point in triumph . . . by my will alone' " (*NN*, xlvii). Fortunately such non-entities do not have the stature to have a major effect on main characters. They contribute to an atmosphere of self-serving gratification. They are the shadows of threat that flicker in the Dickens world as externalized projections of the anxieties that the Dickens hero senses surround him in a very ambiguous environment. But they also threaten to transform him from within. He may become the victim of some combination of his own weaknesses and the fallen models that the world presents for him to pattern himself after. Something could easily go wrong; some unpredictable turn in the road could be taken; and what awaits one there is oneself transformed into the "goroo, goroo" nightmare man who cheats David Copperfield, or into the cheap confidence man who sells Martin Chuzzlewit mutually self-serving commercial illusions. Such characters are warnings of what we may become at our most minimal.

Miss La Creevy remarks to Nicholas Nickleby that " 'the power to serve is as seldom joined with the will, as the will is with the power . . .' " (*NN*, xx). In the Dickens opus the power to serve is rarely joined with the will to serve others. But the power to serve is often joined with the will to serve oneself. For every character like Sydney Carton, who "with wonderful quickness, and with a strength both of will and action, that appeared quite supernatural . . . forced all these changes upon" Charles Darnay (*TTC*,

III:XIII), there are dozens who use their wills to manipulate others for self-serving ends. In the Dickens world the use of mesmeric energy and will for the repression of the selfhood of others to serve the pleasures of the corrupted self is evil. Like the very kind of operator the Victorian anti-mesmerists feared, Fagin rejoices in the prospect of Oliver's being " 'ours! Ours for his life . . . my power over him,' " and ponders how " 'can I increase my influence with her [Nancy]? What new power can I acquire' " (*OT*, XIX:XLIV)?

When two operators clash, even as uneasy allies, the stronger predominates. Ralph Nickleby controls Squeers through the superior force of his will, channeled into devices that communicate his power. "Ralph . . . once more regained the hard immovable inflexible manner which was habitual to him, and to which, perhaps, was ascribable no small part of the influence which, over many men of no very strong prejudices on the score of morality, he could exert almost at will" (*NN*, LVI). To control Squeers he appeals to Squeers' desire to control Smike. " 'The knowledge that he was again in your power would be the best punishment you could inflict upon your enemy' " (*NN*, LVI). And it is in terms of this brute psychological domination that Ralph Nickleby explains the world, seeing his enemies in his own terms, simply as variants of himself. He imagines that Mrs. Nickleby is an automaton manipulated by her son, " 'because I don't believe that under his control, you have the slightest will of your own' " (*NN*, XLV). Ralph's may be a small explosion in comparison to the cannonade assault of a Quilp, but the principle is the same: human relationships are determined by the way in which will power is used as an effective instrument of the energy level of one person to dominate another.

In the Dickens world the will to control for self-serving ends is usually ultimately frustrated—but not without great cost to the innocent and to the ordinary balance of man's affairs. The trivial Merry Pecksniff discovers that she is under the power of a demanding master who dominates by force of will to make her a slave of his needs. " 'I am very humble and submissive. You told me you would break my spirit, and you have done so.' He . . . looked at her, for the moment, through his wicked eyes. For the moment only: for, with the same hurried return to something within himself, he bade her in a surly tone, show her obedience by executing his commands" (*MC*, XLVI). Clearly the person of weakness can be dominated by the person of concentrated strength of will. David Copperfield's horror at a dramatization of this lesson is a major step in his progress toward maturity. He sees the perversion of energy and will, and its potential for both good and evil: "The reversal of the two natures, in their relative positions, Uriah's of power and Mr. Wickfield's of dependence, was a sight more painful to me than I can express. If I had seen an Ape taking command of a Man, I should hardly have thought it a more degrading spectacle" (*DC*, XXXV). But David, on one level of consciousness, resists the main point: that man is both ape and man. Nature contains this universal energy to be utilized by will for evil or for good ends, as the individual and the society will it. David resists the lesson stubbornly. But Dickens does not. He makes David's imperception a stage in the growth of his fictional consciousness. In earlier novels he had dramatized the possibility of the neutrality of the force. In later novels, like *Great Expectations, Little Dorrit*, and *Our Mutual Friend*, he makes it quite clear that it is a natural phenomenon that man can use for whatever purpose he chooses.

An astounding character like Quilp makes the point for Dickens as early as the beginning of the 1840's. He dominates *The Old Curiosity Shop* the way he dominates the other characters in the novel: with the force of his will. He draws upon resources of energy so immense that only the ultimate need of Dickens and his readers for a comic reconciliation and the defeat of evil triumphs over him. Quilp will not accept any attempt to place boundaries on his expression of his energy. Meanly heroic, a twisted representation of the modern ethos, he is a mock Byron reduced to dwarfism. He believes that all relationships are contests based on the exertion of will. The force is there to be used and he would rather be a master than a slave. For there are those who have the power to reduce others to psychological insignificance as well as to physical servitude. An individual can be made into an automaton or an animal or a slave, his sense of self diminished. Estella "came back, with some bread and meat and a little mug of beer. She put the mug down on the stones of the yard, and gave me the bread and meat without looking at me, as insolently as if I were a dog in disgrace. I was so humiliated, hurt, spurned, offended, angry, sorry—I cannot hit upon the right name for the smart . . . that tears started to my eyes" (*GE*, viii). Pip cannot quite identify what has been done to him. Estella wishes to keep him the way Mr. Jaggers keeps her mother, as "a wild beast tamed" (*GE*, xxv), the way Sikes keeps his dog, Uriah Heep Mr. Wickfield, and Steerforth Rosa Dartle. Fanny Dorrit proclaims that she'll " 'make a slave' " of Sparkler: " 'I shall make him fetch and carry . . . and I shall make him subject to me' " (*LD*, II:vi).

But not all domination is achieved so aggressively. Special wiles can be used. To serve her own ends, Mrs. Lammle discovers that the recently wealthy Bella Wilfer "had a fascinating influence over her" (*OMF*, III:v). Cissy Jupe's greatest triumph, unusual in the Dickens canon, is that through "her plain faith in the truth and right of what she said . . . she had asserted . . . influence over" Mr. Harthouse beyond what a more cunning effort would have been able to achieve (*HT*, III:ii). But Cissy is unusual. Innumerable Dickens characters are consummate fabricators of situation and self to serve their own needs. Sometimes the effort is quite conscious and purposeful, as with Mr. Pecksniff, and with Silas Wegg, who uses his proletarian cunning to hoist himself up into the graces of the middle class. At other times, the effort is a spontaneous expression of some great gift of personality that permits the individual to bring others into the orbit of his influence. Steerforth has a natural charisma, "an ease in his manner . . . which I still believe to have borne a kind of enchantment with it . . . in virtue of this carriage, his animal spirits, his delightful voice, his handsome face and figure, and, for aught I know, of some inborn power of attraction beside (which I think a few people possess), to have carried a spell with him to which it was a natural weakness to yield, and which not many persons could withstand" (*DC*, VII). But Steerforth, of course, is a master at exploiting other people's need to subordinate themselves to superior human beings who have been divinely favored with such gifts. And Dickens shared the myth. He believed himself to be one of those favored human beings.

Human nature and circumstance, however, are such that people of strong will are often in conflict with themselves and others. They feel the pain of inner struggle when they attempt to repress their natural energies. Unusual characters like Mr. Chester dominate almost effortlessly, epitomizing Dickens' view of the corrupt sophistication of aristocracy at its worst. Hugh is baffled by Chester's maneuvers and his "submission was complete" (*BR*, XXIII). Usually a Dickens character resorts to violence mainly because his will has failed. Hugh kidnaps Dolly Varden because he cannot subdue her in any other way. Orlick attempts to murder Pip because he has no other means of power. Jonas Chuzzlewit murders Tigg Montague because his will power has failed him in his contest with the swindler. Bradley Headstone and Rogue Riderhood become violent because they see no other way to accomplish their ends. They act with the bitterness of frustrated losers, appealing desperately to their last disastrous weapon. And in certain instances, like those of Ralph Nickleby, Bill Sikes, and Bradley Headstone, it turns upon them or they turn it upon themselves.

"Power (unless it be the power of intellect or virtue) has ever the greatest attraction for the lowest natures" (*OMF*, III:VII). Dickens' world is filled with such "low natures," with those who have an inherent predilection for the misuse of the energy that is made available to them through their willpower. Mr. Wegg, like a parodied and asexual Marquis de Sade, exalts in the rhetoric of domination. Mr. Boffin " 'should be severely handled by them his masters, and should be kept in a state of abject moral bondage and slavery' " (*OMF*, III:vii). When the opportunity arrives, "Mr. Wegg . . . walked him out by the arm, asserting a proprietorship over his soul and body" (*OMF*, IV:iii). Often the power relationship involves some commercial element, "the lowest nature" striving to exert control to enrich itself. The urge to dominate may be translated entirely into symbols of economic power, Dickens' hated "cash-nexus," the Midas touch of men like Merdle, who exist as the projections of other people's greed. For wealth is the power of buying and selling in a society in which almost everyone and everything is for sale. Cash is a tool of control as powerful in some instances as mesmeric force. The great merchants are dealers, like Wegg, in human flesh. Edith Skewton will not let her mother escape with euphemisms. " 'You know he has bought me. . . . Or that he will, to-morrow. He has considered of his bargain . . . and he will buy to-morrow' " (*DS*, xxvii). Ralph Nickleby, Fagin, Mr. Dombey, Mr. Chuzzlewit, Mr. Bounderby, Mr. Merdle, the entrepreneurs of the Dickens world are dealers in the master-and-slave trade.

But in Dickens' fiction cash is an unnatural instrument of control in competition with the natural forces of energy and will. The most dramatic conflicts occur when the two forces come into opposition, often within the same individual. Money power and mesmeric power are at best uneasy allies, more often hostile competitors for the same territory. Edith Skewton, like Lady Dedlock, has an extraordinarily strong sense of self. Her normal mode is to control others rather than to be controlled. But the force of money is in conflict with the natural force of her personality. She confronts the possibility that she must suffer the defeat of the natural energy and will that define her individuality: "Compress into one handsome face the conscious self-abasement, and the burning indignation of a hundred women, strong in passion and in pride" (*DS*, xxvii). For " 'there is no slave in a market; there is no horse in a fair; so shown and offered and examined, as I have been.' "

In contrast, Lady Dedlock represents the attempt of the possessor of natural power to make an accommodation with economic power. The results are equally disastrous. Though "the power and force of this woman are astonishing" (*BH*, xli), she has had to destroy her own child and to suppress her instincts in order to possess wealth and status. She eventually learns that the accommodation is an unnatural and hence destructive one. The suppressed forces of willful self-assertion within her need more expression than that afforded by social position alone. They eventually demand that the accommodation be destroyed. As the wife of Sir Leicester, she has renounced the natural expression of her willpower; she is reduced to expressions of an aristocratic social will that is hard to distinguish from snobbery. Ultimately her position becomes untenable. The energy and will of Hortense, Tulkinghorn, and finally of Mr. Bucket defeat Lady Dedlock's efforts at accommodation. Finding herself forced to face the needs of her suppressed will, she becomes master of herself only at the cost of her life.

When will and energy are in the service of some generous impulse they are sometimes potent enough to defeat the destructive use of economic power or the evil use of mesmeric force. The defeat is often partial and temporary, but it is a moment precious enough in its realization and hopeful enough in its promise to be the dramatic moment of climax and sometimes resolution in Dickens' fiction. But it is not often there. When Madame Defarge, a woman of great willpower, who has made it the essence of her own self-definition to have power over other people's lives, confronts the determined Miss Pross with her request for information about "the wife of Evremonde," she is rebuffed and prevented from searching the house. "Madame Defarge made at the door. . . . Miss Pross, with the vigorous tenacity of love, always so much stronger than hate, clasped her tight" (*TTC*, III:xiv). But "love" has such victories only rarely in the Dickens world. In their struggle against the willpower of the evil, the innocent and good often find their salvation through accident or contrivance or the assistance of some third party or most often through the self-destructiveness of their enemies.

Two of Dickens' most energetic and willful women, Miss Wade and Mrs. Clennam in *Little Dorrit*, represent those who become the victims of their own misuse of their inherent powers. Strong of will to translate desire into energetic action, they act out of pained disappointment to make others their slaves. In doing so they make slaves of themselves, bound in their own fetters of psychological limitation. Each begins with what she thinks of as thwarted love but which Dickens describes as self-serving pride in self. Mrs. Clennam is "a female Lucifer in appetite for power . . . a lady of strong force of character . . . a resolved lady, a stern lady, a lady who has a will that can break the weak to powder" (*LD*, II:xxx). Despite her self-willed entombment in her dark room, she exercises influence through time and space over all those whose lives touch hers. So indomitable is she in the perverse force of her conviction that when her enemies close in on her, she attempts to reveal her long-concealed secrets to Little Dorrit. It is the last act of her will to dominate. But so unnatural has been her use of natural energy, so evil the repression of normal instincts, that the paralysis that she had been master of now becomes her master. She falls insensible, permanently paralyzed, destroyed by her misuse of her great gifts.

Somehow in the Dickens world the neutral force of the mesmeric fluid has inherent within it the potential to become the instrument of the destruction of those who misuse it. The force does not take retribution in some objective way. It is too internalized for that, too closely connected with energies that are self-defining and self-revealing. The force does not self-destruct. But the person who misuses it destroys himself, a total act of the personality working itself out in all its ramifications. The responsibility is not that of the natural force but of the individual who has determined how he or she shall use it. Miss Wade's history is that of "a Self-Tormentor" (*LD*, II:xxxi). Dickens implies that the torment is chosen in a world in which the individual has certain opportunities to be a free agent. But the triumph of such freedom comes rarely and only through an exertion of will and energy towards that end. It must be based upon the renunciation of any accommodation with economic and social power. It must be based on a definition of self that places emphasis on the serving of others. It is not societal but individual. Though difficult to achieve, and few are in a position to make the attempt, it is possible.

But Miss Wade has rejected and denied the possibility. Her will is in the service of self-gratification through the establishment of her mastery over those whom she resents. The expressions of her resentments are so central a part of her that she can define herself only in terms of the extent to which she lives them. Having experienced snobbery and poverty, and the power of men to mistreat women, she has transformed her lesbian experiences into a code that is not only anti-male but anti-humanistic. She will eschew all relationships that she cannot control. She will inform the spirit of her relationships with the tension of her aggressiveness. Her primary external victim is Tattycoram, who deserts the Meagles household and enters into a sexually charged relationship with her in which the struggle for mastery is the natural expression of both willful personalities. Miss Wade correctly insists that she has not " 'spirited away' " the young lady, " 'bereft of free choice' " (*LD*, II: xx), for Tattycoram has a will of her own. She nevertheless found " 'it worth her while, for my own pleasure—the gratification of a strong feeling.' "

Like Miss Wade, Tattycoram misuses her will and energy. She constantly imagines slights. She resents Miss Wade's ability to help her and her own vulnerability as much as the Meagles' failure to accept her as a substitute for their lost daughters. The two women are constantly in conflict. "Clennam felt how each of the two natures must be constantly tearing the other to pieces." Miss Wade attempts to reduce her to a servile animal: " 'You are no higher than a spaniel, and had better go back to the people who did worse than whip you.' " But Tattycoram will not accept such dehumanizing servitude. She accuses Miss Wade of being " 'as bad as they were, every bit. But I will not be quite tamed, and made submissive' " (*LD*, II:xx). The power that Miss Wade possesses is not strong enough to destroy Tattycoram, but it is strong enough to create for herself a depraved self, determined to take pleasure in the pain that it inflicts on itself and others. Like Dickens, she recognizes the effectiveness of will and energy in the service of evil. Miss Wade's is no small accomplishment, an indication of Dickens' knowledge that will and energy are central to human relationships and to our understanding of the positive and negative forces within us. Tattycoram concludes that " 'she had got a power over me, through understanding what was bad in me, so well' " (*LD*, II:xxxiii).

[3]

John Jasper folds his arms on top of the parapet and in the moonlight "watches Neville, as though his eye were the trigger of a loaded rifle, and he had covered him, and were going to fire. A sense of destructive power is so expressed in his face . . ." (*ED*, xii). To have the power to dominate others is potentially corrupting. Others may sense and fear that power. Rosa recognizes that Jasper can "bring down the irreparable mischief that he threatened he had the power, and that she knew he had the will, to do" (*ED*, xx). But Rosa attracts to herself people of power; she is sensitive to their emanations; they feel the magnetism of her potential as a subject of their manipulations. " 'O, I am such a mite of a thing, and you are so womanly and handsome. You seem to have resolution and power enough to crush me. I sink into nothing by the side of your presence even.' " Helena responds, " 'My pretty one, can I help it? There is a fascination in you' " (*ED*, vii).

But Jasper attempts to exercise *his* control over Rosa through mesmeric trance. Rosa resists his attempt to mesmerize her. She "shrieked out, with her hands over her eyes: 'I can't bear this! I am frightened! Take me away!' " (*ED*, vii). Jasper's will is to deny her any self but the self of his desires. People and powers, however, do come to her assistance. She seems able to protect herself at the edge of domination by the interruption of hysteria. It works, though, only at crucial moments. She herself is not a creature of aggressive force. On the other hand, Lady Dedlock opposes with determined resources the attack of Tulkinghorn. The lawyer nevertheless imposes his will on hers, until "he has conquered her" (*BH*, xli). The force of his will to expose her and the weakness of her will in the fear of exposure defeat her. She enters into a mesmerized responsum of will-lessness and capitulation. "She asks all her questions as if she were repeating them from memory, or calling them over in her sleep." But Tulkinghorn's imposition of his will is temporary. Lady Dedlock has entered into the rhetoric of mesmerization at least partially voluntarily, as a strategy, and the mood of trance and sleep-waking that she seems to speak from lasts only as long as it is useful to her. Like the O'keys, Lady Dedlock is an actress of great self-control, a "prima donna of the magnetic stage." She destroys herself before she permits herself to be destroyed.

There is no more potent device of mesmerization than the glittering teeth of James Carker, through which he expresses his will to control those who are susceptible. The most vulnerable victim is Rob the Grinder, who becomes Carker's slave, totally in the power of his influence and eager to serve his commands. Dickens does not directly dramatize the process of Rob's coming under Carker's control. But Carker gets his power not only "through understanding what was bad" in Rob but through communicating "a sense of power and authority" that "exacted his most implicit submission and obedience" (*DS*, XLII). Rob becomes an automaton in the control of his master, eagerly anticipating his every wish. Rob himself is not clear about the sources of Carker's power, and dares not ask. But he suspects that perhaps his yielding is the manifestation of his respect for Carker's mastery of the arts of control that he himself "had been a poor scholar at."

Rob admires Carker for the possession and use of self-serving powers that he would wish to emulate. And that admiration then, necessarily, contains fear. In so far as he knows how he would make use of such power if he possessed it, he knows what Carker may do to him. Rob is perfectly suited to be Carker's slave, "watching his pleasure," because he is indeed a proto-Carker, the older man a model of what the younger would like to be. But, of course, Rob can hardly think these things through. One doubts that even under such tutelage he would have achieved the influence of his master. Only vague possibilities of explanation for his "enthralment" faintly glimmer in his consciousness; and Dickens emphasizes the *secret* source of Carker's control over him and its effectiveness, all lost on the boy: "Mr. Carker, perhaps, was better acquainted with the sources of his power, which lost nothing by his management of it" (*DS*, XLII).

The sources of evil, then, are within the human being's manipulation of the mesmeric fluid that suffuses all things. And in the Dickens world the force is so often used negatively that one senses that the struggle within Dickens' life and fiction to assert the victory of the beneficent forces is realized only at the price of dramatizing the evil forces so vividly that the threat of control in the human world remains a stronger reality than the occasional rare balance between shadow and sunlight in the lives of fortunate individuals. For example, two vigorous dramatizations of great energy and will, Mr. Gashford and Lord George Gordon, are complementary forces of destruction. The former attempts to control the latter, the latter to control the populace. But Dickens is at his novelistic best in *Barnaby Rudge* in the interaction between them, as Gashford uses mesmerism quite self-consciously to keep George Gordon in his power and Lord George Gordon quite unself-consciously uses mesmerism to influence a large popular movement. Lord George's motto on his coat of arms is "called and chosen and faithful." The words of this motto of electness are used as the very tools by which Lord George is dominated by Mr. Gashford, who perceives the weaknesses of his master and knows that the seeming master can become the actual slave. Gashford is a mesmerist. Lord George proclaims that " 'I will be worthy of the motto on my coat of arms.' 'Called,' said the secretary, 'by Heaven.' 'I am.' 'Chosen by the people.' 'Yes.' 'Faithful to both.' 'To the block!' It would be difficult to convey an adequate idea of the excited manner in which he gave these answers to the secretary's promptings . . . something wild and ungovernable which broke through all restraint" (*BR*, xxxv). But it is just this that Gashford has learned how to control.

Lord George is given to strange states of consciousness in which he seeks a new self, for his present self is unstable. It is in Gashford's interest to keep this unstable personality collected for the time being into its present persona. For Gashford has use for him. When Lord George tells Gashford one of his dreams, Gashford makes clear to what use he has put the motto on the coat of arms. Lord George awakens and expresses surprise that Gashford is not a Jew for " 'I dreamed that we were Jews, Gashford. You and I— both of us—Jews with long beards.' " Gashford remonstrates deceitfully:

" 'I hope my lord—' the secretary began. 'Hope!' he echoed, interrupting him. 'Why do you say, you hope? There's no harm in thinking of such things.' 'Not in dreams,' returned the secretary. 'In dreams! No, nor waking either.'—'Called, and chosen, and faithful,' said Gashford, taking up Lord George's watch which lay upon a chair, and seeming to read the inscription on the seal, abstractedly.

"It was the slightest action possible, not obtruded on his notice, and apparently the result of a moment's absence of mind, not worth remark. But as the words were uttered, Lord George, who had been going on impetuously, stopped short, reddened, and was silent. Apparently quite unconscious of this change in his demeanour, the wily secretary stepped a little apart, under pretence of pulling up the window-blind . . ." (*BR*, xxxvii).

Gashford has used the motto and the watch ("if I hide my watch . . .") as mesmeric tools of control. Lord George is brought into the submission of mesmeric trance in which Gashford's will controls his own. The operator imposes himself on another self, for self-serving ends.

This is the action of evil. But what is its source? It is not the mesmeric fluid. That force is natural and neutral. It may be used well, it may be used badly; it may serve others, it may serve the self's narrowest needs. The source of evil, then, is totally within human beings. So perhaps the place where evil comes from is more closely connected to the human will. For the will seems in Dickens' world to be a volitional force, under the control of the individual. But why do certain wills demand control and create personalities, relationships, and personal histories that would be called by Dickens and his contemporaries "morally wrong"? Is there some mechanism that determines how one shall use one's will, to what ends? If "the chosen" are given strong wills, what or who is to determine how they use them? If the control of that energy is within the power of the individual, then what within individuals determines that one shall use his will for good and another for evil ends? The questions multiply. They are Dickens' questions.

CHAPTER

VIII

The Sexuality of Power

⟦ 1 ⟧

One special kind of control that pulses through Dickens' fiction with all its ambiguities, threats, and anxieties is sexual domination and submission. Do we really find "so little suggestion of sexual or sensuous love in his novels"?[1] Of course we must distinguish between manifestations of the sexual drive on the one hand and sexual love-making on the other. Across the beds of the latter Dickens draws an obscuring curtain, just as he does across the "passions" of his own marital and extra-marital "affairs." Sometimes Dickens creates characters who make no appeal to the erotic imagination; at other times the sexual content is so strong that we sense indeed that Dickens intends these characters to have the dimension of sexual force that only the reader's imagination can help create. It is not a question of direct depiction of overt sexual acts but of characters whose sexuality is such that we cannot deny them the inevitable but undepicted completion of their basic drives.

In Dickens' fiction we are frequently in the world of indirect eroticism, the passions, the manipulations, and the potential violence of a sexuality deeply embedded in power

[1] Pamela Hansford Johnson, "The Sexual Life in Dickens's Novels," *Dickens 1970, Centenary Essays*, ed. Michael Slater (N.Y., 1970), p. 193.

relationships. Individuals of strong will and aggressive energy seek to impose themselves on others, to control the psyches and the bodies of those to whom they are attracted. One of the basic drives is to manipulate others for one's own gratification, to satisfy the needs of the self to have itself constantly affirmed through having other selves in its control. The threat is one of nullity: the self may not exist. What better way to provide demonstration of its existence than through the reactions of others to its assertive acts? But the assertion of the self is an act of the will, drawing upon the resources of energy made available by nature through the mesmeric fluid. So many of the relationships in Dickens' fiction that dramatize the Victorian concern with mesmeric force are implicitly sexual. They are relationships in which the dynamic of the dominating operator and the submissive subject convey the implications of the pleasure-giving and the pain-receiving that we associate with sado-masochistic sex. Dickens and his contemporaries had their own framework and vocabulary for such sexuality, and obviously saw it as central to human consciousness.

The early hostility to mesmerism, among the moral arbiters of Victorian society, came from a general sense of the potential danger of one human being's holding concentrated power over another. For the Victorians found unpersuasive the claim that the mesmerized subject would not perform acts contrary to his normal standards of behavior. Normal standards were not all that high, and, at any rate, the danger came from the possibility of a humanly fallible if not corrupt operator forcing his desires upon a vulnerable subject who could not have the resources to resist successfully. Even the distinguished Dr. Elliotson could not escape the connection between mesmerism and sex that was inherent in the minds of experienced people who insisted that domination and submission are sexual impulses. Dickens must have felt deeply, as he had suffered with Elliotson the slanders of Wakley's attacks in *The Lancet* in 1838, the anonymous pamphlet that made the allegations brutally clear: *Eyewitness. A Full Discovery of the Strange Practices of Dr. E. on the Bodies of his Female Patients! At his house . . . with all the secret experiments he makes upon them. . . . The whole as seen by an eye-witness, and now fully divulged!*[2] News accounts of the period luridly described

[2] *The Lancet* (Sept. 1, 1838), 805-811; reprinted (Aug. 7, 1841), 694-699. Characteristic of the sensationalized association of mesmeric power with exploitative sex are these accounts of seductions that appeared in *The Lancet* (Dec. 8, 1838), 414-444; (Dec. 15, 1838), 450-451: "Long before the days of Mesmer and his deluded followers, the effects of certain manipulations, now called 'passes,' on the frames of delicate or nervous females, were known to libertines. That such effects may be readily produced, at the present time, is familiar to every physiologist, and to many of the 'men about town.' The latter, however, influenced by a salutary fear of the law, avoid practicing in public their mesmeric tricks, lest some common-sense view of the case might construe them into what they really are, *indecent assaults*; and, on the other hand, we venture to affirm that there is not a single physiologist in the kingdom, possessed of moral feeling, who would excite, day after day, the nervous systems of young and artless females by a series of manipulations which not only injure the body but frequently lead to a loss of virtue. Many examples of the latter melancholy effect of mesmerism might be adduced. One will suffice; we relate it on the authority of the President of the French Institute. A young French lady, the daughter of a wealthy banker, was placed under the care of a Mesmeriser. The follower of Mesmer was a Polish quack, professing to be a physician. We know not, of course, what may have passed between the impostor and his patient; suffice it to say, that, by some species of 'dislocation,'— or other 'anomalous transposition of the senses' which Mr. Herbert Mayo alone could explain—the young lady was thrown into a profound sleep, and the quack stole her honour. On the discovery of his infamy the Mesmeriser fled to *London*. . . . We mentioned last week, on the authority of the President of the French Institute, the circumstance of a quack having effected the ruin of a young and artless female through the 'mighty magic' of animal magnetism. Since then we have been informed that the seducer is in London, where, under the pretence of disseminating the knowledge of a new science, he is, probably, engaged in seeking fresh food for his libidinous propensities. Another example occurs to our memory: the Hospital St Louis, in Paris. . . . The apothecary of the hospital was a man of strong passions, unscrupulous and without moral principle. The result may be easily imagined. The Parisian Okeys[sic] were thrown into a state of real, or pretended, sleep, and the hospital was disgraced by a series of orgies which only occur amongst licentious enthusiasts. The question of mesmerism and its effects, is one which, in a moral point of view, admits of no debate. . . . What father of a family, then, would admit even the shadow of a mesmeriser within his threshold? Who would expose his wife, or his

seductions in which mesmeric force, often in the hands of las-
civious pseudo-professors, was used to put young women completely at the mercy of sexual advances. The power to usurp
the other's will was seen as inseparable from sexuality, the
assumption being that the strongest male drive is the desire

---

sister, his daughter, or his orphan ward, to the contact of an animal
magnetiser? . . . Should any persons doubt . . . we assure them that a
physician in London, a man of high character and standing in his
profession, was applied to, some time since, by several Russian officers
of rank and fortune, temporarily residing in this country, for instruction in the art of putting persons to sleep, by mesmeric processes, with
the express view, as it ultimately appeared, of exercising their newly-
acquired knowledge in their own country, on unsuspecting females who
might fall within their power. The 'knowledge' was refused on discovery of its object, but what shall we say to a continuance of instruction in this scandalous 'science' in the *private wards of one of our
public hospitals*, where wealthy and, perhaps, libidinous men, are daily
invited to witness the easy mode of producing 'sleep' which has been
invented by one of the physicians? If we even reflect on the *excuse* for
'going to sleep' which mesmerism affords to young and sanguine girls,
we must condemn unsparingly the vicious imposition."
   These are typical of the rumours that the popular as well as the
medical press gave great currency to throughout the 1840's. Dr. Francis
Hawkins in his Harveian Oration responded to Elliotson's defense of
mesmerism made in the Harveian Oration of 1848: "Do not quacks hunt
out the vices or infirmities of mankind to turn them to profit . . . ?
Among quacks, the IMPOSTORS, called MESMERISTS, are in my
opinion the especial FAVOURITES of those, both male and female, in
whom the SEXUAL PASSIONS BURN STRONGLY, either in secret
or notoriously. DECENCY FORBIDS ME TO BE MORE EXPLICIT"
(*The Zoist*, Vol. vi, No. xxiv [Jan. 1849], 404). In his poem "Mesmerism," which DeVane suggests was composed in 1853 (*A Browning Hand-
book*, N.Y., 1955, p. 225), Browning dramatizes some of the fears about
the connection between mesmeric will and power on the one hand and
sexual domination on the other. "Outstanding in the poem in particular is stress on the sexual theme and expression of sexual impulses"
(Jerome M. Schneck, "Robert Browning and Mesmerism," *Bulletin of
the Medical Library Association*, Vol. 44, No. 4, 443-451). While Browning's poem clearly deals with the threat of sexual domination, it provides very little of the titillation that was essential to the effectiveness
of the increasing number of pornographic books that drew upon mesmerism as the century advanced, such as *The Power of Mesmerism, A
Highly Erotic Narrative of Voluptuous Facts and Fancies*, "Printed for
the Nihilists, Moscow, 1891," but somehow copyright in 1969 "by Grove
Press, Inc.," and remaindered by Marboro Book Stores with *Laura Mid-
dleton* as "Two Novels of the Victorian Underground."

190

to succeed in fulfilling sexual needs, often with an unwilling or resisting partner.

But there need be no resisting partners for the male possessed of mesmeric abilities, so the Victorians feared; his power to communicate this force allowed him the opportunity to control the will of his subject. And many of Dickens' most dynamic characters seem to desire nothing as much as the dominance of others for the gratification of their own needs. To subjugate others to their wish is inseparable from their sexuality; indeed, often it *is* their sexuality. Dickens usually does not permit us much more than a carefully veiled description of their heterosexual and autoerotic acts. But their desires are often vividly depicted; and their use of mesmeric will and energy is manifest expression of the inseparability of their drive to dominate and their sexual being.

Evil has its own dynamic in the Dickens world, inseparable from sexual needs. Daniel Quilp's physical repulsiveness is the outer garment of his domineering will, a whirlwind of subjugating energy that seems to represent a perversion of the natural mesmeric force of the universe. He represents the power of doing and having what one wants, particularly in his relationships with women. Quilp most wants the attainment of the gratification of the self that comes from absolute possession of a particular chosen woman. This drive is usually inseparable from other general desires— to control people, to humiliate one's enemies, to achieve wealth and security, to use the power of one's will to satisfy the needs of the ego across a wide range of human activities. But for many Dickens characters the most concentrated desires of will become focused on a single sexual object around which revolve ancillary wide-ranging efforts in many areas and relationships. For Quilp, Rosa Dartle, Bradley Headstone, and John Jasper, the concentration on their single object of sexual gratification is almost monomaniacal; for James Carker, Simon Tappertit, and Uriah Heep, such intensity of focus is lessened by factors of personality and fields of social action, by the equal prominence of desire for economic success or social status.

Gifted with certain natural powers that are only dramatized, not explained, Quilp has an ability to subjugate others through force of energy and will that transforms this deformed specimen of human corruptibility and Philistinism into an irresistible pursuer of women. The one extraordinary woman in the novel escapes his dominance only through her weapon of last resort. But it is she whom he pursues, clearly excited sexually and eager to achieve gratification even through marriage. Of course, such marriages are euphemisms for legalized control, for the institutionalization of the Victorian male impulse to dominate women as an expression of gender and sexuality. Quilp cares nothing for marriage as sacrament. The resonances of the institution established by its traditional position in Judeo-Christian society mean nothing to him. For his pursuit of Nell is an improper one, if only from the point of view of eligibility. But the existence of a current marriage makes no difference to him at all. He sees no reason why the current Mrs. Quilp, whom he brutally tyrannizes, cannot be disposed of at the moment of convenience: " 'How should you like to be my number two, Nelly?' 'To be what, sir?' 'My number two, Nelly; my second; my Mrs. Quilp,' said the dwarf. . . . 'Say that Mrs. Quilp lives five years, or only four, you'll be just the proper age for me. Ha ha! Be a good girl, Nelly, a very good girl, and see if one of these days you don't come to be Mrs. Quilp of Tower Hill' " (*OCS*, VI). He finds Nell " 'such a fresh, blooming, modest little bud . . . so small, so compact, so beautifully modelled, so fair, with such blue veins and such a transparent skin, and such little feet' " (*OCS*, IX).

She is a bud to be plucked, the way Rosa Dartle's name suggests a rose that is destroyed through its unwilling escape from Steerforth, the way Rosa Bud is a young female flower threatened by John Jasper. Nell too is passive, an excitation to the aggressive male who in the Dickens world finds such receptivity more exciting and irresistible than the advances of women who are directly available for sexual gratification. Retreating, unavailable women—like Lizzie Hexam to Bradley Headstone and Eugene Wrayburn, Kate Nickleby to Sir Mulberry Hawk, Emma Haredale to Hugh, Estella to Pip, and Lucie Manette to Sydney Carton—intensify more often than they discourage their pursuers' desires. And with rare exceptions, the aggressive man, using his resources of will and energy to possess a woman for self-gratification, is unsuccessful, though the amount of damage done along the way is often so great as to cast permanent shadows on the lives of the survivors. Little Nell must die to escape Quilp's desires.

Like Simon, Sikes, Hugh, Sir Mulberry Hawk, Carker, Uriah Heep, Pecksniff, James Harthouse, Blandois-Rigaud, Bradley Headstone, John Jasper, among others, Quilp of course has no beneficent ends in mind. His desire to possess Nell, like his desire to dominate all those with whom he comes in contact, is for the gratification of power. The trial of his will against that of others gives him the pleasure of battle, the anticipation of conquest, the self-expansion that comes with absolute dominance. When Quilp proposes a macabre matrimony to Nell, based on his anticipation of the death of his first wife (where "there's a will there's a way" must be Quilp's maxim as well as Nicholas Nickleby's), he notices that "so far from being sustained and stimulated by this delightful prospect, the child shrunk from him, and trembled" (*OCS*, vi). But her manifestation of fear of what it must be like to be possessed by Quilp (even Little Nell is capable of fantasying what life in bed and out with Quilp would be like) actually stimulates the dwarf, who seems to get such pleasurable excitement from similar situations with Nell and others that he appears often on the brink of orgasmic explosions of energy or over the edge into gloating satisfaction.

With the exception of Little Nell, women respond to this Quilpian urge, and it is irresistible. Mrs. Quilp has learned on the bed and with the bruises of experience the close relationship between repulsion and attraction, the conspiracy between dominating male and subjugated female, between operator and subject, that flourishes in a certain psychological-sexual ambiance so common to both the fairy tales and the actual arrangements of Victorian culture. She knows Quilp's power, the force of his will and his sexuality: " 'It's all very fine to talk,' said Mrs. Quilp with much simplicity, 'but I know that if I was to die tomorrow, Quilp would marry anybody he pleased. . . .' There was quite a scream of indignation at this idea" from Mrs. Quilp's female friends gathered in her parlor. "They would like to see him dare to think of marrying any of them; they would like to see the faintest approach to such a thing. One lady (a widow) was quite certain she would stab him if he hinted at it. 'Very well,' said Mrs. Quilp, nodding her head, 'as I said just now, it's very easy to talk, but I say again that I know— that I'm sure—Quilp has such a way with him when he likes, that the best-looking woman here couldn't refuse him if I was dead, and she was free, and he chose to make love to her. Come!' " (*OCS*, iv.)

Quilp hopes that the same techniques of persuasion that are effective with all other women in his and in his wife's real and imagined experience will be successful with Little Nell. For Mrs. Quilp's servitude is made more intense, her position more precarious, by her knowledge of the power that Quilp possesses not only over her but over potential replacements; to the extent that she senses that Quilp would even murder her to fulfill his desires, her subjugation is the more complete. The compensating satisfactions are many, however. She is beaten, mocked, jailed, humiliated, physically teased and taunted, often in the presence of her mother, a member of the household who recognizes that her daughter " 'daren't call her soul her own.' " Such treatment produces not rebellion but submission, not pain alone but some combination of pleasure and pain that Mrs. Quilp finds satisfying indeed. Quilp hopes that he will have with

Little Nell the same responsum of servitude that he has with his wife: " 'Mrs. Quilp! . . . Am I nice to look at? Should I be the handsomest creature in the world if I had but whiskers? Am I quite a lady's man as it is?—am I, Mrs. Quilp?' Mrs. Quilp dutifully replied, 'Yes, Quilp'; and fascinated by his gaze, remained looking timidly at him" (*OCS*, IV).

Quilp's power is mesmeric, his "visual ray" the vehicle through which he transmits to Mrs. Quilp the force of his will. Like many Victorians, she perceives that the vital cosmic energy that certain special people possess with more intensity than others is inseparable from sexuality. Something within her as well as something communicated from Quilp makes it impossible to resist this force. She engages with her husband in a conspiracy of mutual need. Operator and subject, the self and the other, are two sides of the same coin, the self in search of the self's complement, the double needed for self-completion. The subject's submissive response to the operator's mechanisms of control are the manifestation of the subject's desire to be controlled, to find fulfillment through the gratifications of submission.

In the Dickens opus the most interesting relationships are those in which the seeming polarities show the natural affinities and those in which, the natural affinity revealed, the struggle for power is dramatized. Fagin and his boys, Sikes and Nancy, Squeers and Smike, Jonas Chuzzlewit and Merry Pecksniff, Mr. Murdstone and Mrs. Copperfield, Jeremiah and Affery Flintwinch, Jasper and Rosa Bud, among others, are operators and subjects whose complementary needs reveal a shared source of self-definition and gratification. Different Dickens characters do confront themselves and such situations in very different ways. Some are permanently lost in the lure of submission, their selves diminished in the Dickens moral ethos and definition of human potential. Others, like Rosa Bud and Affery, find the resources of self (and the assistance of others) to escape total submission and affirm the possibility of less servile relationships. But

195

characters who seem in conflict often have a natural affinity, the need for the operator to have his subject, for the subject to have his operator. And the repulsion that a victim usually feels for his potential victimizer in Dickens' fiction is the correlative of an equal impetus of attraction, the weak attracted to the strong and the strong to the weak.

Women, however, hardly seem to have the potential to utilize mesmeric force and the will to channel it for beneficent ends. Whenever they seek to assert themselves in the Dickens world, some disappointment, almost like a natural force working from within, frustrates their desires. Only Helena Landless seems ostensibly to possess mesmeric power and the motivation to use it for ends consonant with the moral vision of *Edwin Drood,* or the way in which we imagine it would have been if it had been completed. But women of energy and will, like Lady Dedlock, Rosa Dartle, Edith Skewton, Miss Wade, and Mrs. Clennam, find that something inherent within themselves and their situations destroys them, frustrating their ends, often their lives. Their explosive energy is too connected to sexuality to permit the society of Dickens' fictional world to allow them free and successful expression of their needs. For women are not to be pursuers; they are to be the pursued and the dominated, except in those extraordinary situations in which the pursuer is redeemed through the reconstitution of himself in the exertion of his will for non-self-serving ends. There is the possibility of such relationships, like those of Little Dorrit and Arthur Clennam and Lizzie Hexam and Eugene Wrayburn, in which will power and the dynamic of operator and subject are used finally for constructive purposes.

But usually the burden of the moral quality of the expression of mesmeric force is man's: cultural conditions have given him the opportunity to express himself in ways denied women. And the trial, then, is the man's in such male-dominated fiction; only he has the opportunity to go through fire and water to prove himself worthy. Little Nell, Florence Dombey, Agnes Wickfield, Cissy Jupe, Lucie Manette, and Little Dorrit are worthy by right of birth, as special kinds of women. If Bella Wilfer is the exception, who must be tested and proved, she may be taken as a dramatization of a new attitude towards women that Dickens developed late in his career and might have dramatized quite effectively in the contrast between Rosa Bud and Helena Landless.

In Dickens' fiction there are, of course, strong attraction-repulsion relationships between young girls and older men, sometimes threatening domination (as with Jasper and Rosa Bud), sometimes benevolence (as with John Jarndyce and Esther Summerson). In these cases the sexual content is unmistakable, if only because of the genders of the protagonists and the possibility within the plots of marriages in which male aggressiveness would be fulfilled. However, in the relationship between Rob the Grinder and the manipulative James Carker the normal conventions of the period as they express themselves in Dickens' works do not permit the obvious indications of a sexual relationship. But the relationship of the older man and the young boy (the relationship of Fagin with his boys, of schoolmasters such as Squeers, Creakle, Mell, Blimber, M'choakumchild and Headstone with their boys, of Captain Cuttle with Walter Gay, Edward Murdstone with David Copperfield, and John Jasper with Edwin Drood), a pattern almost as frequent in Dickens' fiction as the older man and the young girl, sometimes vibrates with the latent sexual implications of dominance and control, of operator and subject.

Dickens' knowledgeability about sexual relationships between males (particularly between older men and young boys) can hardly be doubted, though the general Victorian reticence about public discussion throws an obscuring veil over the range of such activities in Victorian upper middle-class and aristocratic London society. The absence of references to such experiences in Dickens' letters suggests that it was hardly a topic of major concern for him. But his wide range of intense male friendships and the special freedom

197

of emotional expression that the Victorians felt appropriate make it rather likely that Dickens was well aware of
the possibilities of such relationships carried to an extreme.
They existed in extreme form all around him, in schools
and clubs, in the examples of otherwise quite respectable
members of the society, and in some detail in the fantasies
of the private mind and the extensive and easily available
night life and pornography of the period. Probably Chauncy
Hare Townshend's relationship with Alexis, his mesmeric
subject, was a sexual one. Dickens could not have been unaware of Townshend's predilection for male relationships,
of Elliotson's bachelor life and male entourage (in contrast to the complications of his own married household),
and the relative ease with which private male lives found
male satisfactions in a society of rather strict public conventions.

[2]

Carker has no difficulty subjugating Rob, his teeth taking
the place of the usual "visual ray" as the vehicle of the
transmission of his mesmeric power. For Rob "admired him,
as well as feared him," his attraction to this force of will
an expression of his own desire to be like Carker, "a master
of certain treacherous arts." There is no battle here between two strong wills; the natural affinity may be revealed,
but Rob's own powers are too minimal at this stage in his
young life to permit a contest between them. Rob completely capitulates into servitude, Carker's sadism and
Rob's masochism finding an appropriate language of domination and submission in the metaphors of mesmerism:

"Inmate of Mr. Carker's house, and serving about his
person, Rob kept his round eyes on the white teeth with
fear and trembling, and felt that he had need to open
them wider than ever. He could not have quaked more,
through his whole being, before the teeth, though he had
come into the service of some powerful enchanter, and they
had been his strongest spell. The boy had a sense of power

and authority in this patron of his that engrossed his whole attention and exacted his most implicit submission and obedience. He hardly considered himself safe in thinking about him when he was absent, lest he should feel himself immediately taken by the throat again, as on the morning when he first became bound to him, and should see every one of the teeth finding him out, and taxing him with every fancy of his mind. Face to face with him, Rob had no more doubt that Mr. Carker read his secret thoughts, or that he could read them by the least exertion of his will if he were so inclined, than he had that Mr. Carker saw him when he looked at him. The ascendency was so complete, and held him in such enthralment, that, hardly daring to think at all, but with his mind filled with a constantly dilating impression of his patron's irresistible command over him, and power of doing anything with him, he would stand watching his pleasure. . . ." (*DS*, XLII.)

But what is it within Carker that prompts him to exercise his will for the purpose of domination? How are we to understand what operative forces are at work within the Dickens world to determine that such a character will use his powers for immoral ends and another for beneficial purposes? If there is some natural power available to the individual, and if "the will is the grand agent in the production of magnetic phenomena," what is to determine the moral quality of the acts of the mesmerist? "Great mental energy, sustained concentration of the will, is necessary to control its influence," Baron Dupotet and other Dickens acquaintances insisted.[3] But what is to determine the moral direction of the will? For he who has mesmeric power, like "the swimmer, who learns at length to surmount the boisterous surf, or to stem the adverse stream, will revel in the consciousness of awakened power. How much more must the mental enthusiast riot in the display of energies so long concealed, so wondrously developed."[4] Dickens had no

[3] Dupotet, p. 341.
[4] Townshend, p. 36.

doubt that his own "riot in the display" of his mental energies was soundly based in a personality and a morality that placed the interests of others paramount, that his efforts on behalf of Madame de la Rue, for example, were not contaminated with the self-serving satisfaction of dominance, the expansion of the self at the expense of another. Certainly he would have agreed with Dupotet that "if anyone should ask what is the moral tendency of the doctrine of animal magnetism, I should answer, that it obviously tends to establish the spiritual ascendency of man over . . . material conditions . . . and affords a precursory evidence of a future state of being, which belief in itself cannot fail to suggest those principles of self-government and moral conduct which alone can promote the real welfare and happiness of society."[5]

But the facts of his fiction deny the theory. For those possessed of such special powers of mental consciousness and control generally use them for self-serving and immoral ends. Such forces of will and energy in concentrated and unmistakably mesmeric forms in the Dickens world are often instruments of control, rarely mitigated by other impulses, rarely turned to beneficent and self-sacrificing ends. So the question remains: why?

Sydney Carton, Arthur Clennam, Little Dorrit, Cissy Jupe, and Esther Summerson save and are saved by the self-sacrifice of their lives, by some principle of love that provides happiness: they do not have the strong impulse of the will; they are not aggressively active; they do not seek to control others. And certainly they are not sexual creatures. There is no suggestion of sexual forces working within them to find channels of psychological and physical satisfaction. Without being submissive, they are sexually passive. Their final triumph depends upon their self-sacrifice, their search for a life of good deeds, and their renunciation of the sexuality of dominance and submission. Why is it, then, that Carker, and so many others, use their special

[5] Dupotet, p. 341.

mesmeric powers for self-serving ends? Is the impulse basically the need for sexual satisfaction?

Sexuality, however, is much more a process of the will in the Dickens world than it is of the body. Even acknowledged lovers go to bed with one another off stage. But such love relationships are less erotic in Dickens' fiction than those contests of the will between unequally gifted but perfectly matched pairs and those between almost equally gifted exponents of willpower whose interests are so opposed that they must engage in a major conflict for dominance. For example, between Tulkinghorn and Lady Dedlock there is a latent sexual relationship, a battle of the wills for absolute control. Tulkinghorn subjugates Lady Dedlock to his will in a pattern not dissimilar—once one makes allowances for differences in class, education, and age —to Quilp's subjugation of his wife and Carker's of Rob the Grinder. The main difference is that Lady Dedlock provides the additional excitement of formidable resistance.

But why does Tulkinghorn do it; what distinguishes him and other mesmeric operators in the Dickens world? He is "a man so severely and strictly self-repressed" that to say of him "that he is triumphant, would be to do him as great an injustice as to suppose him troubled with love or sentiment, or any romantic weakness. He is sedately satisfied. Perhaps there is a rather increased sense of power upon him, as he loosely grasps one of his veinous wrists with his other hand, and holding it behind his back walks noiselessly up and down" (*BH*, XLI). Tulkinghorn has the self-appreciatory ego of one whose gratification derives from his successful domination of others through his insight into their weaknesses. He possesses them through the secrets they cannot keep hidden from him. His loveless self-love is represented imagistically in the metaphor of hands and touch that Dickens so often uses to indicate the quality of human communication. Tulkinghorn holds his own hand, the blood of his "veinous wrist" controlled by the tourniquet of his own self-serving and self-loving grasp. His pleasures are psychically masturbatory, the mind turned in upon itself, his hands clasped together rather than reaching out to touch others. Tulkinghorn's self-love is a metaphor for the ways of a society of self-love that horrifies Dickens.

Not that in the Dickens view all self-love is as damnable as Tulkinghorn's, for his is the conscious, purposeful product of repression of self and others. There are those whose self-love is the victim's response to the purgatory into which they have been forced. Bolder, a victim of Squeers' tyranny at his Yorkshire school, dramatizes self-love in terms that Dickens' Victorian contemporaries would have recognized as a euphemism for masturbation: "An unhealthy-looking boy, with warts all over his hands, stepped from his place . . . and raised his eyes imploringly to Squeers's face . . . 'Bolder,' said Squeers . . . 'why, what's this, sir?' As Squeers spoke, he caught up the boy's hand by the cuff of his jacket, and surveyed it with an eddifying aspect of horror and disgust. . . . 'I can't help it, indeed, sir. . . . They will come; it's the dirty work I think, sir—at least I don't know what it is, sir, but it's not my fault.' 'Bolder,' said Squeers, tucking up his wristbands, and moistening the palm of his right hand to get a good grip of the cane, 'you are an incorrigible young scoundrel, and as the last thrashing did you no good, we must see what another will do towards beating it out of you' " (*NN*, viii).

Squeers may be right about the iconographical origin of the warts, but in the mode of sympathy that Dickens creates the boy is right: it is not his fault. Such self-love has the justification of repression, the semi-conscious gratifications of the exploited. Tulkinghorn communes with himself consciously, to realize gratifications within relationships that he has the power to control. He has the strength of the operator, not the weakness of the subject.

Tulkinghorn purposefully represses "love or sentiment, or any romantic weakness." Such repressions are the actions of a man of strong will who has committed himself to a view of human personality and society that assumes that the desired rewards will come from acting without "any romantic weakness." Why and how he makes this decision Dickens does not answer. The ontology of the circumstance for Tulkinghorn, and other Dickens characters, is unclear, though the teleology is unmistakable: the rewards of self-satisfaction and societal praise that Tulkinghorn believes will result from such actions. And, of course, the eschatology is what Dickens dramatizes as well, for he is enough of a moralist to insist that more or less in every circumstance of such purposeful manipulation of other human beings for self-serving gratifications the character's fate will be a terrible one. He is either torn apart by those forces within him that he has repressed, or turned into a dehumanized vacuum, or defeated eventually by those who possess the qualities of "love or sentiment" that he has rejected.

Tulkinghorn can transform intuition and experience into "clairvoyance." Through the baseness within himself he can recognize weakness within others to use for his own advantage. But he is matched against a strong, though flawed, antagonist whose resources of will are almost equal to his own. Though he recognizes the "power and force of this woman," he is still able, for the moment only, to crush her under his own will ("He has conquered her"), to subjugate her to his desires in a ritual of mesmeric response. "She asks all her questions as if she were repeating them from memory, or calling them over in her sleep." Lady Dedlock is described as if she were in mesmeric trance, the force of the operator's will reducing the subject to a passive responder to the suggestions of the mesmerist. She answers his questions obediently. This is Tulkinghorn's moment of triumph, his "increased sense of power" most intense and heightened, followed by "an expression on his face as if he had discharged his mind of some grave matter." But such release is the Tulkinghorn version of an "expense of spirit in a waste of shame," a special kind of "lust in action." There is no answer to the "why," but Dickens is brilliant at depicting what "is."

[3]

The use of will and mesmeric energy for the gratifications of self-love and the control of other people for one's own self-serving end is the common temptation, the frequent choice, and the often suicidal impulse of strong men. The most tempted, the most responsible, and ultimately the most suicidal is John Jasper. Unlike Tulkinghorn, his impetus towards the gratification of self has an explicitly physical basis. His central obsession, which occupies him ceaselessly and which determines the plot and imagery of *Edwin Drood*, is erotic. He wants total possession of Rosa Bud. Though he does indeed propose marriage, it is quite clear that his impulse is not sacramental. His sexual-copulative drives are implied as fantasies. They are left to the extended novel of the reader's imagination, as is so often the case in Victorian fiction. But Jasper's sexuality is the expression of intense energies within him to dominate, to take pleasure and to give pain both to himself and others through a psychological and political sex in which sex is power and power is sex. His lust for Rosa is inseparable from his desire to manipulate all those with whom he comes in contact. His use of mesmerism is inextricably a part of his sexual desires, the power of his mesmerism indistinguishable from the personality that contains it and the ends for which he uses it.

Though Jasper ultimately is to be exposed through the efforts of Helena Landless and Canon Crisparkle, his destruction comes from his impulse towards self-destruction, which finds its correlative in his effort to murder his nephew. His desire to possess Rosa can be accomplished, he believes, only after he has eliminated Edwin Drood. Ignorant of the fact that Edwin and Rosa have agreed to release one another from the pledge of matrimony made for them by their parents, he plots to kill the obstacle to the completion of his desire. Despite his great powers, his energy and will have failed him; he cannot accomplish his ends through an exertion of the force of his personality, through his use of techniques of domination. Even with the disappearance of Edwin, assumed by the community to be dead, Rosa resists Jasper's attempt to control her. Jasper's love for Rosa transcends the terms of love Dickens and the Victorians could accept. It is an all-consuming, a self-consuming, and an other-consuming love. Passion and the desire to possess are intensified into a physical and psychological desire in which the normal conditions of love are renounced and violence is the next condition of communication: " 'There is my past and my present wasted life. There is the desolation of my heart and my soul. There is my peace; there is my despair. Stamp them into the dust; so that you take me, were it even mortally hating me!' The frightful vehemence of the man, now reaching its full height, so additionally terrifies her as to break the spell that has held her to the spot" (*ED*, XIX). For Jasper his sexual desires and his mesmeric powers are inseparable. But when such powers fail to accomplish his ends, violence is his next weapon, and it too is an expression of his sexual needs.

Certainly he has murdered Edwin Drood. Over and over again in his mind, and then in reality, he has done the deed. He tells the opium lady while in a drugged trance the truth of his fantasies. And the fantasy is orgiastic, masturbatory, ultimately more satisfying than the reality of the murder. Jasper has come " 'on purpose. When I could not bear my life, I came to get the relief, and I got it' " (*ED*, XXIII). For Jasper's life is painful. He deeply feels his lack of completion. His sense of his own self is a fallen and lost one. He can hardly bear his life; his impulse is suicidal. And he has already begun to act on the impulse before the beginning of the novel, in the life of his fantasies in the opium haze with which the novel begins. Each time he enters an opium trance he does so with the knowledge that before the gratifying visions of release can come he must act and reenact in his mind the most pleasurable of his fantasies, the murder of Edwin.

This fantasy is inseparable from the pleasures of the self

whose deepest needs are sexual and psychological: the domination of Rosa, the triumph of Jasper's ego, the elimination
of Edwin, the expression of violence. " 'Yes,' " he tells the
opium lady, " 'I always made the journey first [his euphemism for the fantasy of the act of murder], before the changes
of colours and the great landscapes and glittering proces-
sions began. They couldn't begin till it was off my mind.
I had no room till then for anything else' " (*ED*, xxiii). In
the fantasy the act " '*was* pleasant to do,' " a gratification
that Jasper emphasizes. " 'Should you do it in your fancy,
when you were lying here doing this?' She nods her head.
'Over and over again.' 'Just like me! I did it over and over
again. I have done it hundreds of thousands of times in
this room.' 'It's to be hoped it was pleasant to do, deary.'
'It *was* pleasant to do!' " (*ED*, xxiii). But unfortunately the
fantasy proves more satisfying than the reality, the psychological drama more fulfilling than the physical one. " 'I did
it so often, and through such vast expanses of time, that
when it was really done, it seemed not worth the doing, it
was done so soon. . . . It has been too short and easy. I must
have a better vision than this; this is the poorest of all. No
struggle, no consciousness of peril, no entreaty' " (*ED*,
xxiii).

For Jasper the act of the mind has a greater reality than
the act of the body. What is done in the mind can be done
over and over again, infinitely renewable, without physical
and finite consequences, no effect from the cause, no direct
responsibility resulting from the non-action. It can be done
with masturbatory renewal, with the minimum of human
responsibilities, the self triumphant in itself and for itself.
This is Jasper's world of pleasure, his response to his frustrations. Whatever fantasies he has about Rosa would, if
he could translate those also into reality, seem less satisfying to him, would seem " 'done so soon . . . that when it was
really done, it seemed not worth the doing.' " Whatever
those fantasies are, however, they are certainly sexual. For
Jasper epitomizes the extreme of the relationship between

sex and power in Dickens' fiction: I will have my way or there will be at least three literal or symbolic deaths—yours, my own, and someone else's.

Eugene Wrayburn indeed almost dies as the victim of just such a sworn threat. For a considerable portion of *Our Mutual Friend* he lacks the will to be a threat to others, a self-destructive victim of a "pernicious assumption of lassitude . . . which had become his second nature" (II:VI). He has no center in a world in which the center is falling apart, semi-consciously and with quasi-aristocratic affectation having assumed that there is nothing worth caring enough about to warrant the exertion of his will. Having no ends, he has neither good ends nor bad ends. While his neutrality helps maintain his redeemability, it is expressive of a death-in-life that can be as terrifyingly reprehensible as the most manipulative actions of domineering men, short of the violence of murder.

But Wrayburn exists in a world of swirling power struggles in a novel that contains a number of subplots depicting variations on the themes of dominance, will, and energy. Who will have whom " 'in a state of abject moral bondage and slavery,' " as Silas Wegg puts it, and who will conquer whom for wife and bed? For the subordinate cast consists mainly of characters who accommodate whatever vital force they possess to their economic ambitions, their will for power inseparable from avarice. Fascination Fledgeby's supreme inflation of ego takes the form of a secretive use of capital to dominate others, " 'to work a lot of power over you and you not know it, knowing as you think yourselves, would be almost worth laying out money upon. But when it comes to squeezing a profit out of you into the bargain, it's something like' " (*OMF*, III:I). His attempt to marry Georgiana Podsnap is an attempt to bring profit and power to bed together. It is frustrated, like the Lammles' similar venture, a sexual symbol potent in its significance precisely because there is no sexual passion in the effort. But Wrayburn, at first, will have nothing to do with desire of any kind.

Strong desire demands the effort to work towards fulfillment beyond fantasy.

Such fantasies are the pleasures of innumerable Dickens characters who find sustenance in the pleasures of anticipation: the extent to which their psychic energies remain encapsulated within unacted imaginings may determine the degree to which they are successful in fulfilling their desires. Characters like Gamp, Micawber, Flora Finching, and Jenny Wren have rich imaginative lives precisely because they have allowed their fantasies such freedom (often because of disabilities and frustrations so severe that the fantasy life is more satisfying than any possible real one). They are created to be able to afford such fantasy lives without causing harm to others. But the fantasies of Jonas Chuzzlewit, Uriah Heep, Orlick, Fascination Fledgeby, John Jasper, Rogue Riderhood, Bill Sikes, among others, are the first step in their expression of their will to dominate others and ultimately to use violence to achieve their ends when their wills fail them. The minds of Dickens' characters are intensely busy with fantasies of self-creation and self-destruction. They are filled with comic creations of less vulnerable selves through language, gloating anticipations of dominance and the fulfillment of avarice, wild hopes of sexual satisfaction, vain expectations of the fulfillment of dreams of success. These minds constantly leap ahead to anticipate, initiate, and help create the reality that will be the fulfillment of their needs.

For Bradley Headstone such anticipations are the sheer torture of insecurity, intensified because he is a man of strong will and sexual desire who feels the possibility that both may be balked. His energy also seems to be self-destructively turned upon himself. The field of action for such forces within the individual is, of course, the mind, fantasies of desire and fear creating a special kind of frenetic potential for violence. In such cases, the object of desire is feminine and sexual; and strong forces of will are so frustrated in their effort to establish dominance that the pulsating waves of energy that these characters emanate and that Dickens depicts so effectively demand physical manifestations. Their feelings and fantasies are depicted in a way that resonates with the attitudes toward mind and self that mesmerism helped Dickens to discover.

When Bradley, "grinding his words slowly out, as though they came from a rusty mill," attempts to persuade Lizzie Hexam not to accept Wrayburn's assistance but his own, his fantasies take the form of physical quirks that are the outward signs of his fragmented psychic life: "His lips trembled and stood apart . . . furtively wrenching at the seat of his chair with one hand, as if he would have wrenched the chair to pieces . . . [he] sat contending with himself in a heat of passion and torment" (*OMF*, II:XI). Headstone's great powers of energy, so severely repressed in his years of fitting himself into "his decent black coat," are now released by the strength of his desire for Lizzie. But the conventional middle-class Headstone cannot co-exist with the Headstone of strong passions. The repressed other, once given head, breaks all restraints, so that Bradley insists that the only explanation for this other self is " 'that there is a spell upon me.' " When denied fulfillment, this repressed self explodes, transforming Headstone into a man of monomaniacal willpower, attempting to get what he desires first by persuasion and then finally by force.

But Bradley's sense of his own destruction is not passive. "The wild energy of the man, now quite let loose, was absolutely terrible." The fury of his energy is the intensity of the will to dominate and subjugate balked. And it is in those very terms of mesmeric subjugation that he describes himself. For it is the passive, quiet, and humble Lizzie whom Headstone accuses of having the power to subjugate him. She is like the magnetic loadstone that has concentrated within it all the focused mesmeric force of the universe, irresistible and undeniable. That attraction is produced by his desire for her. His frustration comes from his knowledge that he is being controlled not only against his will but against her desire. She involuntarily demands his submission. She attracts him and does not even want him. He suffers without the release and reward such suffering implies.

That she does indeed "draw" him to a horrible end is the result of his will to create such a power over himself to fulfill his suicidal needs. It is also partly the result of his unwillingness to believe that the self that he offers is so unworthy that she would not choose to have him if she could. He then reasons that she could and would if only a rival did not stand in the way. But Eugene Wrayburn begins with no energy, with hardly any life of the mind at all. He has renounced the fantasies of expectation as simply not worth the effort. One cannot be disappointed in failing to achieve what one does not attempt. Eugene begins without commitment to anything but vague self-indulgence, much more a lost soul than a potential villain. His ultimate destiny is to depend on whether or not the energy for purposeful goodness that is within him can find stimulation and model in the people and circumstances of his life.

Eugene's salvation comes from the one impulse that Dickens always placed confidence in, the love that increases and defines the self through comparative selflessness. Wrayburn does not begin with the desire to dominate but as a vacuum, a nihilist of the imagination and of the act. When he is attracted to Lizzie Hexam, the obstacles to their union come from external conditions and moral scruples that Lizzie considers insurmountable. Stirred by the prospect of fulfilling his love, Wrayburn, heretofore a pale ghost of purposelessness, refuses to accept that the obstacles cannot be overcome. He discovers himself by discovering that there are available to him vast resources of energy that his willpower can direct to accomplish the seemingly impossible. Like Bradley Headstone, then, Eugene had repressed the vital forces within him and around him in the natural order of the cosmos. Simultaneously discovering these powers and his will to use them, he is energized to "revel in the consciousness of awakened power," to "riot in the display of energies so long concealed."[6]

Since the obstacles seem to exist only in Lizzie's mind, he determines that it is Lizzie's mind, her independent volition, that he must conquer. Clearly he is sexually drawn to her, strongly attracted. Marriage, to which he at first gave little thought, now becomes a consideration, so confident grows his sense of the power of his will. It would be a marriage across class lines, of unequals in birth, training, and status. But the unexpected has happened. The growth of his own consciousness of the power of his will has been paralleled by his realization of her admirable uniqueness as a human being.

The tension of the Hexam-Wrayburn relationship results from the unresolved possibilities of how Eugene shall use his power—for brutish or for virtuous ends. For the growth of his commitment to act ethically towards Lizzie lags behind his sense of his power over her. The tool of control that comes to hand is Lizzie's fear for his life. " 'I beg you to take me home, Mr. Wrayburn,' " Lizzie says, moments after Bradley Headstone's impassioned threat to the life of Eugene. " 'I have had a bitter trial to-night, and I hope you will not think me ungrateful, or mysterious, or changeable. I am neither; I am wretched. Pray remember what I said to you. Pray, pray take care.' " But the revelation of concern implicit in the warning is just the advantage that Eugene is seeking. " 'My dear Lizzie . . . of what? of whom?' 'Of any one you have lately seen and made angry.' He snapped his fingers and laughed. 'Come,' said he. . . . He knew his power over her" (*OMF*, II:xv).

For Eugene begins as a variant of Sir Mulberry Hawk twenty-five years later: the predatory aristocrat in pursuit of lower middle-class virtue has become the upper middle-class professional in pursuit of proletarian integrity. No matter how different they are, Eugene begins where Sir Mul-

---

[6] Townshend, p. 36.

berry ends; they are both pursuers whose implied aim is rape, the imposition of their will on a vulnerable female of inferior class status. They are political marauders, their sexual fulfillment inseparable from their will to exploit the power derived from economic and social structures. Eugene, of course, shares mainly an impulse with Sir Mulberry. He too wants the girl and he too works with certain sexual and social givens. But the scheme of *Our Mutual Friend* is to show, among other things, the redemption of Wrayburn through trial and suffering. He is transformed from a man without energy to a man who discovers within himself vast resources of power. His first impulse is to use this power for the satisfaction of sexual needs without the qualities that would turn sexuality into love. But, finally, he develops a sufficiently strong sense of the selfhood of the other to permit him to use his powers in relationships in which constructive ends guide their use.

This is most unusual in Dickens' fiction. In the transformation of Eugene, Dickens provides one of the rare instances in which he dramatizes his own sense of his confidence in his ability to use such powers effectively. In his complexities Eugene is much more a portrait of Dickens in his fullness than any other character in his fiction, including David Copperfield; in Eugene's eventual moral control over his power to dominate others, one senses one of the sources of Dickens' own satisfaction with his use of his energies both in his life and in his art.

When Wrayburn "snaps his fingers," remarking to himself that "he knew his power over her," he has not yet found some balance between his lust and his love, between his awareness of his self's needs and his growing sense of Lizzie as some "other" with whom to enter into a relationship in which his selfhood would be defined in a way that would augment rather than diminish it. He is in danger of becoming a more threatening Bradley Headstone, with the power to use Lizzie callously. The balance begins to come even when Eugene recognizes the extent of her power over

212

him, an admission that he makes rather late in their relationship. " 'Lizzie,' " he says, " 'You don't know what my state of mind towards you is. You don't know how you haunt me and bewilder me' " (*OMF*, IV:vi). The words and the tone, though not quite as impassioned with despair, echo Bradley Headstone's hysterical complaint in an earlier scene: he is irresistibly attracted to the woman, like a magnet, constantly preoccupied with her image and her presence. But Dickens suggests that Wrayburn's transformation is dependent upon his ability to give himself up to Lizzie's power over him while retaining his over her. For that exertion of mutual power is a commitment to the other. It is a bond of attachment that once given cannot be withdrawn and once given carries with it obligations of intimacy and union.

Not that the dynamics of Lizzie's choosing to exert power in the one case and not in the other can be explained. Dickens seems to believe that such emotions and commitments can be dramatized. But some mystery still exists beyond and behind the dramatization. Lizzie chooses to love Eugene and not Bradley; Eugene becomes worthy of her love. Would Headstone have become worthy of it? It hardly seems likely. Dickens has not given him that potential. Eugene chooses to use his will for moral and constructive ends; Bradley chooses to use his in a destructive manner. Could Bradley have done otherwise? No matter how driven these Dickens characters may be, the element of choice always seems to be there, though it may be the result of forces so strong that the individual is hardly to be blamed for the decision when it is destructive but much to be praised when it is constructive.

Dickens straddles two worlds, the modern and his own, when he deals with the nature of evil and the relationship between sexual drives and the impulse to dominate others for self-gratification. When sex cannot be brought into the balance of love, it is a pure power impulse, the glorification of self at the cost of damaging or destroying another. It is

213

evil. But why one individual chooses to use his will for self-serving purposes alone and why another does not— that Dickens does not answer, though no one has dramatized these forces better than he has.

For the moral desideratum of Dickens' imagination to become viable in *Our Mutual Friend*, Eugene must learn to direct his power toward the end of Lizzie's good as she towards his. Both of them are unaware, of course, that at this moment of recognition of the other's needs murderous violence lurks in the bushes in the form of Bradley Headstone, disguised as Rogue Riderhood. Headstone's repressed desire for control of Lizzie must find an outlet. He has come to the last resort of the frustrated mesmeric and sexual will, a masturbatory act of self-love and self-destruction. Lizzie calls for an act of renunciation, of which Bradley is incapable, of which Eugene is first beginning to grow capable, on behalf of the other as well as on behalf of the self. But Eugene's transformation is not yet complete, though the terms of the possibility of their relationship have become clearer to him. He remarks now: " 'Yet I have gained a wonderful power over her, too, let her be as much in earnest as she will' " (*OMF*, IV:vi). Though the vocabulary of dominance has been transformed, it is still applicable. Now dominance, submission, and sexual desire are to be brought together in a rhetoric that represents a relationship in which these forces are under the control of the pledged impulse of each member of the union to use his powers on behalf of the other. In one of the dramatic ironies of the novel, Wrayburn is to have his old notions of power beaten out of him, almost to his death, to be replaced by mutual and voluntary domination and subjugation. Lizzie and Eugene finally give each other this special power, as a gift of love and confidence.

So in the end both have it and both do not, simultaneously. Bradley Headstone's near murder of Eugene, following almost immediately the expression of his "wonderful power over her," makes Eugene totally dependent on Lizzie for a long while. But hers is the power of love, as his finally becomes—with an emphasis for each of them on respect, loyalty, and commitment to the flourishing of the full personality and self-identity of the other. When they marry they bring power—energy and will—to a harmonious bed whose metaphor is not rape but sexual respect. They each make the voluntary gift of some substantial portion of selfhood into the trusted possession of the loved one. They bring the mesmeric fluid or life force out of the conflict of single wills into the balance of mutual needs.

Dickens' Century

" 'It must have been a dream, Oliver,' " Harry Maylie attempts to persuade the boy who has just been in a special kind of sleep in which "reality and imagination become so strangely blended that it is . . . almost a matter of impossibility to separate the two" (*OT*, xxxv, xxxiv). Fagin's manipulative eyes have become a part of Oliver's consciousness, piercing through the external and the internal windows. Though it was indeed Fagin out there whom Oliver saw, Harry Maylie is right, and Oliver is beginning to learn the truths that surface through even the submerged language of cliché and rationalization. "I am here, as in a dream," the self-tortured haunted man proclaims; for "my mind is going blind," he fears, at the very moment when his mind has grown new eyes, has taken on new powers of perception about the self and about reality, painful though the new vision may be (*HM*, ii).

Dickens claimed about dreams that he had "read something on the subject, and had long observed it with the greatest attention and interest."[1] Wide reading in varied subjects made him a formidable Victorian autodidact whose reading was important nurture for his novelistic imagina-

---

[1] *Nonesuch*, ii, 267, to Dr. Frank Stone, 2/2/51.

tion. He created a synthesis of varied kinds of experiences about the occult, the strange apparitions of nature, the meaning and power of dreams, phrenology, mesmerism. He was not boasting. The dream state was his domain, permeating his fiction and non-fiction to the extent that it became a metaphor for his exploration of what he considered the most meaningful aspects of human consciousness and the human predicament.[2] Dreams are special states of consciousness, Dickens believed, in which we can know more about ourselves and our environment than in times of normal functioning, when fundamental truths are hidden from us by mechanisms of deceit.

For the central mesmeric experience is that of sleep-waking, in which we awaken from the dreams of illusion and see the truth of reality. But to the everyday consciousness these moments of insight within mesmeric trance are like dreams, so different do we feel ourselves and so special is the quality of what we see. In the trance state the mesmeric fluid dominates our consciousness, the vital force is given opportunity to express itself. Trains of association and dislocation break through the restrictions of daily realities, expressing natural impulses and desires, the way the O'key sisters in public mesmeric trance revealed feelings that suggested to the Victorians that the scandal of repressed needs would be more manageable if kept private.

"Considering the vast extent of the domains of dream-land, and their wonderful productions" (*ED*, XII), so great are the powers of mind that the threat of what may be revealed is equally as formidable as the hope of what may be discovered. Pickwick hardly dreams, so often is he blessed with "a sound and dreamless sleep" (*PP*, VII). But the possibility of the dislocation of consciousness in the dream metaphor quite clearly exists within the language he has

---

[2] See Taylor Stoehr, *Dickens: The Dreamer's Stance* (Ithaca, 1965). Stoehr briefly mentions Dickens' involvement with mesmerism toward the end of his study in which, as a whole, he tries to demonstrate that many of the peculiarities of Dickens' distinctive style are analagous to dream states.

inherited to express states of anxiety: " 'It's like a dream
. . . a hideous dream. The idea of a man's walking about,
all day, with a dreadful horse that he can't get rid of!' "
(*PP*, v). The dislocations of Pickwick's consciousness that
intensify beyond comedy remain comic even in the events
that lead to his incarceration in debtor's prison.[3] The world
of his cell only threatens to become the nightmare of the
dream states of many Dickens characters from Oliver Twist
on. The "domains of dreamland" are those within which
we either deceive or liberate ourselves, in which we have
the opportunity to explore the past, present, and future,
to discover the forces of will and energy within us, and to
use power and knowledge for good or for evil ends.

The metaphor has many sub-territories: dreams of mesmeric transfixion within trance, the way Annie Strong is
"looking up" at her husband "with such a face . . . so full
of a wild, sleep-walking, dreamy horror of I don't know
what" (*DC*, xvi); dreams of dislocated anxiety, the way
Trotty Veck "looked from face to face as wildly as a sleeper
in a dream" (*TC*, i); dreams of the consciousness of the
loss of ability to comprehend, like Michael Warden, who is
"like a man in a dream at present. I seem to want my wits"
(*BL*, iii); dreams of no longer dreaming, like those of Mr.
Redlaw, who pronounces that he is "quite ready . . . waking
as from a dream" (*HM*, i); dreams that are clairvoyant and
prophetic, like Mrs. Nickleby imagining the prosperity of
her hopes. Others are the reification within dream imagery
of the tremendous anxieties of the moment, like Ralph
Nickleby's sense that he could not have been more shocked
"if some tremendous apparition from the world of shadows
had suddenly presented itself" (*NN*, LIV).

But after *Pickwick* the dreams are often nightmares, fears
of what has been or what is to come. Barnaby's dreams are
the reality of his madness flowing into currents of truth

[3] See Fred Kaplan, " 'Magnanimous Revenge': Reason and Responsibility in *The Pickwick Papers*," *Victorian Newsletter*, 37 (Spring 1970),
18-21.

unavailable outside special states of consciousness. " 'I dreamed just now that something—it was in the shape of a man—followed me—came softly after me. . . . You never saw me run as I did in this dream' " (*BR*, vi). This has been a dream with open eyes, under the influence of an operator with mesmeric powers: " 'Softly—gently,' said the locksmith, exerting all his influence to keep him calm and quiet. 'I thought you had been asleep.' 'So I *have* been asleep,' he rejoined, with widely-opened eyes" (*BR*, vi). So too George Gordon's dreams are those of special vision, under the influence of an operator who has helped the subject achieve unusual power over others. Lord George has made his and Gashford's illusions the realities of the lives of many people. Finally those dreams which had seemed only harmless fantasies become the ultimate reality. They reveal what he is.

These dreams also have their comic and satiric form, particularly in the gallery of secondary characters who exist for the refraction of major themes into minor bodies as seemingly casual amusement. Mr. Perch, whose "act of somnambulism" is to talk cryptically in his sleep, anticipates the reversal in the fortunes of the Dombey firm, his dreams stimulated by "the impression made upon him by the change in Mr. Dombey's face" (*DS*, LVIII). But even when the language is comic, the dream is serious. " 'I'm dreaming . . . that's clear. When I went to bed, my hands were not made of egg-shells; and now I can almost see through 'em. If this is not a dream, I have woke up, by mistake, in an Arabian Night, instead of a London one. But I have no doubt I'm asleep. Not the least' " (*OCS*, LXIV). Such states of special insight often reveal basic corruption: the reduction of the individual to the service of debased economic needs; the use of will and energy for self-serving gratification, like Carker's dream of "people . . . on the ground at his feet" (*DS*, XXVI); the elevation of position in society into an affirmation of the worth of the self.

Or what may seem comic invocations of mesmeric trance

and dream atmosphere turn out to be deadly serious. Dick Swiveller's Arabian Nights dream becomes the actuality of his rebirth. Mrs. Gamp's mumblings about Mrs. Harris act as the replenishment of her psychic needs, her nightly re-creation through dream dialogue with her double of self-necessity. The comic Affery Flintwinch is made serious by her searing contact with deadly things. Disguised as illusions, her dream states hover on the edge of important realities. She "happened in her dreamy state to look at him [Blandois] as he said these words, and to fancy that she caught an expression in his eyes which attracted her own eyes so that she could not get them away. . . . Thus a few ghostly moments supervened, when they were all confusedly staring without knowing why" (*LD*, I:xxx). Mr. Peggotty thanks his " 'Heav'nly Father as [his] dream's come true!' " (*DC*, L). The metaphor of the romantic primitive in search of the fulfillment of his dream has sustained him through his travels in search of Em'ly. Simple good-heartedness cannot be denied the completion of its vision of reunion, though such success becomes the exception in Dickens' imaginative world after *David Copperfield*.[4] But Dickens still believes in the reward, at least in its possibility, for the man of certain powers. Such dreams are not only permissible but realizable, through suffering and trial and transformation of the self. The long journey of Mr. Peggotty is the long journey of the Dickens hero whose fall and loss of self may not be irretrievable, providing that he discovers the core of energy and will within him and without from which to regain vital life.

For the dream of such possibilities may be almost visionary, so intensely seen in apocalyptic terms as to reverberate with the battle between the life and the death in-

[4] Perhaps it is dubious that they were the rule even before *David Copperfield*. But Dickens' projection of himself into David as man and artist and the relative ease with which David obtains his desires has to be compared to the increasing difficulty with which Dickens' heroes after David, especially prototypical artists like Pip and John Jasper, achieve or fail to achieve fulfilment.

stincts, drawing resonance from the tradition of dream visions in Christian culture. Fascination Fledgeby, incapable of dreaming of anything but power and profits, cannot respond to the vision that appears so close to him, so apposite is Dickens in his ironies. In the Dickens world often he who has the most need will be the least attended to, and he who has the potential of spirit will be most assisted. When "Fledgeby went his way, exulting in the artful cleverness with which he had turned his thumb down on a Jew . . . the old man . . . mounted" the stairs. "As he mounted, the call or song began to sound in his ears again, and, looking above, he saw the face of the little creature looking down out of a Glory of her long bright radiant hair, and musically repeating to him, like a vision: 'Come up and be dead! Come up and be dead!'" (*OMF*, II:v).

This vision is frighteningly ambiguous, part of the irony of the late Dickens world. Fledgeby misses it all the time, being dead already. Yet it is available to the Jew for whom the Messiah has not yet appeared, promising him the possibility of heaven and rebirth that comes with death. It is the death-in-life and the life-in-death of the Christian dollmaker Jenny Wren, who has reversed the normal order of the generations by becoming the metaphoric father to her father. She constantly dreams: children, a lover who may come, some paradise of fulfillment. She constructs the particulars of this paradise in response to the lessons she has learned about how life ought not to be from her experience of how life is. Like the dream of Blake's chimney-sweepers,[5] hers gives sustenance and hope. But she too is the victim of a reality so much the given of her physical limitations and the meanness of her environment that she serves as a reminder of the possibility of rebirth for others in a world in which such possibilities are denied to her except in vi-

---

[5] Blake's chimney sweeper (in "The Chimney Sweeper" in *Songs of Innocence*) has been brain-washed to believe that "If all do their Duty, they need not fear harm." Jenny has a self-consciousness about her fallen world that Blake denies his innocents.

sions. Like the Romantic poet, she can sometimes see and hear, in special states of consciousness, what she cannot be.

The reality of certain dreams, however, like that of the self and those who threaten it, is devastating. Often the nightmare patterns that appear are the truths of the psychic life. Sometimes normal consciousness is too fragile to admit the reality of what is actually occurring. So the mind transforms reality into a dream, like Affery Flintwinch's "curiously vivid dream" that was "in fact . . . not at all like a dream, it was so very real in every respect" (*LD*, I:IV). Reality must be seen as an illusion for the self to survive. But Affery has collaborators who assist her in evading reality, those who would like her visions of consciousness not to exist at all. She is controlled by Jeremiah through his knowledge of her weakness. But at the point when the reality that is a dream becomes unbearable, she confronts the truth of the ghostly figures and the dream-like transactions of the night of the Clennam household. Some latent force of will within her rebels against the devitalization that the acceptance of the dream as illusion has forced upon her. Dickens makes Affery's perception a moral one, the catalyst her loyalty to Arthur Clennam. "Affery tell your dreams!" The way out of the dehumanization of this transformation of reality into illusion is to give the illusion the credibility of language, to reveal the dream world as a communication of truth.

But while Affery's dreams are truths that eventually set her free, Little Dorrit's Italian dreams are truths that threaten to destroy her. So the most apt metaphor for their expression is that of states of consciousness in which what is most revealed is the insufficiency of the present reality and the necessity for changing it. All of Italy is to Little Dorrit a "crowning unreality" that threatens to cut her off from the roots of her life, a permanent and useless orphan without the ties of work, loyalty, and responsibility to others that formerly have given her her sense of worth. "Such people were not realities to the little figure of the English girl;

such people were all unknown to her" (*LD*, II:III). England is real; Italy is illusion. Only within realities can we discover the meaning of our lives. Cut off from the London of her reality, where she felt in close contact with the sources of her life, she now has a need to search for something that has been lost. She constantly dreams of her childhood as an expression of her desire to contact once again the reality of what she is. While Venice is the dream of illusion, leading only to loss of self, her childhood is the dream of reality, leading perhaps to the rediscovery of self.

But "dark intangible presentiments of evil" (*ED*, x) suffuse the atmosphere in which Dickens' characters breathe: the brutal givens of social conditions and the human tendency to use will and energy for expansion and gratification at the expense of the independence and integrity of others. Jenny's vision contains the ambiguity of hope without hope, of life in death. Her invitation to Riah and all others is an invitation to die, suggesting the extent of the despair of those who in this increasingly secular society of earthly gratifications discover that fulfillment for them can occur only in a dream vision inseparable from death. For Jenny is a "queer little comicality" (*OMF*, IV:xvi), and Dickens can hardly manage the happy tying up of ends and lives in *Our Mutual Friend* that would persuade us that she, like the Marchioness, will discover her Dick Swiveller. That aspect of Nature which condemns us to physical and psychological deformities Dickens cannot explain, though the institutionalization of such deformities in the weapons of society against the individual he unhesitatingly denounces.

The nightmare is totally human, like the dream vision of possible release for the tortured souls who find the dark shadows of themselves too stark to bear without relief. " 'I was dreaming at a great rate, and am glad to be disturbed,' " Jasper says, " 'from an indigestive after-dinner sleep.' " The metaphor of explanation comes with the return to complete waking consciousness. Just a moment before "Jasper sprang from the couch in a delirious state between sleeping and

waking, and crying out: 'What is the matter? Who did it?' "
(*ED*, x). Dickens' world is filled with the unsettling visions
of indigestive sleep in which the excitement comes from
the distortions of the novelist's mind, like the giant Albion
in his fallen and totally human slumber. Our reality is his
dream.

The constant question is, "Who did it?" But we know
that the questioner asks himself the question in a dual state
of mind, sometimes knowing indeed that the answer is that
he has done it, sometimes having concealed from himself
his own guilt, other times in that curious state of double
consciousness in which he believes in two contradictory
things simultaneously. In one state of consciousness Jasper
quite seriously searches for the perpetrator of the murder that
he has committed, eager to bring him to justice or to destroy him.[6] The dream state, like mesmeric trance, both
conceals and reveals. It helps us to find ourselves as well as
to lose ourselves. When Madame de la Rue in mesmeric
trance told Dickens about the dislocations of her consciousness in swiftly changing, surreal settings with strange but
familiar creatures threatening her, Dickens certainly recognized that she was in that state of consciousness shared by
both mesmeric trance and the dream world. In this state the
anxieties of the present are illumined by the images of the
past. There is a loosening of the restrictions of repression
and convention; the self seeks the self more intuitively and
spontaneously.

Like mesmeric trance, the dream state ultimately becomes
a metaphor for the human condition and the powers of

[6] As many interpretations of the Drood mystery exist as there are
clever spokesmen for ingenious theories. The key unanswerable question
is whether or not Drood has *actually* been murdered. I believe that he
has. But the fact that Jasper has at least in his mind murdered Edwin
and is in the process of destroying himself supersedes all questions
about an actual murder. The complexities and divisions of Jasper's
consciousness dominate the novel. He is perfectly capable of pursuing
the murderer of a murder he has already committed. He is pursuing
himself. His divided consciousness permits him to do this without any
sort of hypocrisy.

mind. To dream is not necessarily pejorative in the Dickens world. Often it is a yearning towards a better reality, sometimes as pathetic and impossible as the dreams of Jenny Wren, sometimes as filled with tortured guilt as those of John Jasper, other times as ultimately redemptive as those of Arthur Clennam. Jenny is to be pitied, Jasper despised, Arthur encouraged; but all are better and more human for the fact of their dreams. Even nightmares are attestations of the power of those special states of consciousness in which the drama of confrontation with the self occurs. This is part of the humanness of Dickens' world, almost a totally psychic world in which human will and energy are the subjects that can be dramatized.

For example, despite the deprivations of Arthur Clennam's psychic life from childhood on, "it had been the uniform tendency of this man's life . . . to make him a dreamer, after all" (*LD*, I:III). But this is dreaming with the eyes open, day-dreaming, a substitute for will and energy. Though Clennam is eventually to be both dreamer and doer, the potential for such unity is inherent from the beginning in his state of mind when he returns to England. He has the capability, despite all the attempts to destroy it, to attain special states of consciousness. He can be brought into contact with truths that the rational and waking mind cannot glimpse.

Why has Clennam retained this capability and others not? Why does he have it in the first place? Why is Cissy Jupe, the child of the circus, born with intuitive sources of vital life, and Bitzer, the child of the schoolroom, born with a mind that will not admit anything but hard facts? Dickens will blame society for only so much and no more. His ultimate rejection of utopian visions and his failure to tie up the plots in a happy solution for all, including the community, in his later novels, seem a dramatization of his acceptance of what is outside human control. The way we are is only partially "our" fault. Some may dream and some may not; some may enter into special states of consciousness and some may not. While Dickens finds whatever little hope there is for constructive lives in the former, he has no explanation for the absence of this faculty in the latter, any more than the mesmerists like Elliotson could explain why certain individuals were potential subjects, others potential operators, and others totally unreceptive to the mesmeric influence.

Unlike some of the people from whom he learned about mesmerism, Dickens lost belief in the ultimate "reforms." Despite the utopian impetus from various sources as the century advanced, many of the most prominent of the scientific mesmerists became increasingly sober about the possible results of the revolution that Mesmer had begun. Without losing faith in the reality of the phenomenon, Dickens, for example, became more restrained in his opinion about what this new force could actually achieve in the way of change. It brought knowledge, which was a kind of power. But because it contained unresolvable mysteries about human nature and the mesmeric fluid, it proved more excitingly descriptive than therapeutically prescriptive. There were too many unanswered questions about the nature of the force; and the question of distribution and utilization was hopelessly unfathomable: who could explain why one individual had it and another not, and who could explain why one individual chose to use it for beneficial ends and another for self-serving gratification?

Fortunately Dickens did not have to, though he would have been as excited as Elliotson and Townshend would have been to have discovered more specific answers to these questions. To Elliotson particularly it indeed must have been frustrating to observe constantly the phenomena in his experiments without obtaining the indisputable explanations of origins and functioning that the scientific community demanded. But the novelist has different imperatives. He need only describe the human reality to reveal us as we are. The assumptions about the forces that work within us are unchallengeable starting points, not ends in themselves. These assumptions indeed need not be either

226

true or false, for they exist on the level of first principles in a fictional world. They are metaphors for the currents of human behavior whose scientific truth or falsity no more invalidates the observations of human behavior and the human condition based upon them than a failure to believe in the Elizabethan theory of humors invalidates Shakespeare's plays or a denial of the factual truth of Wordsworth's notion of the existence of the forms of beauty within Nature makes his poetry any the less effective.

[2]

The great city rose from the water like a Xanadu for the English Romantic imagination, the fire of western creativity and the icy perfection of Byzantine form. Shelley, Byron, Turner, Browning, Dickens, Ruskin, George Eliot, Henry James, Ezra Pound stood on the "Bridge of Sighs" and "sat on the Dogana's steps." The pigeons that rose and made sweeping orifices over St. Mark's Square for Merton Densher in the *Wings of the Dove* and confirmed the "crowning unreality" for Little Dorrit were those which made "concentric circles in the sky" over the steps of the Dublin library. Continuity and dislocation, the ancient traditions and the modern instabilities, the perfection of form and the tumultuousness of the emotions, the seeming permanence of Classical and Renaissance art and the transience of the modern Romantic creation glittered from golden cupolas and drifted on moving waters. To Dickens, Venice was "An Italian Dream," the place where the western consciousness confronted "what is past, or passing, or to come."

Venice is a special city. Only dream imagery can reveal the complex resonances of its interaction with the imagination caught between the Romantic inheritance and the modern world. To Dickens, Venice was a dream that must be seen as a symbolic reality, not a place to live in, but a center of the consciousness that needs to explore itself and its traditions, its past and its possibilities. Little Dorrit, like Dickens, must return to London, for everything else was less real and more dream. The dream had its uses; but London was the reality, the place where the uses must be created. Venice and London: they are the charged opposites of Dickens' imagination, the two connected poles across which the mesmeric current flows.

Unlike the rest of Italy, Venice was the past. Dickens' absorption into a philosophy of progress was far advanced when he came to the city on the Adriatic. His associations of Catholic Medieval and Renaissance culture with inquisitional intolerance and brutality were strong. He was most susceptible when young and hopeful to Victorian visions of progress. The decay of a previous civilization appeared to him in the imagery of unities fragmentized that Pickwick saw in his prison environment, half-broken utensils, chipped bowls, things that were conceived as entities but exist now only in parts: "Sometimes, alighting at the doors of churches and vast palaces, I wandered on, from room to room, from aisle to aisle, through labyrinths of rich altars, ancient monuments; decayed apartments where the furniture, half awful, half grotesque, was mouldering away" (*PFI*, 335). It was a city almost without people, commercial life, and vitality, so strange to the modern consciousness that only the dream image can communicate the dislocation Dickens felt as he glided along insubstantial canals and wandered through cavernous vaults. "I dreamed that I was led on, then, into some jealous rooms, communicating with a prison near the palace; separated from it by a lofty bridge crossing a narrow street; and called, I dreamed, the Bridge of Sighs" (*PFI*, 332).

For Dickens, Venice was the prototype of the museum of the mistakes of the past that every modern city was in danger of becoming, except that it still had within it the permanent life of the artistic imaginations that created a culture rich with art and its associations. For the western mind brings to Venice not only a horror of the barbarities of the past but an appreciation of the great culture that flourished there once: "Past plots of gardens, theatres, shrines, prodigious piles of architecture—Gothic—Saracenic—fanciful with all the fancies of all times and countries. . . . There, in the errant fancy of my dream, I saw old Shylock passing to and fro upon a bridge, all built upon with shops and humming with the tongues of men; a form I seemed to know for Desdemona's, leaned down through a latticed blind to pluck a flower. And, in the dream, I thought that Shakespeare's spirit was abroad upon the water somewhere: stealing through the city" (*PFI*, 336). So England and Italy were brought together, London and Venice, by a dream image that made inseparable the "accursed instruments of torture" and the imaginative expansions of the human mind. Dickens came out of a Romantic tradition in which the great art of the past could be meaningful in a present that was not so desiccated that it could not contain the possibility of a better future, at least for the individual who could see the connection between the two cities.

In Venice the horrors within man's psychic capabilities were reified in the artifacts of the past, his prisons, armories, dungeons, and instruments of torture. It was a calcified museum of the horror that London threatened to become, "London, gloomy, close and stale" whose "melancholy streets in the penitential garb of soot, steeped the souls of the people who were condemned to look at them out of windows, in dire despondency" (*LD*, I:III). But the petrified city was not immutable. Forces greater than its resistance were eroding even its marble solidity. "Like an old serpent" that was coiled around it many times, the symbol of ultimate continuity, like the natural force whose constant energy was a sign of its inhuman permanence, "crept the water always . . . waiting for the time . . . when people should look down into its depths for any stone of the old city that had claimed to be its mistress" (*PFI*, 336). The dream context reinforced the impermanence of this seemingly permanent city: "I have, many and many a time, thought since, of this strange Dream upon the water: half-wondering if it lie there yet, and if its name be VENICE" (*PFI*, 336).

Dickens suggests that Venice is the prototype of the civilization of western man, simply a later stage in the development of London and of all our cities.[7] We and our creations exist in a reality, the most appropriate metaphor for which is the dream city. Inherent within it is the beatific vision and the dreadful nightmare, expressions of the need of the human mind to express its hopes and its disappointments. And it is the human mind with which Dickens is concerned. All cities, past and present, are reflections of human states of consciousness, man's vision of himself and his anti-self, his creative and his destructive capabilities: the power of his mind to effect results as opposite as the traditional distinction between life and goodness and death and evil.

Dickens was a man of his century. There is no better representative. The Romantics discovered the need to emphasize the mind as a power independent of rational deliberations and syllogistic movements. The Medieval and the Renaissance dream vision, the notion of life as most fully lived in special states of consciousness to be best rendered through dream and imagery—this is what the Romantic poets whom Dickens read so intently in his formative years focus on, from Wordsworth's notion that we half create what we see, to Keats's sense of the despairing nightmare of relativism in "La Belle dame sans Merci" and "Ode to a Nightingale," to Blake's absolute affirmation of the power of mind to create a myth that would be the ultimate psychic reality. For the Romantics, real life, ultimate life, was mental life. One created the self through the projections of the mind, the favored word for which was imagination. Dickens learned from the Romantics that the mind was often complex and inconsistent, and that the outer signs that mind sought and created were sometimes perfect representatives of the contradictions within the mind itself. For in it, past, present, and future could come together in percep-

[7] See Alexander Welsh, *The City of Dickens* (Oxford, 1971), for a discussion of Dickens' literal and symbolic use of London.

tions that existed with a simultaneity that suggested time-
lessness, that made one feel the mighty powers of the mind,
"its bounding from earth and spurning time and space"
(*OT*, IX). It could bring together the cities of the past and
the present, just as it could bring together the past and the
present of the individual, and in doing so could help create
the future.

Dickens urged Macready, whose son was seriously ill, to
permit Elliotson and Townshend to assist him with mesmerism, for "I have a strong belief that if you try that
remedy under good superintendence . . . that it will do him
an amount of good that nothing else will, humanly speaking."[8] At certain times in his life Dickens had faith in the
possibilities of divine assistance, within the rhetoric of his
tenuous Anglican Christianity, though his institutional alle-
giance was weak. There does hover in the background of the
Dickens world the semblance of a God of Love. But his function is minimal, more as a reminder of possibilities for the
fallen than a promise of redemption for every man. Because
his ability to believe in this force was less than his desire
to do so, Dickens could be inconsistent. The day of the
reconciliation of God and man could be so far off that "so
deep a hush was on the sea, that it scarcely whispered of
the time when it shall give up its dead" (*LD*, I:1). But in
his death "the star had shown" Stephen Blackpool "where
to find the God of the poor; and through humility, and
sorrow, and forgiveness, he had gone to his Redeemer's
rest" (*HT*, III:VI).

There are things that are beyond human control, but
"humanly speaking" establishes the main boundaries of
Dickens' world. The metaphor is man, not God. If Christ
can be a living force, he can be so for Dickens chiefly as an
image of the capacity within man to love and be loved,
which can provide the counter-balance to the capacity
within man to use his will and energy to exploit others.
The Christian consolation flickers dimly in the main fires

[8] Morgan MS., Dickens to William Macready, 5/30/54.

of the Dickens world, Jenny Wren's invitation to "Come up and be dead" much too ambiguous to provide a satisfactory eschatology. The movement Dickens established as his typical pattern is not upward towards Heaven but downward towards earth, the way Little Dorrit and Arthur Clennam "went down into a modest life of usefulness and happiness . . . went quietly down into the roaring streets, inseparable and blessed; and as they passed along in sunshine and in shade, the noisy and the eager, and the arrogant and the froward and the vain, fretted, and chafed, and made their usual uproar" (*LD*, II:xxxiv). Neither God nor society could deliver salvation; both had lost their capability to assure the human imagination of their efficacy. The field of action that Dickens accepted as real was the human mind and the sense of self of the individual who in rare instances found his fulfillment in his other self, unity with whom created wholeness, purpose, and meaning.

The Romantic background quickly became the Victorian foreground for Dickens, who not atypically embraced simultaneously the Romantic variant of the metaphor of man that emphasized intuition, spontaneity, man as God, the role of mystery and magic in the cosmos, and the Victorian variant that, as the century advanced, more and more emphasized order, social norms, centralized reform, progress, and science. The attempt to domesticate Romanticism met the resistance of divided minds, which sometimes felt that they were "wandering between two worlds, one dead,/ The other powerless to be born," though such solipsistic dramatics were much more Arnold's style than Dickens'. As much as he detested the Victorian machine and the excesses of progress, the novelist sensed the necessity of the new as well as the untenability of the old, in a century of rapid changes that he himself epitomized in the movement from the stagecoaches of *Pickwick Papers* to the polluted wasteland Thames of *Our Mutual Friend*. Mesmerism was an offspring of the Enlightenment that promised solutions to man's problems through man's rational control of the natural phenomena of self and cosmos. But it grew up in the days of the Revolution, in which science was transformed into magic and back into science again in a process in which the mind of the Enlightenment mixed with the new Romantic impetus and eventually produced the paradox of Victorians like Dickens.

For mesmerism, they felt, put them in touch with the secret powers of the universe that had always been there. That force which had been hidden in the mysteries of magic and religion could now be made clear. The great prestidigitations of western myth and rumor, from Christ to Joan of Arc and beyond, were now seen by the mesmerists as simply instances of unusual individuals stumbling onto the existence of mesmeric fluid in the universe and discovering how to harness it through their own special gifts of energy and will. Dickens' main contacts in the mesmeric movement were with scientific mesmerists, like Elliotson, who genuinely believed that they had discovered a scientifically verifiable phenomenon. In this sense, then, the emphasis was on man and man's control of natural forces. The impulse that came out of the Enlightenment and grew to maturity during the Romantic fervor that the Victorians inherited was utopian and progressive: better days for all mankind through man's use of his mind. Magic, they assumed, was the first step in the movement to religion and then to science, the three great attempts of Western man to deal with the natural forces of the universe.

But Dickens himself was always uneasy with what seemed a point of view inconsistent with his sense of human nature and the human predicament, whose answers were plausible but not totally convincing, particularly as the century advanced and as he himself became more conscious of the complex contradictions within himself and his contemporaries. In his novels, mesmerism as science and utopian promise does not speak to the needs of his characters and their world. Despite his own involvement for a considerable period of his life in progressive, rational movements, the given materials of human nature and the natural forces of the cosmos in his fiction seem only minimally amenable to the kind of improvement that is implicit within scientific mesmerism and other utopian visions of the nineteenth century. Unlike Elliotson, Dickens was intensely suspicious of the results of man's attempt to control natural forces within the environment and within himself. This was not mainly his reaction to the pollution of the environment, the absolute offense to his aesthetic sense in the sights, smells, and sounds of modern urbanism. His tolerance for such degradation was less than that of many of his contemporaries, particularly those who believed that they possessed the answers to the problems of progress, whether within mesmerism or any other ideology or methodology. But Dickens ultimately believed in Romantic, not scientific, assumptions. In his exposure to mesmerism early in his career and his continued belief in the reality of the phenomenon all his life, Dickens became, not a mesmerist, and certainly not a scientific mesmerist, though he often admired and hoped for the success of their work, but a novelist who could use the mermerists' emphasis on will, energy, and mind as intensified metaphors for his exploration of the condition of man.

Clearly mesmerism does not explain or account for Dickens' view as novelist about the nature of man. It contributes to it and helps him to find metaphors to express it. But it does not explain it. For Dickens dismisses within his fictional world scientific and spiritual mesmerism and concentrates almost totally on a special application of the image of man that was to become more frequent in the movement of the nineteenth century toward the twentieth: on the psychic state of the individual as the key to his personality and his actions. The community is given its due, the social structure shown to contribute either negatively or positively as the instance may be, but the essence of what the individual is and how he reveals himself is the manifestation of internal mental forces. Dickens' characters have the vitality and the reality of psychic life. He is not a formal realist. But he does contribute significantly to the development of psychological realism that is the direction of his age, moving towards a fiction that ultimately in the twentieth century became a dramatization of the forces of the mind, dealing primarily with the power of mind over matter. Dickens' interest in special states of consciousness is part of a larger movement in which human personality is conceived and evaluated mainly through a focus on the actual processes of individual thought. In this movement poetic forms—like the dramatic monologues of Browning and the interior monologues of Joyce—are developed to bring us inside the mind of a character to search for his reality within the special conditions of his psyche. The movement that Mesmer began becomes, through the contribution of James Braid, the tool of Charcot and the early Freud. It flows into the mainstream of twentieth-century preoccupation with mind in Freud, Jung, Frazier, Wittgenstein, Proust, Sartre, Joyce, Lawrence, Beckett, and a cast too large and too obvious to name.

Dickens was part of this movement. Intuitively he could not accept Elliotson's utopian view of the role of mesmerism in solving man's problems. Mesmerism could help reveal them, but no more. For Dickens felt he was dealing with an elemental force, regardless of whether or not the metaphor for its elaboration be mesmeric, and ultimately this force was neither right nor wrong, good nor bad. Man had to make of it what he could. And the seeming agency of his control of this power, made available to some more than to others in an inexplicable pattern that hardly implied objective or benevolent principles of distribution, was the human will. Dickens was certainly not alone in recognizing the importance of this factor. But he was more puzzled by it than many of his contemporaries who were made secure against potential fears by the optimism of their scientific assumptions, by their dismissal of the possible existence of the permanently unknowable.

Dickens' imagination contained within it an ineradicable, powerful, myth-making capacity in which the mysterious could never be dismissed. His fictional world is an expression of the wonder and complexity of human phenomena. It assumes that our most extraordinary qualities are ultimately unexplainable, deeply connected to the hidden sources of magic and mystery, the occult powers from the cosmos that touch us all the time. We can sense and feel these forces. We can see them working in and through us. But no science will ever explain or account for them fully. They are inseparable from the creative and the imaginative faculties. Dickens needed to believe in the existence of unknown forces in the universe for which the artist is a conduit. Most of all he needed to believe in the artistic imagination. These were his Romantic inheritance. So too was mesmerism.

But the human will creates problems that Romantic assumptions and optimism could not overcome, that scientific mesmerism evaded. The agency of this great source of energy and influence was tainted. Not to have will at all was to be reduced to plastic enervation, vulnerable to the manipulation of those whose gratification came from the exercise of their will to dominate others. To be will-less was essentially to have been deprived of the opportunity for life, completely out of contact with the underlying forces of the universe, the mesmermic currents that created the reality of the natural and the human world. Those without will were either corpses or victims. In the latter form they were often the necessary complements of those who possessed extraordinary willpower, so forceful that attempts to suppress it were self-destructive, while its full expression outside the controls of ethical structure often destroyed others.

Dickens was a novelist of the will who warned against the will's excesses. The Romantics applauded the expression of the heroic will in a struggle in which the oppressor was the stultified human environment that needed to crush the individual will to its narrow measurements of repression, whether in life or in art. Mesmerism discovered that this human will knew no bounds when once its power had been understood. Man could transform himself from individual Romantic rebel into a species whose aspirations could be achieved en masse through the use of willpower to harness the cosmic energy for universal good. But Dickens saw that despite the potential beneficial uses of this energy those who had extraordinary powers of will were more likely than not to use them for self-serving ends. So the Dickens world is populated with threats of domination and exploitation. The problem was an immense one. In a century in which man and his powers become the foreground of primary concern, what is one to do when experience and intuition suggest that mankind cannot use these vast powers for positive ends? Dickens felt these forces throbbing all around him, in himself and in others. He used them for what he assumed were beneficial and therapeutic ends. But his fictional world is filled with the fears and threats of misuse. The instances are rare in which potential misuse is overcome.

Dickens' concern with will embodies his century's fascination with the problems of this force. The social and philosophical determinists, like Spencer and Marx, and even Thomas Hardy, provided the opposition that gave the philosophers of will impetus for dramatic expression. The scientists, among them Elliotson, who anticipated the social scientists and the psychologists, believed that they had discovered a new tool that would make clear what was already implicit in the natural order of things, and they all assumed that man would use the new power for beneficial ends. They were in the long run hardly different from the scientists, who as the century advanced became increasingly possessed of the view that man is no more than the product of his bio-chemistry. This element of nineteenth-century psychology quite naturally combined with scientific materialism to create a therapeutic psychology whose main tool was not the human will but the power of chemicals and drugs. Elliotson himself anticipated the combination. He experimented boldly with what his contemporaries considered excessive doses, sometimes of unusual combinations, in cases not only of physical but also of nervous disorders.

The philosophers of the will, who became the most dramatic voices of the new vision of man's powers, were not mainly English, except as disciples, but continental. Romanticism became the expression of the absolutely unlimited powers of the special man who was in touch with and could control the cosmic force in the universe. He could use it on behalf of his vision of a new and better world, which might be seen in social or utopian or religious or aesthetic terms, as the case might be. Carlyle, for example, attempted to check the Romantic impulse, epitomized in Blake, to go so far as to make the notion of divinity and consequently God identical with the notion of man. But he believed that special men could embody within themselves the power of the natural order of the cosmos and its energy through revelation, through the use of will and its manifestation in the prophetic voice. Dickens felt strongly the attraction of Carlyle's message, especially in its social applications.[9] Like many Victorians, his reactions to the conditions he observed were often so negative that what might have been otherwise unacceptable solutions became palatable enough to be taken seriously. He admired Carlyle, as writer and friend, just as he would have been fascinated, despite eccentricities of personality and social behavior of a kind he himself could not share, with Nietzsche, Wagner,

[9] When Dickens travelled from Genoa to England in December 1844, it was, among other things, for the gratification he expected to feel reading *The Chimes* for the first time in the presence of Carlyle himself: "Shall I confess to you, I particularly want Carlyle above all to see it before the rest of the world, when it is done; and I should like to inflict the little story on him and on dear old gallant Macready with my own lips . . ." (*Nonesuch*, I, 632, to John Forster, 11/3/44). For recent discussions of Carlyle's pervasive influence on Dickens, see William Oddie, *Dickens and Carlyle, The Question of Influence* (London, 1972) and Michael Goldberg, *Carlyle and Dickens* (University of Georgia Press, 1972).

D'Annunzio, and others, who embraced philosophies of the primacy of the human will.

But certain Victorian norms do, of course, run through Dickens, and one of them he could see better than any of his contemporaries: the threat of the human will to the individual life and to the social harmony of the community. Neither scientific determinism nor utopianism nor the promises of the new social scientists nor the exponents of the philosophies of the will as the century advanced seemed to be able to convince Dickens that they had the solutions to the problems of the human personality and the growing problems of this particular society. Indeed, as his imagination developed its full range and intensity over a career that covered thirty crucial years of our civilization, his fictional vision revealed that his personal sense of loss and bafflement increased considerably. He sensed that the cracks in the armor of western civilization had become chasms, huge ulceric sores and dark wounds of self-destructiveness. His humor, his Christianity, his evident delight in his own creative energies were set against not only his personal losses but his strong sense of the failure of the entire enterprise, which turned his humor dark, confounded his Christianity, and forced his creative energies in upon himself in the personal depression he countered through the self-destroying hard work of his exhausting obligations.[10] Like his

10 The mesmeric or hypnotic element in Dickens' relationship with the audiences he read to has been indirectly revealed in the frequent use of the terms "mesmeric" and "hypnotic" in contemporary accounts. As early as his first private-public reading of December 1844 Dickens seems to have associated his affective abilities with power over his audience, an inflating sense of dominance. He wrote to his wife that "If you had seen Macready last night, undisguisedly sobbing and crying on the sofa as I read, you would have felt, as I did, what a thing it is to have power" (Dexter p. 117). The frenetic, anguished, and self-transfixed manner in which Dickens seems to have performed the murder of Nancy and the death of Sikes from *Oliver Twist* suggests a kind of self-hypnosis as well. In these last years Dickens seems to have manifested some of the compulsiveness, self-destructiveness, and power over others, particularly in his readings, that he was to depict so brilliantly in the final year of his life in the character of John Jasper.

great Russian equal, Tolstoy, he was a novelist of the relationship between the individual and himself and the individual and society, though unlike Tolstoy he remained so all his life.[11] Dickens never found the same kind of all-consuming persuasiveness in the Christian millenarianism that terminated Tolstoy's career as writer. To that we are indebted for the intensity of an oeuvre that no other major novelist has matched in comprehensiveness, development, and consistent brilliance.

Despite the cosmic complexities of much of formal mesmeric theory, Dickens learned from mesmerism what he needed to know, what he was learning from other sources as well, about human nature and the human situation. In mesmerism he discovered a terminology and a series of related images through which to express his major perceptions: that the field of action for man's imagination is the here and now; that within the world of man's needs all aspects of his situation can be expressed; that the center point of this field of action is mind; that in the special states of the mind, where past, present, and future come together, the individual creates his self-identity and his sense of worth; that there is some special correlation between the mental forces within and the cosmic forces without; that man expands himself to his utmost limit when he experiences this connection, for it gives him a sense of his own potential powers and purpose; but that this energy has as its agent the human will, which can use the force for good or for evil ends. When the ends are good, then love, forgiveness, loyalty, and self-sacrifice operate; when the ends are evil, then the desire to manipulate, subjugate, brutalize, and deceive others and oneself in patterns that are basically self-destructive predominates. And the main gratification that results seems to be sexual. But why one individual

[11] For an illuminating discussion of Dickens and Tolstoy as novelists, see Q. D. Leavis, "Dickens and Tolstoy: The Case for a Serious View of *David Copperfield*," in F. R. Leavis and Q. D. Leavis, *Dickens, The Novelist* (N.Y., 1970).

rather than another will have the power of will and why one will use his power for beneficial and another for destructive ends, there seems to be no way of determining, no way of explaining. All the novelist can do is to perceive the reality and to dramatize it. And in the dramatization he warns us that central to our vital lives is our potential to destroy or to create ourselves and others.

INDEX

Library of Congress Cataloging in Publication Data

Kaplan, Fred, 1937-
  Dickens and mesmerism.

  Includes index.
  1. Dickens, Charles, 1812-1870. 2. Mesmerism—England. I. Title.
  PR4581.K27   823'.8   75-2994